TREASURE
of the Merrilee

WHISPERS
in the Wind

HEART
of the Warrior

Cover design by Gerald Lee Monks
Cover illustration by Marcus Mashburn

Treasure of the Merrilee originally published in 1993.
Whispers in the Wind originally published in 1993.
Heart of the Warrior originally published in 1994.

The author assumes full responsibility for the accuracy of all facts
and quotations as cited in this book.

Additional copies of this book can be obtained by calling toll-free
1-800-765-6955 or by visiting http://www.adventistbookcenter.com.

ISBN 978-0-8163-6154-0

February 2016

TREASURE
of the Merrilee

Charles Mills

Pacific Press®
Publishing Association
Nampa, Idaho | Oshawa, Ontario, Canada
www.pacificpress.com

Dedication

To my treasure

Dorinda

Whose creativity and enthusiasm

Make these books possible.

Contents

CHAPTER ONE

BARRIERS

If the object hadn't caught her eye for that brief moment, the girl wouldn't have noticed it at all. But something was definitely there, hidden in the thick underbrush.

Wendy pulled gently on the reins, bringing her horse to an immediate halt. The animal turned and glanced back at his young rider as if to say, "Why are we stopping out here in the middle of nowhere?"

"Look, Early," the girl breathed. "Do you see it? Down there, hiding between those bushes. It's not a branch or fallen log. It looks like some sort of board."

The brown horse with the white star between his eyes ignored Wendy's words. He had much greater interest in the late summer grasses that grew by the long-abandoned logging road.

Wendy slipped from the saddle and walked slowly toward the thick growth at the base of a living wall of pine. Carefully, she pushed back the tangled vines and branches to reveal a sturdy, skillfully-cut length of timber half buried in the soil.

"Now, how'd this get here?" she asked no one in particular. "There's not a house within five miles. It couldn't have fallen off a logging truck. It's already cut."

Early glanced over at his companion while slowly munching a mouthful of yampa blooms and dried grass. The early autumn sun, filtering through the cottonlike clouds, freckled nearby meadows and hillsides with bright splashes of light. The air hung cool and refreshing, a welcome change from the hot breath of summer.

The girl tugged at the board, trying to dislodge it from its earthen trap. She pulled as hard as she could, but the strange object remained firmly gripped by the rich Montana soil.

"Whatever it is, it's been here for a long, long time," Wendy called to her horse. "And look, there're nail holes on this end. Mother Nature certainly didn't put them here."

Wendy tilted her head to one side, a smile spreading across her young face. If there was one thing in the whole world this 10-year-old girl loved, it was a good mystery.

Here at her feet was a puzzle, an object that didn't belong by the old logging road this far up in the Gallatin Mountains. The girl shivered just a little, letting the excitement of her discovery fill her with a delicious tingle.

It was the same sensation she'd felt when Joey had shown her the small pile of bones and feathers in the Station's dusty attic, and when she'd seen the eyes of the Squaw shine in the moonlight. Yes, Wendy loved a good adventure. The more mysterious, the better.

The girl spit on her hands and rubbed them together. Gripping the end of the board with all her might, she pulled hard.

Early watched her strain and groan, her teeth

clenched tightly. Suddenly, her feet slipped and she sat down hard, her legs straddling the object that jutted out of the ground.

"Ouch!" the girl cried, rubbing the stabbing pain in her tailbone. "So that's how it's going to be, huh?" She addressed the weatherworn object with a frown. "You want a fight. Well, you've come to the right place. I'll give you—"

Wendy's words caught in her throat. From her new position she could see the underside of the object for the first time. She bent low to the ground until her cheek touched the soil. Running her hand along the rough surface of the wood, she could just barely make out some letters carved into it. The girl let out a low "H-m-m-m." This was getting more interesting by the minute.

Forgetting her aching posterior, Wendy rolled onto her back and slid her head under the board. Early blinked at the strange sight. He shook his head and snorted as if to say, "Hey, Wendy. Quit playing ground-hog and take me back to the ranch."

The girl studied the rough carving, poking her index finger into each nook and cranny. Her lips moved silently as she tried to decipher what she was seeing.

"L—E—E. Yeah, that's it. L—E—E. Lee." She sat up. "Who's Lee? I don't know anyone by that name. Wait, I'm just seeing one end of the word. Maybe there's more down in the ground." Wendy gripped the board and pulled again. The object refused to budge.

By now, Early had waited long enough. He trotted over to his rider and stood looking down at her, an impatient expression on his handsome face.

"Yeah, I know," the girl sighed, stumbling to her feet. "We gotta go. I'm kinda hungry myself. Lizzy should be putting supper on the table right about now. But we're coming back tomorrow." She turned and faced the half-buried object at her feet. "And I'm coming prepared."

With that she slipped her foot into the stirrup and hoisted her stocky frame onto the horse's back. With a last glance toward the bushes, she kicked gently against Early's sides and together, horse and rider thundered away, leaving a cloud of dust hanging in the cool mountain air.

The object of Wendy's puzzlement waited patiently beside the long-abandoned logging road, as it had for years. One more night would make no difference at all.

* * * * *

"What is that heavenly odor?" Debbie asked as her smiling face appeared at the top of the broad, curving staircase in the foyer. "Lizzy? Are you making squash bread again?"

Mrs. Pierce looked up from the neat row of supper plates she was placing along the length of the table in the dining room.

"Yes, dear," she replied to the girl on the balcony. "Squash bread with peach jam."

"*Peach jam?*" Another voice—this one from a suddenly excited child—echoed from the den. "I *love* peach jam!" The words were followed by running feet as a little Black girl burst through the door and raced across the foyer.

"Save me some, Samantha," Debbie called after the breathless youngster.

Joey, walking up the hallway from his room, caught the diminutive runner in a big bear hug. "Where you goin' so fast?" he teased. "She didn't say peach jam. She said bleached ham."

"No she didn't!" the little girl giggled.

"Bleached ham?" Tyler Hanson queried as he exited the Station's second-floor office and joined his daughter at the railing. "We're having bleached ham for supper?"

Debbie chuckled as she tucked her long, dark hair

12

behind her ears. "Yeah, and I thought we were vegetarians."

"Well, if it's bleached . . ."

The girl groaned. "Yuck. I'll stick to fruits and
vegetables, thank you very much."

Mr. Hanson smiled over at the teenager. "You know
I was teasing. So, Miss Fashion Designer, how's your
latest creation coming along?"

The girl stepped back a few paces. "You tell me," she
said with a twirl of her slender body. The soft, blue cloth
of the dress she was wearing flowed about her legs like
waves on a shore. She wore at her waist a narrow, white
belt, held in place by tight loops of cloth.

A pair of puffy sleeves hemmed with lace bracketed
the gently curving neckline, also outlined with delicate
needlework. The dress was pure Debbie—elegant, carefully created, beautiful.

"Oh, my," Mr. Hanson sighed with a shake of his
head. "What are the boys at the Bozeman Mall going to
do when they see you in that pretty new dress? They'll
line up just to say hello."

Debbie reddened. "Oh, Daddy."

The man encircled the girl in his arms. "Have I ever
told you that you—"

"Get even more beautiful every day?" Debbie finished
her father's sentence for him. "Yes, Daddy. You've told
me that a few hundred times."

The man smiled. "Well, it's true. Both you and
Wendy are growing up much too fast." His brow furrowed slightly. "On that note, I think it's time for us to
have that talk I promised you in New York, before we
came out to the ranch."

Debbie blinked. "What talk?"

Mr. Hanson motioned for his daughter to follow him
into his office. They strolled out onto the second-floor

porch and stood looking up the valley, toward the distant mountains.

"What are you talking about?" Debbie asked again.

The man turned and faced his daughter. "Remember when I said we were moving to Montana you didn't want to go? You argued that I should've talked to you about it first. You were right."

Debbie nodded. "It's OK."

Mr. Hanson drummed the wooden porch railing with his fingers. "Well, we made a deal then."

Debbie lifted her hand slightly. "You mean about giving Montana one year, and if I didn't like it you'd let me—"

"I'd let you return to New York and attend that school for ladies, the one—"

"That makes 'women of distinction' out of their pupils?" the girl grinned. "Oh, yeah, I remember."

"So," the man said slowly, "the year is about up."

Debbie stood silent for a long moment. Mr. Hanson studied his daughter carefully, hopefully, looking for an indication of what she was thinking.

"You're 17 years old," he said quietly. "You'll turn 18 during the winter. I'm not one of those overly protective fathers who makes his children do everything his way."

The girl giggled. "Yes, you are."

"Oh, well, in spite of that, a promise is a promise," Mr. Hanson said firmly. "I'll stick by my word. If you want to go back to New York, you can."

Debbie looked over at her father. "Do you want me to?"

"Are you kidding? I worry if you're out in the far pasture. If I don't see you at least once a day, I have withdrawal pains. Really. It's not a pretty sight."

The teenager rolled her eyes. "Oh, sure."

Mr. Hanson placed his arms around the girl's narrow shoulders. "I love you, Debbie," he said. "Wendy and I

14

would be lonely without you. I was kinda hoping to keep you around until you were, oh, say, 37 or so. I know it wasn't your idea to come out here. It was mine. So, as I promised, you have the choice of staying or leaving."

Debbie gazed into her father's eyes. *Could there be a kinder, more gentle man in the whole world?* she thought to herself. For as long as she could remember, he'd always been there for her. Sometimes his life as a lawyer made him a little less available than she would've liked, but she easily forgave him when she saw his dedication to the clients he served.

The girl let her mind drift back to her life in New York City. There'd been lots of excitement, many friends, much to see and do. And the fashions! The city provided endless avenues lined with clothing stores and exquisitely dressed windows to prowl each day after school. Some store managers, inspired by their frequent visitor's knowledge of clothing design and her friendly, outgoing nature, had promised her a full-time job when she completed high school.

New York had everything she'd possibly need to fulfill her dream of becoming a working fashion designer. Montana had little to offer a girl with such fantasies.

Debbie smiled. "Let me think about it a little more," she said softly. "The year isn't up quite yet." She gave her father's hand a squeeze. "I just need some time to make my decision."

"Fair enough," Mr. Hanson said as he planted a kiss on the fair skin of his daughter's forehead. "You choose. I'll support your decision, whatever it is."

The two walked arm in arm back inside the Station. Together they crossed the balcony and headed down the curving staircase leading to the foyer, where supper sounds echoed from the dining room. Big decisions and young girls' dreams could wait a little longer. Right now it was time to enjoy Lizzy's fresh-baked squash bread smothered with heaping helpings of "bleached ham."

* * * * *

Joey looked up from his early morning chores and watched Wendy cross the footbridge and head in the direction of the horse corral. Early stood expectantly by the gate.

The boy chuckled to himself. How did that silly horse know what was going to happen before it happened? Wendy hadn't called him, yet there he was, waiting for his saddle and bridle. Maybe they had a secret way of communicating through brain waves or something.

Joey laughed out loud. Who'd want to establish a mind-link with a horse? Or, for that matter, with Wendy!

"Hey, Joey," he heard the girl call. "Where's the geologist's pick? You know, that gadget for cracking rocks?" It was the best thing she could think of for the job ahead—she could dig with it, but it wouldn't be too heavy to carry up into the mountains.

The boy's eyes opened wide. "Going prospecting, are we?" he asked, walking in her direction.

"*We're* not doing anything," she responded. "I'm just taking a pick with me for my morning ride. What's so strange about that?"

Joey shrugged. He'd come to expect Wendy to make some rather unusual requests from time to time. Just last week she'd insisted that he cut a willow stick for her. She said she was going to witch for water. Must have worked. She came back bragging that she'd found a whole lake.

"OK, OK," Joey said, swinging the corral door open wide. "One geo-pick comin' up." He found the requested piece of hardware as Wendy hurriedly saddled Early.

"Now, don't lose this," he begged, handing the small tool with its pointed blade on one side of the head and a hammer face on the other up to the rider. "Wrangler

16

Barry says I'm responsible for all tools in the corral."

Wendy grinned down at her friend as she grabbed the pick. "Oh, don't have a heart attack. I'll have it back safe and sound before lunch. Thank you, Mr. Dugan. See ya."

With that she gave Early a firm jab with her heels and the horse and rider lunged toward the pasture gate. With a wave of her free hand, they galloped over the footbridge that spanned Shadow Creek and raced down the long driveway that led from the Station to the dirt road.

Joey shook his head slowly from side to side. That Wendy. She lived in a world all her own. The boy looked across the distant meadow to the towering mountains ringing the ranch. *At least*, he thought to himself, *in Montana any world can be beautiful.*

* * * * *

Early grazed contentedly in a small meadow by the old logging trail. Every once in a while he'd lift his head and gaze at the determined figure digging steadily into the hard mountain soil by the bushes across the road. He could hear Wendy huffing and puffing as she bent to her self-imposed task.

"Trying to keep a secret from me?" he heard her say. "Well, I've got news for you. This is Wendy Hanson you're dealing with. I'm on a quest, a mission, a . . . a . . . sacred duty to myself to discover all the mysteries in these mountains. So you may as well just give up, come out of that ground, and show yourself to me right now."

Early snorted softly and returned to the sweet grasses that carpeted the meadow.

Wendy leaned heavily on a nearby tree trunk. This was harder than she had figured. The object must have been lying on the ground when the logging road was widened. One end of it had been buried deep in several feet of earth, which had hardened.

She lifted the pick high over her head and brought it

17

down sharply. Rocks flew left and right as she worked, chipping away at the ungiving earth.

Slowly the soil began to lose its grip. With sweat lining her top lip and staining her shirt, she felt the board give just a little when she tugged on it. "YES!" she cried. "You're mine. Not even the mountains can hide their secrets from me!"

Early shifted his position and studied the figure. It seemed as though he could sense that a great break-through was about to happen.

With a mighty tug, Wendy succeeded in pulling out the long wooden object. Its sudden release from the soil sent the digger falling backward. She landed with a painful jolt on her tailbone.

"OUCH! AGAIN! What do you have against my rear end?" she groaned at the object.

Gritting her teeth, she regained her feet and surveyed the reward of her hard labor. At her feet lay a rough, weathered board, about six feet long and 12 inches wide. Nail holes pierced both ends of the object, She could tell also that it had once been covered with a coat of white paint, although sun and soil had all but erased the evidence.

Slowly the girl bent and turned over the new discovery. Immediately she saw that a word, a rather long word, had been carved the length of the board.

Wendy brushed away the earth and carefully studied each faded and obscure letter. She worked slowly, like a surgeon exploring the depth of a human body.

"M—E—." The girl's finger traced the lines and crevasses etched into the board. "R—R—I—." She whispered each letter as she deciphered it. "L—E—E. ME—RR—IL—EE. MER—RI—LEE." Wendy blinked. "Merrilee. That's what its says. MERRILEE!"

She sat back on her heels. "What's a Merrilee? Sounds like a boat or something. How did a boat get up into the Gallatin Mountains?"

Wendy rubbed her chin with the back of her hand. "Maybe it's a secret password for the cavalry. Or maybe there was a fort here! Yeah, Fort Merrilee." She glanced up at the wall of bushes that lined the abandoned road. "I'll bet you there's a fort in there!"

Ignoring her aching posterior, the girl jumped to her feet. "Hey, Early," she called to her horse. "I've discovered an army fort right here by this road. Neat, huh?"

The horse snorted as if in response, then continued its grazing.

Wendy turned and studied the green leafy wall and began pacing back and forth, looking for a passageway through its protective barrier. She could find none. She just knew that beyond the thick wall of green waited a huge military fort, complete with stables, barracks, and parade grounds. So close, yet so far!

In frustration she grabbed the geo-pick and threw it at the wall. The tool flew above the tangle of vines and branches and into the trees above. Seconds later Wendy heard the sound of breaking glass.

"EARLY!" she screamed, causing the grazing horse to jump sideways. "There's something in there. Did you hear that glass? There's definitely something in there." She clawed at the foliage. "But I can't get through. It's too thick."

She paused. "A machete. I need a machete to cut through this stuff. Joey has one." Then she gasped. "The pick. I've lost the geo-pick. He'll kill me." The girl began pacing back and forth again. "Yup, Joey will kill me for sure. He'll drown me in Shadow Creek." She lifted a finger. "But if I had a machete I could cut through this wall and find the pick. But Joey won't give me a machete if I've lost the pick."

Wendy sank to the ground. "Oh, what a dilemma," she moaned. "I'm on the verge of discovering a great secret and now Joey won't give me a machete." She brightened. "So, I won't ask. I'll just take it. I'll race up here, cut through the wall, find the pick, and hurry back before he even knows what's going on."

The girl shouted for her horse. In a moment she and Early were pounding down the old logging road toward the Station five miles away.

If Wendy had stayed by the green wall just a little longer she would have heard another sound coming from behind its leafy face. First there were a few sniffs, then a low growl, like some ancient beast awakening and preparing to defend the secrets that lay behind the barrier.

CHAPTER TWO

MAIL CALL

Mr. Hanson's red minivan ground to a halt beside the Station. The driver jumped out, hurried up the front steps, and entered the foyer, a big smile lighting his face.

"Hey, everybody," he called. "Mail's here."

Running feet echoed down every hallway as the Station inhabitants answered his enthusiastic announcement. Ever since Shadow Creek Ranch's summer guests had gone, mail call brought excitement to everyone as letters arrived, detailing the continuing saga of the friends they missed.

Eager hands sorted through the postal pile, looking for familiar names. Wendy, fresh from her morning adventure on the mountain, had decided to wait until later in the day to return to the old logging road and whatever was hiding behind the wall of bushes. She was hoping Joey would be working far enough from the corral for her to sneak in and get the machete without him seeing her.

A big, fat envelope printed with her name greeted her search. She tucked it snugly under her arm and headed for the den with the rest of the group.

Little Samantha was left standing in the foyer, bottom lip trembling.

"What's the matter, Sam?" Joey called back to his "adopted sister."

"I didn't get a letter," she sighed. "No one wrote to me."

Mr. Hanson shuffled through the remaining memos. "Here, Samantha," he said with a smile. "*This* one's for you."

The girl brightened. "OH!" she cried enthusiastically. "Where's it from?"

The lawyer glanced at the return address. "Looks like Bozeman. Must be important."

Samantha tucked the letter under her arm as she'd seen Wendy do and walked triumphantly into the den to join the others.

After everyone had settled into a favorite chair, the sound of ripping envelopes and fluttering paper filled the room. "Looks like everyone reported in," Mr. Hanson observed. "There's even a postcard from Grandpa and Grandma. They say they're enjoying their vacation in Seattle but are looking forward to getting back to Shadow Creek Ranch in about a week. See, here's a picture of the big airplanes that are built near the city."

The lawyer held up the postcard so everyone could admire the picture of a silver jetliner flying above a snowcovered mountain. Then he read on. "Grandpa said he enjoyed visiting the aircraft assembly plant while Grandma went shopping at a mall. She bought gifts for everyone."

A cheer rose from the assembly.

Debbie lifted her letter and waved it. "Hey, Janet and Joyce are having a great time with their new foster parents, the Tomlinsons. Say they went shopping on Broadway and picked out some new material for a matching pair of dresses they're putting together on their sewing machine. The store specializes in French patterns. Look, they sent me a swatch." The girl proudly held the small piece of cloth for all to see.

"Oh, that's be-u-ti-ful!" Wendy teased, clutching her hands to her chest, trying to act like it was the most wonderful piece of fabric she'd ever seen. "Looks like it would make a divine saddle blanket."

Debbie rolled her eyes. "I'll have you know this is very exquisite material. They don't have this kind of quality in Bozeman." She glanced at her father, then reddened. "But I can have them send me some if I want. It's no big deal."

Mr. Hanson smiled back at her, but the concern in his heart deepened just a little. He knew how his daughter loved fabric stores, and Bozeman wasn't exactly the cloth capital of the world.

"Anyway," the girl continued, running her finger along the lines scrawled across the paper, "they'll be starting in a new school soon and will write more when anything neat happens."

"You mean as soon as they meet all the guys," Joey chuckled.

Debbie, ignoring that last comment, folded the letter and fingered the cloth thoughtfully. "They sound really happy," she said, studying the delicate patterns printed in the material.

Wendy gasped. "Well, I'll be a ground hog's nose," she blurted, pointing at her letter. "Ol' Ruben got to meet the Cubs' first baseman. Had lunch with him and everything. Says Captain Perry took him to a game last Tuesday night. Guess the good captain knows the man's brother. Neat, huh? Ruben says he told him all about Shadow Creek Ranch. Seems the guy was impressed.

Even sent some money to Project Youth Revival." She looked up. "Now Ruben Manuel Alfonso Hernandez says he's going to help raise funds for summer camps like ours. That's cool."

A round of enthusiastic applause rose from the group as each one remembered first meeting the happy boy who proudly wore a colorful Cub's T-shirt. "Good for Ruben," they cheered.

"Speaking of fund-raising," Mr. Hanson announced, "I got this on my fax machine this morning. It's a brochure designed by none other than Andrew Morrison the Third of Beverly Hills, California."

"Yeah, Andrew!" the children shouted.

"Seems he's passing these out to all his well-to-do friends and neighbors," the lawyer continued, "insisting that they send money to Ruth Cadena for Project Youth Revival. A note that arrived with the fax says he misses everyone and hopes we can come visit him. He wants to be remembered to Lizzy and Grandma and Grandpa Hanson, all you kids, and all the horses."

Joey laughed. "He's the only guy I know that would travel all the way to Montana to shut himself up in an office and pound on a computer all day."

"Don't knock it," Mr. Hanson chuckled. "My office equipment enjoyed the workout. Everything operates faster and better. I have no idea what he did up there, but I can get things done a lot more efficiently now. That kid was a computer genius."

Samantha waved her letter over her head. "What's mine say? What's mine say?" she pleaded.

Lizzy took the envelope and studied it for a moment. "Oh, Samantha. It looks very important," she confided.

"It does, doesn't it?" the little girl grinned. "Read it quickly!"

The old woman tore open the letter and studied the writing. "It *is* important," she announced enthusiastically. Samantha sat on the edge of her chair.

"Your letter," Lizzy said, "says you owe U.S. West Communications $138.89." She turned to the little girl sitting beside her. "Been making a lot of phone calls lately, Samantha?"

The girl blinked. "One hundred and how much?"

"Thirty-eight dollars and 89 cents."

Samantha looked around the room. "I only have $14." She lifted her hands to her head and fell back into her chair. "What am I going to do? I'm ruined!"

Joey burst out laughing. "That's the phone bill, Sam. You don't have to pay it. Mr. Hanson will."

"But why did they send *me* the letter?" Samantha asked, her head tilted to one side.

Mr. Hanson jumped to his feet. "Oh, dear," he said with a wink in Lizzy's direction. "I must have given you the wrong one. Here. *This* letter's for you. It says you can buy fruits and vegetables at 15 percent off the regular, everyday low price at the Safeway store on Main Street." He handed the girl a brightly colored envelope with pictures of food and a smiling checkout woman on the front. "Silly me. Sorry 'bout that, Samantha."

The girl gladly accepted the new letter. "Whew," she said with a big grin. "Thought I was broke for sure."

Lizzy gave Sam a big hug while trying, unsuccessfully, to suppress her giggles. Shifting in the big overstuffed chair by the window, she turned to Joey. "Looks like you got another letter from New York."

"Yeah," the boy said, his face flushed from laughing. "It's from Darick Tanner. I've been so busy listening to you all I haven't had a chance to read it."

"Well, then take it away," Mr. Hanson invited. "We're all ears."

The teenager cleared his throat. "Dear Joey." He looked up. "That's me."

Wendy nodded. "How glad we are that you recognize yourself."

Joey sighed, then continued. "How is everything on the ranch? I still miss you guys and think about my visit often. Tell Wrangler Barry that I remember when he saved me from going over the waterfalls. He saved my life, and I really appreciate that."

The boy looked up. "Scared me to death," he said softly. Shaking his head as if to clear unpleasant memories, he continued reading. "I'm doing pretty good at staying out of trouble. Wish I could say the same for some of the guys I know. I hate to tell you this but—" Joey paled, his eyes not leaving the paper. "But The Reaper's been arrested."

Lizzy glanced up suddenly, all smiles vanished from her face. Joey looked across at her, then back at the letter. His voice became hesitant, strained. "Seems he had some stuff on him. I hear he insists he was set up. Could be. There's some pretty nasty dudes in his neighborhood. Be just like them to let him take a fall for something they were into."

Joey glanced around the room nervously, his face tight, uncharacteristically somber. "Then he just says to say hello to everyone. That's all."

Mr. Hanson leaned forward in his chair. "Son, what's the matter?"

The teenager stood and walked to the door. "I gotta get back to work," he said softly. "I gotta go."

With that he hurried out into the foyer. The group heard his footsteps in the den and then the front door opening and closing. No one moved.

"Mrs. Pierce?" the lawyer asked. "What's the matter? Who is this Reaper fellow that Darick mentioned in his letter. Do you know him?"

The old woman nodded slowly. "Oh, yes," she said quietly. "I know him."

26

"Well, who is he?" Mr. Hanson pressed. "And why did Joey get so concerned? He looked more frightened than I've ever seen him before."

Lizzy turned to face the bright window. Sunshine flooded the silent room with bright autumn light. After a long moment she brushed silver hair from her forehead and faced the lawyer.

"You all don't know this—few people do—but Joey has a brother, an older brother. He's about 20 or so. Name's Troy, Troy Dugan. But because of his, shall we say, aggressive fighting habits, those on the streets call him The Reaper."

* * * * *

"You want to talk about it?" Mr. Hanson stood in the wide doorway of the corral, his form silhouetted against the bright Montana sky.

Joey sat with his back to the door, hands resting in his lap.

"Mrs. Pierce told us about your brother." The lawyer leaned against the open door. "It was kind of a shock to know there's another Dugan running around. Tell me about him. What's he like?"

The teenager's head nodded slightly. "He . . . he's tall, strong, smart—a tough fighter. You gotta be a tough fighter on the streets, or you're dead."

A cool wind drifted through the cracks of the corral, whispering its passage. "Ever since I was a kid, he'd come by the apartment—leave food and sometimes a jacket or pair of socks." The boy's shoulders sagged. "He was all the family I had, other'n Sam and Dizzy. 'Cept he was real family, know what I mean?"

"Yes, I know," Mr. Hanson said.

"I ain't heard so much from him during the last couple years. Thought maybe he moved away, you know, upstate, or down to Florida—a lot of the gang bangers want to live in Florida—not so cold in the wintertime."

27

"Was he a gang member?" the man asked.

"Yeah. They called themselves 'Reaper's Revenge.' Word was they were pretty tough. But I didn't think they were into doing stuff."

The lawyer lifted his hand. "You mean—?"

"Yeah. Drugs, cocaine, crack, the usual." The boy turned to face his companion. "Mr. H, if he said he didn't know nothin' about it, he didn't. I trust him." The boy turned away. "He's my brother."

Mr. Hanson took in a deep breath. "I'm sorry, Joey," he said quietly. "If there's anything I can do—"

"It's OK," the boy interrupted. "He'll prove that he was set up and they'll let him go. You see, he won't last too long in prison. He don't like little rooms with no windows. I remember that about him. Even when he came to the apartment, he always had me open all the windows and curtains so he could see out. He was kinda strange that way. I hope Captain Abernathy lets him look out once in a while."

"Abernathy?" the lawyer looked up in surprise. "Captain Abernathy's got him?"

"Yeah. The letter said he was arrested on the street where me and Dizzy used to live. Maybe he was comin' to see me. I don't know. I didn't have a chance to tell him I was leaving. He probably found out later from some of my buddies."

Mr. Hanson walked over and placed a hand on the boy's shoulder. "I'm really sorry, Joey," he said. "Your brother sounds like he has a lot of good in him. We'll all pray for him tonight at evening worship."

The boy nodded slightly. "You think God can see through all those walls?" He turned and faced his friend. "There ain't no windows in the Third Precinct jail, remember."

Mr. Hanson studied Joey's face. "God can see in, even

if your brother can't see out. He's kinda strange that way."

Joey smiled sadly. "You're probably right," he said. "But Troy don't know that."

*   *   *   *   *

Wendy stood, hands on hips, surveying the wall of bushes and limbs. Her face reflected a mixture of frustration and determination, a duet of emotions she experienced often.

Around her waist she wore a leather strap. Hanging from it, attached with shiny brass fittings, a long sheath snugly embraced Joey's razor-sharp machete. Her dusty riding boots, worn blue jeans, loose-fitting cotton shirt, and old felt hat she'd found in the Station attic made her look like an explorer ready to march into the Amazon basin to hunt for lost civilizations.

"Now," she said, addressing the barrier, "you still think you can keep me away from your secrets?" Slowly she pulled the machete from its sheath. "Well, secret this!"

Letting loose a yell any Confederate soldier would be proud of, Wendy attacked the living wall like a battalion of troops trying to rout an enemy. Leaves flew high into the air. Severed branches dropped at her feet. Bushes parted at her passing, left to wither where they fell. Her hands and arms worked in rhythmic jabs and thrusts as she tunneled through the barrier with little regard for man or beast.

The wall didn't stand a chance.

With a final swing of the machete, Wendy broke through the last of the undergrowth and vines that separated the road from what lay beyond. Suddenly she found herself standing on a dark patch of ground. There was no sound, only an occasional call from an unseen hawk high overhead.

What she saw seemed at first like a forest laden with

thick bushes and scattered brambled borders. There was nothing to distinguish her surroundings from any other spot in the shadowy woods.

Then the tangled forms of brush began to reveal themselves as objects not natural to the woodland. The mass of vines to one side seemed to melt right before her eyes into the shape of a small, boxlike form. Bush clusters a dozen or so feet in front of her suddenly had corners with abnormal protrusions and sharp angles. Tilting back her head, Wendy followed a bunch of climbing vines as they spread up, up, up to a rectangular shape over her head. In the shadows she could just barely make out the muted gleam of broken glass.

"What *is* this place?" she whispered, not wanting to dispel the dark intrigue that gripped her heart with a delicious fear. "What is this place?" she repeated, this time a little louder.

Reaching out her hand, she carefully took hold of a small batch of branches and pulled. At first they refused to budge, as if clinging to something. Then they broke away with a snap, revealing several white boards running horizontal to the forest floor.

Wendy wrapped her excited fingers around other patches of brush and pulled. They too resisted at first, then gave way, widening the gash, showing more weatherworn wood dressed in dry, peeling paint.

Stepping back a few paces, the girl suddenly realized that the thing in front of her was not a formation of weeds, vines, and branches, but rather a wall—a wooden wall, tall and straight, hidden behind years of forest growth.

"It's a building," Wendy breathed. "A white building. Yes. I can see it better now. The window, the corners, and the peak of its roof." She moved further away, her eyes searching the nature-wrapped structure.

"Hey! I know what it is. It's a house. I can see another

window behind those branches. And there's a section of a porch or something." The girl spoke slowly, listening to her own words as if waiting to hear an explanation for what she was discovering.

Her backward movement was abruptly halted as she felt herself pressing up against something hard. Turning, she stared at another bramble-shrouded structure, this one much smaller. She pulled back the branches and found more wooden boards, carefully fitted together to form the side of a small shed.

Realization flooded through the girl's senses. "It's a farm! I'm standing in a farmyard." Wendy's words cut the stillness. She pointed first in one direction then another. "That's the house . . . that's the barn . . . there's the shed. Oh, my. Oh, my! It's an old farm buried in the forest and I found it. I FOUND IT!"

She began running from place to place, jumping over rock piles and bushes, stumbling to first one vine-covered object then another, pulling at the years of green growth that covered the faces of the silent structures.

Wendy whipped the machete into action, slicing at thick stands of young fir and spruce, carving wide impressions in bramble-guarded openings, rooting out the stubborn stems of alpine grass and weeds. Vegetation wilted under the heat of her attack.

Before long, the girl stopped, her breath coming in short, heavy pants. There was no question now. She had, beyond the shadow of a doubt, discovered a long forgotten homestead cradled in a little valley in one of the folds of the towering Gallatin Mountains.

Wendy dropped her weary body onto the newly revealed steps that led up to the small porch of the old house. She sat for a moment, letting herself enjoy the solitude of the forest. She could now make out the shape of the yard with its different outbuildings—pump stand, well shelter, feeding trough for animals long gone, and chicken pen, its wire fencing intertwined with vines.

As she sat there, waiting to catch her breath, her mind wandered, filling in the missing details that the years had erased. She imagined the lilting laughter of children echoing from the base of the big tree by the barn, the snap of a whip wielded by a man guiding his sharp-tongued plow and broad-muscled mare across the north pasture—an area now filled with small, second growth trees. The mother would be in the kitchen, baking a pie—cherry pie, of course.

The girl sighed as a sad feeling mixed with her imaginings. She had had a mother, once, who made pies. But that was before the morning she found a note on her dresser telling her and Debbie and Daddy that Mother had left to "find herself" with a man from Connecticut.

It had frightened her, not like an adventure or mystery or secret discovery frightened her. That's a pleasant fear, like riding on a roller coaster. With an adventure fear you know you're going to be all right in the end.

But that morning the fear had been different. In her young mind the world was unwinding and she couldn't stop it. What had she done that was so awful, so unforgivable, so mean, that her mother had to leave?

Wendy shifted her position on the rough, wooden step. Sure, Daddy had explained that it was not her fault, that Mother felt she had to make a change in her life. To the little girl clutching the handwritten note that morning in their Manhattan apartment, it was impossible to fathom how life, any life, could be better than it had been.

Now, all she had from the woman she called Mother were fading memories and an occasional letter saying how much she missed her daughter. It just didn't make sense.

Wendy straightened. But the family who lived on this

farm had been different. She just knew it. They stayed together and stayed together and stayed together until the forest came and wrapped its green arms around the house and the barn and the tool shed, and buried them all while love still lived and moved among the vines and branches, sealing them forever in happiness.

That's what happened here, she decided silently, confidently. That's what happened at Merrilee.

The girl's eyes opened wide. Merrilee! The sign. The sign says the name of the *farm*.

Wendy jumped to her feet and raced across the cluttered farmyard and through the opening she'd slashed in the barrier. She emerged by the road and grabbed the long board lying in the weeds.

Triumphantly, she hurried back through the opening and paused by the old shed. Looking around frantically, she called across the yard. "Where are you? Where are you?"

Then she saw it, just off to her right. Two tall beams leaned drunkenly, supported by the branches of nearby trees. Between them a gate lay crumpled in the weeds. Wendy hurried to the spot and held the board over her head. Yes! If the beams were standing upright, the distance between them would be identical to the length of the plank. This was the front gate. And the proud piece of wood had announced to one and all with deeply carved letters and bright, white paint, that this farm had a name.

The girl turned and faced the old homestead, board still held high above her head. "Merrilee," she called, her voice strong and triumphant, "you're alive again. I'll bring you back to life with my command. You'll be my own secret place, where I can come and imagine stories and pretend adventures, where no one will laugh at me and say I'm silly. You're mine. From this moment, you're only mine!"

A clattering sound in the direction of the house made Wendy jump back with a start. From behind some timbers on the first floor a low growl disturbed the stillness.

Wendy's face turned ashen as she watched the branches covering the front door move slightly. Was there something inside, trying to get out?

The girl screamed, dropped the long plank, and dove through the opening she had cut in the vines. Early, who'd been grazing contentedly in the little meadow across the road, looked up and saw his rider sprawl across the old trail.

Sensing danger, he galloped toward the frightened girl. Wendy jumped to her feet and grabbed the horn of the saddle as the horse swept by. In one movement she was astride the animal, laying leather to flank, thundering down the logging road, raising clouds of dust in the cool mountain air.

Back in the brambles, something moved. Then, as suddenly as it had begun, the commotion ceased. Afternoon shadows wrapped the forgotten homestead in a deep, fathomless silence.

* * * * *

"Hey, Wendy," Joey called when he saw the girl and her horse trotting up to the corral, "I wanna talk to you."

Wendy panicked, suddenly realizing that not only had she failed to retrieve the geologist's pick she'd thrown into the trees on the mountain, but now here she was, wearing the machete she hadn't ask permission to borrow. Joey most certainly was going to kill her right then, right there.

"Hello, Mr. Dugan," Wendy called, all smiles. "What is it you'd like to discuss? The weather? Politics? State of the economy?"

"How 'bout, where's my geo-pick!" Joey gasped when he saw the long object hanging from the rider's waist.

34

"And *that!* I don't remember giving you permission to take my machete."

Wendy patted Early lovingly. "Oh . . . well . . . guess I forgot. But I knew you'd understand. You're such a wonderfu—"

"Cut the gooey talk," the teenager interrupted. "You did it on purpose and you know it! If you dinged or messed it up in any way, Wrangler Barry's going to string me up under the nearest cottonwood tree. You promised to return the pick safe and sound. I suppose you left it up there somewhere!" He pointed toward the mountains. "I'm responsible for all this stuff, or have you forgotten?"

The girl nodded. "Calm down, Joey. I know where everything is, sort of. You'll get your precious tool back."

"I want it *now!*" The boy's face reddened as he slammed his fist hard into the corral gate. "Everybody thinks they can just run all over me anytime they want. 'Ol' Joey won't care. He'll just smile and say, "That's OK." ' Well, it's *not* OK. Those things are my responsibility and I want them back."

Wendy frowned. She'd never seen her friend this upset.

"You think I work out here, day after day, because it's a hobby or something?" the boy continued. "I'll have you know Grandpa Hanson *pays* me to work here. He trusts me, he and Wrangler Barry. Now both of them are on vacation and I'm in charge. *I'm in charge!*" Joey picked up a bucket of oats and threw it against the wall with shattering force, sending showers of grain across the worktable and feed sacks. "So what happens? In one day I lose a geo-pick and who knows what else, thanks to you. Doesn't anybody think about what's important to me? Doesn't anybody care?" The boy sank to his knees, face in hands. "I have responsibilities too, you know. There are people who depend on me."

Wendy felt a hand touch her leg. Glancing down she saw Lizzy standing beside her, motioning for her to take Early out into the pasture. With a nod, the girl reined her steed and together they moved quietly away from the corral.

The old woman stood for a long moment, studying the kneeling form on the dusty floor. Joey's muffled sobs tore at her heart and brought tears to her own eyes.

"He'll be OK," she said softly. "Captain Abernathy is a kind man. He'll watch over Troy."

Joey sank onto his heels, a tired moan escaping his lips. "I always figured my brother would really be something, you know? He'd get off the streets, be a teacher or artist, something really great." The boy looked up at the woman. "He was my hero. I wanted to be just like him. Now he's going to spend years and years in prison. It'll finish him off, for sure. He won't make it. He'll just shrivel up and die. That's what he'll do. I feel so helpless, so totally helpless."

He gazed into the eyes of his lifelong friend. "Does he know that I worry about him? Does he know that I wonder about how he's doin' and stuff?" The boy paused. "Does Troy know that I love him?"

Lizzy moved through the sunstruck columns of dusty air and sat down on a bale of hay. "I'm sure he does," she said. "He's proud of his little brother. He's said so many times." The old woman chuckled softly. "I've heard him say the same things about you that you just said about him. Seems you two have a mutual admiration society going here."

Joey smiled weakly. "He always told me I was gonna be president of the United States some day. And I could hire him as FBI chief so he could throw all the bad guys like us in jail where they belong." The speaker saddened. "Guess Troy figured wrong. He stayed a bad guy a little too long."

Lizzy sighed. "Maybe Darick was right. Maybe he was set up."

"Doesn't matter," Joey responded. "You think anybody's gonna try to defend him, to prove him innocent? And besides, what was he doin' with that gang, anyway?" The boy shook his head. "Nah. He's done for. My brother's gonna rot in prison while I live in Montana ridin' horses and enjoyin' life. It's just not fair."

"Joey," the woman brightened, "why don't you write him a letter? Tell him how you feel. He'd like that."

"Oh, sure. I'm sittin' here on my mountain with the birds singin' and the grass growin' and he's in a dark cell with no windows and I take time from my busy schedule of havin' fun to tell him I'm thinkin' 'bout him. He's gonna believe that real fast. Words don't mean nothin' when you're hurtin' deep inside, when you think you've blown it big time. Maybe a letter would help, but it won't change nothin'."

Lizzy nodded. "Perhaps you're right." She thought for a long moment. "We all make choices, Joey," she said slowly. "And sometimes we have to live with the results of those decisions." She brushed a stray strand of hair from the boy's forehead. "And sometimes those results hurt other people, too."

Joey nodded, then sighed and rose to his feet. "Well, enough feelin' sorry for myself. I gotta get back to work and clean up this mess." He paused. "And I guess I gotta go talk to Wendy and apologize for blowin' my stack like I did. Probably scared her half to death."

"Wendy's a smart little girl," the old woman said. "I think she'll understand."

Joey nodded and started walking toward the grove at the far end of the pasture. Lizzy watched him go. She knew the turmoil in his heart was far from over. But her young friend was learning that sometimes pain is part of the package called life.

CHAPTER THREE

Facing
The Dragons

✳ ✳ ✳

Dawn crept in with the mist that rolled and drifted above Shadow Creek. Night-cooled ripples murmured along the winding waterway as it cut through the mountain valley like an ancient scar.

Pine trees dripped dew from their needles while cottonwoods stood motionless in the cold, gray hint of a new day.

The big Station, its proud face moist from the passing fog, sat waiting for the sun to rise, watching the morning glow as it touched the distant mountain tops.

If the inhabitants of the old stagecoach inn had been awake they would have noticed one of their number slip silently through the front door and lightly descend the steps. They would've seen the shadowy form move up the hillside and join the dusty road running beside the broad-shouldered dwelling.

Had they been watching, they would've seen the figure pause and stare down at the Station for a long moment, then turn slowly and begin walking away from Shadow Creek Ranch toward the county road three miles to the west.

But no one took notice of the silent departure, for sleep held eyes captive, and dreams still drifted with the early morning mist.

* * * * *

Breakfast dishes rattled and clanked as Lizzy rinsed remnants of scrambled eggs and hash browns from the china plates. Mr. Hanson stood in the doorway, sipping a cup of herb tea, watching the old woman work.

"Wonder why Joey didn't come out for breakfast?" he said thoughtfully. "Not like him to miss a meal, especially when hash browns are involved."

Lizzy chuckled. "That boy would eat a whole potato patch full of 'em if we'd let him. Can't say as I blame him. Grandpa Hanson's spuds are the best around. Some of those 'taters are as big as boulders."

The man nodded. "They are good, that's for sure. Do you think he's sick?"

"Who, Grandpa Hanson?"

"No, Joey. He didn't come to breakfast, remember?"

Lizzy laughed. "I know who you're talking about. I'm just pulling your leg. Guess our assistant ranch hand had a late night with the horses. I saw the corral light on until past midnight. Don't know what he was up to. Musta worn himself out. I'll check on him if he doesn't creep from his den in a couple hours."

Mr. Hanson lifted the cup and drained it. "Sounds good. I'm a little worried. He took the news of his brother's arrest pretty hard."

The old woman nodded slowly. "Yeah, I know. Joey has strong feelings when it comes to Troy. I kinda admire him for it. Troy hasn't exactly been the best role model through the years."

39

"Captain Abernathy says they caught him with drugs in his pockets," the lawyer sighed. "I called him yesterday just to see if there was anything I could do. He said it's basically an open-and-shut case. He'll probably get 10, maybe 15 years behind bars. The district attorney is no pushover when it comes to possession charges. He hits 'em where it hurts."

Lizzy picked up a dishtowel and dried her hands. "It's a real shame, too. Troy could've made something of himself."

The man grinned. "There you go again," he said, "thinking every bad boy is a good boy waiting to get out."

"Well, don't you?" Lizzy responded, sharing a smile.

"Guilty," the lawyer admitted. "And look where that line of thinking got us—out here in the hinterlands of Montana trying to keep groups of city kids on the straight and narrow a few weeks at a time."

The old woman placed the dishrag over the faucet. "Tyler, we're a couple of pushovers, that's all there is to it. But I wouldn't change you or me for all the money in Andrew Morrison the Third's Beverly Hills bank account."

Mr. Hanson laughed and turned to leave. "Speaking of money, I'd better go earn some so we can continue trying to keep city kids on the straight and narrow. See ya."

Lizzy waved, gave the sparkling clean kitchen a visual once-over, and walked out into the hallway. Pausing as she passed Joey's door, she lifted her hand to knock, then lowered it again. She knew her young friend would come out when he was good and ready.

* * * * *

Wendy licked her lips and drew in a deep breath. Pulling the felt hat tightly over her ears and adjusting her grip on the machete, she plunged boldly through the opening in the barrier.

Once inside, she stopped and looked around, eyes narrow, searching, scanning every bush and tree for the beast she knew lived within the green boundaries of the old homestead named Merrilee. Everything was as she'd left it. The buildings stood silent and empty, surrounded by tall trees and mountain meadows.

She held the machete stiffly at her side. Maybe whatever had frightened her the day before had gone, she told herself. Maybe the beast was unhappy with the intrusion of the adventurer with the long, sharp knife and had decided to move on. A twig snapped nearby. Then again, maybe not.

Turning, she saw one of the branches covering the front entrance to the house move slightly. She crept forward without a sound. It was time to face this . . . this . . . whatever it was, once and for all. There wasn't enough room for both her and it in Merrilee. Somebody would have to go, and it wasn't going to be her!

She was tired of her world being filled with people and things that insisted on snatching her dreams away. In her young mind, Merrilee was more than an old, abandoned homestead. It was a symbol of her hopes. They, too, had become overgrown with vines of sadness and thick barriers of uncertainty. As far as she was concerned, her mother had left her to fade back into the forest just as this farm had been forced to do.

Now, whatever dragon lived here, whatever beast roamed the long-forgotten rooms of the little two-story home, she'd confront it right here, right now. The girl lifted her chin. It was time to face the dragon and let her dreams live on.

Sniff, sniff. A strange sound came from behind the leaf-shrouded door. It sounded like an animal breathing. This was followed by a low growl that sent shivers up and down the girl's arms and legs. But she didn't back

41

off. Instead, she walked slowly in the direction of the porch.

Growl . . . growl. Her feet climbed the steps, hands holding the machete above her head.

Wendy stood on the porch waiting, staring at the doorway. Slowly the branches near the bottom of the entrance began to move apart. The girl felt lightheaded, weak. She could feel her heart pounding in her chest, but she remained frozen to the spot. She wasn't going to run away this time.

Wendy saw a moist, black nose and a shiny eye immerge from the leaves. A face sporting a black mask-like arrangement of hair turned toward her. Clawed fingers gripped the branches and held them away from the furry countenance. The creature lifted its snout and growled a low, gurgling growl.

Wendy's eyes opened wide. "YOU!" she cried, her voice high with tension. "*You* scared me away from here?"

The creature pulled itself the remainder of the way through the branches and ambled over to the feet of the girl holding the machete above her head. It sat down and sniffed the air as if to say, "You plan on using that thing on little ol' me?"

"A *raccoon?*" Wendy lowered the sharp weapon as relief flooded her body, leaving her arms and legs tingling. "A *raccoon* made me run away like a scared dog? I don't believe this!"

The animal licked its front paws and studied the intruder carefully as if to say "Believe it, sister. That little growl of mine has made it possible for me to live in this dump for quite some time now. I was doing just fine until you showed up."

Wendy started to giggle. Then she tilted back her head and laughed long and loud, filling the farmyard with a happy noise it hadn't heard for years upon years.

42

The raccoon sat and watched this strange visitor rock back and forth, holding her stomach as her pent-up fear and tension found release in gaiety.

When she could control herself, the girl sank heavily onto the top step. She glanced over at her far-from-scary companion. "You got me," the girl giggled. "You got me good. I thought for sure you were some ancient beast with long, sharp tusks and beady eyes ready to eat me for supper."

The animal lifted its nose as if to say "My, oh my. You humans have such imaginations. I'm a raccoon and nothing else. If you want to think I'm some kinda monster, that's your problem."

Wendy leaned her tired head against the rough porch railing. Scared by a raccoon. If that didn't beat all. Maybe her dad was right. Maybe she shouldn't let her imagination get the best of her.

She sat for a long moment, letting the peace and rustic beauty of the old homestead soak into her thoughts once again. *Maybe not all dragons turn out to be dragons*, she pondered, watching her new forest friend rummage about the porch. *Could it be that some fears, maybe most, when faced head-on turn out to be a whole lot less scary than first imagined?*

The young girl sighed, then rose quickly to her feet. She'd give this new revelation more thought later. Right now, with the growling beast taken care of, she could continue her adventure.

With a light step she walked to the door, the raccoon at her heels. This was no time for dragons. It was time for discovery. Wendy reached out and began pulling away the vines and branches that guarded the entrance to the old house. Maybe there were more mysteries hiding behind the musty walls of her new secret kingdom.

* * * * *

"Joey?" Lizzy knocked on the boy's bedroom door,

her hands stained from cutting and canning fresh vegetables. "Hey, Joey, it's Dizzy. You up?"

There was no response.

"You planning on sleeping all day?" Her call was interrupted by the sound of a car arriving in front of the station. With a shrug, she continued down the hallway, through the foyer, and out onto the broad front porch.

Wrangler Barry was just closing the door of his pickup when he heard Lizzy's cheery greeting. "Well, hello, stranger. We didn't expect you for a few more days."

Barry smiled up at the woman. "Didn't plan on coming back," he said. "But Joey called last night and said he needed some help on the ranch. He sounded a little—I don't know—funny, so here I am." The tall, muscular horseman glanced in the direction of the pasture. "Where is our ex-New Yorker anyway? Out riding?"

Lizzy frowned. "No, he's still sleeping, I guess."

"Sleeping?" Barry looked up in surprise. "It's almost noon!"

Mr. Hanson appeared on the second-floor balcony. "Hey, Barry. What are you doing here?"

"Tyler?" Lizzy called, moving down the steps a few paces and looking up at the man standing on the upper porch. "Barry says Joey phoned last night and asked him to come to the ranch."

"Odd," the lawyer said, scratching his head. "He didn't tell me anything about it. Maybe we'd better have a little talk with Joey. Where is he?"

"Still in his room, I guess," came the reply. Mr. Hanson and Lizzy stood for a moment, confused. Then the man's face paled. "Mrs. Pierce, you don't think—"

The woman's mouth dropped open. "Oh, Tyler!"

"What's going on?" Barry asked.

The old woman and young lawyer spun about and

44

raced back into the building, the wrangler following close behind. The group arrived at Joey's bedroom at the same time.

"Joey?" Mr. Hanson called, pounding loudly on the door. "Joey, open up."

No response.

"Joey, I'm opening the door," the lawyer warned as he twisted the knob. The three pushed into the little room together.

The bed was neatly made and the boy's favorite hat hung on a hook by the window. Mr. Hanson hurried to the dresser and pulled open the top drawer. It was empty.

"I don't believe it!" the lawyer gasped. "He's gone. Joey's gone."

"Where?" Barry pressed. "What's going on?"

"Look, Tyler," Lizzy said. "He left a note on the nightstand."

Mr. Hanson sat down on the bed and unfolded the piece of paper. He read slowly, his voice unsteady.

Dear Everybody. I'm going back to New York City. Don't worry. I'll be OK. I can't sit around and do nothing while my brother is in such trouble. He needs to know someone is worried about him, so that's why I'm going. Sorry, Dizzy, but I decided that a letter just weren't enough.

I asked Wrangler Barry to come out and take care of the horses. Tell him Tar Boy scratched his left-front knee the other day, so that's why there's medicine on it.

I'm going to stop by the bank in Bozeman and get my money out that Grandpa Hanson paid me. It's enough for my airplane ticket and some food. Darick Tanner said I could stay with him in East Village, so I won't be out on the streets or anything like that.

The man's hands trembled as he read on. *Mr. H, don't worry about me. You always told me I should face the challenges that come to me. That I should not wait for*

45

someone else to do something, but do it myself. Well, this is a big challenge, and I'm going to face it just like you said.

One more thing. When I'm done, can I come back to Shadow Creek Ranch? I want to come back, you know. So please don't let anybody else have my room, OK?

I love you all, even Wendy and Debbie.

Your friend and assistant ranch hand, Joey.

Mr. Hanson looked up at the woman, his eyes moist with concern. "Oh, Mrs. Pierce, I never meant for him to do something like this. He doesn't know what he's up against. Lizzy, what have I done?"

* * * * *

The big jetliner skimmed the low collection of scattered clouds spreading like a tattered blanket over the city. A young boy's face pressed against one of the small, oval windows that lined the aircraft as the plane slowly descended toward a distant runway.

To the observer watching from above, the city looked neat and orderly, its streets and boulevards crossing at measured intervals, like designs on a beautiful tapestry.

Tall buildings, their odd-shaped forms moving silently as the airplane passed, pointed heavenward, as if trying to reach beyond the landlocked boundaries of the city to the clean air and bright afternoon sunlight high above their heads.

The boy recognized many of the landmarks he'd seen only from ground level. He could trace the long finger of Manhattan stretching from the Bronx to the Battery. Across the Hudson River sat Jersey City. There was Queens, and right below it, Brooklyn and Coney Island. And sure enough, there was Lady Liberty out in the harbor, her golden torch surprisingly small as seen from the plane.

Soon the sandy island dunes of Jamaica Bay slipped below the wing. Closer and closer they came. The boy unconsciously lifted his feet, as if trying to keep his boots from skimming the blue waters.

Then solid land rushed by, followed by a firm thump, thump as the jetliner settled onto one of the long runways at Kennedy International Airport. The pilot deployed the aircraft's thrust reversers; with a mighty roar, the sleek jet slowed to a comfortable taxiing speed.

In minutes, the aircraft rolled up to a terminal gate, and the boy heard the engines spool down to a whisper.

"Ladies and gentlemen," the voice on the cabin speaker called cheerfully, "welcome to New York City."

The arrival area swarmed with passengers and well-wishers as the young man stood off to one side, his eyes scanning the crowd, searching for a familiar face. He was beginning to wonder if he'd misunderstood the directions he'd heard early that morning when "Hey, Joey" called a friendly voice from across the crowded room.

The boy turned to see Darick Tanner running in his direction, hand waving above his head. "Sorry I'm late. The bus had a flat tire. Wouldn't you know it, a flat right in the middle of Queens. Had to grab a taxi. Hope you brought some cash. Driver's waiting out by the curb. I told him I'd pay him when we got to the airport. Had to do some smooth talking, man."

Joey laughed. "No problem, Darick. I feel rich today. Let's take the taxi all the way back to East Village. We're a couple of high-society types, at least for this afternoon. Whadda ya say?"

"Great by me," Darick chuckled. "If you got the bread, let's have a picnic."

The two friends hurried out to the waiting cab and dropped Joey's small suitcase into the trunk. The driver, who didn't speak English too well, finally understood where the boys wanted to go and said he'd take them there if they paid in advance. Joey handed the man a small pile of bills. Satisfied, the man turned the key and moved out into the line of cars inching past the arrival area. He didn't get too many requests to take passengers to East Village, especially a Black and an Italian boy riding together.

As the vehicle sped along the expressway toward Manhattan, Darick brought Joey up-to-date on the latest news concerning his brother.

"I talked to Abernathy this morning after you called. He said Troy's first meeting with the judge will be tomorrow. Some yo-yo from the DA's office has been assigned to defend him. I'm sure Troy was thrilled to hear that."

Joey nodded. "Yeah, probably made his day."

"Anyway," Darick continued, "Abernathy said Troy's doin' OK, considering. Says during his calmer moments he just sits in his cell a lot and stares at the wall."

"He don't like rooms with no windows," the passenger wearing pointed-toe riding boots stated flatly. "Makes him nervous. Always has."

They sat in silence, watching the streets and buildings rush by. In the distance, the spires of Lower Manhattan were rising into view.

"So, Joey, why'd you come?" Darick asked the question without letting his eyes leave the passing scenery.

His companion shrugged. "He's my brother."

"But you were in Montana, on that beautiful ranch with horses and Mrs. Pierce and all the rest. You had it made, man. What if you get into trouble here and can't go back? What if someone turns on you, makes you do something stupid? Do you trust yourself that much?"

The boy didn't answer for a long moment. "I ain't the same Joey Dugan who left here a year ago. I've changed."

"Yeah? But the streets ain't changed. They can grab you and hurt you and make you do bad things even if you fight 'em."

48

"Then I'll stay away from the streets." Joey lifted his chin slightly.

"I ain't talking about just roads and avenues. I'm talking about what's hiding in here." Darrick pointed at his heart. "You got streets in you, man, just like I do. Survival, hate, anger. I'm working hard to keep it under control, but it ain't easy. What makes you think you can beat the streets that run inside your own mind?"

Joey felt his throat tighten. That was a question he'd asked himself a hundred times since the moment he decided to return to New York and help Troy. Being the good, kind, thoughtful Joey Dugan he was on the ranch was easy. He was surrounded by goodness, kindness, thoughtfulness. But in East Village the ranch and its collection of people were far, far away. Would he survive as the Joey Dugan he'd become? Or would the streets, inside and out, snatch him back again?

"He's my brother," was all the boy could say.

The cab sped across the Williamsburg Bridge, which abruptly emptied its burden of cars, buses, and trucks onto Delancey Street. Within seconds, the taxi and its passengers had disappeared into the steel and concrete jungle of Manhattan's Lower East Side.

* * * * *

Wendy looked about the room, a smile of satisfaction spreading across her dirt-stained face. The downstairs section of the old homestead was being transformed by her busy hands.

She'd quickly discovered that the furnishings were simple, made from wood, and carefully pieced together. The girl figured that whoever had lived here before, boasted a talent for creating chairs, tables, desks, and shelves from fallen trees found in the surrounding forests. For the most part, everything in the sturdy home was still in place, like something unexpected had happened to the people who used to live there. Only the ravages of time and the frequent visits of woodland creatures had disturbed the abandoned dwelling.

She found an open book on a small table by the cobweb-covered rocking chair, an empty glass setting by the sink. One of the windows in the tiny dining room was propped open, as if to let in the cool, fresh air of some long-forgotten summer evening.

Rows of well-used books, their titles faded and covers worn, lined the glass-fronted bookcase in the corner. An old timepiece, its ornate hands pointing perpetually at the 6:00 hour, gazed down from the mantle above the small fireplace, its pendulum hanging limp and silent.

Wendy had carefully removed piles of leaves and twigs from the living room rug and brushed aside seasons of dust and cobwebs from the small collection of furniture. Under her gentle attack, a spark of life was returning to the abandoned rooms. The old homestead was feeling the touch of human hands for the first time in many, many years.

The girl's furry companion insisted on inspecting her work, usually while she was in the process of performing it. The raccoon would stick its nose into the corners as she was dusting there, examine every twig and load of leaves she collected, and climb all over the sections of furniture his newfound friend was attempting to piece together.

"Get out of the way!" Wendy commanded for the two-hundredth time as she was picking up an overturned chair by the window. "You're not exactly helping, you know."

The raccoon looked up at her as if to say, "Well, I'm not as big as you, but I'm doin' the best I can."

At one point the animal squeezed between Wendy's feet as she was carrying a load of rubbish in the direction of the front door. The girl almost tripped.

"Would you *please* get out of the way? You're always

50

under my feet." Wendy paused. "That's it! I've been trying to think of a good name for a pest like you. Now I've got it. Since you seem bound and determined to stay here, I'm going to call you Mr. Underfoot. How do you like that?"

The little creature stopped dead in his tracks and tilted his head to one side. Wendy was sure he was thinking about what she'd just said. The animal scratched his head twice, then sniffed the air. "If it would make you feel better," he seemed to say, "you can call me Abraham Lincoln. But Mr. Underfoot isn't so bad. I can live with it."

That item of business settled, the two continued in the direction of the door, the furry creature zig-zagging between the young girl's feet.

As she worked, Wendy let her imagination wander, a practice she'd perfected long ago. Who lived here? Probably a young man and woman from back east. They'd come west in search of adventure. Maybe even gold. Wendy gasped. Perhaps they'd found some and it was hiding right here in the house!

She shook her head. If they were so rich, why didn't they have fancy stuff lying around, like fine crystal goblets in the kitchen instead of those tin cups, or foreign carpets instead of the thin throw rugs dotting the floors. No, they weren't rich, that was for sure.

At one corner of the room, under the open window, Wendy discovered a cedar chest. The wood was faded and stained by countless days of rain or fog. During the cold winter months the little chest more than likely wore a blanket of snow across its upper surface.

Some of the wood slats had shrunk, pulling apart from each other.

Wendy knelt beside the chest and brushed aside the coating of dust. Peering between the boards she could see odd-shaped objects inside.

"What's this?" she called to Mr. Underfoot, who was busy examining a spoon lying at the bottom of the washbasin in the kitchen. Wendy saw the little animal's eyes and nose appear above the rim of the basin, ears poised high with curiosity.

"Looks like some sort of chest maybe," Wendy continued. The animal sniffed, then returned to his spoon. Anything remotely shiny was of much greater interest to him than an old dusty box.

Wendy bent low and began searching for a latch. "Maybe there's money in here. Yeah, that's what this was for, to hold all the money they brought west with them. They were saving it to buy more land. There's probably a million bucks in here and if I find it, it's all mine!"

The raccoon's head suddenly appeared at the top of the basin again. "*And* yours," the girl added, eying her companion. "I know, you were here first."

Sniff.

Finding the latch on the front of the chest, the girl disconnected it and slowly lifted the lid. The late afternoon sun filtered through the window and formed tiny pools of light in the dark recesses of the chest.

Wendy saw a faded and tattered blanket resting in one corner and a collection of books in the other. But what caught her eye was something hiding under a pile of darkly stained pillowcases and bed linens. Only a corner was visible.

The girl reached down and pushed aside the cloth. What she saw made her gasp. There, resting among the faded folds, was a rectangular object, about the size of a shoe box. But no pair of loafers ever had such a beautiful container. The object's gleaming silver surface was covered with skillfully etched markings—flowers and trees, hills and valleys, towering mountains. Some sections of the box reflected its surroundings like a mirror.

52

Wendy could see her own amazed face in the shiny surface.

"It's ... it's ... just ... beautiful," she breathed, words failing her for the first time she could remember. "Oh, it's simply beautiful!"

Mr. Underfoot scampered down from the washbasin and hurried over to join his companion. Wendy saw his face appear beside hers in the box's gleaming lid.

"Look at that, Mr. Underfoot," Wendy gasped. "Have you ever seen anything so beautiful?"

The animal growled, thinking the little masked face he was seeing was another raccoon trying to edge in on his territory.

Wendy laughed. "That's you, silly," she said, pushing her furry friend to one side. "Now, get out of my way. I've gotta see what's in that box. If what's inside is anything like what's outside, I'm one rich dude. I can probably buy Montana and parts of Wyoming."

The girl lifted the box from the chest and carried it cautiously to the dining room table. She set it down and hurriedly drew up a chair. With tongue firmly planted in one corner of her mouth, Wendy raised the lid and peeked inside.

* * * * *

By the time the taxicab had dropped the two friends off at Darick's apartment, the sun had settled behind the Jersey shore and night stars had blinked on above Manhattan's celebrated skyline. Not much had changed in East Village during the past year. For Joey, it was like slipping back in time. The process made him feel uncomfortable.

The front door of the third precinct police headquarters squeaked open as Joey and Darick entered the two-story brick building. The structure was set in among rows of other buildings that looked identical to it. The only distinguishing features singling out the precinct from its neighbors was a lighted sign above the door and the occasional police officer climbing or descending the stoop.

"I never thought I'd be coming here without an escort," Joey chuckled.

Darick nodded. "The only reason I'm here is for you and Troy, believe me. This place and me aren't on the best of terms."

"Well, what do you know," the officer behind the desk called as he caught a glimpse of the two visitors. "Joey Dugan and Darick Tanner—the neighborhood's very own dynamic duo. Strange. I didn't send a squad out to any robbery during the last 20 minutes. You two just giving yourselves up?"

Joey grinned. "No, Sergeant Horowitz, we didn't do nothin' this time. I'm here to see my brother."

"Oh, yeah, Troy Dugan. Bad dude." The officer leaned forward. "You sure you want to pay him a visit? He ain't exactly in a . . . how shall I say . . . receptive mood tonight. If you keep your eyes open, you'll probably see one of our staff wearing Troy's supper on his chest. Your brother insisted the steak was too rare. Hey, we put it in the microwave for at least 45 seconds. I don't know what his beef was." The man burst out laughing. "Get it? Steak? Beef? Who says cops aren't funny?"

Darick smiled. "I've always thought cops were a barrel of laughs."

The man coughed, then frowned.

"Is Captain Abernathy here?" Joey asked, jabbing an elbow into Darick's ribs.

Sergeant Horowitz nodded. "He's in his office. You know where it is. Now get outta here before I dump you two in the cooler and toss away the key."

Joey and Darick smiled and waved as they walked past the big reception counter and headed down the hallway.

"I've been expecting you," Captain Abernathy called from behind his desk. "How you doin', Joey? Aren't you a long way from home?"

The boys entered the room and closed the door. "Sorta, I guess," the teenager said with a nod, then looked around. "I sure spent a pile of time in here."

"Don't get too used to it," the policeman chuckled. "I'm going to get you back to Montana as fast as I can." The man turned. "And you, Darick, you're in on this caper, too, I see."

"Yes, sir," the Black boy said. "Just trying to help out a buddy."

"Montana must be some kinda place if it made friends of you two," Captain Abernathy added with a warm smile. "I was half expecting to hear from Tyler that you'd done each other in this summer. Glad you made peace. Does my old heart good to see you two fellows in the same room without weapons drawn."

The boys grinned at each other. "Let's just say we worked stuff out," Joey encouraged. "It was sorta touch and go for a while."

"I'll bet it was," the captain nodded. "So," he leaned back in his chair, "now you want to see Troy. As you might imagine, I got this frenzied long-distance phone call from our lawyer friend this afternoon. He's worried sick about you, Joey. You shouldn't have just snuck out like that."

"I know," the youngster admitted. "But he would've tried to talk me out of comin' and all. But I just had to. You understand, don't you?"

The officer nodded slowly. "Yeah, I understand. Tyler does too. You don't have to apologize. We'd probably have done the same thing if we were in your shoes . . ." the man glanced down at the floor, "or boots, in your case."

Joey laughed. "Sneakers just don't feel right no more."

Captain Abernathy reached over and pressed a button by his phone. A voice called out from a tiny speaker resting above it: "Basement."

"Has Mr. Dugan calmed down enough to have visitors?"

The boys heard a chuckle. "Just come down with full riot gear, Captain, and you'll be fine."

The officer lifted his hand in the direction of the door. "Shall we?" he invited.

Joey and his companions moved through the first-floor corridors and then descended the stone steps leading to the basement. The building had been renovated to include several jail cells where the old furnace had been. The walls were painted white, and someone had hung a few pictures along the wide, brightly-lit hallway that ran the length of the chamber. To the left were thick-barred rooms labeled with numbers. Captain Abernathy and his guests walked to the far end of the area and paused before cell number 4.

"Hey, Dugan," the policeman called. "You got visitors."

A bed mattress slammed against the bars, followed by a stream of obscenities. Joey jumped back and shouted. "Troy! It's me, Joey!"

The cursing stopped. A form moved in the shadows at the far end of the cell. "Joey?" a rough voiced called. "Is that you, Joey?"

The boy smiled weakly. "Yeah, Troy. In the flesh. Came to see ya."

A young man, chin covered with a week's worth of beard, stepped forward into the light. Joey gasped when he saw the deeply lined cheeks and sweat-stained face approaching him. He wanted to run away, but he didn't.

"Hey, Joey," the man called, his eyes opening wide with wonder. "Whadda you doin' here? I thought you was in Alaska or something."

56

"Montana," the boy said softly. "I was in Montana."

"I stopped by to see you a while back and your neighbor, what's her name, Peterson, yeah, Mrs. Peterson, she said you and Lizzy Pierce had flown the coop, gone out west to ride horses."

Joey's hands trembled. He'd never seen his brother so frail and worn. His clothes were dirty, his hair long and uncombed. "I live on a ranch called Shadow Creek. It's really nice."

"Shadow Creek," the older boy repeated. "Sounds pretty."

"It is."

The two stood staring at each other through the bars for a long moment. "So, you came to see your big brother?" The man laughed weakly. "I'd invite you in, but I ain't got the key."

Captain Abernathy stepped forward. "If you'll behave yourself, Troy, I'll let your brother come inside."

The young man backed away from the door. "Hey, I wouldn't try nothin' with my kid brother here. It'd be a bad influence on his young mind. If there's one thing I don't want to be, it's a bad influence. It'd ruin my reputation, right, Joey?"

The boy grinned shyly. "Whatever you say, Troy."

The metal door slid back noisily and Joey stepped inside the cell. With a loud clank the door slammed shut again, causing the boy to jump.

"Sorry 'bout that," the captain said. "This stupid door sticks. Gotta be firm with it sometimes." He glanced at the prisoner. "Must need oiling."

Troy shrugged. "I hate sticky doors," he responded. "Sorta grates on your nerves, know what I mean?"

Darick lifted his hand. "Hey, Joey, I'm gonna go up and entertain Sergeant Horowitz. Maybe I'll tell him a few jokes. I'll wait for you up there, OK?"

Joey nodded. "Thanks. I won't be long."

Darick and the captain walked down the hallway and climbed the steps. Soon the room was silent.

Troy settled on the bare springs of his bed. "So, little brother," he said, "you come to save me, or what?"

Joey righted an overturned chair and sat down. "You need savin'?"

Troy grinned. "Nah. Got everything under control." He paused. "Why'd you come?"

The boy was still for a moment. "You're my brother and I love you. When I heard you was in jail, I had to come."

Troy sighed and studied the heel marks on the floor. "You gonna try to get me out?"

"That's what your lawyer's supposed to do."

"Lawyer?" Troy laughed. "Oh, I got a real winner there. The district attorney assigned him to my case 'cause no one else would take it. I've only seen him once and he didn't even ask if I was guilty or nothin'. But I know what he's thinkin'. He just said he'd make sure I got a fair trial, then ran off."

"Well, are you?"

"What, getting a fair trial?"

Joey leaned forward slightly. "No. Are you guilty? Did you have stuff on you?"

Troy shrugged. "Hey, half the guys in the neighborhood are stoned most of the time."

"Did you have drugs on you when they picked you up?" Joey repeated.

"What difference does it make?" the older boy said.

"It makes a difference to me!" Joey urged, his voice a little louder than he'd planned. "It . . . makes a difference."

Troy nodded slowly. "Yeah. I had a few ounces. So what?"

"So, that's against the law."

Troy stared at his brother. "I don't believe this! Since

58

when are you Mister Perfect, tellin' me that I'm breakin' the law? I don't recall you ever gettin' a good citizen's award, you arrogant little punk." The young man rose to his feet. "Where you get off, judging me like some high-class, fine, upstanding Boy Scout? The law didn't mean too much to you, if memory serves me correctly."

Joey reddened. "Hey, I never did drugs. I may have done stupid things. I may have broken the law. But I never messed around with drugs. They kill people, man. They make people do crazy things. I ain't perfect, but I never done that stuff. And you shouldn't have, either."

"You take the cake, you know that?" Troy kicked at the bed frame. "What makes you think you can waltz in here and preach at me? I'm your brother. I done plenty for you."

"I know," Joey shot back, "and I appreciate what you done."

"Well, you got a real interesting way of showing it. You're no better than me, Joey Dugan. We're just alike."

"That's not true!" the boy shouted, his voice a mixture of anger and frustration. "I changed. I really changed. And you can, too. That's why I came. You gotta change before—"

"Before what?"

Tears stung the teenager's eyes. "Before you get killed. Before they find you beat up in some dumpster like a pile of trash. I don't want you to die, Troy, that's all."

"Hey," the young man countered. "I can take care of myself, so don't worry your little head about me."

"And there's somethin' else," Joey blurted. "I want you to know that God sees you here, right now. Mr. H says He does. He sees you right here in this cell."

"God?" Troy spat out the word like he was ridding his mouth of something bitter. "What're you talkin' about? What're they feedin' you out on that ranch? If you got religion, just keep it to yourself." His voice rose to a shriek. "I ain't interested in God, or Jesus, or that whole save-you-from-your-sins pack of lies. You people think you're so holy. Well, go peddle your bleeding-heart garbage someplace else because I ain't interested!"

Troy rushed to the cell door. "Hey, guard. Come get this preacher outta here. You hear me?" Turning to his brother he shouted. "I don't need you, I don't need God, I don't need nothin'."

Joey lifted his hands. "Troy, I didn't mean no harm. I just want to help."

"Then get outta my face! You hear me? GET OUT!"

The prison guard slid the door open, reached in, and grabbed the young visitor by the collar. Joey found himself being pulled forcefully from the cell as Troy exploded into a frenzy of swinging arms and stinging curses. The guard slammed the door shut and hurried the teenager down the hallway and up the steps. The cries of the prisoner echoed along the stone walls.

Once in the safety of the precinct lobby, Joey sank into a chair and wept. He hadn't meant to anger his brother. Now he'd turned a bad situation worse. Troy hated him. The boy felt suddenly lonely, very lonely.

A hand touched his shoulder. "Come on, Joey," Darick said softly. "Let's get outta here, OK?"

Joey looked up and nodded. Together they walked out onto the stoop and descended the steps. Above them, the night sky had filled with stars, and the sound of traffic moaned in the distance.

CHAPTER FOUR

LOVE LETTERS

The beautiful box with the mirrored face and silver etchings rested open and empty on the old dining room table. The late afternoon sun had continued its silent journey westward, causing shadows on the forest floor to move slowly to the east, toward approaching night.

Mr. Underfoot snoozed in his favorite corner of the kitchen, between the icebox and counter. The animal's furry sides expanded and contracted slowly as he stored up energy for the night's hunt. Like all raccoons, Mr. Underfoot would spend the coming hours roaming the forests and meadows, looking for food and enjoying the protection from predators that darkness provided. His new human friend seemed harmless enough. He'd chosen to leave her alone, at least for the time being.

Wendy sat on the floor by the open window, holding fragile pieces of paper up to the fading light. Supper time had come and gone but she hadn't even noticed. The contents of the box held her in a fascinated embrace.

She'd found several items of interest—an old fountain pen and a glass ink well; a lovely broach with a horse on it; a few postcards with pictures of a world's fair held in Chicago a long, long time ago; and a ticket stub announcing a train's departure from Kansas City to Denver.

But what had caught the imagination of the girl and held it for so long was a stack of letters folded neatly in their envelopes. The collection was about six inches high, and had been tied securely with a length of blue silk ribbon. Each letter was addressed to a Mrs. Grant, Route 5, Box 179, Bozeman, Montana. There was no zip code.

As the sun had eased earthward, Wendy had become lost in a mystery so deep, so tantalizing, that time didn't matter. Only the words she was reading were real; everything else simply didn't exist.

Her first discovery was that the letters had been put in order according to their dates—she could tell that by their postmarks. The girl had decided to explore them from the beginning, so she'd flipped the pile over, laid it down beside her, and selected the oldest envelope first.

In the beginning, the mailers contained only simple drawings—a house with crooked windows, a dog with pointed ears, and some figures Wendy decided were people, although the legs and bodies were huge and the heads tiny. She immediately surmised that this was a child's depiction of the world as he or she saw it. Samantha insisted on drawing from the same perspective.

But before long, carefully formed letters began to appear—big, tall renderings drawn with colorful crayon.

Soon letters of the alphabet began to be grouped together, forming words. The girl recognized HORSE, APPLE, MOM, DAD, and BOUNDER. Wendy decided the last word must be the name of the dog with pointed ears.

Then emerged the very first memo composed entirely

of words, no pictures. It said boldly, "GRANDMA, I LOVE YOU. PLEASE COME VISIT ME. YOUR FRIEND, LITTLE M."

"Little M?" Wendy frowned. "Who's Little M?"

From that point on, each letter was signed the same way. But Wendy recognized that the child who drew the colorful pictures was growing up. Seven years had past according to the postmarks. Someone's history was slowly unfolding right before her eyes. She shuddered with excitement as she lifted the next item of correspondence and slipped the folded paper from inside.

"Dear Grandma," it said in carefully formed letters. "I like second grade. See, I can write good. No one is helping me."

The next letter showed even more improvement in handwriting skills. "Dear Grandma, Today we played baseball. I hit the ball and hurt my finger. Teacher put a bandage on it. Thank you for writing to me."

Then abruptly came a Western Union telegram printed in uneven type. The message was formal and to the point: MRS M GRANT STOP WILLIE AND MAR-GAREET BAKER KILLED IN AUTO ACCIDENT STOP DAUGHTER PLACED IN FOSTER HOME STOP REGRETS STOP. It was sent by the sheriff's department of Pendleton, Oregon.

Wendy closed her eyes and sighed, trying to imagine the shock this telegram had brought to whoever this Mrs. Grant was on the little homestead so far away from the scene of the tragedy. The girl, who apparently was the writer of the letters, had lost her parents and had been moved to a new home with people she probably didn't know.

The reader quickly picked up another envelope. The date was about a year later. That would mean that the little girl had entered the third grade.

"Dear Grandma," it said in small, practiced letters. "I

have not written for a long time because I was too sad. I miss Mommy and Daddy everyday and sometimes even while I am eating.

"My new parents are nice but they are very busy. A lady told me that you wanted me to come live with you but that they would not let me because you are old. I don't care. I love you and want to live with you on your farm in the mountains.

"Please write to me often. I like your letters and read them many times. They make me feel happy again."

Wendy held the letter up to the window to catch the last rays of the setting sun.

"I decided that I want everyone to call me by my other name instead of Little M. It makes me feel grown up, OK?

"I love you, Grandma. I love you lots and lots. Your granddaughter, Merrilee."

Wendy gasped. "Merrilee! The little girl's name is Merrilee!" Mr. Underfoot stirred, his long nap coming to an end. The reader glanced around the room and spoke quietly, somberly. "Is this farm named after her?"

It was now too dark to read anymore. Wendy carefully gathered the letters and rebound them with the blue ribbon. She'd return tomorrow and continue her exploration into the history of two people she'd never met.

What happened to the little girl with the big name? What became of Mrs. Grant? Wendy knew the answers would be hiding in the pile of letters she gently placed in the mirrored box on the old table.

After depositing her discovery in its proper place deep in the cedar chest, the girl hurried away to find Early and return to Shadow Creek Ranch. She'd search for the answers at first light.

* * * * *

The city stirred. Early morning joggers moved with

measured pace along the deserted streets and avenues lining Manhattan's villages and parks. Garbage trucks clattered and banged their way along the miles of curbs, picking up the refuse of millions of people who lived in tightly packed tenement houses and apartment buildings.

A homeless man sifted through a dumpster, searching for something to appease the hunger that was his constant companion. He didn't look up as a young boy hurried past with a large sack clutched tightly under his arm.

Several minutes later, the man on duty at East Village's third precinct police station looked up to see that same boy enter the building and present himself at the reception desk.

"Yes?" the officer on duty asked with a yawn. "May I help you?"

"Good morning," the visitor announced brightly. "I'm Joey Dugan and I've come to have breakfast with my brother, Troy. You know, the prisoner down in Cell 4."

The policeman blinked. "Weren't you here last night, before my shift began? I heard about your first visit. Didn't go so well, huh?"

"I guess not," Joey shrugged. "But Captain Abernathy said I could see Troy again if it's OK with the officer in charge and I don't go inside the cell."

"You sure you want to visit him again, kid?" the policeman queried, a touch of concern in his voice.

"Sure," the boy smiled. "He was just a little upset last night. I'll be OK."

"A little upset?" the policeman laughed. "I'd hate to see what he'd do if he got good and mad."

Joey pointed in the direction of the door leading to the basement. "So, can I see him?"

The man behind the desk sighed and pressed a button on the little box by the phone. "Hey, Barnhart, you awake?"

A tiny speaker rattled to life. " 'Course I'm awake, you idiot. Whadda ya want?"

"Dugan's got a visitor."

"Again?"

"Same kid as last night. Is the beast up?"

There was a short pause. Then the speaker rattled again. "I don't hear nothin' from that end of the room. Guess he's calm enough."

Joey smiled. "Thanks," he said as he turned and walked to the door.

Descending the steps he paused by the guard who sat behind a small desk under a bright light in the corner. He passed the bag he was holding to the man who pulled out each item and inspected it carefully. Joey knew the routine well.

"Listen, kid," the guard said quietly. "Why don't you just forget about that creep? You seem like the smart type. Let the law do its thing and take care of him. Why bother yourself?"

Joey accepted the return of the bag and smiled. "Because someone didn't give up on me when I was in big trouble once. Want to return the favor."

"Suit yourself," the man said, lifting his hands. "But be careful. Troy Dugan ain't exactly worth the effort, in my book."

Joey paused. "I guess I got a different book," he said.

The man shrugged as the visitor made his way down the long, wide hallway to the far cell. He watched as the young boy found a chair and pulled it up to the bars. Resting the bag on his lap, the visitor called quietly, his voice warm and friendly. "Hey, Troy, wake up. I got breakfast."

The guard heard his prisoner stir. "Go away," came the groggy response.

"Hey, it's your favorite," the boy pressed. "Scrambled eggs and toast. Hot chocolate, too. Cost me a fortune. You try to find a diner open this time of day."

The officer behind the small desk in the corner shook his head. "One thing's for sure," he mumbled to himself. "The kid's got guts."

Troy Dugan opened his eyes and glanced across the cell. He saw Joey sitting on the other side of the bars, a big smile spread across his young face and a plate of warm food held in his outstretched hands.

The prisoner chuckled softly and shook his head. "You remember Christmas about, oh, six years ago? It was cold, real cold. We was sittin' in that drafty apartment building trying to get into the holiday spirit."

Joey nodded. "Sure, I remember. You brought dinner that day—a Caesar salad and breadsticks. Then Lizzy made some bean soup and we all ate together in her kitchen by the stove 'cause it was warm there."

"Then we gave each other gifts," Troy continued. "I got you a pocket knife and you gave me a new pair of gloves—big, thick, red ones with a black stripe across the top. I still got those gloves. Wear 'em when it's blowin' cold outside."

Joey sighed. "Yeah, those were the good ol' days."

Troy blew a puff of air between his lips. "Leave it to my optimistic little brother to think those days were good. We were cold, man, and that was the biggest meal we'd had for months."

"We had a good time, anyway." Joey lifted his hands out in front of him. "Speaking of food and good times, how 'bout your breakfast? I got some, too. We can eat together, like before. Whadda ya say?"

The prisoner slipped his legs out from under the thin blanket that lay draped across the bottom half of his bunk. He yawned broadly. His brother watched as he stood to his feet and stretched long and hard, first his arms, then his legs. The younger boy found himself smiling. He did that very same thing each morning when he got up. It was sort of a ritual to him, an unchanging activity in a constantly changing world. No matter what he faced that day, the morning ritual remained constant.

Troy righted a toppled chair and slid it to the front of the cell. He settled himself heavily on the chair's metal seat and studied his younger brother for a long moment.

"Aren't you mad at me about last night?" he asked, reaching through the bars and taking the plate of food. "I was pretty rough on you."

Joey shrugged and began unwrapping his own meal. "Yeah, well, we got good days, we got bad days. I'm not too civilized myself sometimes."

Troy nodded and spooned a heaping pile of scrambled eggs into his mouth. "You kinda made me mad with all your big talk about breakin' the law and stuff. Then when you threw God at me, it really set me off. Guess I kinda lost my temper."

The younger boy chewed thoughtfully. He realized he'd blown it big-time the night before. He only wanted to tell his brother about what life was like beyond the streets, in a world where people respect you and give you important responsibilities. He wanted to tell him how good it feels to wake up in the morning and know others are depending on you to do your job, to pull your weight, to make a difference.

But, most of all, he wanted his brother to know that he was loved, even when he was in trouble, even when he did something really stupid like take drugs.

Joey glanced through the bars at his companion. "How are the eggs?" he asked.

The prisoner nodded and pointed with his fork. "These are good. Where'd you steal 'em from?"

Joey laughed. "I didn't *steal* 'em. I bought 'em fair and square, with money and everything."

"With money, no less," Troy smiled. "You're really comin' up in the world. Not bad for a dumb kid from East Village."

Joey grinned. "Hey, I *work* for a living out on the ranch. Take care of horses, mend fences, you know, cowboy stuff."

"My brother the range-rider," Troy teased, warming to his visitor. "I suppose you got a horse?"

"Yup, partner," Joey responded in his best western drawl. "Name's Tar Boy. Let me tell you about him."

The boy leaned forward and began painting a word picture of a valley with a big, white way station, pastures green with summer grasses, and mountains stretching into blue, cloudless skies. As the sun slowly rose above the city, Joey and his brother sat separated by steel bars, yet for the first time in years finding themselves growing closer and closer together.

The teenager's heart sang as he saw his older sibling responding to his description of a world beyond the streets, and to the love he was holding in reserve just for him.

* * * * *

The door to the abandoned farmhouse creaked open as Wendy entered. Mr. Underfoot paused his rummaging in the soft soil under the open window and pulled himself up onto the ledge. When he saw the girl standing in the doorway, he let out a friendly growl and returned to his digging.

Wendy hurried to the cedar chest and lifted the lid. Sometime during the night, an uncomfortable feeling had crossed her mind—the feeling that a girl named Merrilee was just a dream, a figment of an overactive imagination.

But standing there, looking down at the mirrored box tucked safely away in the chest, she felt a great sense of relief. It was real, and so were the letters she knew waited for her inside.

Wendy retrieved the mirrored box and sat down below the window ledge. She could hear the raccoon digging outside, his powerful paws searching for grubs in the mountain earth. At least he'd be occupied. Maybe she could attend to business without the creature's constant interruptions.

The next letter in the series was dated a few weeks after the one she'd ended with the day before.

"Dear Grandma," it began. "I got your letter yesterday when I came home from school. Thank you for writing to me.

"When you told me about your mother and when she died, I knew you understood about when I am sad. And I liked it when you told me about the flowers growing under your window in the dining room. They sound pretty and I'm sure they smell nice too."

Wendy paused and glanced up at the open window above her head. She was sitting at the far wall of the dining room, so the flower box must have hung outside, just below the ledge. The girl drew in a deep breath as if expecting to catch the scent of the old woman's spring blossoms. But only the musty smell of the forest drifted in through the opening.

"Guess what?" the letter continued. "I made a 100 on my math test. Everyone else missed at least two, but I got them all. My teacher says I'm smart. I think I was just lucky.

"Tell me more about your farm. I live in a big building with lots of people around. I think living on a farm would be nice.

"Please write to me soon. Merrilee."

Wendy slipped the paper back into its envelope and picked up the next letter in the stack. Inside she found a birthday card with a note attached.

"Grandma. I don't know when your birthday is, so I thought I'd give you this card that my friend Beth Ann gave to me just in case it's soon. It has a pretty picture on it and I hope you like it.

"When is your birthday anyway? Merrilee."

There followed a collection of letters telling about school life, friends, and Christmases passing one by one. Each note was like spinning the hands of a clock forward from the past, sometimes a week, sometimes several months. Each envelope contained bits and pieces of a little girl's life put into words. Wendy could only imagine the joy such messages brought to their reader.

In a matter of an hour, Merrilee had grown from 9 years old to a teenager. Her letters began to reflect a changing view of the world.

"Grandma. Got your correspondence today. I checked my mailbox and there it was. You are the only one who writes to me from Montana. Of course, you are the only one who writes to me period, so, keep it up!

"Thanks for your advice about Harry Parker. You're right, he isn't treating me very good. I told him to grow up or move on (I believe those were the words you suggested that I use). Well, he just stood there looking at me like a bomb had fallen on his foot. I about cracked up.

"To make a long story short, I'm dating someone else now. Harry's off bothering another poor soul.

"You should meet Andrew. Isn't that a sophisticated name? He's about six feet tall, plays football, and drives a Ford convertible. Man, he's really cool, I mean really cool.

"Gotta run. Love ya. Merrilee."

Wendy rolled her eyes. This girl was beginning to sound just like Debbie. Boys, boys, boys. You'd think there was nothing else in the whole world of any importance at all.

The girl leaned her head against the wall. What was so great about boys, anyway? To her, the opposite sex served very little purpose except to lift heavy things and provide a degree of competition in baseball.

She thought about the group that had spent the summer with them on the ranch. Hey, there'd been an Andrew in that bunch, too, although "sophisticated" was the last

71

thing she thought about when she uttered his name.

Wendy sighed. She didn't ever want to grow up if that meant becoming all mushy and giggly like Debbie got sometimes, especially around Wrangler Barry. It was embarrassing.

She unfolded the next letter and read the words printed skillfully across the faded paper.

"Grandma. Something awful happened. Last night was Junior Festival and Andrew took me as his date.

"Everything was going along fine until about 10:00. I went to the bathroom to check my hair, and I heard two girls talking about some guy who was going to dump his date for another girl he'd met and wanted to take to the festival but couldn't because she had a date. But then her date cancelled at the last minute and she came anyway and just stood around looking beautiful in a blue dress with no shoulders or sleeves so all the guys were falling over themselves trying to bring her drinks and sandwiches and stuff.

"Anyway, I go back out into the gymnasium and who do you think she's got her claws into? That's right, Andrew—dear, old, sophisticated Andrew. I go up to him and say, 'Come on, *date* (I said "date" real loud). Let's go check out the fall fashion show (Jackson's department store puts on this really stupid fashion show each year at the Junior Festival).'

"Well, Andrew turns to me and says, 'You go ahead. I'll catch up.'

"So I'm thinking, *Oh, sure you will.* And Grandma, he leaves me and goes off with Miss No Sleeves for the whole rest of the evening.

"I cried all night. I mean, what's so awful about me that Andrew would just dump me like that? I'm pretty, at least that's what you told me when you got my class picture. I spent all my savings for the Festival dress. You'd think guys would at least stick with their date for just one evening. I felt so ashamed. I just knew everyone was laughing at me because I had to catch a ride home with a friend.

"Oh, Grandma. It hurts to think about what happened. It hurts so bad. Will I ever be happy again?

"Your very sad granddaughter, Merrilee."

Wendy studied the words on the page. She could feel the anguish of the writer, the loneliness, the despair. Hadn't she felt it, too? Not because some selfish guy had dumped her at a party. Her hurt centered around her mother. Hadn't she dumped the whole family?

The reader slowly folded the letter, slipped it back into its envelope, and let out a deep sigh. Why must people always suffer? Why are little girls and big girls left crying when everyone else seems to be having such a great time? Why are some left alone to face a hurt beyond words?

Merrilee understood what it was like to be forgotten, left behind, pushed aside by someone she cared for.

Wendy bent forward and rested her face against her knees. She cried softly, the way she'd taught herself to cry so her dad and sister wouldn't hear. It was a familiar pain, one she was almost used to, but not quite. Tears tended to ease the loneliness. Here in the old abandoned farmhouse she felt strangely comforted, as if the walls and ceilings had been witness to such sadness, and survived.

After some time had past, she brushed aside the tears and reached for the next letter. That's what she would do too—survive.

"Dear Grandma." The words spoke from the neatly folded paper. "You're the very best there is in the world. I read your last letter over and over again. It was like you could see into my heart.

"I've been trying your idea for about a week now, and you know, you were right—I'm not the only one who gets sad and hurt. Like you suggested, whenever I got to feeling sorry for myself I looked closely at the people around me to see if anyone seemed troubled or worried. Then I talked to them and tried to encourage them. And just like you said, I forgot my own troubles for a little while.

"Grandma, I found out that EVERYONE has sad days. Everyone gets hurt. I thought I was the only person in the whole world who cried at night, or had a broken heart. But I was wrong. There's more sadness in the world than I ever imagined.

"When I talk to other people, and try to encourage them, I find that it makes me feel better. The more I help the other person, the happier I get.

"I like what you said that love is—thinking of the other person first. How did you get to be so smart, Grandma?

"Thank you for helping me see that I'm not the only one who cries. I love you very much. You're so special to me.

"Your granddaughter, Merrilee."

Wendy sat for a long moment staring at the paper. Outside the window, a blue jay chattered in the trees, scolding a squirrel that was busily storing nuts for the winter. The wind whistled softly, adding a soothing background to the activity high in the branches. Then the bird flew away, leaving the old farmstead wrapped in the gentle sound of autumn breezes.

* * * * *

The courtroom buzzed with afternoon business as groups of people came and went, each standing before the stern-faced judge who sat gazing down from her lofty perch behind the bench.

Her desk was cluttered with papers and file folders. This was Wednesday, and that was the day for setting trial dates. The judge wanted to make sure each person who was charged with a crime had someone to represent him or her and that all legal requirements were met before the case was heard.

Troy and the defense lawyer who'd been assigned to his case sat by the door that led to a secured area of the building. The prisoner transport bus was parked in the alley by the courthouse.

Joey waited on the other side of the room, where friends and family could gather to watch the proceedings. This was the first time he'd seen his brother's lawyer, and he wasn't impressed. The man fidgeted and kept looking at the clock, as if he wanted to be somewhere else. His lack of interest in his client was very apparent, even from across the room.

"City of New York versus Troy Dugan," the judge called out without looking up from a file folder in her hand. "He's charged with breaking and entering, theft, possession of stolen goods, possession of an illegal substance, and possession of illegal substance with intent to distribute." She looked over at Troy. "How does the defendant plead?"

"My client pleads not guilty on all charges," Troy's lawyer responded, rising to his feet.

"He pleads guilty to at least one of the charges, Your Honor!" another voice called from the back of the courtroom. "Troy Dugan pleads guilty to possession."

Joey spun around and gasped. Mr. Hanson had burst through the door and was walking down the aisle to the front of the chamber. He paused at the small gate that separated the visitors' area from the rest of the courtroom. "I have reason to believe that it is in the best interest of the accused to plead guilty to that charge, if he will let me represent him."

Joey sat speechless, unable to utter a word. He watched as a smile spread across the face of the judge. "Well, Tyler Hanson! I thought you were in Wyoming or somewhere."

"Montana, Your Honor," the man said. "It's very near Wyoming."

"Hey," the assigned lawyer called out angrily.

75

"Who's this character and what's he doing, barging in on my case?"

Mr. Hanson turned to face Troy, ignoring the irate attorney. "I'm here to represent you if you want. I'm a good friend of Joey's. That means I'm a good friend of yours, too."

Troy glanced over at his brother, a questioning look on his face. Joey nodded eagerly, his mouth still hanging open.

"Well, you can't come busting in here like this," the other defender insisted. "This is my case."

Mr. Hanson nodded. "According to the law, someone accused of a crime can choose his own lawyer *or* have one assigned to him. I'm just giving Mr. Dugan that choice." The man paused. "Besides, I think you'd rather be somewhere else, wouldn't you? An associate of yours told me that you had an important matter to attend to concerning your last case. Maybe he was mistaken."

The counselor paled and started gathering his small pile of papers. "Well, yes," he stammered. "Perhaps I *should* see to my other affairs . . . uh . . . responsibilities. This assignment caught me a little off guard. Didn't have much time to prepare."

With a wave, he was gone, leaving Troy standing alone and staring at Mr. Hanson. "So, you gonna save me from the big bad city?" he asked coldly.

The lawyer smiled. "I'm going to try to save you from yourself, young man." Turning to the judge he added, "For the record, my name is Tyler Hanson, and I represent the accused in this case."

"So noted," the judge said, jotting down a few words in her file folder.

Joey leaned back in his chair and closed his eyes. It seemed Mr. H had a habit of showing up just when he needed him most.

76

CHAPTER FIVE

DEAL OF
THE CENTURY

"Well, I think it stinks." Troy dropped his tired body onto the cell bunk and rubbed his forehead with his palms. "Since I pleaded guilty to one of those charges I may as well tell the guard to toss the key in the trash. I'll be in here 'til I'm an old man, slobbering down my chin. Some lawyer you are."

Mr. Hanson looked up from the open briefcase that lay across his lap. "But you are guilty. The crime report says you had the cocaine in your jacket pocket when they picked you up. Can't argue with the facts. Pleading not guilty to possession under these circumstances would be like calling the arresting officers a pack of liars. Judges frown on that. Trust me."

"Yeah, trust you," the prisoner laughed. "I don't even know you and here I am puttin' my future in your hands."

"Mr. H is OK," Joey called from outside the cell. "He ain't much of a horseman. But a lawyer? He'll stick by you to the bitter end."

"Oh, that's encouraging," Troy sighed.

Mr. Hanson smiled. "Look. The legal system is very complex. I'm just trying to make sure you get a fair trial and that your punishment isn't more than you deserve."

"That's what the other joker said before you fired him," Troy shot back.

"First," the lawyer responded, "I didn't fire him. You chose to have me represent you. And that other 'joker,' as you call him, was taking your case for a paycheck and nothing else. He didn't care what happened to you as long as he got his money from the city." The man closed his briefcase and began to rise. "But if you'd rather have him take your case, I'll see if he's still available."

"*No!*" Troy said, quickly lifting his hand. "No. I want you. Forget him."

"Then you're going to have to cooperate, Troy," the lawyer warned, returning to his seat. "You're in serious trouble. You've got to be honest and open with me so I can help. If you've broken the law, then you must be punished for the extent of your actions and nothing more. If you're innocent of some of the charges, I'll get you off. I'm after truth, not excuses. So, let me ask you again. What were you doing with the drugs?"

The prisoner glanced over at his younger brother. Joey sat silent in the hallway, his eyes searching the man on the bunk.

After a long moment, the accused spoke. "I was gonna sell 'em."

Mr. Hanson sighed. "OK. Where did you get the drugs from?"

"I don't know. Some guys down by the river."

"Which river?"

"Whadda ya mean, which river?"

The lawyer spoke slowly. "The Hudson or the East?"

"The East River. And what difference does it make?"

"Do you remember what they looked like?"

Troy stood to his feet. "They looked like guys, you know, two eyes, two legs, two arms. What're ya askin' me all these questions for? You already said I'm guilty. What's the big deal?"

"Sit down, Troy," Mr. Hanson commanded.

"Forget it, man. You've already judged me."

"Sit *down!*" the man repeated firmly.

Troy pointed in Joey's direction. "Hey, you might be able to order my kid brother around, but this is The Reaper you're talkin' to. Nobody tells me—"

Hands grabbed the speaker's shirt and he suddenly found himself lying on his bunk, a face held inches from his nose. "Look, Mr. Reaper," the lawyer whispered. "I didn't come all the way from Montana to baby-sit a spoiled brat who thinks he's tough. The court systems will have you for lunch if you don't wise up and let me help. Understand?"

Troy struggled to get up but the man held him down. "This is no time to stroke your inflated ego. These aren't the streets and you're not The Reaper anymore. You're a confused young man facing a whole lot of years in a very small penitentiary cell unless you drop the I-could-care-less act and cooperate. The sooner you get that through your thick skull the better."

Mr. Hanson moved his face even closer. "Now, who do you want to tell your story to? Me, or the judge?"

The prisoner lay still. It was strange to have someone who insisted he was there to help treat him so roughly. Looking into the eyes of the lawyer, Troy saw frustration but no real anger. He realized the man's words were not a threat but a plea. He didn't think people like this existed. No one had ever tried so hard to do him *good.*

Mr. Hanson released his grip on the young man's

shirt and walked back to his seat. Troy reached up and adjusted his collar. "Take it easy, hot shot," he said, his words suddenly empty of aggressiveness. "Let me think for a minute, OK?"

The lawyer lifted his hands. "It's your decision."

Joey pressed his face against the bars. "Please, Troy. He means what he says. I didn't believe him at first, either. I thought he was crazy or somethin' when he tried to help me a year and a half ago. But he stuck by me. He really did. I know Mr. H. He believes in God and prays and stuff. He wouldn't lie to you. Really. Me and him are all you have left. Don't blow it, Troy. Don't blow it."

The prisoner nodded slowly. "OK. I'm sorry," he said quietly. "I ain't used to bein' around nice people."

Mr. Hanson glanced over at Joey and shook his head. "What is it about you Dugans?" he said with a slight grin. "You guys keep making me do really weird stuff like go to Montana, come back from Montana . . ."

Joey chuckled. "I don't know about Troy, but it's my cute baby face that makes you crazy."

The lawyer sighed. "And your modesty, too."

Joey grinned.

"Now," Mr. Hanson said, turning back to Troy, "let's talk about those guys who sold you the stuff by the East River. Tell me everything you know about them and their connections. I want to know what color their eyes were, what their breath smelled like, and what they had for breakfast, if you can remember. Tell me everything."

Troy nodded and rubbed his forehead with his hands. Mr. Hanson took notes as the prisoner talked. Word by word, Troy Dugan drew his listeners into the back alleys and mean streets of New York City, into a world that tourists, and even most residents, never see.

Joey sat outside the bars, his chin resting on his fists. It was a world so familiar to him, yet now so foreign. He thought of Tar Boy and the Station, of Wendy, Debbie,

Lizzy, and little Sam. Suddenly, for the first time in two days, he felt terribly homesick.

* * * * *

Mr. Underfoot waited patiently at Wendy's side. The girl had brought a sack lunch with her, not wanting to disturb her adventure by eating a regular meal. The envelopes and enclosed messages had captured her imagination as nothing else she could remember.

"Merrilee is in college, according to the last letter I read," she called to the raccoon between chews. "She's going to be a nurse."

The animal tilted his head to one side as if to say, "Well, that's all fine and good, but are you going to finish that orange or what?"

"And," the girl continued, "she has a roommate named Jessica Blackwell. They have lots of fun together. Jessica wants to be a lawyer. That's what my dad is, you know. She also likes chocolate pie and pineapples."

Wendy threw a slice of her fruit in the raccoon's direction. Mr. Underfoot lifted the offering in his hands and turned it over and over, inspecting it carefully. Then he bit into the sweet tasting orange, letting its juices flow down his whiskered chin.

"I'm not going to be a lawyer," the girl added. "I'm going to be a cowboy like Wrangler Barry. I'm going to ride horses all day and fix saddles and go searching for lost people in the mountains." She paused. "And maybe I'll buy an airplane so I can fly around looking for hurt or dangerous animals for the forestry department.

"You know what they do? They shoot bears with tranquilizer darts, then take them to another part of the state so they can roam around and start new families. Neat, huh?"

Mr. Underfoot sniffed the air, then licked orange juice off his paws.

"Or maybe I'll run a ranch like Shadow Creek. Yeah.

81

I could charge tourists a whole lot of money so they could stay there. I'd be rich. Then my dad wouldn't have to work all day, or go flying off to New York to chase down Joey Dugan. And I could buy Debbie an apartment on Broadway so she could make dresses until she dropped over dead.

"Whadda ya think, Mr. Underfoot? Sound like a plan to you?"

The raccoon ambled over to the empty bag by the window and examined it. Finding nothing inside, the creature settled himself by the old table and rolled up into a ball.

"Sleep tight, you silly animal," he heard Wendy call. Then all sights and sounds disappeared as he slipped into slumber.

The girl wiped her mouth with a paper napkin and stuffed the remnants of her lunch into the bag. Adjusting her position on the torn throw rug, she picked up the next letter in the stack and began to read.

"Dear Grandma. Boy, do you have to work hard in college! Sometimes I think I do nothing but study, study, study.

"Jessica and I did go skiing two Sundays ago. That's when I met someone I want to tell you about. His name is John Dawson. He's a senior this year and hopes to graduate with a degree in public health. He's really great with people—always wants to help them. I think you'd like him a lot; I know I do.

"In your last letter, you mentioned that you were sick but you didn't say what was the matter. Are you OK? Now you take care of yourself. That's an order! You're my grandma and I love you, so take your medicine (if that's what the doctor said) and don't leave your windows open so high at night. You're not as young as you used to be. Keep those precious bones warm.

"Thank you for the lovely birthday card. I have it

taped to my headboard where I see it every night when I go to bed ·and every morning when I wake up. You'll never know how important you are to me.

"Your granddaughter, Merrilee."

Just a few letters later, Wendy picked up an envelope that was much more fancy than the rest. She had a feeling what was inside.

"Mr. John Dawson and Miss Merrilee Baker
Invite you to share in their joy
As they join their lives in Holy Matrimony."

At the bottom of the invitation, the girl saw that someone had hand printed these words: "Grandma. Oh, I wish you could come, but I understand you're not feeling up to it. John is such a wonderful man, so kind and loving. I'm the luckiest girl in the world."

Wendy smiled. Merrilee was happy, so very happy. Her words fairly shouted her joy.

As Wendy stuffed the announcement back into the envelope something fell onto her lap. It was a tiny photograph. Holding it up to the window light, Wendy looked into the faces of a smiling couple, the man young and handsome with dark hair and laughing eyes. At his side stood a beautiful girl with long brown curls and rosy cheeks. She had her arm looped through the man's and was pressing her chin against his broad shoulder. Carefully scrawled across the bottom of the picture were these words, "Love at last."

Wendy studied the photograph, holding it tightly in her hands. Now she had an image, a smile, a form she could attach to the words she had been reading. The woman looked very contented. Maybe all this love stuff wasn't so bad, after all.

But more letters waited. Did Merrilee stay in love, or were there tears waiting to spoil the smiling faces in the little picture?

The girl reached for the next letter. Just how long could love last?

* * * * *

A gentle knock sounded at the door of New York City's district attorney's office. Jerry Diel looked up from a memo and called, "Come."

Mr. Hanson slipped into the room and closed the door behind him.

"Tyler." The man behind the desk grinned when he saw his visitor. "I've been expecting you. Have a seat."

The lawyer sat down and glanced out the window. Lower Manhattan lay at his feet, its tightly packed collection of skyscrapers bunched together as if trying to ward off the cold wind that whipped past their glassy faces.

"City's pretty from up here," Diel said, also admiring the view. "You miss it?"

Mr. Hanson shook his head. "Nope. You should see the view from my office at the Station. Not a high rise in sight. Just trees and mountains."

"To each his own, I guess," the DA shrugged.

"How's Sarah?" Mr. Hanson asked.

Diel chuckled. "Still complaining that I work too hard trying to put bad guys behind bars."

Mr. Hanson nodded. "You continue to do that with amazing regularity, I hear."

"I try," came the modest reply. The man looked straight at his companion. "That's where bad guys belong."

"You'll get no argument from me there," the visitor agreed, "as long as it's best for everyone involved."

The DA grinned. "And that brings us to Troy Dugan, right?"

Mr. Hanson spread his hands. "Hey, he's guilty of possession, no problem. But breaking and entering? Theft? The cops found a boombox in his apartment when they arrested him. Just so happens somebody broke into a Radio Shack three blocks from his building the night

84

before. There were no witnesses, no fingerprints, nothing to connect my client with the break-in."

"Hold on there, Tyler," the attorney pressed. "It just so happens that the boomer found in Troy's apartment was identical to the one stolen."

"Jerry, Jerry, Jerry," Mr. Hanson sighed shaking his head. "All you've got is circumstantial at best. The only thing my client is guilty of, in this particular case, is owning a very popular boombox. So let's stop worrying about his shopping habits and deal with the real issue here—drug possession and intent to distribute. Tacking on a silly theft charge to help you clear up another case doesn't do *you* justice."

Diel studied his visitor for a moment. "Whew! Montana hasn't softened you up any," he said. "You're just as determined as ever to prove me wrong."

"I'm not trying to prove anything except my client's innocence of half the charges you dumped on him. Maybe your wife is right. Maybe you do try too hard."

"But," the attorney responded, "even without those charges I've got an ironclad case against your boy. The City doesn't like people buying and selling drugs on the streets. Gives us a bad name."

"That's exactly what I wanted to talk to you about," Mr. Hanson said, leaning forward in his chair. "You and I both know that Troy is just a middleman, a spoke in a very big wheel. But spokes do one important thing—they connect the rim with the hub, or in this case, the user with the source."

"So?"

"So, what if I tell you that my client is willing to give you complete descriptions of the guys who supply most of the drug dealers from Delancey to 57th? *And* he can supply names and descriptions of *their* suppliers in Long Island."

The DA drummed his fingers on his desk. "Go on."

"You drop breaking, theft, and stolen goods and be

open to some creative suggestions on the possession and intent charges." Mr. Hanson settled back in his chair.

"That's all?" Diel asked. "You sure you don't want me to elect Mr. Dugan mayor or something?"

"Not yet," the lawyer replied.

The attorney shook his head. "What is it with you, Hanson? Don't you believe that people do bad things on purpose? Hasn't it ever occurred to you that some folks break the law and try to get away with it because they're just no good to anyone, including themselves?"

"I believe in law and order," the visitor replied. "I believe in punishment. But I also believe in forgiveness and second chances. Our prisons are jammed with offenders who are truly sorry for what they did and would live a very different life if they were given the opportunity. You don't hear about those people when they're paroled. They just fade into the background, get lost in the crowds. But let one ex-offender get out of line and everyone cries for more severe punishment and tighter locks on the doors. The system stinks and you know it. That's why I do what I do."

Jerry Diel remained silent for a long moment, studying the man who sat across from him. When he spoke, his words sounded tired. "A system that stinks is better than no system at all."

"I agree," Mr. Hanson said softly. "But it shouldn't make us all victims."

The district attorney picked up a file folder and studied its contents. "Five years, max."

"One."

The man gasped. "Come on, Tyler!"

"One year and assignment to a rehab program."

"You really like to dream, don't you?"

Mr. Hanson smiled. "Ever heard of Project Youth Revival? They've got a chapter in Pennsylvania. It's a two-year work program connected with the state. Participants build roads and parks. It'll get Troy Dugan out of the city."

"So will prison."

The lawyer didn't respond.

"Oh, all right," Diel sighed. "But your man better have some really juicy stuff for the police chief. I mean, really juicy."

"He does." Mr. Hanson rose to leave. "Why don't you send the good chief down to the jail later this afternoon? My client has nothing better to do."

When the visiting lawyer reached the door the man at the desk called out, "Is it worth it, Tyler—all this hard work for a guy who'll probably stab you in the back when it's over? Is it really worth it?"

"He won't," the man stated flatly. "I live with a constant reminder that forgiveness and acceptance is a stronger security than any prison the system can build."

"What do you mean?"

"One of the people who helps run our ranch in Montana is a good friend of Troy's. It's his brother, Joey."

Diel nodded and waved his hand weakly. "Get out of here. I've got some phone calls to make."

Mr. Hanson smiled and left the office, closing the door quietly behind him.

* * * * *

Samantha stood waiting for Tar Boy to get into position. The horse wasn't exactly sure what was expected of him, but the little girl on the sporty-looking bicycle seemed determined to set everything in order.

She had pushed his ribs and pulled his long, dark mane in an attempt to move him over a few feet from where he was standing. That's when he'd noticed a patch of autumn grass growing nearby, and moved. The girl had seemed pleased.

"Good," he heard her say. "That's exactly where I want you to be."

Then his companion had postioned her bike by his side and straddled it. "Now when I say go," she directed, "you run as fast as you can to the corral and I'll see if I can beat you. Understand?"

The horse shook his head, more in an attempt to rid himself of a collection of flies than in agreement to the girl's words.

This would be a very exciting race. Samantha was sure of it. She'd been practicing up and down the long driveway all morning and just knew she was speedier than any horse alive.

She figured if she could ride her bike as fast as a horse could run, that would impress Joey and Wendy with her ability and they'd always take her with them when they rode off into the mountains, like Wendy had done that very morning. She could race along beside her friends, they on their horses and she astride her trusty two-wheeler.

"On your mark!" Samantha lifted her right foot and placed it on the pedal.

"Get set!" Tar Boy stomped his hoof in an effort to shake biting bugs from his knee.

"GO!" The sharp command startled the big animal. He launched himself straight across the pasture, hooves pounding the earth like wood on a drum.

Samantha raised herself up on her pedal and started pumping furiously. She zigged one way, then zagged another, trying to find the rhythm that would catapult her toward the corral with blinding speed.

The horse skidded to a halt by the gate and turned to see where his little companion had gone. There she was, out in the middle of the pasture, working the pedals as hard as her legs would allow.

She was making pretty good progress when he saw her suddenly skid to a stop. The girl was looking at something in the grass.

Then she screamed. *"Snake!"*

Samantha leaped from her bike, letting it drop to the ground, and began running, her legs and feet a blur over the clumps of grass.

"*Snake!*" she screamed again as she rushed by the animal, her eyes opened wide in terror. Within moments, Samantha was across the footbridge and stumbling up the steps to the Station.

Tar Boy saw her rush into the building and slam the door. Then a little face appeared at the den window, its mouth open wide, trying to draw breath into hurting lungs.

The horse ambled to the center of the pasture where the bike waited on its side. Sure enough, there in the grass lay a snake, its smooth scales reflecting the sunlight in multicolored patterns.

As Tar Boy approached, the reptile lifted its head and flicked its tongue in and out as if to say, "Did you see that? *Did you see that?* I was minding my own business out here, enjoying the warm sun, when a little Black girl threw her bicycle at me. Boy, you're not safe anywhere in the pasture. If a horse doesn't step on you, some little girl will surely run you down with a bicycle. I'm going back to the forest where hawks and skunks are all I have to worry about!"

The creature slithered through the grasses and disappeared under a fallen log.

Tar Boy sniffed at the bike, then continued grazing. Humans. They were certainly a silly lot.

Lizzy Pierce strode into the den and noticed Samantha by the window, her little sides huffing and puffing.

"Hi, Sam," she called. "Why aren't you outside playing?"

"I was," the girl sighed. "But then a snake attacked me."

"A snake attacked you?" the woman queried. "Where?"

"Out in the pasture. I was riding my bike when this

89

big snake reached up and grabbed me."

"It did?" Lizzy gasped. "How awful! Strange. Grandpa Hanson says most snakes are afraid of people and slither away when someone comes by. Are you sure this horrible creature reached up and grabbed you?"

"Well," the girl confided, "maybe it didn't, but it was thinking about it. I could tell."

"Oh. That's possible," the woman agreed, "although it's pretty hard to know what a snake is thinking. Maybe it was just sunning itself on the ground and you saw it there. Do you think that's what happened?"

Samantha nodded slowly. "Probably. But it scared me. That's why I jumped off my bike and ran here as fast as I could."

"You jumped off your bike? Why didn't you just ride away? Wouldn't it have been a lot faster?"

"Are you kidding?" the girl gasped. "My bike is the slowest one in Montana."

Lizzy looked surprised. "What makes you think so?"

Samantha turned away from the window and headed for the door. "Because it can't even beat a horse," she moaned.

As the little girl continued out into the lobby, the woman heard her mumble, "Besides, I think Tar Boy knew that snake was there all along."

* * * * *

Debbie sat watching the shoppers saunter by, their arms laden with bulging, brightly marked plastic bags. Bozeman Mall seemed especially crowded today, with old and young alike searching for the "Fall Bargain Bonanza" items everyone had been hearing about on the local radio stations.

One department store insisted that it was having the "Sale of the Century." Debbie smiled to herself. She'd discovered that the ad was right—you could get great deals on clothes that had been designed and manufactured at least a century ago. The latest fashions cost just as much as ever. And that was always more than she could afford.

She'd ridden into town with Wrangler Barry, who was off in some hardware store looking for a fence post or something. She liked being with him, not only because he was incredibly handsome and strong but also because she felt comfortable in his presence. Barry wasn't a fake like many of the guys she'd known. He didn't make himself out to be anything more than he was—a hard-working, outdoor-type young man with dreams of running his own ranch some day.

Other than his total lack of taste when it came to clothes, he was perfect. Debbie secretly fantasized that someday he'd suddenly notice her as a woman, not just as a friend. The young man would sweep her off her feet and carry her away to some mountaintop where they'd share a picnic lunch and walk hand in hand through meadows of spring blossoms, while birds sang from every limb.

"I can't believe the price of manure spreaders," a familiar voice called. Debbie looked up to see her dream man approaching, a frown wrinkling his suntanned face. "They've gone up 15 percent in the last six months." Barry sat down beside her. "Grandpa Hanson wants me to get one for the ranch, but they're so expensive. Maybe I should look for a used one. What do you think?"

Debbie nodded thoughtfully. "I believe that's exactly what you should do." She paused. "Did you say *manure* spreader?"

"Yeah, you know, the tractor implement that can take a load of horse manure and spread it on the ground. Great fertilizer. Doesn't hurt the environment, either."

The thought of a device that throws animal sewage all over the place made Debbie shudder.

"Your grandfather wants to start a big field of corn in the meadow beyond the cottonwoods, come spring. Needs

91

lots of fertilizer. Spreader's the only way to go."

The girl shook her head decidedly. "Well, I guess so! And I think used would serve our purpose just fine."

Barry put his arm around her shoulders and gave her a friendly squeeze. "You're really somethin', Debbie Hanson—pretty, and a sharp business mind to boot. I'll go check with the dealer down the street. I think I saw a spreader setting out behind his lot. Wanna come?"

"Oh, I don't think so," the girl responded. "I'll just look around here a little longer. Pick me up when you're done."

"OK," the wrangler agreed as he stood to leave. "Be back in about 30 minutes. Meet me at the sporting goods store. Need to pick up some bug repellent. See ya."

Debbie watched the young man disappear behind the fountain in the middle of the mall. She sighed. Barry Gordon wouldn't know what romance was if it sat on his head.

The girl stood and began walking along the front of the stores, glancing at the items arranged so tastefully in the passing windows. Soft music played from unseen speakers, and the voices of shoppers drifted by in a warm and soothing manner.

She loved to be here, where everything was new and fresh, where endless varieties of merchandise begged for her attention. It was as though all the store windows whispered, "Debbie's coming. Debbie's coming! Everyone look sharp, now. She may decide to buy."

Since leaving New York, the girl wasn't that hung up on things anymore. Not really. She didn't insist on having *new* all the time. In her closet hung beautiful dresses, most of which she'd made with her own hands. Even the contents of her dresser drawers reflected a careful shopper with an eye for value, not extravagance.

But she still enjoyed coming in contact with lovely things whose price tags put them far beyond her reach.

To the young girl with the long dark hair, soft brown eyes, and slender body, shopping was fun even if no money changed hands.

As she moved along, her mind wandered back to New York. She remembered the little stores tucked in out-of-the-way places along the back streets of Manhattan, where shop owners spoke little English but whose establishments were a Disneyland of fashion and fabric.

She thought of her old friends with their ever-changing parade of new clothes and designs, each trying to outdo the others in style and sophistication. It'd been fun—all the attention she'd received, with her careful consideration of every detail of dress and decorum.

But had she been really happy there? Time has a way of erasing the bad and leaving only the good. Shadow Creek Ranch had much to offer. So did New York.

Debbie paused in front of a window display of leather handbags. A woman was carefully arranging the merchandise so they'd catch the eye of passing shoppers. She waved when she saw the girl watching her.

Debbie waved back then pointed with her finger. "Over there," she said, moving her lips so the lady could see what she was saying. "Move that one over there."

The woman in the window turned and studied her display. Reaching down, she picked up the bag Debbie had pointed to and moved it to the spot suggested. The display was now perfect.

"Thank you," the woman mouthed with a grateful smile.

Debbie nodded and moved on. Barry could have his spreaders. She could still design fashion displays with one hand tied behind her back. Even in Bozeman, Montana, she hadn't lost her touch.

CHAPTER SIX

RISKING IT ALL

The Staten Island ferry slipped from its berth in New Brighton and began its journey to the northeast, toward the distant tall towers crowding Manhattan's island.

The lights of Brooklyn glowed a mile or so to the right, and Jersey City could be seen up ahead on the left. Liberty Island waited in the darkness, the famous statue with the torch looking small and lost in the nighttime reflections of the Upper Bay.

Joey, Darick, and Mr. Hanson stood at the bow of the boat, letting the cold, moist air rush over their faces. It felt good, like a fast-flowing river washing away all the worries and frustrations of the past few days.

The three had spent the afternoon exploring Great Kills Park and walking along the deserted beaches of Gateway National Recreation Area, a stretch of sand and stone facing the waters of the Atlantic.

Now it was time to return to the city, to the challenges waiting in East Village. All that could be done for

Troy had been done. His meeting with the police chief had gone well. The officer seemed impressed with the information the prisoner had offered and equally amazed at what he'd learned. Troy's testimony had much "juicy stuff," as the district attorney had required. It was now up to the judge to decide whether a proper deal had been made to reduce the young man's sentence.

Joey watched a freighter glide by in the darkness. "Can I ask you something?" he said to Mr. Hanson, not letting his gaze drift from the passing boat.

"Sure," the lawyer encouraged.

After a long pause the boy continued. "Did I do the right thing—you know, coming back to the city? Do you think I helped Troy any?"

The lawyer nodded. "I think so. I would've rather had you talk to me about it before you left, but you did what you thought you should do."

Darick turned his back to the wind and adjusted his collar. "I never had no brother do somethin' like that for me. I was impressed."

"You don't have a brother," Joey reminded him with a grin.

"Oh, yeah. But if I had, and he did what you did, I'd be impressed."

Mr. Hanson watched the lights move slowly in the distance. "It's a good illustration."

"Of what?" Joey wanted to know.

"Of what Jesus did."

"Jesus came to New York?" Darick gasped.

The lawyer chuckled. "Sort of. You see, Joey decided he was needed someplace far away from where he was. Even though he was living in Montana, out on a beautiful ranch filled with people who cared about him and loved him like a son or brother, he left it all behind for one man in a distant city who was alone and frightened. Joey risked everything to be with his brother. Nothing

95

else mattered—not the ranch, his horse, his close friends, nothing. He just knew his brother needed him, so he packed up and left, thinking he might never see Shadow Creek Ranch again.

"That's what Jesus did a long time ago. He looked down from heaven and saw you and me wasting away in sin, guilty of breaking His laws, mad at the world and ourselves. Suddenly heaven didn't look so beautiful to Him. The angels' songs weren't as pretty. The golden streets had lost their luster.

"So one day He left it all and came to earth as a tiny baby, to grow up in our streets and towns, to feel our sadness and our pain. He wanted to show that He loved us and was willing to risk everything to tell us so."

Joey pushed droplets of moisture across the railing. "And we killed Him," the boy sighed. "Grandpa Hanson said so."

"He's right. We didn't understand all He'd sacrificed for us, so He gave what He had left—His life."

Darick kicked at the railing support and cleared his throat. "Nobody ever told me that before. Jesus came to help *me*?"

"All of us," the man nodded. "You, me, Joey, Troy, all the people in those buildings out there, all the business-men and women, kids on the streets, aristocrats living in the fancy houses on Long Island, the garbage collectors and taxicab drivers, the guy piloting this boat—Jesus left heaven for each one of us. He didn't know whether He'd ever see His Father or His homeland again.

"Couple of times, the devil almost had Him. But He wouldn't give in, even when He was hanging on the cross."

The lawyer shook his head slowly. "The city has a way of crowding out such thoughts. Sometimes it's hard to remember what Jesus did when the streets are so noisy and busy, when trying to survive fills every mo-

96

ment of every day. But we *must* remember. Even if we're sitting in a jail cell for some stupid mistake we made, we must remember that Jesus sees us, and longs to hear us call out to Him."

The Brooklyn Bridge loomed into sight as the big boat turned slightly and headed in the direction of Battery Park. The huge wall of structures forming the pointed end of Manhattan rose like a bright partition separating the dark waters of the bay from the hustle and bustle hiding behind it.

Joey let out a long sigh. The lawyer saw the boy's shoulders sag just a little as he lifted his chin and let the cold breezes wash by. The distant city cast a glow over his young face as the boat continued its journey through the darkness. "I love you, Troy," he heard the boy whisper into the wind.

* * * * *

Wendy sat in the den of the old way Station, listening to the mantle clock tick quietly in the background. The weekend had come and gone and with it the usual journey to the little brick church resting by the highway.

She liked the church, with its collection of farmers and ranchers and their families. There were always visitors from Bozeman in attendance, too. They considered the chapel a sort of spiritual hideaway from the fast pace of the town where they lived and worked.

Wendy found the singing strangely soothing. Although there were few strong voices, those that were tended to be slightly off-key. But it didn't matter. The vocalists' faces always shone with an inner joy as they praised God with the words and melodies printed in the old, faded hymnbooks. The little electric organ that stood under the broad stained window at the front of the room added a feeling of hominess to the gathering each week.

The sermon had been about love—God's love—and

how He wanted His people on earth to share it with others. It was a much-used theme, one that popped up no matter where the group from Shadow Creek Ranch attended church. But Wendy had had a hard time keeping her mind on the message. She kept thinking of the old, abandoned homestead up in the mountains and the pile of letters still waiting to be read.

Every once in a while Debbie would poke her in the ribs and tell her to pay attention. She tried, but soon she was wondering what was going to happen next in the saga of Merrilee and John Dawson.

The girl leaned her head against the softness of the high-backed chair by the fireplace. She'd even considered bringing the letters home to the Station with her. But it just wouldn't be right. They belonged in the little two-story house resting in the folds of the mountains. Reading them elsewhere would diminish the mystery they offered.

The author of the letters had finished college and moved with her husband to Salt Lake City, Utah. Things were going pretty well. She stayed at home as he went off to work each morning at the local welfare department. Merrilee had even started a special savings account at their bank in the hope of someday traveling to Montana to visit the grandmother she'd never met. Years of correspondence had been the two women's only connection.

The happy couple also wanted to start a family, but no children came to bless their lives. Disappointment was obvious in the letters.

Merrilee spent more and more time worrying about her grandmother's health. Wendy wasn't sure what the problem was, but it seemed to get worse as the years passed. First, there'd been cards addressed to a hospital in Bozeman, then to one in Denver. Finally, the old woman had returned home to the farm. It seemed the doctors had given up on her.

During this time, life wasn't too easy for Merrilee, either. John lost his job because of government cutbacks. He worked as a carpenter, then as a truck driver. Needless to say, the "Go See Grandma" fund dried up in a hurry. The last letter Wendy had read before returning to Shadow Creek Ranch mentioned a job possibility in Boise, Idaho. "It's all we can find," the writer had scrawled across the page.

But something else had struck the girl as unusual. The letters kept talking about the love Merrilee had for her husband, and the care and gentleness he showered on his wife. Wendy thought that when two people faced hard times they automatically got divorced. She'd seen it happen over and over again in the lives of neighbors at her apartment building in New York, and to her friends at school.

And hadn't her own mother grown weary of the long hours her dad was putting in with the law firm? The woman had decided that life with the family wasn't worth the effort, so she'd left. Isn't that what everyone did? A husband and wife who faced trials together and still kept their love alive was a new concept for the girl.

Those were her thoughts when the weekend arrived, and those were her thoughts now as she sat listening to the clock tick on the mantle.

"Hey, Wendy," she heard someone call from the doorway. "You want to play with me?" Samantha strode into the room, her face smeared with remnants of ice cream, her after-supper treat. "We can play anything you want."

"No, thanks, Sam," the girl said smiling. "I just want to sit here and think for a little while."

"That's no fun," Samantha protested. "Thinking is boring. I once sat down and thinked for a while and you know what?"

"What?"

"I went to sleep. When I woke up I thought, *Did I really go to sleep or do I just think I did?* I thought about that for a while and finally decided not to think anymore 'cause it was boring."

Wendy giggled. "So now you don't think about anything?"

"Well, sometimes I *wonder* about stuff, but that's different."

Debbie walked into the den and settled herself in her favorite chair. "Hey, guys," she called, "whatcha doin'?"

"Wendy is thinking and I'm not," Samantha called out. "You want to play with me?"

"Not right now, Sam," the girl answered warmly. "Maybe tomorrow. I just want to sit here and enjoy the fire. Isn't it pretty?"

Samantha skipped over and dropped onto the floor in front of the crackling flames. "It's beautiful," she said, lifting her hands to feel the glow. "I like the fireplace. It makes me think I'm camping in the woods with wild animals all around but they won't get me 'cause I'm near the fire."

Wendy laughed out loud. "No, you don't think anymore. I can tell."

Debbie glanced at her sister and smiled. "So, half-pint, what's going on in that over-energized mind of *yours?* You've been acting strangely all weekend. You wouldn't be in love or anything, would you?"

"Hardly," came the quick reply. Wendy paused. "But I have been wondering about it."

The older girl blinked. "What? Did I just hear you say you've been wondering about *love?* Are you feeling OK? Are you dying or something?"

"No," Wendy groaned. "Give me a break, Debbie. I'm a woman too, you know. I'm just trying to get hold of my feelings."

100

"Now you sound like Mother," Debbie chuckled. "She got hold of her feelings, all right. They were in Connecticut."

Wendy ignored her sister's sarcasm. "Let me ask you something, Debbie. Do you think it's possible for two people who are married to each other to have problems and still stay in love, and not get a divorce?"

Debbie's eyelids rose just a little. "Well, sure, if they work at it."

"What do you mean, 'work at it'?"

The older girl turned and gazed into the fire. "Grandpa says if two people *both* want their relationship to succeed, it will. Also, you have to forgive each other when you make mistakes."

"Then why didn't Mom and Dad stay together? They both worked at loving each other."

Debbie sighed. "No, they didn't, Wendy. Mom didn't like it when Dad spent so much time at the office. She thought he didn't love her, and refused to forgive him."

"That's not true!" the younger girl called out. "It wasn't all her fault."

"I agree, but Dad forgave her when she got mad and said those awful things. You remember, don't you? They'd argue late at night, after we'd gone to bed. Mom would say Dad didn't care about her, that all he wanted to do was go to the office. Dad would insist he was working hard for all of us so we could have a nice apartment and half-decent clothes. Then Mom would start to cry and Dad would say he was sorry. But not once, *not once*, did I ever hear Mom say *she* was sorry."

Wendy looked down at her feet. "Well, she was. She just didn't say it out loud."

Debbie studied her sister for a long moment. "Wendy, listen to me. Mom was a great mom. She took good care of us when we were little. But she broke the first rule of love. She didn't work at it hard enough. And no matter

101

what you think, she didn't forgive, not so Dad could notice. He couldn't read her mind."

Wendy sat still, listening to the clock tick away the seconds. She turned to her sister and spoke slowly, her voice strained. "Don't you miss her at all?"

Debbie smiled a sad smile. "Sometimes. I miss hearing her voice waking me up in the morning. I miss her combing my hair and insisting that I'm beautiful. Most of all, I miss having someone to talk to when I have questions Dad can't answer. That's when I wish she was still here."

Wendy brushed back a stray strand of hair from her cheek. "I wish it was different. I wish they still loved each other," she said softly.

The older girl rose and walked to her sister's chair. She settled at her feet and rested her chin on the girl's knee. "So do I. Sometimes," she whispered.

Debbie and Wendy sat looking into the fire, each lost in their own thoughts as Samantha dozed in the warm glow of the flames.

* * * * *

Monday morning dawned clear and unseasonably cold in New York City. A weather front had passed through during the night, leaving the metropolis shivering under a blanket of frigid, Canadian air.

Joey was up at first light, racing around Darick's tiny apartment, trying to rouse everyone.

As he entered Darick's room his host opened one eye and glanced over at the intruder. "Go back to sleep," he yawned. "Birds ain't even up yet."

"Yes, they are," Joey called, throwing open the curtains. "See? There's a pigeon sittin' right there on the ledge. And if you'll look closely, his eyes are open!"

"He's probably frozen." Darick rolled over and covered his head with his blanket. "Call me when he thaws out."

Undaunted, the boy sped out into the living room. "Hey, Mr. H. It's time to rise and shine."

A voice moaned from under a pile of tattered blankets on the couch. "It's still dark in Montana," it said. "Even Wendy isn't up."

"Hey, but this is New York," Joey enthused. "And today Troy's going to see that lady judge. She'll reduce his sentence and everything will be OK."

The blankets shifted and a hand appeared. "Now, listen Joey." The appendage moved about as if searching for something. "She may not go for it. The judge may think Troy needs to spend more time in prison." The hand stopped its wandering and disappeared back inside the pile of cloth. "Don't get your hopes up."

Joey spread his arms. "Hey! I'm a hopeful kinda guy. So let's all get up and have breakfast. Whadda ya say?"

The hand appeared once again. "I can't find those ear muffs Darick loaned me last night. Do you see my ear muffs anywhere?"

"Over to the right a little." The bodyless extremity moved according to the instructions. "There, that's them."

Quickly the muffs disappeared under the covers only to reappear snugly clamped over the lawyer's ears. "Don't poor people have heat?" he said hoarsely.

"Sure," Joey nodded, "when the furnace kicks in. That ain't for another 10 minutes. You'll hear the pipes rattle right at 6:30 sharp. It was the same in my apartment building. You get used to it after a while."

Mr. Hanson looked around the small dwelling with its torn wallpaper and sparse, aging furniture. "I don't want to get used to it. I want to go back to my room in the Station where things sitting on the stand by your bed don't freeze solid during the night."

Joey chuckled. "You rich dudes would never make it where I came from."

Mr. Hanson nodded. "Let us not forget that you're now one of us, Joey Dugan. It's OK to wake up in a warm room."

Darick stumbled down the hall and stood in the kitchen doorway, a blanket pulled tightly around his shoulders. "Morning, Mr. Hanson. How was your night?"

The man moved his legs back and forth. "I think I slept with something furry."

Darick chuckled and walked to the stove. He set all the burners on high and pulled a carton of milk from the refrigerator. "I told you you wouldn't have hurt my feelings if you continued to stay at that fancy hotel on Houston Avenue. But you insisted on coming here for one night."

The lawyer lifted the pile of covers and let his well-socked feet drop to the floor. "Wanted to see how the other half lives," he said. "Don't like it. I'm glad I'm rich."

Darick grinned broadly. "Well, you can stay here any time you want. You and Joey are always welcome."

The man smiled over at the boy. "Thanks, Darick," he said with affection. "You're a good host and I appreciate your hospitality."

Joey poured himself a glass of milk. "So, let's get goin'. We should leave before Darick's roommate comes in. He's usually kinda drunk."

Darick nodded. "Good ol' Jason. But he pays half the rent."

The three set about preparing themselves for the day. Sure enough, at 6:30 sharp the heat came on with a bang. Pipes shuddered and clattered all over the building. Morning had officially arrived in East Village.

* * * * *

The courtroom buzzed with activity as cases were brought before the magistrate. It had been decided that, because of the rather unusual particulars of the Troy

Dugan proceedings, the judge would render her verdict in her chambers outside the courtroom.

Troy would be arriving soon, hopefully with his hair neatly combed and chin cleanly shaven. Mr. Hanson had told him that he'd have a better chance of impressing the judge with his potential if he didn't show up looking like "something from a slasher movie."

Joey, Darick, and Mr. Hanson sat waiting in the magistrate's office. They stared at her broad desk and the shelves of books that lined each wall. A pile of newspapers rested on the coffee table.

To one side of the room hung a picture of George Washington, and against the far wall a bust of Martin Luther King topped a tall stand. Joey nodded to himself. This lady was serious about her work. The only thing that confused him was a photograph of a pretty young girl on the desk. He leaned over and examined the photograph carefully.

"That's me when I was a girl," he heard a coarse, deep, female voice call from the doorway. Everyone looked up to see the judge enter the chamber, her black robes flowing.

"I keep it there to remind me of my roots," the lady added as she seated herself behind the desk. "Do you think I'm pretty?"

Joey blushed and glanced back and forth between the photo and the questioner. The years since the photo was taken had not been kind to the magistrate.

"I . . . I . . ."

"Oh, go on," the woman grinned. "You can flatter me."

"You're . . . you're very smart looking," the boy stammered.

Mr. Hanson burst out laughing as the judge stared at Joey. "Smart looking?" she said with a straight face. She glanced at the lawyer. "Fifty bucks I spent on my hair

105

yesterday and all I get is *smart*?"

The door at the far end of the room opened and Troy walked in with Jerry Diel and Captain Abernathy. The judge leaned in Joey's direction. "I'll take care of you later," she said.

Joey cast a worried glance at Mr. Hanson, who gave him a shrug and winked at the judge.

Troy had heeded his lawyer's advice. He looked like a completely different person. Even his brother was impressed.

"Welcome, gentlemen," the magistrate called, pointing where each should sit. "Because of the legal maneuverings that have taken place in this case, I felt it better to have our session in here, away from the press, et cetera, et cetera.

"I've reviewed the files and the recommendations of those involved and have reached a verdict. But before I administer that verdict, I'd like to ask the accused a few questions."

The woman glanced at Mr. Hanson. "Tyler, I don't want you to say anything. Just sit quietly and don't prod your client. Agreed?"

"Yes, Your Honor," the lawyer responded with a respectful nod. "He's all yours."

"Good." The judge turned to face Troy. "Mr. Dugan, do you realize the seriousness of your crime?"

"Yes."

"Tell me why your crime is serious."

The young man blinked. "Because it's against the law?"

"Don't answer a question with a question," the woman said firmly.

Troy looked over at Mr. Hanson, then back at the judge.

"Because breakin' the law don't help nobody."

The judge nodded slowly. "Why'd you break it?"

106

Troy squirmed in his seat slightly. "I don't know. 'Cause the law never did nothin' for me before."

"Oh, really?" the woman asked. "You've never been helped by the law?"

The young man didn't answer.

"Well, maybe you need to understand what the law is. This city has decided that certain activities do more harm than good to its citizens. For instance, you're not supposed to carry around a gun on public property. Guns aren't evil things in and of themselves. They're just pieces of metal stuck together in such a way as to fire a bullet. Totally harmless, unless that gun is in the hands of someone trying to hurt you. Then that same contraption suddenly becomes deadly. So, just in case some creep wants to kill his neighbor because he plays his stereo too loudly, we make it against the law for people to carry guns on the street. You with me?"

Troy nodded.

"So the law doesn't make something evil, or harmful. The law simply helps identify potential problems, and tries to keep bad things from happening to people."

Troy stared at the speaker. Her words were beginning to make sense.

"Now," the judge continued, "you were caught dealing in drugs. You had the stuff on your person, right?"

Troy nodded again.

"Answer me out loud."

"Yes," he conceded.

"If the city had looked the other way, and allowed you to take, or sell, those drugs, could any harm come of your actions?"

The young man shifted in his chair. "Maybe if I sold 'em, but what if I took 'em myself? That wouldn't be hurtin' nobody."

"Oh, but you're wrong, Mr. Dugan," the woman said leaning forward on her elbows. "You'd be hurting *you*.

107

You'd be risking the life of one of New York's own citizens. You'd be putting someone's health and well being in jeopardy. And that's against the law."

"Wait a minute," Troy chuckled. "You mean to tell me the law is trying to protect me from me?"

"Sometimes, if you need protection from yourself. So let me ask you again, why is your crime serious?"

The accused thought for a long moment. Joey watched his face, looking for the answer before it was spoken. "Because I could've hurt somebody, or myself."

"Bingo," the woman announced. "I want you to remember something, Troy. The law is not a toy to be played with until you tire of it. It's an attempt, imperfect as it may be, for neighbor to care for neighbor, and friend to protect friend."

The room was silent except for the traffic noises that filtered through the tightly shut window.

"Now, here's what the court has decided. I hereby sentence you, Troy Dugan, to five years in the state penitentiary with the possibility of parole after 12 months. Upon your release, you will report to a probation officer of this city and will then volunteer your services to—" the judge glanced at some papers on her desk— "Project Youth Revival, an organization that can 'help you learn to help others,' this according to the cowboy lawyer sitting beside you." She flipped her file folder shut. "Any questions?"

Troy looked at the woman behind the desk. "Thank you," he said in a low voice. "I appreciate your not sending me away for a long time."

"You can thank your friends there," the judge smiled. "They stood by you. Don't let them down."

The young man stood to his feet. "I ain't never had such good friends before. I ain't never—"

Joey ran and threw himself into his brother's arms. He pressed his face into the older boy's chest and hung on for a long moment. "I'll write you a letter every week," he breathed. "I promise."

Troy rested his chin on the boy's head. "Forgive me, Joey," he said, his words strained. "Forgive me for gettin' mad at you. You was just tryin' to help. I know that now."

"It's OK," the younger boy said softly. "And Troy, I'll pray for you each night before I go to sleep. I'll pray that God will come and sit by you all night long so you won't feel alone."

"You do that," Troy said, tears moistening his eyes. "I'll know He's there because you're asking Him to."

Captain Abernathy took his prisoner by the elbow and gently led him to the door. Troy turned and looked at Mr. Hanson. "You're OK, hotshot," he said with a smile. "Joey was right. You're OK."

The lawyer nodded and blinked back a few tears of his own. With a wave, Troy Dugan was gone.

Joey felt a hand on his shoulder. Turning, he gazed into the eyes of the judge. "Your brother will survive," she said softly. "You gave him something to look forward to."

She walked to the door leading into the courtroom. "The proper papers will be mailed to you," she called to Mr. Hanson. The man nodded.

"Your honor," she heard Joey call.

"Yes?"

"I . . . I think you're beautiful."

The judge lifted her chin and glanced at the lawyer. She gave her hair a couple of strokes. "This style," she said. "It gets 'em every time."

With a broad smile creasing her timeworn face, she turned and disappeared through the doorway.

CHAPTER SEVEN

TREASURE

The jetliner seemed to hang motionless in the thin atmosphere high over Idaho. Salt Lake City had long since faded to the south. Below, Rocky Mountain ranges rose and fell, wearing remnants of autumn's colorful glory on their rugged chins.

Mr. Hanson sat reading a magazine. He'd found an interesting article about a new technology set to shake up the computer industry. The man chuckled to himself. Andrew Albert Morrison the Third probably already had the device the magazine was reviewing tucked in one corner of his bedroom that overlooked the Hills of Beverly. The lawyer knew he'd get an urgent fax from his young friend sometime in the next couple days, enthusiastically suggesting that he purchase this latest and greatest high-tech marvel.

Mr. Hanson turned to the teenager seated beside him. The boy sat with his nose pressed against the Plexiglass window, soaking in the passing parade presented by Mother Nature 35,000 feet below.

Joey sighed a long sigh. He'd done it. A satisfied smile brightened the young passenger's face. He'd really done it, and survived.

When the teenager left for New York, he'd carried with him a fear that the streets, the neighborhoods, his old friends, would offer such enticements that he'd be caught up into his past lifestyle again.

But it hadn't happened. Why? Joey knew the answer. It was because he'd found something much better, much more satisfying. He'd discovered a life with a promising future. Since leaving the city more than a year ago, he'd found the joy of honest labor, and the self-confidence that came from the fact that people relied on his abilities and valued his judgments. At Shadow Creek Ranch the young boy had uncovered a purpose for his life. No street, no gang, no city, could compete.

Joey nodded thoughtfully. That's why he'd survived the last week. That's why he couldn't wait to get home to his little room in the big Station, to Tar Boy, Wrangler Barry, and all the people who meant so much to him.

The lad knew he'd never be satisfied unless he was actively involved with things that made a difference in the lives of others. During the past year, the New Yorker-turned-cowboy had discovered an important truth: being a positive force in the world, as hard as it may be sometimes, is the very best way to live.

He recalled the words the woman judge had spoken that very morning during her talk with Troy. She'd insisted that the law was designed to help people care for other people. Joey smiled. The woman had almost sounded like Grandpa Hanson. Hadn't he said over and over again that *God's* law was for the same purpose, that when we obey it, we're really revealing our love and concern for others as well as our respect for the Creator?

In that judge's chamber, surrounded by the noise and activity of the big city, the teenager had suddenly

111

realized that keeping the law was much more rewarding than breaking it.

Surprisingly, he also found himself agreeing that punishment for breaking a law is *necessary*. It makes people stop and realize what they've done, and how their actions have affected others and themselves.

And even though Troy's crime had been very serious, the judge understood that the accused had something few can boast—a caring, forgiving support system waiting for him. That's why, in 12 months, Troy would get the opportunity to start life new again, if he proved he was ready for parole. The court system was offering him a second chance.

"Your nose will be flat against your face when we get to Bozeman," Joey heard his seatmate say. "You'll look like a bulldog."

The boy chuckled. "Wendy will insist it improves my appearance."

Mr. Hanson leaned forward and glanced out the window. "What's down there?"

Joey studied the route map printed in the back of the airline magazine and checked his watch. Using the suggested time-distance table from the previous page, he reported confidently, "My calculations put us over the Continental Divide . . . or" he squinted at the map, "Argentina. I think I'll go with the Divide. That means we're entering Montana right on schedule." The lad pointed out the window. "Over there's the Madison Range and just beyond it, our very own Gallatin National Forest. Just think, Mr. H, somewhere down there is Tar Boy waitin' for me to ride him up into those mountains."

The lawyer lifted his chin and sniffed. "I think I smell Lizzy's vegetable stew cooking, too."

Joey pressed his nose against the window once again.

"And best of all," he said quietly to himself, "down there is home."

* * * * *

Wendy studied the letter thoughtfully. It was dated almost 15 years ago, so she knew whatever was about to happen had taken place before she was born. But still she felt uneasy as she read.

Much time had passed. Years. Merrilee and her husband had worked hard, trying to build a life for themselves, but they'd been repeatedly struck down with hardships and disappointments.

Somehow, through it all, the writer had remained confident that things would improve.

As the pile of unread letters dwindled, the young girl sitting under the window ledge in the old, abandoned farmhouse began to realize that not all stories have happy endings. It seemed that Merrilee and John were two people born to suffer while others escaped the cruel clutches of reality. They'd been given no advantages.

But most amazing of all, the couple had remained deeply in love with each other. Time and time again, Wendy marveled at the strength of their devotion.

Now she held the next to last letter in her hands. Her eyes studied the words written neatly across the page.

"Grandma, please tell me what's going on with you. I know something isn't quite right.

"It's your health, isn't it? Oh, if you only had a telephone, I'd call. Hasn't the phone company decided, as I have, that you're the most important person in the Gallatins? They should rush right up there and put in a line just for you so I can call and insist that you *go see a doctor*! He'll give you medicines. Forget this silly notion that you have in your head that you're too old to get better.

"OK. I'll get off my soapbox and let you be (for a little while).

"John and I are both working, at least temporarily. He's building cabinets for a new apartment complex going up north of Boise, and I'm doing some part-time nursing at a local retirement home. Our hours are such that we don't see much of each other. Neither one of us likes the arrangement, but you gotta pay the bills, right?

"We've started another 'Go see Grandma' fund, so you must keep well until I can come to take proper care of you. We want to fix up a room in our apartment just for you. Those cold Montana winters can't be doing you any good. Of course, cold Idaho winters aren't a whole lot better, but I'd be around to watch out for you every day.

"News flash! John just came in and told me that he may have a job opportunity in Missoula, *Montana*, in about six months! The Social Services offices there reviewed his résumé and may be interested in hiring him after one of their workers retires. That's just 200 miles from Bozeman and not far from your little farm. Oh, I hope it works out!

"Grandma, you've been my best friend for over 25 years, yet I've never gotten a chance to hug your neck and look into your eyes. Your letters have seen me through some pretty rough times. The unshakable faith you have in God and your words of encouragement have brought me such comfort through those years.

"Now, if all works out, we may be living in the same state with you! I've got my fingers and my toes crossed and I'll pray every night that this job comes through. John is a wonderful man and deserves all the breaks he can get. I love him so much. And I love you too.

"Please, grandma, go see the doctor. I want you well and happy when I come to give you the hug my arms have ached to give.

"You will always be my very best friend.

"Your granddaughter, Merrilee."

Wendy slowly slipped the page back into its envelope

114

and then picked up the last letter. She was about to open it when her eyes caught the name written across the front. This was not a letter *from* Merrilee to her grandmother. It was a letter written by Mrs. M. Grant and addressed *to* Merrilee Dawson.

The girl gasped. The words she was about to read were penned by none other than the old grandmother herself!

A sudden chill swept over the girl. Why wasn't the letter ever mailed? What was it doing here in the mirrored box with the rest?

Breathlessly, Wendy pulled out the neatly folded pages. For the first time, she'd see words placed on paper by the woman who'd lived in the long-abandoned house, the lady who'd been so important to a granddaughter she'd never met.

"My dearest Merrilee." The writing was a little unsteady but still very readable. Wendy could tell that a multitude of years weighed heavily upon the hand that pushed the pen across the paper.

"How I love to read your letters. They fill my life with such joy and I thank God every day for my precious granddaughter.

"Throughout your life you've always been so brave, so giving. I know you and John can face anything together—hard times, moments of frustration, great disappointments. You've chosen to make your love for each other strong. My heart sings when I think of the two of you standing hand in hand, facing whatever the future brings.

"Each night, before I tuck myself into bed, I kneel and pray for you. I ask God to place His loving arms around you and John and bring you peace in these troubled times. I know He hears my prayers.

"Life is quiet on the farm today. Most of the birds have flown to warmer skies, and the trees are laying a carpet of leaves to cradle the coming snows.

"When you're old, you seem to notice the seasons more. They pass away like friends you've known, leaving only reminders of themselves to wander through your thoughts.

"Don't worry about me, Merrilee. The good Lord says He's building a new homestead just for me up in the mountains behind the New Jerusalem. I've asked Him to build one for you and John too, right next to mine. Then we can see each other every day with no distances separating us. Won't that be wonderful?

"I think it's time I tell you something. When the day comes that I fall asleep in Jesus, I'm leaving behind a treasure for you. It's more valuable than gold, and nothing can take it away as long as you live. It's all I have to give. Please accept it without tears, for it's my way of loving you until the Lord comes and we can be together for eternity.

"I keep the key to the treasure in that mirrored box I've told you about, the one my husband gave me years and years ago before he died. It's hiding in an old cedar chest under the dining room window. I'll be sending the key to you soon with instructions of what to do.

"Must rest now. I feel so very tired. I'll put this letter away and mail it tomorrow when the postman stops by.

"Good-night, sweet Merrilee. I'll think of you again when I awake.

"Grandmother."

Wendy reached into the now empty box and her hand touched something hiding in a dark corner. The sun's rays, filtering in through the window above her head, struck the object as she lifted it into the light. In her trembling fingers she held a bright, shiny key.

* * * * *

It seemed like homecoming at the Station. First Wendy and Early returned from their ride into the mountains, then the lawyer's red minivan pulled up and out jumped Joey, followed by Grandpa and Grandma Hanson. They'd made arrangements to arrive at the airport at the same time as their returning son and young ranch hand.

Samantha bolted from the Station with Pueblo and Lizzy at her heels. Wrangler Barry jogged across the footbridge, and Debbie appeared on the upstairs porch, her arms waving excitedly.

What had been a quiet, peaceful ranch became a chaotic mixture of hugs and shouts as friends and families were reunited.

Everyone was eager to know what had happened in New York. As soon as the suitcases were lugged to their proper quarters and Wendy had put Early out to pasture, the whole gang filed into the den and took their seats, each waiting to hear every detail of the past week's adventures.

Joey and Mr. Hanson told their story, drawing words of encouragement and thanksgiving from their listeners.

Next, Grandpa and Grandma Hanson shared the excitement of their vacation trip to Seattle. They told of walks along Pacific beaches and of visits to museums and novelty shops. Grandpa insisted his favorite part was seeing those huge airplanes being built.

Then Debbie shocked everyone with an announcement. "I've got a part-time job," she said smiling.

Mr. Hanson looked up surprised. "Where?" he wanted to know.

"At the mall."

"That figures," Joey chided.

The girl ignored her friend's jab. "I'll be working two afternoons a week for the company that designs and decorates store windows. I called them on the phone and gave them the names of some of the shop owners I knew in New York City, the ones I used to help with their window displays after school. Well, they called back this morning and offered me a job. I can ride in with Barry or

Grandpa when they go for supplies."

She turned to her father. "So, what do you think?"

The lawyer searched his daughter's face. "But what about—"

"I'm going to build my *own* future," she said resolvedly. "If New York fits into my plans, then maybe later."

She turned to the others. "You see, Dad had promised me that if I wanted to, I could return to New York after being here in Montana for one year. He'd send me to a real nice school for girls near Central Park."

The speaker glanced at her father. "Then I got to thinking about you, Daddy. I've never seen you so happy before, at least when you're not chasing ol' Dugan here halfway across the country." Joey blushed as the girl continued. "See, you were my dad in New York, and you're my dad here at Shadow Creek Ranch." She paused. "You're a much better dad here. So I figured there's something about these mountains and trees and rivers that change people and make them even kindlier and more loving than they were before. Well, I want them to change me, too."

The man studied his daughter's face. "Debbie," he said, his voice trembling just a little, "you know I'd love you no matter where you chose to live."

The girl nodded. "I know. But during the past year you've shown me what choices work best. I guess you're stuck with me for a while longer."

Mr. Hanson reached over and gave his daughter's hand a squeeze. "You're all grown up, Debbie," he said softly. "And I'm very, very proud of you."

Joey glanced at Wrangler Barry. The horseman had a big smile spread across his suntanned face. Seemed others in the group took Debbie's announcement with a degree of pleasure, too.

There was a moment of silence in the room, then Wendy stood to her feet. "I've got a story to tell," she said. "But I don't know how it will end."

"What do you mean?" Lizzy asked.

The young girl walked out into the hall and returned with something in her hands. Everyone gasped as she placed a beautiful mirrored box on the coffee table by the fireplace.

"Wow," Joey breathed. "Where'd you get that?"

The girl turned toward the window and pointed to the east. "Up there," she said. "And there's a treasure, too."

"A treasure?" Debbie asked. "What treasure?"

Slowly, with careful attention to every detail, Wendy related the adventure of the past week and a half. The whole group sat listening as if spellbound, marveling at her every word.

She told of the old homestead, of Mr. Underfoot and the box of letters. As evening stole across the meadow and wrapped the Station in darkness, her voice carried her listeners back through the years. They met a little orphan girl named Merrilee and a grandmother who lived in a farmhouse in the mountains.

Then Wendy read aloud the last two letters in the box and lifted the key so everyone could see it.

When her story ended, she closed the box. No one spoke. They, like Wendy, had come to know two extraordinary people, one of whom had lived just five miles from the Station.

Grandpa Hanson sat silent for a long moment, lost in thought. Suddenly, he looked up. "I may know who she is . . . or was."

"You do?" Wendy breathed.

The old man nodded. "When we first moved here I heard of an old woman who was found somewhere up in the mountains. Folks said she died peacefully in her sleep." He shook his head. "Yes, I remember. The mail carrier stopped at her farm and sensed something was wrong. When there was no answer to his knock, he went inside and discovered that she had died. No one knew

119

who she was. No one ever came to claim her belongings or anything. She just faded away."

Wendy spread her hands. "But she has a grand-daughter. And that granddaughter has a treasure wait-ing for her."

"It would seem so," the old man agreed. "Whadda ya think, Tyler? Should we investigate? Maybe the woman they found was the same lady who received all these letters."

Wendy rushed over to her dad. "Please! Let's find out. Please?"

The lawyer nodded. "I suppose I could make some phone calls. But don't get your hopes up for some kind of buried treasure or anything. The way you describe the farm, the lady wasn't rich."

"I know," the girl agreed. "But Merrilee may have something from her grandmother that she doesn't even know about. The letter was never sent." The girl paused as her face paled. "Oh, my. OH MY!" She glanced at the mirrored box. "The old woman died the night she wrote the letter. Merrilee never knew what happened. She doesn't know about the key, about the treasure! No one knows but us."

Wendy pressed herself into her father's arms. "We have to find Merrilee. We just *have* to!"

* * * * *

Interstate 90 runs through the valleys of western Montana like a river seeking the sea. On both sides of the highway rise towering mountains, their summits painted white by early snows.

Deer and elk had left the higher elevations to seek the diminishing grasslands, which still offered a final feast before winter arrived and buried the meadows until spring.

A sign appeared up ahead, then flashed past the little red minivan as it moved along in the thin current of traffic. **Missoula—30 miles**, the marker announced.

Mr. Hanson glanced down at his only passenger. "What are you going to say to her?"

Wendy studied the distant peaks. "I don't know."

The vehicle sped along, leaving a small whirlwind of leaves fluttering on the shoulder of the super highway.

During the past week, the lawyer had made good his promise to search for the missing granddaughter. He'd also checked with the authorities in Bozeman, trying to dig up as much information as he could about the old woman who'd died in the mountains years before.

Referring to the last letter received from Merrilee Dawson, he contacted the Social Services Department in Missoula. Sure enough, their records showed that a John Dawson had indeed worked for them, beginning about the time that the letter had indicated.

But three years ago, the man had been seriously injured in a freak automobile accident. As far as the agency knew, he and his wife still lived in town, although the address they had was no longer valid.

That's when Mr. Hanson had tapped into a medical database with his computer and found that a nurse by the name of Merrilee Dawson was presently employed at a community hospital in Stevensville, a town 25 miles south of Missoula at the base of the Bitterroot Mountains. A quick call to the hospital yielded an address and phone number.

The lawyer had made contact with the woman and told her he'd like to pay her a visit. He said he had some new information about her grandmother.

The minivan turned south on Highway 93. In a short time another sign heralded the approach of Stevensville.

Before long, the vehicle stopped in front of a small brick house in an older part of town. Wendy and her father strode up the neatly swept walkway and paused at the front door. Mr. Hanson smiled down at his daughter.

"Well, go ahead and knock," he encouraged.

Wendy rapped lightly on the door. It opened to reveal a woman in her early 40s. She was wearing the blue-white dress of a nurse.

"Are you Mr. Hanson?" she asked.

"Yes. And this is my daughter Wendy."

The woman looked surprised. "Oh, hello," she said smiling. "I wasn't expecting two visitors. Please come in."

The front room was thoughtfully decorated with simple furnishings and colorful pictures hanging over slightly faded wallpaper. A man appeared at the kitchen door, leaning heavily on a cane, hand outstretched. "Good afternoon," he said warmly. "I'm John Dawson, Merrilee's husband."

Wendy recognized him from the tiny picture she'd seen before. Both the man and woman carried vivid reminders of much younger years. Their smiles had not changed at all.

"Wendy?" The girl heard her name spoken and she looked up into the woman's face. "Would you like something to drink? Some soda, maybe?"

"No, thank you," Wendy responded. She stared back into the kind eyes. "I know you," the girl said softly. "I know you."

"You do?" came the surprised reply.

"Yes. I know you had a dog named Bounder and that you used to draw pictures of people with big legs and little heads. I know that your mom and dad died when you were young, and that a guy named Andrew left you at the Fall Festival and made you cry."

Merrilee's mouth dropped open as she sank onto the couch. "How . . . ?"

"I know you had a roommate named Jessica that liked pineapples and chocolate cake, and that you wanted to have a baby but . . ."

The woman looked over at her husband, then back at

122

Wendy. "My dear girl," she gasped. "How do you know these things?"

Wendy lifted an object from the bag she was carrying. "Because of this."

Merrilee's eyes opened wide when she saw what the girl was holding. "The box," she gasped. "The mirrored box! It belonged to—" the woman couldn't continue.

"Your grandmother," Wendy said, her words not much above a whisper. "She lived in the mountains near our ranch. I found her house one day beside an old logging road."

The girl opened the box. "See? These letters were from you to your grandmother. I read them. I hope you don't mind."

Tears stained the woman's cheeks as she reached over and took the pile of envelopes from the girl's outstretched hands. "My last letter to her was returned with a kind note from the postman. He said grandmother had died. It broke my heart."

Wendy pointed at the stack of papers tied with a faded blue ribbon. "There's a letter in there that you never got. Your grandmother wrote it the night she—"

Merrilee pulled out the correspondence Wendy was indicating. "Oh, John, look," she said softly. "It's her handwriting. I'd recognize it anywhere."

"There's something you need to know," Mr. Hanson said, seating himself by the window. "The letter mentions that your grandmother was planning to leave what she called 'a treasure' for you."

The woman tilted her head to one side. "A treasure? My grandmother was not rich. She, like us, had very little."

"That's not quite the case," the man continued, pulling an envelope from his coat pocket. "In that last letter, she mentioned a key. My daughter found it in the mirrored box, just as Mrs. Grant had said. I took the key to the authorities in Bozeman, and they discovered that it fits a safety deposit box in the Western Security Bank on Main Street.

"I took the liberty of assuming legal responsibility for its contents since no one had opened the box for over 15 years. Two items found in it relate to a Mrs. Merrilee Dawson.

"First is this last will and testament, signed by your grandmother a year before she died and still binding at the time of her passing. Because of the impersonal world of high-tech record keeping, no one at the bank connected the reported death in the mountains with your grandmother. As far as the bank is concerned, she's still as alive as her savings account.

"The will names you and your husband, John Dawson, sole beneficiaries of her estate, which includes a fair amount of cash, thanks to 15 years of interest, and this." Mr. Hanson held up a document. "This is the deed to the homestead she was living on, and the 25 acres of timberland surrounding it. It now belongs to you. Of course, there will be some back property taxes to pay, but the money will more than cover that."

Merrilee and her husband sat stunned. All their lives they had faced hardships and heartbreaking disappointments. Even the news of Mrs. Grant's dying generosity had taken 15 years to reach them.

The woman stared at the document in the lawyer's hand for a long moment. Slowly a smile began to spread across her face. "Of course," she said. "Now I understand."

Mr. Dawson looked over at his wife. "What do you mean?"

Merrilee took in a deep breath. "Grandmother used to write a Bible verse across the bottom of some of her letters. All these years I didn't understand what she was trying to say. Now I do. She'd write, 'The Lord shall open

124

unto thee his good treasure, the heaven to give the rain unto thy land in his season, and to bless all the work of thine hand.'

"Don't you see?" The woman took the unmailed letter and pressed it against her heart. "Grandmother's treasure isn't just a piece of land. It's an opportunity for us to see God sending the rain to make things grow. It's the privilege of putting seeds into our own soil and working for the harvest. She wanted us to witness God's power firsthand, there in the mountains, on her precious homestead."

Wendy walked over to the woman's side. "Will you come live there?" she asked. "We can be neighbors. I'll visit you every day with my horse, Early. We can fix it up. I know you'll like it."

Merrilee looked at her husband. "What do you say, John?"

Mr. Hanson lifted his hand. "We at the Station will be more than happy to help you rebuild the homestead. I checked it out the other day. It has real potential. You could stay on our ranch until the work is completed. But be warned, we're kind of a strange bunch."

John Dawson turned to his wife. She saw tears in his eyes. "All my life I've wanted you to be happy, really happy," he said. "I've longed for a place where we could settle down and never have to leave, where I could work hard and build a future for us. I'm almost well now. This could be my chance."

"I know it is," the woman said, taking his hand in hers. "Grandmother knew it, too."

Wendy sat savoring the newfound joy radiating from the couple's faces. The treasure had been passed to its rightful owners. At long last, the old homestead called Merrilee would echo again with the happy voices of love, just as the old woman had planned.

WHISPERS
in the Wind

Charles Mills

Dedication

To the Harold Kuebler clan—
In-laws *extradordinaire*!

Contents

CHAPTER 1

LAUGHTER IN THE RAFTERS

◎ ◎ ◎

"How on earth did *that* get there?" Merrilee Dawson drew in a sharp breath and blinked her eyes, testing to see if what was there actually existed.

"What are you talking about?" her husband asked, not turning from the window, where he was carefully replacing a broken pane of glass.

The woman stepped closer, eying the strange object lying on the floor of the dark, dusty closet. "This . . . this thing."

John Dawson walked across the small, upstairs room and stood beside his wife. "Beats me," he said as his brow furrowed slightly. "I'm sure it's nothing your grandmother would have had lying around the

house, and," he paused, examining the object carefully, "certainly not in her bedroom closet."

Merrilee stepped out into the hall and called
down the stairwell. "Wendy? Could you come up
here for a moment? We've found something very
strange in the closet."

The woman heard not one but four pair of
running feet. Within seconds, Wendy, Joey, Debbie,
and little Samantha were standing around her expectantly, huffing and puffing from their quick journey from wherever in the house they'd been.

Even Mr. Underfoot, the long-time resident of the
old, abandoned homestead scurried up the steps as if
he, too, wanted to see what the announced "very
strange" something might be. The fact that Mr.
Underfoot was a raccoon didn't deter him from
trying to be involved in all the "people" goings-on
that had been interrupting his peaceful forest do-
main during the past six weeks.

"What is it, Merrilee?" the wide-eyed group of
energetic youngsters asked.

"Did you find a hidden safe with lots of money in
it?" 10-year-old Wendy breathed.

"Is it a big box where old clothes with lace and
fancy embroidering could hide?" her older sister,
Debbie, asked.

"Did you find an old flint-lock rifle or a bunch of
Indian arrows?" Joey wanted to know.

Merrilee shook her head from side to side and
laughed out loud. "Where do you guys get your

imaginations? It's nothing as exciting as all that. But it is a mystery. Come, I'll show you."

The woman led the ever-curious youngsters into the bedroom and paused before the closet door. "There," she said, pointing into the dark shadows of the small enclosure. "Would you mind telling me what that is, and how it got in here?"

Joey drew in his breath as his mouth dropped open. "My geologist's pick. MY GEOLOGIST'S PICK! I've been looking everywhere for it. How did—" He stopped in mid-sentence. The boy's eyes narrowed as he slowly turned to face one of his companions. "Wendy Hanson?" he said in as pleasant a tone as possible, considering his teeth were clenched together tightly. "As I recall, and correct me if I'm wrong, I seem to remember loaning you that very geo-pick about two months ago. And," he lifted his work-soiled index finger as if to make a point, "you *promised* to bring it back."

The lad's voice began to tremble. "Wrangler Barry thinks that I lost it. Me. He says I left it somewhere. ME! Now, here's my geo-pick on the closet floor of Mrs. Dawson's house up here in the middle of the Gallatin National Forest. I know I ain't the smartest person in the world, and I may be from New York City, but would I be too far out of line to ask you for an explanation?"

Wendy smiled meekly. "Joey, Joey, Joey. You can ask me anything you'd like. We're friends. Buddies. Like brother and sister."

11

"The only thing we are right now is mortal enemies," the boy said, taking a step toward Wendy. The girl didn't budge.

"Just calm down, Mr. Dugan," she said. "I can explain everything."

"I'm listening," came the icy reply.

"Well." Wendy blinked her eyes, trying to look innocent and sweet. "You see, when I found that board out on the road that had 'Merrilee' written on it and when I couldn't get through the wall of underbrush and vines, I got mad and threw the geo-pick at it."

"You threw my geologist's pick at a bunch of vines and underbrush?"

"And trees," Wendy added. "There were lots of trees, too."

Joey closed his eyes.

"But I missed," the girl brightened even further. "That silly ol' geo-pick sailed right over that silly ol' barrier and that's when I heard it."

"Heard what?" Joey asked, his voice not much above a whisper.

"The glass breaking. SMASH—tinkle, tinkle. That's when I knew I'd really found something neat."

Mr. Dawson turned and studied the window pane he'd just replaced. He then looked across the room at the closet. Yup. The two were right in line with the tangle of vines near the road.

"So," the girl concluded, "I guess that geo-pick came right in through the window and landed in the closet and . . . so . . . there it is." She reached down and picked up the tool. "Here's your geologist's pick, Mr. Dugan," she said, smiling sweetly. "Sorry it took so long to get it back to you. But a promise is a promise."

With that she turned and stepped lightly out into the hallway and descended the stairs.

Merrilee's hand shot to her mouth in an attempt to stifle a laugh. Her husband turned quickly toward the window so Joey wouldn't see his uncontrolled grin.

The boy sighed. "That Wendy is crazy. Totally, off-the-wall crazy." He shook his head and left the room.

Behind him, gales of laughter suddenly exploded, the happy sound echoing through the little rooms and broad-beam rafters of the old homestead. Joey glanced down at Mr. Underfoot. Even the raccoon seemed to be overflowing with giggles as he scurried past the boy and followed Wendy down the stairs.

The youngster sighed again. How was he going to tell Wrangler Barry that he'd found the long-lost geologist's pick in a musty, dark closet on the second floor of an abandoned farmhouse? He brightened. Not to worry. He'd just mention to his ranch-hand boss that he'd loaned the tool to Wendy. That should be explanation enough.

* * * * *

Mr. Hanson steered his red minivan along the

13

bumpy, mountain road that led from the Station to the old homestead nestled in a fold of the Absaroka Range in southwestern Montana. He hummed an unending tune as he sat watching the last remnants of autumn drop lazily from the passing cottonwoods and aspens.

Even the small stands of white birch moving slowly by the vehicle no longer wore their fall finery. Winter was coming. You could feel it in the October air. You could see it in the frenzied activity of the small forest creatures that lived among the fallen logs and grassy patches of the mountains and meadows.

The lawyer settled back in his seat and let his mind wander freely. So much had happened during the past five months. Shadow Creek Ranch had welcomed its first small group of teenagers from across the country. Joey had surprised everyone and gone back to New York to help his streetwise brother. Wendy had found a farm and a person, both named Merrilee. The Dawsons—Merrilee and her husband—had moved from Stevensville to the farm and were preparing to start their new lives in the old home that the woman's grandmother had willed to them. Debbie had found a part-time job in Bozeman with a company that designed window dressings for department stores. And somehow, through it all, he'd managed to maintain a busy workload at his home office in the old way station.

Life was full. Sometimes too full. But he and his

mom and dad seemed to be holding down the fort with some degree of success. Hadn't Lizzy Pierce said just the other day that life on Shadow Creek Ranch was as overflowing as a mountain stream in spring?

Mr. Hanson nodded. Life was good, and worthwhile. But he secretly hoped that the coming winter would be a time for relaxing, for recharging his inner soul. As during the winter before, the only challenge he wanted to face was making sure the children studied their school lessons and did all that Mrs. Pierce, their housemate-turned-teacher, told them to do.

The little minivan continued up the old logging road, making its way through the tall stands of spruce and fir. Yes, this winter would hold no surprises. As the local grizzlies demonstrated, it was time to hibernate in the warm and cozy den of the Station.

Beep. Beep. Wendy looked up to see her father's vehicle slip through the narrow opening among the trees and come to a stop by the newly painted shed.

She waved and turned back to her work. A new section of porch had recently replaced the old, broken portion by the front door. Her job on this cool Sunday afternoon was to apply a thick coat of white paint over the carefully nailed boards, sealing the wood from the weather.

"You 'bout done?" her father asked as he walked toward the girl. "Looks pretty good around here. I

15

see you've finished the shed. We'll start stacking fire-wood in there tomorrow after school."

"Yup," Wendy smiled with satisfaction as she wiped stray strands of blond hair from her forehead. "Merrilee is lookin' great, just like I knew it would. It's hard work, though. Even Joey looks a little pooped around the eyes."

"I heard that," the boy's voice called from inside the rustic living room. "Ask your daughter what we found upstairs, Mr. H."

The lawyer glanced down at his youngest child. "A pot of gold? A treasure map?"

Wendy rolled her eyes. "No. Joey found his geologist's pick."

"Ask her where it was," invited the bodyless voice from inside.

"Where'd you find it?" Mr. Hanson smiled.

"In the upstairs closet."

"Ask her how it got there."

The lawyer's eyebrows rose. "How'd it get there?"

"Through the window, of course," the girl said, dipping her paintbrush in the container of thick, white liquid beside her knee.

"Ask her who threw it through the window."

"Who th—"

"I did," Wendy interrupted. "So, big deal." She faced the front door. "You've got your stupid ol' pick back, so just forget it."

Mr. Hanson lowered his voice and bent close to his daughter's ear. "So . . . why'd you throw Joey's geologist's pick through the window?"

"I'll tell you later," the girl sighed. "Much later."

The man chuckled. "OK. But now you'd better finish up what you're doing. It'll be dark soon. Supper's waiting down at the Station. Grandma and Lizzy have prepared lentil soup with homemade bread and peach jam."

Wendy unconsciously licked her lips. If there was one thing the girl liked more than a good mystery, it was good food, and lots of it. For someone who'd been eating for only 10 years, she could pack it away with the best of them.

Before long, all the workers had been rounded up, tools washed and put away, and door and windows closed against the night air. As the little red minivan descended the mountain road, it overflowed with tired but happy passengers. The old homestead was almost ready. Before the heavy winter snows arrived, John and Merrilee Dawson would be living within its cozy walls, warmed by the newly-installed wood-burning stove and the memory of the generous old woman who'd lived there many years before.

But for now, only one thought held center stage in the minds of the weary travelers: lentil soup and homemade bread with peach jam. What a delicious way to end the day.

Supper was everything it was hoped to be. Bowls of steaming soup disappeared down hungry throats as pleasant chatter drifted with the sweet smell of freshly baked squash bread.

Samantha sat beside Joey, her dark face radiant with pleasure as she heaped top-heavy piles of jam on her third slice.

"Take it easy, Sam," the boy chuckled. "If you eat anymore you'll pop like a balloon."

The 5-year-old stopped chewing and looked up at her companion. "I will?" she said, her mouth full of bread and jam.

"Yeah. We'll have to scrape you off the walls with a shovel."

"Gross!" Wendy moaned.

Debbie wrinkled her nose. "Come on, Joey. We're trying to eat."

Grandpa Hanson nodded. "We'd have Samantha soup."

"Puh-leeze," Lizzy groaned. "I think I'm getting ill."

Wendy shook her head. "No, no. If she popped we'd have Samantha stew."

Debbie lifted her hand. "Enough already. I happen to like the smallest member of our ranch family all in one piece, if it's OK with the rest of you."

Samantha's little black face grinned a wide, peach-jam grin. "Thank you, Debbie. But I'd make a delicious stew, I think. Dizzy says I'm as sweet as sugar and as yummy as candy cane."

Those gathered around the table burst out laughing at Samantha's evaluation of herself. "You're right," Joey said, smiling. He bent down and gave his adopted sister a wet, slobbery kiss on the cheek, then he licked his lips. "One thing's for sure. You do taste like peaches, for some strange reason."

"See?" the little girl beamed. "Sweet. Just like Dizzy says."

Wrangler Barry entered the room and hurried over to his place at the table. "Sorry I'm late, folks," he apologized as he hurriedly began loading his plate with food. "Had a little trouble with one of the horses." He glanced over at Joey and grinned. "The big black one. Didn't want to come in for the night. Had to chase that beast clean around the pasture."

"Hey," Joey said, lifting his hands palms up. "Tar Boy likes the great outdoors. He doesn't want to be cooped up in some corral with a bunch of sissy horses like . . . oh . . . Early, shall we say."

"Early's not a sissy," Wendy shot back. "He's as tough as that Mack truck you call a horse."

Mr. Hanson cleared his throat. "Wendy? Joey? Let's just eat our food in peace. You two can discuss the merits of your horses later, OK?"

Debbie nodded and smiled shyly over at Wrangler Barry. "That's right, *children*," she said, emphasizing the last word. "Supper is no time for silly, *childish* conversations." She lifted her fork and poised it above the plate. "Barry and I would like to eat our meal in peace and quiet."

The wrangler blinked and looked around the table. "Why, thank you, Miss Debbie," he grinned. "I was just telling the horses how totally disgusting *their* eating habits were. You and I are truly kindred spirits." With that he gingerly lifted his milk glass and took a tiny sip. "Now, please pass the soup, if you would be so kind."

Debbie smiled sweetly. "Certainly." She lifted the large bowl of steaming liquid and was in the process of presenting it to the young ranch hand when her fingers slipped and the container dropped with a plate-shattering thud on the table.

A wave of lentil soup rose from the bowl and washed across Wrangler Barry's face, leaving it coated with the meal's main course.

Debbie's eyes opened wide with horror. The horseman remained seated, seemingly unaffected by the hot bath he'd just received.

"And may I have some bread?" he said with a smile. "It's just not proper to eat soup without a few morsels of bread."

Joey sank into his chair, gales of laughter racking his young, muscular body. Wendy buried her face in her hands and shook uncontrollably. Grandpa and Grandma Hanson and the Dawsons didn't even try to hide their merriment as they joined Mr. Hanson and Dizzy in a roaring response to the ranch hand's composure.

But it was Samantha that finally brought the house down and ended all attempts at sanity. "Hey, look," she called out excitedly. "Now Wrangler Barry's as delicious as I am."

Debbie sat silent and red-faced for the remainder of the meal. As much as she loved Shadow Creek

Ranch and all its inhabitants, human and otherwise, she did wish for a more formal atmosphere from time to time.

But it was the ranch's young wrangler who really got her 17-year-old heart racing. He was tall, slender, with sun-streaked brown hair and the bluest eyes she'd ever seen. Someday, Barry would graduate from Montana State University in Bozeman with a degree in agriculture. He wanted to be a rancher. Debbie fantasized that, maybe, he'd include her in his plans. But so far, she'd only managed to throw him into Shadow Creek and drench him with lentil soup.

During their trips into town, he'd shared his hopes and dreams with the young girl as she sat beside him in his speedy four-wheel-drive pickup truck.

She'd listen intently and nod her head thoughtfully. He even said he enjoyed talking with her. But Debbie was beginning to feel that she'd have a better chance of attracting his attention if she knitted her next sweater out of burlap. Maybe if she'd dab a little "Essence of Horse" behind her ears she might succeed in catching his eye.

"Did I mention that you look lovely this evening?" the wrangler was saying as Debbie blinked back her rambling thoughts. The meal was finished and everyone had left the table. She could hear Lizzy and Wendy busy with the dishes at the kitchen sink. "That's a lovely sweater. Did you make it yourself?"

The girl smiled shyly. "Yes." She ran her hand

along her shoulder and let it follow the curve of her arm down to the sleeve. "I tried to capture the beauty of nature with these little leaves and flowers. Do you really like it?"

Wrangler Barry nodded enthusiastically. "I do, Debbie. You're very talented. I've always admired you . . . uh . . . your work."

"Thanks," she said brightly. "Oh . . . and . . . sorry 'bout the soup."

The ranch hand grinned. "Don't worry your pretty little head about it. No damage done."

He gave her a quick wink and rose to leave. "Gotta get to the university. Grandpa asked me to pick you up Tuesday at the mall and bring you back with me to the ranch. Five o'clock all right?"

"Great," Debbie nodded. "I'll make sure I'm done by then. We're working on that new store, you know, the one beside the Furniture Palace? I'll be waiting for you there."

The horseman grinned and waved. "See ya."

He disappeared through the doorway, leaving Debbie alone. She sat for a long moment in the silence. "See ya," she said softly.

* * * * *

In the weeks that followed, Shadow Creek Ranch fell into its usual routine of work, play, and study. Wendy, Joey, and Debbie labored at their school books as Lizzy Pierce skillfully taught morning classes in the den's cozy home school.

22

Mr. Hanson busied himself at his computer and fax machine, maintaining a constant stream of information and guidance between the big white Station and his law firm in New York City. There, associates wearing three-piece suits carefully guided the company's many clients through the intricate mazes of corporate and personal legal actions and defenses.

Grandpa Hanson spent hours each day readying the ranch for the coming winter season, when Montana and the surrounding states would fall victim to the whims of nature, particularly the cold arctic air that would sweep down from the north.

The day-to-day operation of the Station itself was the responsibility of Grandma Hanson. Wrangler Barry saw to the livestock and ranch machinery during his visits on Sunday, Tuesday, and Thursday. He spent all his other time in classes and studies at Bozeman State University, about an hour's drive from Shadow Creek Ranch.

John and Merrilee Dawson worked long days at the homestead, building, repairing, painting, dreaming. Mr. Dawson figured it would be only a week or so before he and his wife could move their meager belongings from the Station to their new home in the mountains.

The house had been repaired and a new wood stove installed in the small living room where Wendy had spent so many hours reading through the pile of letters she'd discovered in the mirrored box. Those letters had introduced her to a little girl named

Merrilee and a grandmother who loved her dearly.

Now, 15 years since the last letter was written, Merrilee Dawson scrubbed and cleaned the home she'd only dreamed about through her correspondence with her aging grandmother.

The old woman had left the farm to Merrilee and John, a last demonstration of love from the special lady who wanted to share God's nature with the child who grew up calling her Grandmother.

Plumbing work had been contracted out earlier in the fall, and all the electrical wiring had been replaced. Repairs on some of the outbuildings had been finished, with plans to complete the rest when spring would blush the cheeks of the mountains with wildflowers.

Merrilee paused at her work and stood by the window, gazing out into the forest. "I can feel her presence," she said to her husband. "Even though she's been gone for 15 years, I can still feel her love in these rooms."

John Dawson walked to his wife's side. "I know what you mean. There's something very special about this place. I remember that whenever you'd get a letter from Mrs. Grant you'd almost sparkle. You'd open the envelope and hold the paper in your hands for a long moment before starting to read."

"I wanted to feel close to her," the woman's voice broke softly. "I knew her hands had been the last to hold that letter. I never got to see her. Not in 30 years. We couldn't afford to make the trip and she was too sick or too old to come see us. All we had were the words on those papers to show our love for each other."

John wrapped his arms around his wife. "Now you have the farm named after you. The two Merrilees are one. In your grandmother's eyes, I think they always were."

Mrs. Dawson smiled. "Thank you for agreeing to move here," she whispered. "It really feels like we're home."

The man nodded. "Yes, it does. But we'd better get back to work or our home won't be ready before the deep snows come."

"You're right," Merrilee sighed. "I'll dream and remember more when we sit by the fire and listen to the winds blowing outside. We'll have to rest up for spring. There's only enough money in our saving's account to see us through to planting time. After that, we'll have to live off the land."

"No problem," John announced with more conviction than he felt. "We're going to have beautiful gardens and cash crops. If Merrilee the farm is even half as giving as Merrilee the woman, we'll be home free. Now," the man twirled his wife around until she stood facing the chair she'd been sanding, "let's get back to work."

"Yes, sir," the woman said, throwing her husband a smart salute.

The two attacked their projects with joyful hearts. There'd be time for musing later. Just now, they had a dream to finish.

Outside, unnoticed by the busy home remodelers, the wind slowly began to shift to a more northerly direction. Animals in the forest paused in their activities and sniffed the air. Birds that had not flown south earlier perched on leafless limbs and studied the distant curves of the horizon.

An unseen force was moving across the face of the mountains and broad alpine meadows.

A squirrel chattered and flicked its tail nervously. A crow called out in a raucous voice and shook its dark feathers. Far to the northwest, a wind rose unseen, sending fingers of chill running along the rivers and streams and through the broad valleys of western Montana.

Something was about to happen—something feared by all the creatures that lived in the forests and fields surrounding Shadow Creek Ranch.

THE LONG DARK LINE

✿   ✿   ✿

Wendy sat on the edge of her bed listening to Samantha's soft, rhythmic breathing. Dawn was just beginning to lighten the eastern sky with a faint silver glow.

Early morning was Wendy's favorite time of day. She would wander about the Station aimlessly, lost in thoughts only a 10-year-old would think. There was no one to bother her, no one to laugh or make fun, no duties to perform or schedules to keep. It was her time and hers alone.

She moved out into the long hallway of the building's south wing and ambled to the balcony that overlooked the foyer. The old clock at the base of the stairs ticked quietly, counting the seconds— endlessly, faithfully. Wendy liked the sound. To her it meant that time was passing, bringing with it new moments to savor, new challenges to face.

The young girl tip-toed down the curving staircase and moved into the warm den where the embers of Grandpa's late-night fire still glowed in the big stone hearth.

She plopped down in her favorite chair and curled her feet up under her. Outside, beyond the big windows that lined the wide wall of the cheery room, rose majestic mountains, their summits dusted by early snows. The tall trees at the far end of the pasture stood stark and bare in the grey, early morning light. It seemed as if they'd been painted against the shadowy backdrop of mountain ranges and deep, distant valleys.

"Grandmother liked the early mornings best," a voice called from the doorway. Wendy spun around and found Merrilee standing in the warm shadows, a smile lighting her face.

"Oh, you scared me," the youngster breathed. "I wasn't expecting anyone else to be up so early."

"I'm sorry," the woman said, lifting her hand. "I didn't mean to startle you." She walked to a nearby chair and sat down quietly. "I couldn't sleep anymore. Guess I'm too excited about the farm. We're almost done. Just a few more days until we can move in."

Wendy nodded. "I think it's lookin' great. It sure isn't the way it was when Early and I found it a couple months ago." The girl chuckled shyly. "At first I thought it might be a fort with barracks and stables and stuff like that. But I'm glad it was a farm."

Merrilee smiled. "You changed our lives, Wendy Hanson. You know that, don't you?"

The girl shrugged. "I guess so. I didn't mean to. I just wanted you to know what really happened to your grandmother, that she died before she could send you her last letter." Wendy paused. "I wish I could have known her. But she was gone before I was even born."

"I think Grandma Grant would have enjoyed knowing you," the woman said. "She was so full of life, so interested in anything and everything, just like you are. You two would've made an intriguing pair."

The thought brought a grin to Wendy's face. "We could've had fun together."

Merrilee nodded. "I'm sure you would have. It's nice to have friends who are older than we are. We can learn a lot from them. They have much to teach if we'll just listen."

Wendy's smile faded. "Maybe. But some don't stay around long enough to teach you anything."

"Oh, I'm sorry," the woman urged. "I didn't mean—"

"It's OK," the girl interrupted. "I don't miss my mother, anymore. She's happy with her new husband in Connecticut and I'm happy here in Montana with everyone on Shadow Creek Ranch. Who needs her, anyway?"

Wendy stood and walked to the entrance of the den. "Besides, I'll just teach myself what I gotta know. Me and Early don't have to have some woman telling us how to act and what to do. We'll make out just fine."

With that she turned and disappeared into the foyer.

Merrilee sat for a long moment staring at the spot where Wendy had stood. She let out a long sigh and slowly laid her head against the tall back of her chair. "You're wrong, Wendy," she said quietly. "You can't do it alone. No one can."

Outside, the first ray from the rising sun pierced the eastern sky. It shot heavenward and disappeared into the vast, open canopy that spread horizon to horizon over the mountains and valleys.

Had Merrilee looked to the northwest, she would have noticed a long dark line of clouds slowly rising, as if a huge army of horse-mounted soldiers were racing down from Canada, creating a rolling, boiling cloud of black dust. In the early morning light, the shadowy line seemed to hover in the far, far distance, as if waiting for the sun to summon it south, into Montana, into the valley where Shadow Creek ran cold past frosted boulders and along ice-rimmed banks.

". . . increasing cloudiness by mid-morning as temperatures prepare to plunge." The little clock radio resting on the night stand beside Grandpa Hanson's bed rattled to life.

"A low pressure system presently situated above Alberta is expected to move southeast today, bringing with it a strong cold front that's being fed with moist air flowing east from Washington, Oregon, and Idaho."

The old man sleepily opened one eye.

"We can expect snowfall, perhaps heavy at times, east of the Divide, with accumulations of eight to 10 inches as far south as Denver during the next 24 to 48 hours.

"Montana temperatures presently range from 25 degrees in Kalispell, 31 degrees in Great Falls; Billings reports 32, and here in Bozeman it's a chilly 30 degrees. You can expect these readings to drop rapidly as the front passes over our area later today. Stay tuned to this station for hourly updates.

"Now, here with world and national news, is—"

The voice snapped into silence as the old man pressed the snooze button. He yawned broadly. After living in this part of the country for so many years, to him all weather forecasts sounded alike.

Grandpa Hanson chuckled softly to himself. Eight to 10 inches. That wasn't even worth waking up for. He pressed his cheek into the soft warm pillow. But he would mention to Tyler that it might be a good idea to dig out the tire chains. May as well be prepared when the *real* weather hit. For now, what the old man wanted most was another five minutes' sleep.

* * * * *

"Breakfast is ready!" Grandma Hanson's cheery voice echoed down the hallways and high-ceilinged rooms of the Station.

Shuffling feet and energetic voices responded from every direction as the inhabitants of the old dwelling left whatever they were doing and hurried to the big dining room. There the breakfast table waited, piled high with bowls of steaming oatmeal, plates of warm toast, and cups brimming with hot chocolate or herb tea.

After everyone had gathered, Grandpa Hanson lifted his hand and heads bowed for prayer.

"Our Father," the old man began, "thank You for this food. Thank You for healthy appetites and strong bodies to do Your bidding today.

"May we all put Your blessings to work in service for others. This we pray in Your Son's name, amen."

"Amen," the group repeated softly. Then with happy smiles everyone dove into the morning feast that Grandma Hanson and Lizzy Pierce had prepared.

After the food had disappeared and the plates were empty, save for a few crumbs, the old man at the head of the table cleared his throat. Everyone knew it was time for the day's activities to be announced. During these few moments, those around the table could encourage each other or share some suggestions. It was a time to feel part of something bigger, something important.

"I'll be driving the Dawsons up to Merrilee right after breakfast," Grandpa Hanson began, with a smile. "We might be having a little bit of snow later today and their car doesn't have chains on it as yet."

"We've got some ordered," John responded, wiping his mouth. "Should be arriving soon."

Wendy drained the last of her milk and lifted her hand. "Can I go up and help on the farm after lunch? I've got my homework for tomorrow already done."

"You do?" Lizzy queried.

"Yup," the girl nodded. "Did it this morning while you all snored in your beds."

Mr. Hanson lifted his chin. "My daughter, the genius."

Joey snickered. "We should make a new rule that all homework done before the sun comes up doesn't count."

"At least I get my assignments completed in the same month they're due," the girl mumbled, a sly grin wrinkling her face.

"Hey, I get my lessons done," the boy protested. "I just study during normal hours, like normal people."

Lizzy nodded. "Fine with me if you want to help up on Merrilee. That'll leave me some extra time to assist Joey with his history assignment."

"History." The boy said the word like it didn't taste good. "How is history going to make me a better wrangler?"

"Studying exercises another part of your body,"

Debbie giggled. She continued before Joey could respond. "This is Thursday, so I'm going into Bozeman this afternoon to work at the mall. I'll be riding in with our neighbor, Mr. Thomas. And Barry says he'll pick me up and bring me back after I'm finished. I figure around 4:30 or 5:00. He called and said he's got some stuff to get for Grandpa at the feed store, so we should be rolling in around supper time."

"Well, I'm going to go riding this afternoon," Joey asserted. "Tar Boy needs some exercise, too." He looked over at Debbie. "All parts of him."

Samantha lifted her hand.

"And you, little bit," Grandpa Hanson asked warmly. "What are your plans for today?"

"I'm going to read five books in the library, then make a cake and then build a boat."

"A boat?" the old man blinked.

"Yup. Me and Pueblo are gonna build a boat and sail to California to see all the movie stars."

"You and that dog of yours might have a little problem around Hoover Dam," Joey teased.

"That's OK. Then we'll walk or take an airplane."

Lizzy leaned down and looked into the little girl's eyes. "But we'd miss you terribly. Please don't go away."

Samantha thought for a minute. "OK," she said. "We'll just sail to Bozeman to see Debbie at the mall."

"Good," Lizzy breathed. "Besides, I wouldn't want

you to go too far away. The radio said we might have some snow."

"That reminds me," Grandpa Hanson said, lifting a finger. "The weatherman did mention the possibility of a few inches of white stuff later today. You all might want to wrap up your work a little early and get back to the Station before dark. It shouldn't be anything to worry about. But better safe than sorry, I always say."

"You never say that," Grandma Hanson chuckled.

"Well, I'm saying it now," the old man grinned.

Everyone pushed back their chairs and began the day with enthusiasm. Joey, Debbie, and Wendy headed for the den to start classes with Lizzy. Grandpa Hanson and the Dawsons left for Merrilee. Grandma Hanson attacked the piles of dirty dishes, while her lawyer son switched on his office equipment and began tapping on the computer keyboard.

Samantha dressed warmly and headed for the tool shed. She figured she'd need at least a hammer and two screwdrivers to build a boat.

* * * * *

Wrangler Barry walked quickly across the campus of Montana State University in Bozeman, on his way to the agricultural field buildings. At the moment his thoughts weren't exactly on schoolwork. He was concentrating on pipe—PVC pipe, to be exact. He and Grandpa Hanson were planning a repair job at the Station, and he had learned that a local hardware store was having a sale on sub-standard lengths of the plastic tubes. He would have to buy extra couplings, but even so it should be a good bargain.

He was just about to cross 11th Avenue and head down Lincoln Road when he happened to glance over his shoulder to the north. Looking past McCall Hall, in the direction of Bozeman, he saw a collection of dark clouds standing motionless above Bridger Range and the distant Big Belt Mountains.

The line loomed silent in the sky, as if brooding over something unpleasant. Barry noticed that the usual drift of air in and around the buildings and tennis courts on campus was gone. The air lay strangely still, unmoving, as if afraid to make itself known to the approaching specter to the north.

Look at that, the young man thought to himself, his eyes scanning the dark horizon. *Last time I saw a line like that was when I was a kid on my father's farm.*

"Hey, handsome," a female voice called from the nearby parking lot. "How 'bout helping a damsel in distress?" Barry saw an attractive coed trying to lift a bulky object from the trunk of her car. Her brown curls were jammed under a brightly colored knit cap and her cheeks glowed with youthful energy. "If I don't get this assignment to class, Professor McIntyre will flunk me for sure, and I'll have to explain to my parents that I failed college because I couldn't get a bush out of my trunk."

The wrangler laughed. "Judy," he called, hastening in the girl's direction, "you didn't have to take your assignment home with you. You could've left it in one of the field buildings like the rest of us."

"And have your yampa throwing spores all over my wake-robin? I think not!" The girl giggled, revealing two rows of straight, white teeth surrounded by naturally rosy lips. "I'll have you know this little ol' collection of plants will someday help modern woman enjoy a more painless childbirth. After all, the Indians used the rootstalks during delivery. Helped, too." She fingered a handful of delicate blossoms. "It will revolutionize medical science."

Barry pursed his lips and puffed a small stream of air. "Since when does medical science care anything about old-fashioned, Indian remedies?"

"Hey, it's becoming the in thing! They got people down in South America studying the rain forests, or what's left of them. I'll just bet that in a few years my little wake-robins will be sold as a high-priced prescription health remedy. You'll see."

Barry shrugged and looked into the friendly blue eyes laughing up at him. "Women everywhere will thank you." He lifted the carefully packed plants from the car and hoisted the bundle over his shoulder. "I hope your wake-robins help hernias, because that's what I'm going to get carrying them to class."

"Nah. For that you'll need salsify or even arrowleaf balsamroot. Helps indigestion, too." Judy smiled at her classmate as they made their way along

37

Lincoln Road. "Flowers and plants, especially herbs, have a lot to offer if we'd just take the time to study them carefully. I mean, animals know what to do when they get sick. They don't rush down to the local drug store."

"Lines are long enough as it is," Barry teased. "Imagine waiting for your prescription behind a bull elk with a headache."

The girl chuckled at the image Barry's words formed in her mind. "Or how 'bout a bobcat with a nervous condition?"

"Or a grizzly with acid indigestion?"

The two paused and laughed out loud, their voices bright and cheery. "Judy, you're really something," Barry said, shaking his head.

"Well, thank you, cowboy," the coed grinned. "You're really something yourself. As a matter of fact," she paused, suddenly shy, "I was wondering if you had a date for the football game this Sunday afternoon? I hear the team from Missoula isn't all that bad. Should give our guys a run for their money."

Barry cleared his throat. "Well . . . I . . . uh."

Judy gasped. "It's true. It's really true!"

"What is?" Barry asked, unsure of his classmate's strange reaction.

"You're shy," the young woman giggled. "I've heard other girls say so, but I thought they were crazy—you being so tough and manly. I thought you'd be the forward one when it came to dating."

Barry shifted the load from one shoulder to the other. "I'm not too good at all this boy-girl stuff," he said. "I feel much more comfortable around horses and crops."

Judy laughed. "Well, speaking for women everywhere, we like to think of ourselves a little bit more interesting than horses and crops."

"Oh, I'm sure you are," Barry blushed. "I've known some very interesting girls . . . I mean . . . I don't mind being around females . . . I mean . . ."

"Take it easy, cowboy," Judy giggled. "You don't have to go into any details. I just want to know if you'd like to go to the game with me. I'll try not to scare you too much."

The wrangler shrugged as best he could with the load on his shoulder. "Well, I guess so, if no emergency comes up or anything."

Judy tilted her head slightly. "What kind of emergency?"

Barry pursed his lips. "Oh, if one of the horses I'm caring for hurts itself, or comes time to foal, or whatever. Those kinds of emergencies."

"I see," Judy's grin tried to hide a giggle. "Well. Let's just hope all the animals stay nice and healthy over the weekend so we can go to the football game. OK?"

"OK," Barry nodded as Judy opened the door to one of the field buildings and let the wrangler and his burden pass by. The young man paused. "Have you ever seen a horse actually being born?" he asked. "It's really fascinating."

Judy walked down the hallway beside her enthusiastic companion, leaving the big, glass door to slowly close behind them. In the distance, the dark line had moved forward imperceptively, covering the mountain peaks with long tendrils of ash-colored clouds. The wind stirred, then died down again, as if giving second thought to its action.

* * * * *

"What time is it?" Wendy asked as she rubbed firmly on the window ledge with a soapy cloth, trying to remove another layer of dirt and grime from the pastel blue paint hiding somewhere underneath.

Merrilee looked up from her work. The doors to the kitchen cupboards all hung open, ready to receive the fresh, brightly patterned drawer paper the woman was cutting to size on the counter. "It *is* getting kinda dark," the woman said, glancing at her watch. She blinked. "Huh? That's odd. It's only quarter after three. Isn't it too dark outside for being only quarter after three?"

Wendy opened and closed her hand, trying to draw some feeling into her cramped fingers. She peered out through the window and squinted into the unusual gloom beyond the panes of clean glass.

"Yeah, it is," she agreed. "But I can't see the sky because of the trees. Grandpa did mention that we might get some snow later this afternoon or tonight.

Maybe it's just clouds drifting in."

Merrilee shrugged. "The days *are* getting shorter. Or perhaps I'm just not used to being in the mountains. Sometimes sunlight has a hard time reaching these little high-altitude valleys."

"Sure. That's all it is," Wendy reasoned. "Shorter days. A few clouds. Mountain valley. I guess I just never noticed how soon it starts to get dark up here, with winter coming. Your husband should be back soon with Grandpa's truck. Hope he remembered to get those nails we need for the upstairs floorboards. They kinda creak a lot."

"I like creaky floorboards," Merrilee said, carefully guiding her scissors along the patterned paper. "Sorta makes a house homey. Know what I mean?"

"Sorta makes a house creepy, if you ask me," Wendy retorted. "There's nothing like waking up in the middle of the night and hearing a floorboard squeak in another room, especially if you think you're the only one in the house."

The woman shivered. "Now, don't go scaring me like that. Besides, if anything," she paused, "or any*body* was wandering around uninvited in our house, John would chase him away. He's a great husband and takes very good care of me."

"I know," Wendy giggled. "I read the letters, remember?"

Merrilee smiled. "You must have thought we were kinda strange people after reviewing our lives together, at least up until 15 years ago. I had a habit of going on and on about how much we loved each other. I knew it made Grandmother happy."

"Well, you did love each other, didn't you?"

"Oh, yes," the woman beamed. "Still do. But those letters didn't contain *all* the facts. We had some rough times, too. Everyone does."

"But you had something special, right? You two were different."

Merrilee laid her scissors down and leaned against the counter. "Not really—no different than anyone else. There are things about John that I wouldn't mind terribly if he changed. And there are things about me he'd be better off not having to put up with. We both can be kinda stubborn and pigheaded. It's not easy for us to admit when we're wrong."

Wendy stopped her scrubbing and listened intently. *Stubborn. Pigheaded.* Those were words she'd heard her mother and father fling at each other late at night, when they thought she and Debbie were asleep.

"John and I decided long ago that there are things about people that can't be altered—personality traits, harmless habits that you wish the other didn't have. Those we call 'untouchables.' We don't even bother ourselves with them anymore."

Wendy's eyes opened wide. "Do you have an untouchable, Merrilee?"

The woman smiled. "Sure. Several of them."

42

"What are they?"

"Well," Merrilee thought for a moment, "this is one." She held up her scissors.

"Mr. Dawson doesn't like it when you cut things with scissors?"

"No," the woman laughed. "I'm just so particular about some stuff, especially the house I live in. I want it to be as perfect as it can be, so I cut out drawer liners, make the curtains just so, try to get as many things to match, colorwise, as possible. I work hard at it.

"Now, John, on the other hand, isn't so particular. He doesn't care if the drawers have liners or if the curtains match the sofa or if the bedspread shares any semblance of color with the throw rugs. To him, a house is somewhere you go to get out of the rain and eat a meal and sleep. What it looks like inside is of no consequence as far as he's concerned.

"Sometimes he gets upset with me for spending so much time trying to get things just right, or as just right as our budget will allow."

Merrilee grinned a comfortable grin. "So, he's learned that I'm not about to change my ways. That's why that part of my personality has become an 'untouchable.' He just lets me feather the nest the way I want it to be."

Wendy chuckled and looked around the room. "Would you be upset if I said I agreed with Mr. Dawson? I like pretty things; not as much as my brain-dead sister, you understand, but a house or a room is just a place to go when you can't be outside doing important stuff like riding Early or breakin' in a new gelding."

The woman nodded. "See? That's one of your untouchables. I'd know better than to pop into your bedroom down at the Station and tell you to make it just the way I want it to be. Oh, I'd insist that you sweep it once a week and keep it clean. Being sanitary is part of being healthy. But for me to tell you to pattern your room after mine just wouldn't be fair. If you wanted a burlap bedspread and feedsack curtains, then that's what you'd have, as long as they were clean."

Wendy's mouth dropped open. "That's neat. That's really neat."

"I call it 'interpersonal survival,'" Merrilee said. "Imagine what kind of world we'd have if everyone just let other people be themselves, without trying to make them conform to their own way of doing things."

The woman thought for a minute. "My grand-mother used to say that's how God is with us. He has certain rules we all must follow. But then He lets us be individuals, with individual ways of doing things. She'd say in her letters, 'Merrilee, the good Lord doesn't want servants—He wants friends, brothers and sisters. That's what He wants.' I believe she was right, don't you?"

Wendy frowned. "Wait a minute. That means I have to let Debbie do what Debbie does without griping at her all the time."

"It would seem so," the woman nodded with a grin. "Sometimes it isn't easy, is it?"

Wendy shook her head, then smiled. "I like talking to you, Merrilee," she said. "You tell me neat stuff."

Mrs. Dawson wiped her forehead with the back of her hand. "But we'd better talk less and work more, right now." She looked around. "It's getting mighty dark outside. Maybe those snow clouds are gettin' here a little ahead of schedule. We'd better hurry, just in case John shows up."

The two returned to their tasks with renewed vigor. But something was very strange. The room grew darker by the minute, as if night were falling over the mountainsides and ravines. And the house seemed a little colder than before. No, not a little — much colder.

Wendy shivered and lifted her jacket from where she'd hung it earlier in the afternoon. "I hope Mr. Dawson comes soon," she said. "I have a bad feeling about this. Maybe we should be heading back to the Station right away."

* * * * *

"Debbie!" Wrangler Barry's voice echoed down the broad expanse of the almost empty Bozeman mall. "Debbie! Where are you?"

"Here I am," the girl with the long dark hair answered. As she looked over her shoulder she saw her friend running at full speed past the drygoods store. "What's the matter?"

"Come on!" Barry shouted. "We gotta go. We gotta go *right now!*"

"Why?" Debbie queried. Hurriedly she gathered her color swatches and drawing pencils and tossed them into a leather satchel. The store window would just have to wait for her to transform it into a beautiful showcase that the client would be proud of.

The wrangler was out of breath. "Don't ask any questions. We've gotta get back to Shadow Creek Ranch, and we don't have a second to spare."

"Whatever is the matter with you?" Debbie protested. "I'm not quite finished. Can't you give me another 15 minutes?"

"NO!" Barry urged. "This one's going to be bad, mark my words. If you want to get home before it hits, we have to leave this instant."

The girl began to scowl but suddenly noticed that Barry's expression wasn't just hurried; it had a look of desperation.

"Let me just say goodbye to my boss."

"OK, but hurry!" Barry called after the running girl. She soon returned and together they rushed past the deserted stores and fast-food restaurants.

"Where is everybody?" Debbie called out. "Guess I was so busy with my work that I didn't notice how empty the mall was getting."

"Haven't you been outside?" the cowboy shouted over his shoulder.

"No, not since I arrived, just after lunchtime."

The two burst through the wide entrance doors and Debbie's breath was immediately swept out of her lungs. A bone-chilling wind struck her as though she'd run into a solid wall, making her stumble and almost fall. Barry grabbed her arm to support her.

The girl's eyes opened wide. Even though it was only a little after 4:00, the sky hung dark as midnight above their heads. A fierce wind whipped across the broad parking lot, whistling past tall, swaying lamp-posts and swinging signs.

The carefully manicured trees and shrubs shivered, while crumpled newspapers and other pieces of trash blew headlong across the flat expanse of asphalt.

"What's happening?" the girl screamed, trying to be heard above the deafening roar of the wind. "Barry. WHAT'S GOING ON?"

The young man pulled harder on her arm and guided her to his big, four-wheel-drive pickup truck waiting by the curb. "Storm!" he shouted, pushing her into the roomy cab. The word was snatched from his lips and blown away.

The wrangler hurried around to the driver's side and jumped in, trying to wrest the door from the icy grip of the gale. With a heave he managed to close it.

"It's a big one, Debbie," he said breathlessly as he turned the key in the ignition. "Fasten your seatbelt tightly." He watched the tachometer spring to life, the only indication he had, in the storm's howl, that the powerful pickup's engine had started.

Jamming the vehicle into first gear, he spun the tires across the wind-swept surface of the parking lot and sped in the direction of the exit. "I should have been here earlier," he moaned, "but I wanted to get the stuff your grandfather ordered at the Co-op."

The truck roared west on Route 84. "I should've just come and picked you up." The young man's words turned to wisps of steam as he spoke. "I thought I could beat it. I should have known better. This is Montana. You don't play with the weather in Montana."

Turning south on Highway 191, Barry pushed the accelerator to the floor. The pickup lurched forward, pressing Debbie against the cool leather of her seat. "We didn't have anything so awful last winter," she said, studying the sullen sky to the south. In the distance she could make out long, wispy, dark grey arms stretching from the lower clouds to the surface of the fields that rushed past her frosted window.

"We haven't had this kind of storm for a long, long time," her companion called over the whine of the engine. "Last time was when I was a kid. Shut the whole state down for a week."

"A week?" Debbie's brown eyes shadowed with concern. "We'll make it to the ranch in time, won't we?"

"We'll sure try," Barry encouraged, pressing even harder on the accelerator. The vehicle roared past a road sign that swayed drunkenly on its pole. "If we can just beat the snow."

"I don't see any snow yet," the girl encouraged.

"Oh, really?" the wrangler shouted. "Well, what do you call that?"

He pointed behind them, to the north. Debbie leaned forward and peered into the outside mirror fastened to the passenger side of the truck. What she saw drained all color from her face.

She spun around and gazed out through the rear window and the cap that enclosed the bed of the vehicle. There, not more than five miles away and closing fast, was a huge wall of white. It rolled and tumbled like an ocean wave, driven by fierce winds. The clouds above it boiled black, illuminated from inside with jagged shafts of lightning. The white wall seemed like a wild beast of some sort, pursuing the truck down the highway.

Debbie tried to say something but the impact of what she'd seen robbed her of words. All she could do was stare at the driver, her mouth hanging open, eyes filled with terror.

"We'll make it," Barry responded to her unspoken fear, his voice not as reassuring as she wished it was. "We'll make it."

Windblown snowflakes began slapping the windshield. Debbie studied them thoughtfully. What if those little pieces of ice and water were only scouts, sent by the storm to seek out helpless travelers in the monster's path? She imagined that their job was to

49

strike any vehicle trying to get to safety, then hurry back into the darkness behind, like worker bees returning to the hive. There they'd dance another dance—this one designed to tell the storm where the little truck and its occupants were.

"I'm scared," the girl whispered.

"What'd ya say?"

"I said I'm scared. I've never seen a storm like this."

Barry licked his lips, his mouth dry. "It's just a few more miles."

The turnoff loomed into view. "See? There's the road that will take us into the mountains, to Shadow Creek Ranch. We're almost home."

The wrangler spun the wheel and skidded his truck onto the frozen surface of the logging road that led from the highway to the ranch. "I can almost smell supper cooking," he yelled.

Suddenly, the world turned from brown and grey to white. Barry leaned forward, trying to make out the path of the gutted road as it wound through the trees and meadows. Debbie shivered as familiar forms of outcroppings and cottonwood groves became ghostlike apparitions, scowling at her through swirling masses of snow.

She was astonished at how fast the world had changed. Where earlier there had been familiar forests and glens, everything was being overwhelmingly altered by the storm. The transition from familiar to terrifying was almost instantaneous.

"It got us!" Barry shouted as he jammed the truck into four-wheel drive. The vehicle lurched as each tire suddenly found itself infused with independent power. The big wheels dug into the snow-covered surface of the road, now gripping and holding, now skidding and slipping.

"What are we going to do?" Debbie cried, her voice thick with concern.

"We're going to keep on," the driver said firmly, his lips forming a tight line across his face. "We can't turn back. Every inch we travel brings us closer to the Station."

By now, few things beyond the windshield were recognizable. Barry drove more from habit and experience than sight. He'd traversed this road hundreds of times. He could feel its curves and dips. The wrangler understood each bump and jolt as the wheels of his truck fought to maintain contact with the rugged surface of the mountain trail.

All at once, the world turned completely white. The winter monster had stretched its lethal arms over the mountains and settled on them like a predator attacking its prey. Barry drew in his breath as everything disappeared into swirling, twisting shadows.

His foot slammed the brake pedal but there was no slowing. The vehicle surged forward at an alarming speed. He didn't recognize the bumps, the jolts, the feel of the road below him.

The truck skidded sideways, completely out of

control. A grinding noise rose from underneath the pickup and the two helpless passengers felt the cab tilt violently to the right.

Debbie screamed as formless shapes rushed by, striking the metal and glass with deafening noise. Then it seemed to the pair that the bottom dropped out from below them. They felt themselves falling, falling, falling.

Barry caught a quick glimpse of something approaching at a very high rate of speed in front of the vehicle, then with a resounding crash the windshield exploded. Snow, ice, and glass struck the pair like a shotgun blast. Finally all was silent, still, unmoving.

Above, the wind howled and shrieked, as if somewhere someone was laughing, the voice echoing in the thunder. Barry watched as his world turned grey, then black. Sinking into unconsciousness, he heard himself cry, "Debbie. DEBBIE!"

There was no response.

CHAPTER 3

MONSTER

✪ ✪ ✪

Joey stared at the sky with unbelieving eyes. He was sitting astride Tar Boy in the far pasture, beyond the cottonwoods, where Grandpa Hanson and Barry had cleared the land in preparation for spring planting.

"Look at that," the boy said to his big, black horse. "I've never seen that kind of clouds before. Must be a storm, and I think it's comin' this way."

The animal sniffed the air, then blew a fine mist of steam from his broad nostrils. He shook his head and snorted again, nervously.

"I agree," Joey nodded, as if in response to Tar Boy's unspoken suggestion. "We'd better get back to the corral *fast!*"

The boiling band of clouds and snow bore down

from the northwest with fearsome speed. As the horse and rider raced along the curving driveway that led from the logging road to the big house by the creek, Joey felt sharp pellets of ice begin to sting his face. He urged the animal to even greater haste and squinted against the tiny obstacles that filled the air. "What's going on?" he called. "Storms don't move this fast."

As the two crossed the footbridge, the world suddenly turned white. In seconds the ground was covered with a thickening shroud of snow and the air turned bone-chilling cold.

Tar Boy skidded to a stop and rose on his powerful hind legs, fanning the gusting winds with his hooves. "Come on," Joey urged, his voice thin and trembling, fear tugging at his heart. "Come on, Tar Boy. We gotta get to the corral."

The young wrangler dug his heels into the horse's flanks and tried to steer his steed in the general direction of the horse barn that waited beyond the tack shed. He could catch only quick glimpses of the structure through the blinding snows. In one movement Joey slid to the ground. The horse snorted and sidestepped, yanking on the leather straps that the determined boy held as he led him along.

"Get in there, Tar Boy!" Joey screamed, trying to be heard above the sudden gale. He slapped the big animal's rump with the loose ends of the reigns. "Get in there now!"

The big stallion impatiently followed his leader

into the enclosure and paced back and forth as Joey tried to wrestle the broad, wooden door closed behind them. It took a mighty shove to slam the portal shut. Snowflakes that had been driven by the howling wind outside suddenly found themselves in a calmer atmosphere and floated daintily to the straw-covered floor.

"MAN!" Joey gasped, leaning against a pile of feed sacks to catch his breath. "What's goin' on? I ain't never seen a storm come up so fast!"

The stallion stomped his hooves and tossed his mane back and forth, eyes wide with terror, ears flattened against the top of his noble head.

A sudden bang on the barn door made Joey jump. He spun around and hurried to the entrance. Leaning against the gale, he forced the door open again. Before he could get out of the way, Early burst into the barn, followed by several other terrified horses. The boy sprawled across the straw, sending clouds of dust swirling in the frigid air.

"Well, come on in," he called, rubbing his elbow. "Don't wait for an invitation." Joey stumbled to his feet. "OK, OK. Let's see, one, two, three, four, five. Yup. Everybody's here."

He hurried back to the door and wrestled it shut, his teeth clenched against the powerful force of the wind. "Good thing we don't keep any more riding horses on the ranch during the winter. There wouldn't be enough room in the barn."

The animals milled about in anxious confusion.

"Settle down, critters," the boy called, trying to sound soothing. "It's just a little ol' storm. We'll wait it out. Haven't you learned that Montana blows make a big noise at first, then settle into your normal, everyday brand of blizzard? In a half hour or so, I'll head over to the Station and leave you guys here to enjoy all this grain and oats. Tough life you beasts live. Real tough."

Tar Boy pressed close to his master, nervously eyeing the closed barn door. "Now, everyone get into your stalls and settle down. Go on, Tar Boy. Move it, Early." Joey pushed against the smooth flanks of the animals. "You too, Sapphire. Come on, White Star. And get off my foot, Pookie." The boy paused. "Why Grandpa Hanson let Samantha name you Pookie is more than I know. That's a stupid name for a horse." He paused again. " 'Course, you're a stupid horse, so maybe that's OK."

The small, dappled animal turned and stared at the boy. "Oh, all right. Maybe you ain't stupid, but that's still the craziest name for a horse I ever heard. Pookie. Sounds like something a rich lady would call her dog."

With a little more urging, all the animals finally took their assigned places in the comfortable barn. Joey scooped oats from the feed bin by the work table and gave a generous portion to each of his four-footed charges. He tried to ignore the rattling, shaking walls that surrounded them.

"Some wind, huh?" he said, trying to keep his

56

own mind occupied, the sound of the gale making him uncomfortable. "Well, you're all safe and sound in here. This old barn's been around for at least a hundred years. Maybe more. When this ranch was a way station, folks on their way to Yellowstone used to bed down their horses in here, you know, the ones pullin' the wagons and fancy buggies. You guys are lucky. You're just ridin' horses. Man, I tell you, it weren't easy being a horse a hundred years ago. No, sir."

The boy walked to the far wall and tried to peer through the wooden slats. Seeing nothing, he carefully pressed the door open a few inches. A blast of frigid air followed by spraying snow hit him hard across the face. He blinked and coughed while quickly relatching the broad portal. "Maybe I'll just wait in here with you," he said to the animals who now were contentedly munching on their oats. "Doesn't look too friendly out there right now."

Joey sat down and leaned his head against the feed sacks. He frowned. What was going on outside the sturdy walls of the horse barn? He'd seen snows, and he'd seen storms. But this? If it kept up any longer, he was going to start getting concerned.

The boy picked up a piece of straw and twirled it in his fingers. "Don't worry," he said aloud. "It'll be over soon. I'll be back in the Station before supper."

* * * * *

The leading edge of the blizzard hit the little farm

in the mountains like a giant fist. Wendy had just returned to the house with an armload of wood for the stove when she felt the air turn suddenly chill.

As she walked toward the open door it slammed shut, driven by a gale-force gust that bent the trees and rattled the rafters. It felt as if the building was in the jaws of an angry dog.

The lighted candles on the newly painted kitchen table flickered out, leaving the room in almost total darkness.

Merrilee was upstairs in the bedroom putting the finishing touches on her wallpaper when a large limb smashed through the window and impaled itself into the chest of drawers like an out-of-control bulldozer.

She screamed as a seemingly solid mass of icy air struck her broadside, knocking her to the floor. Hail the size of golf balls pounded the tin roof of the farmhouse with deafening resonance.

"Wendy!" the woman cried out. "Wendy, are you all right?"

The young girl appeared at the door, face pale, eyes wide with terror. "Are we going to die?" she shrieked. "Are we going to die?"

Merrilee jumped up and pushed the girl into the hallway, slamming shut the bedroom door behind her. Together they slipped to the floor and huddled in the darkness at the top of the stairs. It seemed that nothing around them would survive. They heard wood splintering and snapping, and glass breaking. Downstairs, pots and pans that had been neatly stored in the cupboards rattled and banged to the floor. The building strained on its foundation.

"Oh, dear God! Oh, dear God!" Merrilee called out, holding Wendy close to her. "Help us. SAVE US!"

Her words were lost in the roar of the wind.

* * * * *

"The shutters! Close the shutters!" Grandpa Hanson and John Dawson raced across the broad foyer of the Station and into the den. The big wooden shutters designed to protect the windows from wind and rain were quickly latched, sealing the room in darkness.

"I've got to get up to Merrilee," the younger man urged. "May I borrow your farm truck? It should have pretty good traction."

"Not on your life," Grandpa Hanson shouted over the roar of the wind. "You won't get a hundred yards out there."

"But what are we going to do? They'll be stuck up there in an unfinished house." He paled. "I've got to try."

"NO!" the old man persisted. "You won't make it. I can't let you go. It's best to be either here at the Station or there on the farm, not somewhere in between. Listen to that wind. It's not fooling around. It means business."

Mr. Dawson groaned. "Oh, why didn't I leave an hour ago? I spent too much time working on that new bedframe."

"Look, John," Grandpa Hanson called, straining to latch the fluttering shutter while powdery snow blew hard against his face. "If you'd gone when you'd planned, you all might have been caught out on the logging road. Believe me, you, your wife, and Wendy are a whole lot better off right where you are."

"I suppose you're right," the younger man agreed hesitantly. "I just wish they were here with us in the Station."

Grandpa Hanson smiled. "They'll be all right. We have to leave them in God's hands for a little while." The wind rattled the shutters and knocked a plant from the window box. "I guess we're *all* in God's hands right now," the old man continued. "I've never seen anything like this, not ever."

Throughout the old structure, hurried hands labored, trying to protect the house from the wrath of the storm.

Lizzy locked all the entrance doors on the lower level, then hurried from room to room, making sure windows were closed and shutters latched.

The building moaned almost humanlike as fierce winds pounded its age-old face and broad sides. It had survived other storms, but this one seemed somehow different: angry, mean-spirited, bent on destruction.

"Is it going to crash down on us?" a little girl's thin, fear-filled voice echoed along the upstairs hallway. "Is the storm going to make us fly away?"

Samantha ran along behind Grandma Hanson,

trying to find reassurance from the worried adults who rushed past her, each on an urgent errand. "What if the wall breaks? What if the roof breaks? Is it going to hurt bad?"

The old woman paused and caught the girl in her arms. "Oh, no," she said. "Everything's going to be OK, Sam." Grandma Hanson smiled in the dim light. "We just have to prepare the Station so it will be strong and protect us."

"Oh," the little girl breathed. "So we're not going to fly away and get hurt real bad?"

"No, no," Grandma Hanson said, passing her fingers through the youngster's tightly curled locks. "We're just going to finish our work, then wait for the winds to die down. Would you like to help?"

Samantha brightened. "Yeah. What do you want me to do?"

"Go find Pueblo and take him to the den where you'll both be safe. OK?"

The girl spun around and headed down the long passageway. "Here, Pueblo. Here, Pueblo," Grandma Hanson heard her call. The woman rose and ran to her son's office.

"Tyler," she called as she entered the room. "Everything all right in here?"

The lawyer looked up from his desk. "I've got my data saved and equipment turned off. I was just about to start unplugging stuff. If there's any lightning in this monster storm, it could fry all my computer circuits in a heartbeat. Do the phones still work?"

"I think so," Grandma Hanson called over her shoulder as she headed for one of the two curving staircases. "Make sure your windows are latched and the shutters in place. I'm going to check and see how your father's doing downstairs."

The man nodded and reached for the telephone.

Grandpa Hanson was just coming out of the kitchen when he saw his wife passing by the entrance to the dining room. "Have you seen Joey?" he called.

The woman stopped. "No, as a matter of fact, I haven't."

Grandpa Hanson closed his eyes and tilted his head back a little. "I think he was out riding."

"Oh, my," his wife breathed. "You don't suppose—"

"Joey's a smart kid," he reasoned. "He'd know to head for the corral—that is, if he had enough time."

"I seen Joey," Samantha called from under the table. She emerged with a frightened dog held tightly in her arms. "He and Tar Boy were going across the bridge when everything went white and the wind made me scared."

"Praise the Lord!" the old man shouted.

"Praise the Lord!" Samantha repeated, a happy smile spreading across her face.

Grandma Hanson bent and gave the diminutive dog-catcher a hug. "Then I'm sure he made it to the barn. Even if the snow blinded him, Tar Boy would get them there. Horses can track through anything."

"You're right," the old man agreed. "I think we can safely assume that Joey's in the barn. But there's one way to be sure." He ran to the den and grabbed the ranch's small walkie-talkie from the mantle. "Wrangler Barry keeps a receiver charging beside his cot. If Joey is out there, he'll hear our call."

* * * * *

Tar Boy shifted his weight from one hoof to another as he watched his human friend pacing back and forth in front of his stall.

"I'm beginning to get worried," the boy was saying. "I mean, what if this storm lasts for days and days? I might be stuck out here with you guys 'til I'm old and gray. Spring will come and they'll find me, frozen like a snow cone, propped up by the feed sacks." He turned. "What do you think, Early? How long is this storm going to last?"

"Joey, can you hear me?" A voice sounded from the far end of the barn.

The boy stiffened and looked closely at Wendy's horse. "Did you say something?" He listened, then shook his head vigorously. "Must be the wind."

"Hey, Joey, can you hear me?"

"Wait a minute," the youngster said, scratching his head. "The wind doesn't know my name."

"Come on, Joey, if you can hear me, answer."

The young wrangler blinked his eyes. "Man, I'm

going crazy. I swear the wind is callin' me." He frowned. "Oh, sure. It probably wants me to waltz outside and play with it. It's teasing me, that's what's happenin'. It's trying to get me to leave this warm, yet smelly, horse house and go stumbling around outside. Well, no way."

The boy lifted his chin. "I'll just stay here, thank you very much. After all, I've got a roof over my head, at least for now, and blankets over there, a cot, a walkie-talkie on the shelf, a—"

Joey gasped. "A walkie-talkie!" He rushed across the room. "That's what I heard. I wondered how come the wind sounded so much like Grandpa Hanson."

The boy grabbed the little communication device and pressed the transmit button. "Hey, Grandpa, is that you callin' me?"

"Are you all right, son?" the electronic voice queried. Even above the roar of the wind, Joey could hear relief in the old man's words.

"Yeah, I'm just fine, considerin'. Is this a storm or what?"

"Listen, Joey," the voice urged, "you've got to prepare for cold. Do you hear me? You've got to get the barn as ready as possible for the night hours. Temperatures are going to drop way, way down. Over."

"How do I do that?"

Grandpa's directions crackled with the sound of thunder overhead. "Fill in as many cracks in the walls as you can. Use straw or cloth or whatever. You've got to keep the wind out and body warmth in. How many horses are with you?"

"All of 'em," Joey called, his finger pressing hard on the transmit button. "Over."

"Great! That's terrific! You'll be able to keep each other from freezing. Don't even think of starting a fire in there because you might burn the place down, so just seal the cracks and wrap up in as many blankets as you can find. Over."

"OK," the boy said, looking around. "Don't worry about us." He paused. "Are Wendy and Mrs. Dawson still at Merrilee?"

"I'm afraid so," the disembodied voiced replied. "Over."

Joey pressed the transmit button. "How 'bout Debbie and Barry?"

Grandpa was about to respond when he looked up and saw his son entering the den. "I've just been on the phone with Bozeman," the young lawyer announced slowly. "The mall security guard said he saw Debbie and Barry leave about two and a half hours ago." Mr. Hanson sat down on the sofa. "The police have closed the interstate because of snow and high winds. They said all roads have become impassible across the entire southern portion of the state."

He looked at his parents, his eyes revealing the deep fear in his heart. "That means my little girl is out there in this storm somewhere between here and Bozeman."

"She'll be OK, Tyler," Grandma Hanson said softly. "Wrangler Barry will—"

"That's not all," the man interrupted. "The security guard said the latest weather forecast says we can expect more than eight *feet* of snow. It's being called the storm of the century, and it's only two hours old."

Mr. Hanson rose slowly and walked to the foyer. "I'll be in my office," he called without turning. The stunned group watched him climb the steps and disappear from view.

"Joey?" the old man called, the walkie-talkie still at his ear.

"I heard, Grandpa Hanson," Joey's voice rattled in the device. "I heard what he said."

* * * * *

The meadow bustled with activity. Dazzling wildflowers bloomed in broad expanses of velvet grasses, and squirrels played among the low-hanging branches moving with the gentle breeze. Birds soared in the azure sky, their songs filling the air.

"I found one," a child's voice called out. "Come see, Daddy. I've found one."

Tiny fingers wrapped around the delicate blossoms. "See? It's a beautiful wake-robin. Can I take it home? Can I?"

The child glanced up. The meadow had suddenly

become all white. The trees were gone. There was nothing but a flat expanse of powdery snowdrifts cresting like ocean waves along a beach; rolling, rolling, rolling.

"Where are the flowers?" the little voice called. "Where did they go?"

The boy gasped. The waves in the meadow grew higher and higher. The sky had turned black. He felt something between his fingers. He looked down. The wake-robin blossom had become an ugly, twisted piece of metal, hot to the touch. He dropped it and the object shattered against the white ground, setting the snow on fire.

"Daddy!" the little boy screamed. "It's hot. The fire is hot!"

Above him the waves continued to build until he couldn't see the sky. He jumped up and started to run across the meadow, the bottoms of his feet burning. "*No!*" he shouted. "Go away, fire. Go away, snow. Leave me alone."

The giant wave crested and started falling toward him. He couldn't move. The fire grew hotter. The wave kept falling. He was trapped—trapped between fire and ice.

"*No!*" he heard someone calling. "*No!*"

Barry's eyes opened. Who was shouting? He listened. Wait. It was he. He was the little boy. He was shouting. The white wave descended with a crushing blow.

The wrangler stiffened, pain stabbing his chest.

He wasn't in a meadow. He was somewhere else. Somewhere dark. Somewhere silent and cold.

Slowly he began to remember. The winding road. The racing truck. The snow. So much snow. Couldn't see. Couldn't see the road! Falling. *Falling!*

"*No,*" Barry cried out, his breath labored. "*No!*"

The dream faltered, then faded away in the thick darkness.

Slowly, ever so slowly, the odd-shaped forms surrounding him began to take on recognizable designs. He saw the steering wheel, bent and twisted against the dashboard, compressed by the impact of his own body. Beside him were sacks of grain, thrown forward into the cab of the truck by the wrenching crash. One sack had a large gash in its side. A steady stream of grain flowed from the open wound. The kernels tumbled past a crumpled box of leather straps and through the still, white fingers of a hand that jutted from the pile.

He studied the fingers for a long moment. How strange they looked. How very strange. They weren't his, that was for sure. His fingers weren't that dainty, that smooth. His were rough, work-worn, weathered by the sun and seasons.

But those fingers were gentle, curved so artistically.

The horseman closed his eyes, fighting the painful haze that tried to creep over him. He must stay awake. He mustn't dream again.

Why? He wasn't sure. His work was done. Was

there something else he was supposed to do today? Barry fought to remember. He'd finished his classes on time. Just as he'd promised, he'd stopped at the mall and picked up Debbie. Hadn't he taken her back to the Station, back to Shadow Creek Ranch?

No. Wait. Now he remembered. There was a storm. Yes. A storm. He was driving fast. Very fast. But the storm was chasing him. He couldn't outrun it. It kept coming. And coming. *And coming!*

"We'll make it," he called out loud, his voice choked. "Don't worry, Debbie. We'll m—"

Barry gasped. Debbie? Yes. Debbie was with him when he crashed. He began to tremble as he studied the hand jutting from the feed sacks. Oh, no! That was Debbie's hand.

He reached out and closed his fingers around the pale palm. It was cold, like the air in the cab.

"Debbie?" he whispered, the word sounding thick, unnatural. "Debbie, can you hear me? Please, can you hear me?"

He waited as full realization of what had happened took form in his mind. "Please answer, Debbie," he begged. "Oh, please be OK."

He felt the hand move slightly, and a moan escaped from unseen lips.

"DEBBIE!" he shouted. "CAN YOU HEAR ME?"

"What . . . what happened?" a thin, high voice spoke hesitantly from beyond the tangled collection of sacks and supplies.

Relief flooded the horseman's body as he heard

the words. She wasn't dead. At least he knew that much. But how badly was she hurt?

"We had an accident," he said. "We slipped off the road." The wrangler looked around, trying to get his bearings. "I can't see anything outside and I don't know why."

Suddenly, the truth struck him hard, forcing the air from his lungs.

"Oh my!" he breathed, unbelieving.

"What is it?" the voice asked.

"We're . . . we're buried under the snow, Debbie!" he said. "Do you hear me? We've been completely buried by the storm."

Barry waited in the dim darkness of the cab. The only illumination seemed to be coming from somewhere outside. But where? He glanced down at the controls behind the smashed steering column. Of course. The headlights.

He reached down and pressed a lever. The world went completely black.

"Barry?" the weak voice called. "Will they find us?"

The young man leaned his head against the cool glass by his ear. "That depends."

"On what?"

The wrangler closed his eyes, a burning fear pressing against him like fire. "The storm," he said. "That depends on the storm."

High above, unseen by the two occupants of the buried truck, the monster roared, its icy breath screaming through the trees and howling over mountain tops. Snowdrifts formed cresting waves across the meadows, covering the face of the land with a heavy mask of white.

Night had fallen. Southern Montana lay trapped under the speeding blizzard's tread.

CHAPTER 4

NIGHT WINDS

✿ ✿ ✿

Wendy sat cross-legged in front of the wood-burning stove, trying to coax flames from the partially dried logs stacked neatly inside.

She'd carefully crumpled up some paper plates found in the trash bin. They'd been tossed there a couple days earlier, after the group had enjoyed a pizza feast. For some reason, no one had bothered to take the trash down to the Station.

Outside, in the darkness, the wind whistled through the forest, sounding not so much like a storm as like a speeding train.

Every few seconds, a window would rattle or a loose board would squeak somewhere in the little two-story farmhouse. Wendy tried her best to ignore the strange noises, concentrating instead on getting the fire going.

Even if and when she did, the girl knew that they had only one armload of wood to warm themselves with. Somehow, they'd have to get more fuel, and soon. The only supply of logs was neatly stacked out in the shed, 30 feet from the front door. Usually this would not be a problem. But just now there happened to be a blizzard between her and the woodpile.

"I'm trying to light wet wood with damp paper plates," she mumbled as she struck another match and held the tiny flame against the singed corner of a brightly-colored platter. "Where's a good flamethrower when you need one?"

Merrilee chuckled and looked up from the kitchen table where she was trying to open a can of baked beans with a pair of pliers. "We weren't exactly prepared for this, were we?" she sighed. "I don't remember inviting this storm into our state, do you?"

Wendy nodded. "Squall line. That's what it's called."

"I beg your pardon?"

The youngster struck another match and held it to the plate. "Squall line. That's the leading edge of a cold front that has lots of wind and hail. I learned about it in a book I read about flying."

"Is that what hit us?"

"Yup. The squall line comes first and then the main portion of the storm. If you're a pilot, you keep away from fast-moving cold fronts or you'll crash and burn."

"Oh, dear," Merrilee gasped. "Sounds awful." She rotated the can in her hand and took another grip with the pliers. "Do you want to be a pilot when you're older?"

"Maybe," Wendy responded, watching a thin wisp of smoke curl from the dark circle of burned paper. "I haven't decided yet."

The woman at the table gave her pliers a firm squeeze. "Well, I don't like squall lines or storms or cold fronts or tin cans that won't open."

"I wasn't scared," the girl announced. "I just went upstairs to make sure you were OK."

"Thank you," Merrilee smiled, glancing at her companion then back at the can of beans. "You were a great comfort. I thought the house would blow away."

"Nah. It's a tough ol' building. And our hard work has made it even tougher. No storm is going to knock it down. No, sir." The girl paused. "Even Mr. Underfoot knows that. He's probably in the attic rolled up in a ball, hibernating. He feels safe here."

A tiny flame flickered, then began to grow. "All right!" Wendy enthused. "One warm, crackling fire comin' up."

"Good going, Wendy!" Merrilee responded with a shout. "And I've about got supper ready. Hope you like baked beans. John and I found them on sale in Bozeman. Bought a whole case. I'm afraid that's all we've got to eat until someone rescues us."

The girl held a piece of kindling to the flame. "Right now, I'm hungry enough to eat one of these logs."

Tomato sauce squirted from the jagged hole in the can and sprayed Merrilee in the face. She cried out in frustration. "Remind me to bring a can opener up here our very next trip from the Station."

Wendy giggled. "Isn't the food supposed to go in your mouth?"

Merrilee picked up a dust rag and wiped her forehead. "My mother use to say that when I was a little girl I always insisted on *wearing* my supper. Said mashed potatoes were my favorite. I heard her tell her friends that I could turn into an Idaho spud right before her eyes." The woman smiled. "Mealtime and bathtime were the same when I was a child."

Wendy giggled. "Samantha sort of wears her food from time to time, too. Joey says her mouth is always too busy talking."

Logs crackled and hissed as moisture battled flame within the confines of the new stove set in the corner by the living room window.

"Joey's a pretty nice fellow," Merrilee said, forcing the can's lid open and pouring its contents into two cooking pots. "Your father told us the story of how you all came out from New York. Exciting stuff."

"Yeah. He's OK, for a boy. He's learning horses pretty good. Wrangler Barry said he never saw anybody work so hard to learn the horse business in all his life."

"That's because it's important to him," the woman said, seating herself on the floor beside Wendy. "People always work hard at things they consider important." She handed her companion a small pot of baked beans. "This house is important to John and me, so we don't even think of what we're doing here as work. It's fulfilling a dream."

Wendy nodded slowly. "I kinda thought it would be. You talked about lots of dreams in your letters to your grandmother. Are you sad most of them didn't come true?"

The woman shook her head. "Dreams are funny things. They change as the years roll by. I guess reality makes it so. That's when you create new dreams, new wishes."

"Well," Wendy sighed, looking down at her pile of beans, "right now I wish I had a spoon to eat my supper with."

Merrilee laughed. "That's why God gave us fingers, so that if we were ever caught in a blizzard with nothing to eat but beans, and no spoons in sight, we'd survive just fine until someone came and rescued us . . . or brought us some silverware." The woman took in a deep breath. "And speaking of God, maybe we'd better bow our heads and thank Him for keeping the house standing for another day and, hopefully, for at least another night."

Wendy grinned and closed her eyes. "Our Father," she prayed, "thank You for keeping us safe until now. Thank You for these beans. And be with everyone down at the Station. Help us to figure out how to get that wood out of the shed before we freeze to death and die. In Jesus name, amen."

"Amen," Merrilee whispered.

The fire crackled in the stove, its warmth pressing in on the two diners seated before it. "Next time," the woman announced, "we'll have *hot* baked beans."

"Not *too* hot," Wendy giggled, holding up her sauce-covered fingers.

"Oh yeah. No spoons." The two fell silent as they hungrily devoured the sweet tasting legumes. Outside, the wind continued to howl and the snow fell deeper and deeper against the old homestead.

* * * * *

Joey studied the windward wall of the corral, eyeing the clusters of straw stuck between boards here and there. He shivered a little and pulled the saddle blanket he was wearing tighter around his chin.

"That's almost got it," he called to his four-legged companions. "You guys see any more holes anywhere?"

The horses snorted and stomped their hooves contentedly. "Oh sure, you don't care," the boy quipped. "You're used to being out here in the cold. Well, I ain't. This is not my idea of home sweet home.

I'm hungry. I'm tired. And I'm cold. Not a good combination."

Tar Boy shook his head, his long mane flowing in the frigid damp air. "Yeah, I know," the boy nodded. "I'm not a horse. Thanks for recognizing that fact. I should be in the Station sitting by the fire, eating Grandma Hanson's stew." Joey paused. "Oh, why did I think of her stew! I'll go crazy if I imagine food, especially Grandma Hanson's vegetable stew."

He paced back and forth across the floor. "Why didn't Barry leave any food out here? He slept in the barn all summer. Didn't the guy ever get hungry for some snacks or anything? Why'd we have to hire a healthy wrangler? You'd think he would have stashed some corn chips under his cot, or a bag of candy behind the tools, like normal people."

Joey flopped down on the cot and covered his feet with his blanket. He watched the candle glow on the workbench, its flickering light casting long shadows on the walls. "What I wouldn't give right now for a piece of Lizzy's cornbread just dripping with honey. I'd wash it down with a cold glass of milk." He blinked. "What am I saying? Forget the cold milk. Make that hot milk. Or better yet, hot chocolate. And forget the cornbread and make that soup. Hot soup. Hot stew. Yeah, Grandma Hanson's delicious hot stew."

The boy jumped to his feet. "Aaah! I did it again! I thought about stew. Man, I've gotta stop doin' that." He began pacing back and forth once more. "They're gonna find a frozen *skinny* snow cone in here in the spring." He grabbed the walkie-talkie. "Hey, Grandpa Hanson, you hear me?"

There was a long pause. Then, "Yeah, Joey. How you doin' out there?"

"Terrible."

Grandpa Hanson's voice sounded concerned. "What's the matter? Are you too cold?"

Joey shook his head. "No, I'm OK there. I'm hungry. I keep thinking about Grandma Hanson's vegetable stew and it's driving me bonkers."

He heard the old man chuckle. "I'm sorry, Joey. There's no way we can get food out to you right now. The snow is up to the downstairs windows all around the Station. We can't see more than 10 feet from the house. And five minutes ago we lost power. It's going to be a long night. Over."

Joey sighed. "I just wish there was something to eat around here. I mean anything. I've even considered munching on the horse feed. Over."

"Why don't you?" came the quick reply. "Just take it easy, eat a little at a time, and chew it up good. Over."

The boy shrugged. "I guess I could. I ain't never ate horse food before."

"Sure you have. Only we call it breakfast cereal. Difference is, one's cooked, one's raw."

"Well, if you think it's OK, I guess I'll give it a try. Over and out."

Joey walked to the feed bin and stared at the piles

of wheat stored there. He reached down and picked up a few kernels and held them in his hand. Slowly, he placed them in his mouth and began to chew. He chewed and chewed and chewed and chewed. After what seemed a very long time, he swallowed. Glancing over at the horses standing in their stalls watching him, he smiled weakly. "Needs salt," he said.

* * * * *

Snow swirled above the high banks, forming random patterns across the road and drifting into the deep ravine to one side. There were no traces of anything living except for gnarled, leafless tree branches that occasionally broke the surface of the drifts.

The only indication that a vehicle may have recently passed by were a few broken limbs hanging from the wind-blown trees that guarded the edge of the roadway.

The night moaned like a dying animal as the face of the land sank deeper and deeper under a blanket of white.

Beneath the snow, down in the ravine where a brook used to sing its summer song, Barry's truck lay smothered by the storm. Its front end pointed slightly upward; the frame tilted to the right just a little.

Inside the cab, there was movement.

"Hang in there, Debbie," the wrangler encouraged as he pulled another sack of feed through the shattered back window and let it drop into the covered truck bed. "I've got to check you out. Make sure nothing's broken."

The girl felt the weight that pressed on her shoulders and left side ease little by little as the young man worked to shift the load off his passenger. She nodded in the darkness. "How can you see what you're doing?"

"Flashlight," she heard the wrangler say. "And I've got a first-aid kit in the glove compartment and some other stuff back here. Just as soon as I get you out from under the supplies, I've got to get a line of this PVC pipe up to the surface of the snow. Grandpa Hanson had me pick some up. We're doing some work on the waterlines in the Station."

"You gonna try to call for help?"

"No," the young man chuckled painfully, his chest and sides aching with the strain. "Oxygen. Gotta get some air down here."

Debbie shifted in her seat. "Are we going to freeze to death?"

"I don't think so," her companion replied. "Snow is a good insulator. Just ask the Eskimos. They build houses out of the stuff. We just have to get a constant supply of oxygen into the truck. I think I can do it, depending on how hard the snow is packed. My guess is, not all that hard. Not yet, anyway."

The teenager felt the bag at her back and neck slowly ease away. "Well, hello, young lady," she heard Barry say as a beam of light played on the icy window by her head. "You come here often?"

She grinned slightly. "Not if I can help it."

Barry lifted more bags until none were left in the cab. He carefully arranged the feed sacks in the back of the truck, then appeared at the rear window. "So, can you move everything? Fingers? Toes? Arms?"

Debbie gently exercised her limbs. "Ouch. My shoulder hurts pretty bad."

Barry nodded. "Well, I should think so. You had a two-weeks' supply of oats come in through this window trying to bury you alive. Just make sure nothing's broken. Stiff is OK. Sore is OK. Broken is *not* OK."

The girl flexed her legs and arms. She slowly moved her head forward, then back. "I think I'm still in one piece. Just a little cold."

Barry disappeared then reappeared, a thick blanket in his hand. "Here, spread this over you. Oh, and you can take your seatbelt off. I don't think we're moving fast enough to need it."

Debbie unfastened the chromed latch in her lap and the belt clanked to the floor. "Now just sit quietly," Barry directed, "and I'll get working on the air vent. You still may be hurt and not know it, so just take it easy."

The young man grimaced as he moved back to the rear of the truck bed. "Barry! You're hurt," Debbie called. She grabbed the rearview mirror and quickly adjusted it until she could see her companion's dimly lit form in the back. "Let me help you."

"I'm OK," Barry called. "I think I might have a few cracked ribs or something. Stupid me. Didn't put on my shoulder harness, just the seatbelt. Glad they build collapsible steering columns into these newer trucks or I'd be a shish-ka-bob right about now."

Debbie shivered as she looked at the steering wheel pushed flat against the dashboard. "Mark one up for modern technology," she said.

"You got that right. Now where did those plastic pipes get to? Everything's a mess back here. Grandpa had me pick up a bunch of supplies at the Co-op. I even got some groceries at the store for your grandmother. Are you hungry?"

"No," the girl responded. "Just get us some air down here. It's beginning to get a little stuffy."

The wrangler nodded and gathered several pieces of three-inch-diameter pipe. He was glad now they were not the standard 10 feet in length; several were not more than five.

He pushed at the Plexiglas window at the rear of the pickup cap, but the window wouldn't budge. "Guess I'll have to use the driver-side opening in the cab," he called. "I'll put a cap on this first pipe and use it to bore up to the surface. Here goes."

Debbie watched as Barry wrestled the pipe from behind her and pushed it up through the snow at the "upper" side of the cab. Twisting the tube back and forth, he carefully guided it up, up, up through the drifts.

When most of the first length had disappeared he

joined a second to it with a coupling—no need for glue. This, too, he slowly worked up through the cold, icy mass.

As the third length was about halfway up into the snow, Barry felt the resistance slacken. "That's it. We're at the top." He whistled softly to himself. "There's about 12 feet of snow between us and the storm. And that could become even more. I'll make sure we have plenty of extra tubing up there."

He pulled the pieces back into the truck, separating them carefully, one by one. From the last length to come down, he worked off the cap. Then, working quickly, he reversed the action, pushing the pipe back up through the hole, this time without the cap. As the top section cleared the surface of the snow he could feel a current of cold air blowing from the pipe in his hand. He and Debbie could also hear the echoed sounds of the storm. They sat in silence, listening to the roar as it passed down the length of the plastic tubing.

"Sounds kinda bad," Barry said somberly. "This may be an unusual statement, but I'd rather be down here in the truck than up there in all that wind."

Debbie turned her face as tears moistened her eyes. The wrangler reached through the window and placed his hand on her shoulder. "We'll be OK, Debbie. I promise. They'll come looking for us as soon as they can."

The girl nodded. "But how will they find us? We're 12 feet under the snow. And no one has any idea where we are, to begin with."

Barry searched in his jacket pocket for his handkerchief. "I'll get us out of here," he said softly. "I promise."

He was about to pass the cloth to his companion when he began to cough. He held the handkerchief to his own mouth and bent double in the darkness, his chest searing with pain. It felt like hot knives were stabbing him over and over again. He fell backward into the truck bed, his face contorted with agony.

"Barry!" Debbie screamed, quickly turning and wiggling through the opening between the cab and the truck bed. "What's the matter? You're hurt, aren't you? You're hurt bad."

She picked up the fallen flashlight and shone it on her friend's face. Barry's hand dropped from his mouth, still clutching the handkerchief. The white cloth was stained with bright, red blood.

* * * * *

Tyler Hanson sat unmoving at the end of his bed. A single candle, resting on the nightstand beside an open Bible, illuminated the lawyer's face with soft yellow light and threw his shadow, large and dark, against the far wall.

Outside, the storm howled, occasionally rattling the tightly closed shutters that guarded the room's only window from nature's rage.

The man's eyes were closed, as if he were trying to stop the fearful scenes that his imagination insisted on presenting. The night winds screamed a reminder that both his daughters were in grave danger, and he couldn't do anything about it.

To rush out into the storm in an attempt to rescue either of them would be simple suicide. He knew that. Besides, he wasn't even sure where Debbie and Barry were. They'd left the mall hours and hours ago, just before the blizzard hit. Perhaps they'd found shelter in someone's home. Maybe they'd driven into the city, not away from it. At this moment, they might be sitting by a friend's fireplace, sipping hot chocolate and swapping jokes. Or—the man shuddered—they might not be.

"Tyler?" Mr. Hanson heard a gentle voice call from the doorway. "Are you all right?" The lawyer looked up and saw his mother standing just beyond the candle light.

"No, Mom," he whispered, "I'm not all right. I'm terrified. Totally helpless. The storm has captured me. It's holding me prisoner while my little girls are out there beyond my reach. I can't call to them. I can't hold them." He closed his eyes once again. "I feel so very helpless, so afraid."

The woman moved through the shadows and sat down beside her son. "Wendy's safe at Merrilee. It's a strong house and she and Mrs. Dawson will figure out what to do to stay protected."

"But what about Debbie?" Mr. Hanson's voice choked as he spoke. "What's happening to her? The radio already reported that this storm is killing people, good people, folks who weren't prepared. Are my daughter and Barry in trouble, in danger right now, right this very moment?"

The old woman placed her arms around her son. "Tyler, God knows exactly where Debbie is. We've got to believe He's watching over her."

"I wish I could do something, anything!" the lawyer moaned. "It's driving me insane to just sit here and wait, listening to the gale rattle the shutters. I have confidence in Wendy. She's tough, resourceful. I know she and Merrilee are reasonably safe up there in the farmhouse. They'll do the right things. They've got wood and a stove, and John says he took a case of canned beans up there a few days ago. So they'll have something to eat.

"But Debbie is another story. She's so vulnerable, so delicate, like a meadow flower in spring. What does she know about survival, about fighting a storm like this?"

"Don't forget," Grandma Hanson urged, "she's with Wrangler Barry. He knows *everything* about surviving Montana blizzards. He's lived here all his life. That young man's not about to let anything bad happen to Debbie, you can be sure of that." The old woman smiled. "He's a lot like you. He treats our Debbie with such gentleness, and you can tell he cares about her very, very much. So as long as our wrangler friend is anywhere nearby, no harm will come to our little girl."

"It's all my fault," the man said, leaning forward

and pressing his face into his hands. "I shouldn't have come out here. I shouldn't have allowed Debbie to take that job in town. I shouldn't have—"

"Don't be silly," Grandma Hanson interrupted. "I suppose you think you'd all be better off if you shut Wendy and Debbie up in a secure little room and not ever let them out?"

The lawyer lifted his chin. "Only for meals and holidays."

Grandma Hanson chuckled softly. "Well, trust me, Tyler, you'd have some very unhappy children on your hands. Do you think they're sitting wherever they're sitting right now, blaming you for this storm, for the fact that they're caught in it?"

The lawyer didn't answer.

"Children want freedom. But freedom brings risk, sometimes terrible risk. Your father and I have always been very proud of how you've allowed your girls to grow up following their own dreams. You've provided loving support, advice, guidance, discipline, and both Debbie and Wendy are developing into their own wonderful, individual persons. It takes freedom to do that."

The old woman paused. "Remember when you were a child, your father used to tell you the story of Adam and Eve in the Garden of Eden? It was your favorite." Mr. Hanson nodded slowly as his mother continued. "Well, Grandpa used to say that the Creator gave people freedom because He knew that's the only way they'd truly love Him. God knew the risks. He knew sin would roar like a storm across His beautiful new world, placing everyone in terrible danger. He knew innocent people would suffer. That's why He came to earth and lived right here in the middle of the storm with us, so we'd know He knew what we were going through."

The candle flickered in the darkness. "You love Debbie and Wendy so much that you're willing to let them live their lives outside the safe, secure room you wish you could keep them in. It's true that we can't rush out and help them just now, but God can. So, leave them in His hands for one night, Tyler. We'll bring them home after the storm has passed. OK?"

Mr. Hanson's shoulders sagged and tears slipped down his cheeks. "You're right," he said. "That's what I have to do."

He turned and fell to his knees beside the bed. "Oh, God," he prayed, the words tearing from his aching heart, "be with my girls tonight. Keep them safe. Remind them that I love them very much. In Jesus' name, amen."

Grandma Hanson stroked her son's hair in the dim light. She looked through the shadows in the direction of the shuttered window. The wooden slats beyond the glass shook from the force of the gale. She closed her eyes and leaned forward until her cheek rested on top of Tyler's head. "Amen," she whispered.

CHAPTER 5

MORNING

❂ ❂ ❂

Joey stirred. Frigid air hung in the horse barn like an icy curtain, turning the atmosphere into something heavy that pressed down on the small collection of horses and the young boy.

He opened his eyes and blinked a couple times. At first, the teenager wasn't quite sure where he was. He could hear animals nearby, their slow breathing heralding the fact that some were still dozing. What were animals doing in his bedroom?

Joey pulled the covers up until just the tip of his nose was showing. Everything else lay buried under layers of rough cloth.

I think I need some new bedsprings, the lad thought to himself. *These are gettin' kinda hard.* He squirmed. *And what's that awful smell? Maybe it's time for me to wash my socks!*

Joey shook his head as if to clear his thoughts. Now, where was that big, hot dish of mashed potatoes and gravy he'd been enjoying until just a moment ago?

Early snorted and stomped his hoof on the wooden floor. Joey sat up with a start. He'd *never* heard a horse snort in his bedroom before.

"What's goin' on?" he called out into the dimly lit chamber. He looked around. Hey, this wasn't his bedroom in the Station. This was . . . was . . . the barn?

Slowly, ever so slowly, the boy remembered. "Oh, yeah," he moaned, rubbing his chin with his hand. "It really happened. I thought it was a dream."

He flopped back down on the cot. "I'm stuck out here in the barn with five horses and no food." Early snorted again. "No *human* food," the boy corrected. "Horse chow we got. Mashed potatoes and gravy we ain't got."

He sniffed the cold air. "You guys stink!" he called in the direction of the stalls. "Course, it don't help that we're sealed in here like a bunch of Lizzy's peach preserves." He paused. "Maybe you horses think I stink." He lifted an arm to his nose and drew in a deep breath. "Hey, I smell like a horse." The boy smiled. "This should not offend you."

First one leg then another dropped from beneath the covers and landed with a thump on the cold floor. He looked around. Stray shafts of light appeared between some of the boards overhead.

"Must be morning," Joey called out to his four-legged companions. He squinted at his wristwatch that hung from a nearby nail. "Hum. Nine o'clock. *Nine o'clock?* Man! I overslept!" He jumped to his feet. "I gotta get up and—" Joey glanced around, then sat back down. "—feed the horses. This is going to be a short commute. I'm already here."

The teenager slowly stretched his legs one at a time, then his arms. He was right in the middle of mid-stretch when he noticed something was different, something other than the fact that it was morning.

"Hey, listen," he called out. Early flipped his ears forward and sniffed the air. "Do you hear it?" Joey queried, walking to the corral door. "Maybe I should say, 'Do you *not* hear it?' The wind. The roaring wind. It's gone. *It's gone!*" The young wrangler danced about the space in front of the horses. "Do you know what that means? Food. *Food!* I'm going to get out of here and eat normal, human food like people are supposed to. No more raw wheat and oats."

The boy ran to the corral door. "Freedom, here I come," he shouted as he unlatched the broad wooden gate. But his excitement came to an abrupt halt when the door would not budge, not even an inch.

"Hey, let me outta here!" he called, even though he knew no one was listening except five curious riding horses.

Joey ran across the room and grabbed a stepladder. "I don't believe this," he shouted angrily to himself. The ladder slammed against the small door above the large barn entry. He scurried up the steps and pressed against this secondary opening, which was used to increase the height of the main door when a large object such as a buggy was brought in for repairs. When both doors were utilized, the barn could also accept bulky wagons loaded with hay.

As the smaller portal swung open, Joey's breath caught in his throat. The top of the snow lay just a few feet below his lofty perch. That's why the main door wouldn't budge. It was buried behind a wall of drifted snow. The stuff also covered the pasture, footbridge, creek, orchard, and just about everything else in sight.

Straining to the left, Joey could barely make out the front porch of the Station, beyond where Shadow Creek was supposed to be. The snow had drifted up, almost hiding the first-floor windows. The sight was so unbelievable, so totally incredible, that the boy rubbed his eyes to make sure that what he was looking at really existed.

Slowly, the young wrangler closed the small door and descended the ladder. He went to his cot and sat down heavily on the pile of blankets. "I won't be having breakfast in the Station today," he moaned, glancing toward the stalls. "You'll have to share a few more meals with me. Hope you don't mind."

93

Early and the other horses snorted as if in response.

* * * * *

Wendy scratched her head thoughtfully. She and Merrilee had spent a not-very-comfortable night lying by the woodstove, burning anything that was flammable in the house. The armload of logs the young girl had brought in from the shed just as the storm hit had long ago disappeared up the chimney in the form of smoke and ash, leaving its gift of life-saving heat behind.

During the eternal hours of the night, unused wall paper, burnable building materials, a small pile of yellowing newspapers found in an upstairs closet, one old chair Wendy and Mrs. Dawson had reluctantly decided was of more use to them as heat than a place to sit, a couple of packing boxes used to deliver a load of bathroom tiles and paint supplies, and even the paper labels from the baked-bean cans, including the box they came in, these all had been sacrificed in the stove. The only thing left was the furniture.

"We're not flaming any more of the house stuff," Wendy announced wearily. "You guys gotta have something to sit down on when you move up here."

Merrilee smiled and rubbed her hands together, trying to absorb the last of the heat that radiated from the stove. "What else is there?"

"Wood," Wendy said firmly. "We've got a whole

shed filled with wood right out there." She pointed at the snowed-covered windows. "Let's just go get some."

"We can't walk through that much snow," the woman sighed. "It's over our heads."

"Then we'll tunnel through it," Wendy urged.

"What if it caves in and buries us alive?"

The girl nodded reluctantly. "Good point." She sat silently for a moment, pondering the situation. The house was still a little warm, but in a few hours the temperature inside would drop below freezing. They'd be in danger. Real danger.

Yes. They had to have that wood. It was the only solution left to the problem.

Wendy's eyes suddenly brightened. Merrilee saw a grin begin to twitch at the corners of the young girl's mouth, then a smile that spread from ear to ear.

"Wendy Hanson, what on earth are you mulling around in that brain of yours?" the woman asked hesitantly. "If those stories I've heard about you are true, I don't think I'm going to like what you have up your sleeve."

The girl tilted her head. "What stories?"

"Well, there was this thing about a curse in the attic, a rock with glowing eyes—"

"Oh, those," the girl shrugged. "Ancient history."

"Yeah, right," Merrilee chuckled. "You're not thinking of calling up some ancient spirit to get that wood for us, are you?"

Wendy laughed out loud. "Don't you know there

aren't any spirits *or* curses? That's just a bunch of old-time Indian mumbo-jumbo." She paused. "Besides, we don't need any voodoo, 'cause I've got a plan."

"A plan?"

"Yup. In no time we'll be sitting here as warm as a wooly worm in a tree trunk."

The woman's eyes narrowed. "And just how do you expect to get wood out of a shed that's buried up to its eaves in a drift?"

Wendy leaned forward. "Well, you see all that snow out there?"

"I did notice a few flakes."

The girl grinned. "We can't go *through* it."

"Nope."

"Can't go *under* it."

"Nope."

"Then," Wendy said, rising to her feet. "We'll go *over* it."

"Over it?"

"Yup. Just like Tarzan."

* * * * *

Debbie sat in the stillness of the truck bed, watching her companion sleep. It was dark. Only a faint glow of reflected daylight reached the buried vehicle through the air passage. That's how the girl realized night had finally ended and a new day had begun.

By placing her ear right next to the tube, she could hear that the winds had gone, too. There was no way she could be sure if it had stopped snowing. She could only hope the storm had spent its fury and moved on to the southeast.

The night had been long. Barry's condition had worsened rapidly. He complained of terrible pains in his chest and had coughed up blood several times. After one such agonizing spell, he'd provided his own diagnosis.

"My broken ribs must have punctured something inside me," he'd gasped, his face pale in the harsh radiance of the flashlight. "Maybe even a lung."

At first, Debbie had been terrified, unable to speak. The seriousness of their situation had pressed down on her shoulders like an unbearable weight. But then the terror had passed, leaving behind a stubborn resolve to survive.

She'd made the wrangler as comfortable as possible, covering him gently with as many blankets as she could find. She figured if his ribs were causing the damage, he must not move. This would only make things worse. She also knew that if they were going to be rescued at all, she'd have to be the one to figure out a way to make it happen.

After Barry had fallen into a restless sleep, she busied herself securing the truck. Things useless to them were stored in the passenger side of the big cab. The several bags of groceries Barry had picked up for Grandma Hanson were carefully sorted and placed nearby, ready to provide energy for the hours and perhaps days ahead.

Although she was cold, Debbie discovered that Barry had been right—snow acts as a very effective insulator against freezing winds. She'd even limited the flow of air down the pipe by securing a flap of duct tape over the end of the tube. When it began to get too cold, she'd lessen the flow. If things got a little stuffy, she opened it back up again.

Now, as she sat in the stillness, watching Barry sleep, her mind was busy with thoughts of rescue. She spoke in the cold air even though she knew her companion didn't hear.

"OK. This is the situation. We're buried under about 12 feet of drifted snow. We've got food and protection to last us for a couple days, longer if necessary. Barry's hurt badly and must not move an inch. I can melt small amounts of snow for drinking water by breathing on it. We've got a flashlight with fresh batteries, and all the PVC pipe we'd need to transport water from here to New Mexico."

The girl adjusted her position on the small pile of feed sacks. "What I've got to do is figure out a way of telling people up there that we're down here." Debbie leaned her head against the wall of the truck bed. "But they're not going to know where to look, are they? I'm sure the phone lines are down and the power is off all over this area, so I better not get my hopes for a quick rescue up too high."

She glanced down at her injured friend. She could

just make out the features of his face outlined by the dim light radiating from the air pipe. "I wanted to spend some time with you," she said, "but this wasn't exactly what I had in mind."

Debbie saw the young man's face grimace as the pain in his chest prodded his sleep like a bully poking a classmate with a stick.

"Please be OK, Barry," she breathed. "I don't know what to do to help you. You need to be OK."

The wrangler coughed quietly and stirred. Debbie adjusted the blankets about his shoulders and whispered, "Lie still, cowboy. You've got to stay motionless until help gets here." The horseman's breathing relaxed as he drifted into deeper slumber. "That's right," the girl nodded. "Sleep. Dream of horses and sunny pastures." She paused, then bent low until her lips were close to his ear. "And if you want to, you could even dream of me. I wouldn't mind."

Debbie's voice choked in the darkness. "Just don't die," she said, a tear slipping down her flushed cheek. "Please, Barry, please don't die."

* * * * *

"Base to Joey. Base to Joey." Grandpa Hanson stood out on the freshly shoveled porch that fronted his son's office. From his second-story perch he could make out the upper half of the horse barn.

"Joey to base." The walkie-talkie crackled to life. "Hi, Grandpa Hanson. You guys still kickin' over there?"

"I was just going to ask you the same question. Over."

He heard his young ranch hand chuckle. "Oh, me and the horses are doing just fine. We've started a club. Wanna join?"

"Not right now," Grandpa Hanson laughed. "Looks like you might be able to see out of the upper door if you wanted to. Over."

"Yeah. I already did. Big deal. Just a bunch of snow piled everywhere. Here, I'll show you."

The old man stood waiting, surveying the ocean of white that spread across his valley to the towering mountains beyond. The view was impressive and would have been all the more so if everyone were safe and sound in the Station.

He looked to the east, in the direction of Squaw Rock. He knew that up there, in one of the folds in the mountains, Wendy and Merrilee were being held captive by the incredible drifts of snow.

"Hey, Grandpa Hanson. Do you see me?" The rancher heard a voice calling from a distance. He laughed when he saw Joey hanging out of the upper doorway of the barn. He clicked off his walkie-talkie and cupped his hands to his mouth. "Hi, Joey. You look like you survived well enough. Are the horses taking good care of you?"

"Oh, we're regular pals, except somebody over here stinks to high heaven and it ain't me, no matter what the horses may say."

The old man chuckled. "You'd better clean out the stalls."

He saw Joey pause, then look around. "Just where am I supposed to put the manure?"

"Good question," Grandpa Hanson called back, his voice echoing across the distance "Just carry it up there and throw it out across the top of the snow. Frozen horse pies are a whole lot less smelly than fresh ones."

"You're right," the teenager shouted back. "Excuse me while I get to work." With a wave Joey disappeared into the barn. In a few moments, Grandpa Hanson saw a shovelful of manure fly out of the opening and bury itself in the clean white snow. This was soon followed by another. Then another.

Samantha stumbled out onto the porch and joined the old man at the railing. She stood watching the strange goings on at the distant barn.

"What's Joey doing?" she asked, her words muffled by the scarf she wore tightly wrapped around her face.

"He's cleaning out the stalls," Grandpa Hanson said.

Another load of manure flew through the open doorway and arched out across the snow. "There goes Pookie's poop," the little girl announced. "I can tell."

The old man laughed out loud. "You get back into the house," he ordered with a grin. "It's too cold out here for little girls with lots of curls."

Samantha nodded. "OK. Tell Joey I'll come and visit him just as soon as I get my snow boat finished."

"You're building a snow boat?"

"Yup. Me and Pueblo will just sail out there and rescue Joey and the horses and bring them back here to the Station."

Grandpa Hanson chuckled. "Well, I think I may have a better idea. Come on, I'll show you."

The little girl followed her friend back into the big Station and up the stairs that led to the attic. The old man looked around, lifting a box here and moving a piece of dusty furniture there.

"What are we looking for?" Samantha asked, peering behind a pile of burlap bags.

"These," Grandpa Hanson announced triumphantly as he bent and picked up what looked like a pair of tennis rackets.

"What're those?" the little girl gasped, fingering the tightly strung, wooden frames. "Are you going to play a game with Joey?"

"Nope," the old man said. "Mr. Hanson's gonna rescue him."

"How?"

The rancher searched and found another pair of the strange looking devices. "He's gonna just walk over to the barn and bring him back. You wanna watch?"

"You bet!" Samantha cried.

"Well then, let's get going," the old man encouraged.

102

"Let's get goin'," his companion repeated as they clamored back down the attic stairs and made their way to the office porch.

The young lawyer was waiting by the railing, dressed in layers of warm sweaters and coats. "You sure this is going to work?" he asked his father as the two approached.

"Got any other ideas?" the old man chuckled.

"Fresh out," Mr. Hanson admitted. He turned toward the barn just in time to see something fly through the upper door and disappear into the snow.

"What was that?" the man gasped.

"Pookie poop," Samantha explained.

Mr. Hanson blinked. "Pookie what?"

The old man giggled. "Oh, yeah, you might want to tell Joey you're coming before you get there. Wouldn't want you to get a face full of Pookie poop if you appear at the opening unannounced."

Samantha watched as Mr. Hanson tied those strange looking objects from the attic onto his feet. The other pair he hung over his shoulder. Then slowly, carefully, Grandpa Hanson helped his son ease over the railing and lower himself with a rope to the surface of the snow below.

"Now, keep your feet far apart so you won't trip," the older man called as the rescuer with the funny shoes adjusted his position on the snow. "The drifts have had time to settle so you shouldn't experience too many problems. Just don't fall over. You might not be able to get up again 'til spring."

103

Mr. Hanson nodded. "That's good to know." He let go of the rope and took a few uncertain steps forward.

"That's it," Grandpa Hanson called. "You're doin' fine. Just pretend the snow is rock solid. Don't think of it as something that could bury you alive."

"Enough with the encouragement. Just don't lose sight of me in case you have to come dig me out."

"Can't," the old man stated. "You've got both pairs of snowshoes."

The lawyer paused, then continued. "Remind me to buy a few more of these gizmos at the hardware store next time we're in Bozeman."

"Already on the shopping list," his father responded.

Ever so carefully, Mr. Hanson made his way toward the distant corral. He saw that the surface of the snow dipped slightly and took that to be Shadow Creek. As he stood catching his breath, he could hear the muffled sound of water running somewhere far below.

Joey scooped the last of the manure from the stalls and sent it hurling through the open door above the main corral entrance. He was about to climb the ladder and secure the portal when he heard his name being called.

"Hey, Joey. Stop throwing stuff out the door."

The teenager ran to the walkie-talkie and pressed the transmit button. "Is that you, Mr. H? How ya doin'?"

The lawyer's face appeared at the opening over-head. "You want to get back to the Station, or do you like it out here with the horses?"

Joey sighed. "Man, I wanna be with you guys like nothin' else, but I'm stuck. No way out. Over."

Mr. Hanson realized that Joey thought his voice was coming from the walkie-talkie. He covered his mouth to suppress a giggle. "Tell you what I'll do," the lawyer called, trying to make his words sound electronically reproduced. "You promise to make my bed for a month and polish my boots every Friday afternoon and I'll come out and rescue you right now. Over."

Joey brightened. "Sure!" he gasped. "You get me back to the Station and I'll do anything. But how you gonna do it? Snow's too deep. Over."

A loud clattering made the young wrangler jump sideways, just as something landed at his feet. He looked down to discover a pair of snowshoes in the straw. Glancing up, he saw Mr. Hanson's smiling face grinning down at him from the opening above the main door.

"Mr. H!" Joey cried out excitedly. "You've come to save me. Now I can eat. Now I can be warm!" He paused. "Wait a minute. You tricked me. I thought you were in the Station."

"Details, details," the lawyer called down. "Just slip those do-dads on your big feet and we'll waltz right back to the house."

Joey shook his head and retrieved the snow-

105

shoes. "Man, you got me good. But I don't care." He climbed the ladder and sat on the ledge of the opening. He quickly fastened the devices to his boots and swung his feet out onto the surface of the snow. "I forgot Grandpa Hanson had these. Showed 'em to me last winter. Never needed 'em 'til now."

As the two made their way along the expanse of white, Joey chuckled. "Now I've got to make your bed for a week."

"Month."

"And shine your dirty ol' shoes. Man, you tricked me good. But it's OK. I didn't think I'd *ever* get rescued."

"Now we've got to concentrate on the rest of the family," his companion sighed as they moved along. "Soon as the road crews restore power and phone service, we've got to find Debbie and Barry and get up to Merrilee."

Joey reached over carefully and tapped his friend on the shoulder. Mr. Hanson turned. "We'll find 'em," Joey smiled. "We'll get everyone home safe and sound. You'll see."

The man nodded and continued walking carefully in the direction of the big Station.

* * * * *

"This is not going to work." Mrs. Dawson stood leaning out of the upstairs window of the small homestead, her arms tightly wrapped around Wendy's legs.

The girl studied the length of rope that stretched

between her hands and the tree limb about 20 feet above and away from the house. "Of course it's going to work. Haven't you ever seen a Tarzan movie? He zooms from tree to tree as easy as you please. I just have to swing over to the shed. Piece of cake."

"Tarzan is Hollywood. This is Montana. There's a big difference, you know."

Wendy ignored her companion's complaints. "You just make sure you don't let go of the second rope I've tied to the main rope. I'll tie the logs to the main rope, and with that second rope you can pull them here to the window. And you'll be able to pull me back when we've gotten all the wood out of the shed. I think it's a terrific plan. I got this rope over that limb up there, didn't I?"

Merrilee shivered in the icy air. "I don't like this. I think we should just burn the furniture. You might get hurt or something."

"Don't worry. I've got it all figured out. My swing should carry me right over the shed. I'll just land gently on the roof, knock a whole in the boards with this hammer, ease down through the opening, and start bringing those big, beautiful logs up for you to haul in." She tightened her grip on the rope. "Now, let go."

The woman reluctantly loosened her hold on Wendy's legs. With a war whoop that would make Red Stone the Indian proud, the girl dropped out into space. Merrilee watched as she sailed away from the farmhouse, out across the snow-buried yard. Her feet skimmed the drifts as she picked up speed.

Wendy felt her weight increase as she raced across the snow. She saw the shed rush toward her, then begin to drop as she swung up, up, up. Her hands gripped the rough cord until her knuckles turned white.

Maybe this wasn't such a good idea after all, she thought to herself as she watched tree branches whip past.

Reaching the end of her swing, she felt her body go weightless for a second, then begin to drop again. She glanced down and found she was right above the snow-covered shed. She knew that if she didn't time herself just right she wouldn't land on the structure at all but would be carried past it. There was only one thing to do. Let go.

Merrilee saw the girl release her grip on the line and fall straight down. She screamed as Wendy's body slammed into the roof and disappeared through splintering boards and swirls of snow. A muffled crash reverberated from somewhere inside the structure. Then everything was still.

"*Wendy! Wendy!*" the woman cried, fear straining her words. Oh, why had she allowed such a hair-brained idea in the first place? Now Wendy was badly hurt and she couldn't even go out to help her.

A hand, then an arm, then a head appeared through the large, gaping hole in the shed's roof. "Wow. What a ride!" she heard Wendy call out excitedly. "Landing was a little less graceful than I'd planned, but here I am." The young girl spread her arms apart, a smile lighting her flushed face. "Ta-da!" she trumpeted.

Merrilee sat down on the window ledge, trying to still her racing heart. "You scared me to death," she called. "I thought you were dead for sure."

"All in a day's work," the girl responded gleefully. "Hooray for Hollywood!"

The woman laughed with relief as Wendy leaned back and beat her chest with her fists. "Ahh-ee-aaahh-eee-ahhh." The call of Tarzan echoed through the snow-covered pines and cottonwoods of Gallatin National Forest.

CHAPTER 6

THE SUBSTITUTE

✪ ✪ ✪

The day stretched tiringly into the afternoon hours. Every 15 minutes or so, Mr. Hanson would get up from his spot by the fireplace and walk to the hall phone. He'd pick up the receiver and place it against his ear. Then the lawyer would quietly return the handset to its cradle and walk back into the warm den.

Joey and the others would shake their heads sadly. The man's quick return meant the phone lines were still dead. Communication with the outside world was still impossible.

No one wanted to talk about Wendy, Merrilee, and Debbie, yet the missing members, especially Debbie, were on everyone's mind. It was almost cruel to be able to look out of the upstairs windows and see the mountains, knowing that Wendy and Merrilee were up there—so close, yet so far.

And what about Debbie and Barry? Were they all right? Were they hurt? The agony of waiting began to tell on those gathered by the flickering flames.

"I've got to do something!" Mr. Hanson slammed his fist onto the arm of his chair. "I'll go crazy if I don't."

Grandpa Hanson sighed a frustrated sigh. "There's nothing you can do. All the roads are—"

"I know that!" his son interrupted with a voice charged with anger. "You don't have to remind me. But I can't just sit here while my daughters are in danger." He jumped to his feet. "I'm going out. I can try for Merrilee with the snowshoes. They got me to the barn."

"Tyler, No!" the old man commanded. "Joey was just across the creek. John's homestead is five miles away. And what if there's an avalanche, or darkness comes before you get there? And what if it starts to snow again?"

"DON'T TELL ME WHY I CAN'T DO THIS. TELL ME WHY I CAN!" The man's face was lined with tension.

Grandpa Hanson lifted his hands. "There *is* no *can*, Tyler," he said gently. "And what good are you to anyone if you freeze to death out there? Road crews out of Bozeman are working around the clock. The power and phone people are right behind them, doing their best to restore service to all the hard-hit areas. Don't forget that our very own neighbor, Ned, works for the county. He was away from home when the storm struck. He'll be anxious to get back to his wife, and trust me, he'll bring the big highway snow-blowers with him."

He paused. "Besides, for all we know, Debbie and Barry may be already found. So just sit down and wait with the rest of us."

The lawyer paused at the door and bowed his head. After a long moment he spoke. "It hurts, Dad. It hurts my heart to feel so helpless."

Grandpa Hanson stood and walked over to his son. Placing a hand on his shoulder he said quietly, "All we can do is pray, Tyler. That's the only action available to us right now."

The younger man turned and gazed into his father's eyes. "But I don't feel like praying, Dad."

The old man nodded. "That doesn't mean God won't hear. He knows our hearts are hurting. He understands what it's like to be afraid and feel far from the source of strength that we need. Remember what Christ said on the cross? In His darkest hour, Jesus cried out, 'Father. Why have You forsaken me?'

"God knows what you're feeling, Tyler. He knows . . . and hears."

Mr. Hanson nodded slowly, then walked out into the hallway. Pausing by the phone he lifted the receiver, then placed it back on its cradle and climbed the cold steps leading to the second floor.

Those gathered in the den heard him enter Debbie's room and quietly close the door.

* * * * *

The last log swung from the top of the shed, across the snow-blanketed farmyard, and to the upstairs window. Merrilee pulled it into the bedroom and loosened the knot, letting the chunk of wood thump to the floor.

The room was littered with carefully cut lengths of firewood, enough to see the hard-working, snow-bound pair through days of captivity in their little mountain home.

"That's it," Wendy called, her arms aching from the hours of lifting, tying, swinging, and hauling. "That'll keep us toasty warm for a long time. And look what else I found." She held up a couple of tin cups and an old, bent spoon she'd discovered on a shelf in the shed. "Not exactly uptown, but at least we can drink water out of something other than a cooking pot."

"Only one spoon?" Merrilee responded from the window. "Guess we'll have to share. At least we can have hot beans for supper and give our fingers a rest."

Wendy chuckled. "Don't say the word *beans*. Let's pretend that for tonight we're going to have macaroni and cheese or something." The big rope swung in her direction and Wendy caught it as it passed by. "And we're not going to be drinking

113

water. It'll be hot chocolate or some of Grandma Hanson's steamy herb tea with honey in it."

The girl tied the rope around her waist then took a firm hold on the rough line. "Now you're going to have to get me swinging really high so I can make it up there. Just tug on the secondary rope each time I'm headin' in your direction."

"OK," Merrilee agreed. "But be careful."

Wendy stepped back a few feet from the edge of the shed, then ran forward, launching herself out over the snow.

The woman pulled hard, then allowed her companion to swing away from her.

Back and forth, higher and higher the girl oscillated, like a human pendulum, traveling further and further with each pass. Soon, she could just about reach the window ledge with her toes. Two more arching swings and she dove through the opening. Merrilee grabbed her around the waist.

For a moment, they thought they'd both be pulled back out of the window as Wendy began her return trip, but the woman's strength prevailed. The girl quickly unfastened the rope and they dropped to the floor, tired, happy, victorious.

"See, I told you it would work," the grinning youngster teased. "I may not be the smartest, most talented, or prettiest girl in the world, but I can get wood out of an old shed any day."

Merrilee chuckled. "Well, I think you're smart, talented, and pretty, all rolled into one. You saw a problem, worked out a plan, and got busy. That's how it's done."

Wendy stumbled to her feet and surveyed the random piles of logs scattered about the room. "Not a bad haul, even if I say so myself."

The woman nodded. "But they're not going to do us any good up here. Let's get a couple loads downstairs and make that stove earn its keep. I can feel the temperature dropping. Sun's going down. We'll need all the heat we can get tonight."

The two gathered armloads of the dry logs and clamored down the stairs. "I'm hungry," Wendy moaned. "What's for supper?"

"Bea—" Merrilee stopped mid-word. "Make that macaroni and cheese, with hot chocolate and wheat bread."

"Good choice," the girl giggled. "Fresh strawberry pie would be nice too."

"Oh, no," Merrilee called. "Gotta save that for breakfast."

* * * * *

Night slipped in from the east, covering the frozen land with silvery shadows. Day disappeared without a sound, without a trace; it left nothing in its wake but silent drifts of snow and fearful hearts.

Debbie watched the dim light at the base of the air passage slowly fade. In her silent world, the only sounds were her breathing, and the occasional moan from her fitfully sleeping companion.

She gently stroked the wrangler's hair with her fingers. *Funny how the human body insists on sleeping when it's trying to heal,* Debbie thought to herself. She adjusted the blankets covering the young man's shoulders. *Maybe this is what it's like to die. You just hurt some, then go to sleep. Isn't that what the preacher kept saying last Sabbath at church—death is like sleep? You close your eyes and then you see Jesus coming?*

Dying wouldn't be so bad. Who wants to suffer through life, anyway? Who wants to see friends hurt, watch people die, read about nations murdering nations. Life's hard on everybody. Dying seems like such a good idea.

Debbie shook her head. "What am I thinking?" she said aloud. "I don't want to die. I want to live. I want to be with Dad and Wendy. I want to design pretty dresses and fix up window displays in department stores."

The girl stared into the darkness. "And," her voice softened, "I want to fall in love and get married and have children—two children—a boy and girl. I want to do something important for other people, something that will make them happy, something that will make the world better for everyone."

She sighed. "Most of all, I want to get Barry and me out of this truck. He needs a doctor. He needs to get to the hospital where they can fix his ribs and find out what's wrong inside."

Debbie sat silent for a long moment. "I want to

116

know what it's like to have someone, a guy, love me and think I'm the most wonderful person in the whole world."

"You sure don't want much," a weak voice spoke in the darkness.

Debbie gasped. "Barry? You awake?"

The wrangler chuckled painfully. "How can anyone sleep with all this gabbing going on?"

Debbie reddened. "Oh, no. How long have you been awake?"

"Long enough to know that the world better be prepared when we get out of here. You're a woman on a mission."

The girl buried her face in her hands. "You weren't supposed to hear all that. I was just thinking out loud. Oh, I'm so embarrassed."

"Hey." The girl felt a hand touch her arm. "It's OK. I like what you said. Those were good things, important things. You sounded like Judy."

"Judy?" the word was spoken with not a lot of enthusiasm. "She your girlfriend or something?"

"Nah. Just a classmate, although we were supposed to go to the game this Sunday. Don't think we'll make it."

There was a long pause, then Debbie spoke in the darkness. "What's she like?"

"Oh, I don't know, just a girl. She thinks she's going to revolutionize modern medicine with herbs. Probably will. There's nothing more powerful than a woman on a mission."

117

"Is she pretty?"

The wrangler coughed quietly. Debbie could feel his hand tighten around her arm as the pains in his chest reminded the horseman of his injuries. "She's OK. Not as pretty as you."

"Oh, I'm not all that great."

The girl heard her companion chuckle. "Debbie Hanson, you're about the prettiest thing I've ever seen—especially when you do your hair up, like when I took you to that job interview at the mall. You looked just like a fashion model or something."

The girl reached up and touched a length of long, dark hair cascading past her face. "You really think so? I mean, do you really think I'm pretty?"

"Whadda I gotta do, sign something? Yes. You're beautiful. Any guy would be proud to have you as his girlfriend."

Debbie let her hand drop back to her lap. "Any guy, huh? I'll try to remember that."

Barry shifted his position, groaning as the pain in his chest racked his prone body. "That includes me," the voice in the darkness said softly. "But I know I'm way out of your league."

Debbie blinked. "What? What did you say?"

Barry's hand tightened again as a groan escaped his lips. "Man, I hurt bad, Debbie," he said. "I'm sorry you have to take care of me like this."

"I don't mind," the girl responded breathlessly. "I'll take care of you until we can get you to a hospital. I promise."

118

The man's breathing steadied. "Thanks, Debbie. You're the best. You're the very best."

Weariness and pain overcame the horseman and he slipped into an uneasy slumber. Debbie sat in the darkness, stroking his head with gentle fingers. "I was wrong," she whispered, her words unheard by her injured companion. "What I really want the most . . . is you."

* * * * *

R-r-ring. The sound of a telephone echoed through the midnight halls of the Station. Mr. Hanson jerked, wide awake, listening. Had he heard something?

R-r-ring. He leaped to his feet, hands trembling. "THE PHONE! It's working again!" he cried out, trying to make his way past the stirring bodies scattered across the den rug like leaves in a field.

R-r-ring. Stumbling out into the lobby, the lawyer fumbled for the phone in the murky darkness. "Debbie? DEBBIE?" he shouted into the receiver.

Grandpa Hanson appeared at the doorway, his form silhouetted against the dim glow radiating from the fireplace.

"Yes. This is Tyler Hanson." The man listened intently as he shivered in the cold. "Yes. Her name is Debbie. She's with Barry Gordon, a student at the University. They left the mall around 4:00 or 5:00 yesterday, just before the storm hit. No, I'm not sure which way they were heading, but I assume they

119

were trying for the ranch. Now that the phones are working, she may call in."

Mr. Hanson stood listening to the voice in the receiver. "Yes, please," he said, his words filled with newfound excitement. "At first light. I understand. And we'll call if they make contact with us before then."

Grandpa Hanson could hear a distant, electronic voice buzzing from the handset at his son's ear. "Oh, thank you," the young lawyer called out. "Let me know if anything . . . if you find anything. Just call immediately, OK? I'll be waiting. Goodbye."

The man hung up the phone and turned to face his father. "That was the police in Bozeman. They talked to the security guard at the mall and he told them about Debbie and Barry heading out just before the storm. The officer said that the big snowblowers are clearing Highway 191 as we speak and that they'll send one this way at first light."

The old man wrapped his arms around his son and held him close. "We'll find them tomorrow, Tyler. I promise. They'll be OK."

Mr. Hanson let out a long, heartrending cry. The weight of fear had finally overcome him, causing his knees to buckle. Together, father and son dropped to the floor and sat in each other's embrace for a long moment. "Oh, dear God," the young lawyer sobbed, "don't leave her. Don't let her go. Please. Just one more night. Please, God."

Grandpa Hanson tightened his grip on the weeping man as they sat shadowed by the yellow glow from the hearth. One by one, the other Station inhabitants made their way into the cold lobby and added their arms of support until the crying man found himself completely surrounded by people who cared for him.

Far away, through the hours of darkness, powerful snowblowers driven by dedicated highway workers lumbered along, sending fountains of snow rising into the frigid air. Inch by inch, mile by mile, they moved through the half-moon shadows, closing the distance between them and the little ranch in the valley.

* * * * *

"Merrilee? Are you awake?" The question came softly, like the rustle of dry leaves across the frozen face of the forest.

"Is something wrong?" the woman said, sitting up quickly. "Is the fire going out?"

The living room was warm and cozy, the hard-won logs doing their duty in the stove's crackling, ember-red firebox.

"No. I'm OK. I just wanted to ask you something."

Merrilee lay back down against the rug, her head resting on a rolled-up window curtain. "I was dreaming," she said. "You, me, and John were in Florida, on the beach, enjoying a very hot sun." She chuckled. "Strange. You were swinging from the yardarm of some pirate ship out beyond the breakers. I told you to be careful, but you just insisted you had to get the logs."

Wendy giggled. "Now where did such a silly dream come from?"

"I wonder," the woman grinned.

The two were silent for a moment. "I wanted to ask you something," the girl said softly.

"Well, now that I'm not on a beach in Florida getting a suntan, ask away."

Wendy rose up on one elbow. "When you were my age, did you miss your real mother? You know. When she died in the car crash?"

A stray gust of wind sprinkled snow against the window, then blew past. Wendy heard her companion sigh deeply. "I thought my world had ended," the woman began. "I was at school when the police car pulled into the parking lot. I watched the man get out and slowly close the door. He seemed sad, nervous, as if he didn't want to do what he'd been assigned.

"He came in and talked to my teacher and they kept looking over at me. Then Mrs. Waterman asked me to follow her out into the hallway.

"I remember I had a library book in my hand— one about birds. It had a big hawk on the cover. She told me that there'd been an accident and that my mom and dad wouldn't be coming to get me after school. She said they'd both been killed. To this day, I can't look at a hawk flying overhead without thinking about how much I miss my parents."

Wendy was silent for several minutes. When she

spoke, her words sounded very, very tired. "Sometimes I wish my mother had died. Then I'd know why I couldn't see her anymore. But then I'm glad she's alive because I love her." She turned to face Merrilee. "Is it awful for me to say that I wish my mother had died?"

The woman stared at the firelight dancing across the ceiling. "I don't think so," she said. "Sometimes death is easier to take, easier to understand, than divorce. I've known many children whose parents have split up. It's like they see their security, their happy home, crumble right before their eyes. But then, unlike death, they see someone they love, someone they depend on, simply move out, walk away, start a new life somewhere else." Merrilee looked into the eyes of her young friend. "Death and divorce are very much alike. But when two people stop loving each other, there's no funeral, no memorial service, because both are still alive, still a part of life. In many, many ways, divorce is the harder to accept."

Wendy lay back on her makeshift pillow. "My mom used to take me shopping. We'd go to bunches of stores and she'd buy me lots of dresses and white gloves and shiny shoes. I'd try everything on and she'd get all gushy and stuff about how *won-der-ful* I looked. It made me feel like I was really special, really important."

The woman smiled slightly. "You used to wear

dresses? I mean, real girl-type dresses, with bows and lace?"

"Yup," Wendy said. "But when Mom left, I gave them all to the community welfare store around the corner from our apartment building. They were silly, anyway. I looked like a real jerk in 'em."

Merrilee shook her head. "I'll bet you looked nice."

"Maybe," the girl responded. "But they were sorta like your hawk. They made me remember. That hurt too much."

Wendy slowly got up and walked to the living room window. Through the trees she could see the first hint of dawn touching the distant mountain tops. She stood there, not knowing what to say or even why she'd shared her deepest, most painful thoughts with a woman who'd had troubles of her own when she was young.

"We're a lot alike, you and me," Merrilee called softly. "We both have painful pasts. We both have scars on our hearts from things that happened—things we had no control over."

Wendy studied the dark outlines of the mountains against the soft glow of the sky. "Does the pain ever go away?" she asked.

"No, not really. You just have to learn to live with it."

"How?"

Merrilee joined her friend at the window. "It's kind of a decision. You decide that one part of your life, one important part in this case, is past, gone, finished. But life must go on. You can't relive the years that have vanished. So you cry your last tear, pick up the pieces of your broken heart, and march on, asking the Lord to help you heal. He's good at that. Had plenty of practice."

Merrilee heard her companion sob softly. "Will you help me?" Wendy asked. "Will you show me how?"

"Of course," the woman responded, her eyes glistening.

The young girl turned and gazed up at Merrilee. "There're so many questions I want to ask. So many things I wonder about. My dad doesn't know what to say when we talk about certain stuff. Debbie's always too busy with her dresses and drawings, and I'm too embarrassed to ask Grandpa or Grandma about the things I want to know. Can I come visit you and we can talk about stuff and you can tell me why I feel certain ways and what's going to happen to me as I get older? Then I won't feel so scared all the time. Then I might not miss my mother so much."

Merrilee encircled Wendy with warm, loving arms. "Tell you what, partner. If you'd like, I can be your substitute mother for as long as you want me to. John and I have never been able to have children of our own, even though we've tried for years and years. So you can sorta be my substitute daughter, too. Looks like it might be a good deal for both of us. How's it sound to you?"

Wendy was silent for a long moment. Merrilee felt the girl relax in her arms, then she saw a smile spread across the young, tearstained face.

"You're not going to make me wear dresses or anything, are you?"

The woman shrugged. "Well, maybe once in a while, just to remind me that you're a girl."

"No pink ones," the youngster giggled. "And no bows. I hate bows."

"Deal," Merrilee announced, thrusting out her hand. "No pink and no bows."

Wendy reached out as if to shake her companion's hand, then paused. She looked up into the gentle eyes gazing down at her. "Once I thought that the treasure of the Merrilee might be a pile of gold. But now I know better. It's love, isn't it? Mrs. Grant knew it. Now we do, too. Isn't that right?"

"That's exactly right." The woman smiled. "In this world, there's nothing more valuable than old-fashioned love."

Beyond the ice-rimmed window panes, a new day was dawning. For Wendy Hanson, the storm had finally passed.

CHAPTER 7

RESCUE

❂ ❂ ❂

A sharp *snap* resonated from the embers that lay in small, shimmering piles in the soot-darkened fireplace. The den was silent except for the soft breathing of prone figures snuggled inside fluffy sleeping bags and under blankets.

Grandma Hanson opened an eye, unsure, at first, of where the sound had come from. Slowly she rose on one elbow and looked around the dimly lit den. The room had no color, only silver-gray, the same hue as the eastern sky beyond the windows.

A shadowy form by the door caught her eye. Someone was sitting up in a chair, fully dressed, with hat, earmuffs, gloves, and boots in place. A pair of snowshoes leaned against the nearby wall.

The old woman smiled a hopeful smile. Today her

precious son would be reunited with his daughters, her granddaughters. She knew it. The lady wasn't sure why, but she just knew today would bring an end to the fear and hopelessness that filled Tyler's heart, filled her heart.

The man in the chair nodded, his sleep fitful. Dawn would not catch him unprepared. He'd dressed for the challenge hours ago, after the phone call from the Bozeman police.

"Tyler?" Grandma Hanson called quietly.

She saw her son jump to his feet. "I'm ready. Let's go!" The man looked about the room, then over at his mother. "Oh," he said, "I thought maybe the blowers had come."

"I'm sorry," the woman apologized. "I didn't mean to startle you. I just wanted to suggest that you get some warm food in your stomach before you head out. Joey and Mr. Dawson, too. You'll all need strength for the search."

"Food?" A muffled voice called from deep inside a sleeping bag by the window. "Did someone say food?"

Joey's nose and eyes appeared from under the pile of cloth. "I ain't never gonna refuse chow again in my whole life."

Mr. Hanson chuckled. "I might be too nervous to eat anything, but it sounds like a good idea. I'll get John up, just as soon as I figure out which pile is him."

"Don't bother," came a reply from the direction of

the fireplace. With a quick move, the top of a sleeping bag flipped back, revealing a man completely dressed, with boots and gloves. "And let's pack a supply of eatables for our two castaways at Merrilee. I'm sure they're kinda tired of baked beans by now."

One by one, the other members of the survival slumber party awoke and began readying themselves for the hours ahead. Voices were guardedly cheerful. For the first time in two days, their words carried a hint of genuine hope. Today, the lost would be found. Today, heart-numbing questions would be answered. Today, Wendy, Merrilee, Debbie, and Barry would be rescued from the monster's grip.

Busy bodies moved through the cold, gray-lit halls and rooms of the big Station. Faces were washed in the kitchen sink, using water heated on the gas cooking stove.

Steaming bowls of vegetable stew, along with thick, soft-crusted slices of wheat bread, disappeared down eager throats. Each Station inhabitant wanted to be fully prepared for what the day might bring.

Even as they ate, their ears were tuned to catch the first sounds of the approaching blowers. Tension and expectation mounted as the seconds ticked by.

* * * * *

"Barry?" Debbie leaned close to her friend and spoke softly in his ear. "Barry, wake up."

"What? What is it?"

"I hear something."

The injured man blinked his eyes open and coughed quietly, flinching at the pains in his chest. "I don't hear anything."

"No. Listen. It's coming down the tube." Debbie scrambled to the broken window that separated the cab from the truck's bed. She placed her ear next to the opening of the plastic air pipe and lifted a finger. "There. Do you hear it? Sounds like a machine or something."

Barry tilted his head slightly. Yes. There was a new noise echoing down the airway, one they hadn't heard before. It sounded like a rumbling, a churning, like a train going by. But there were no tracks in this area. What would a train be doing—

"Wait." The wrangler grimaced at the movement his word brought to his chest. "It's a truck. A big truck."

"How can it be?" Debbie questioned. "Snow's too deep. There's no way a truck could be driving by."

"It could if it was pushing a snowblower," the young man said, his words strained.

"A snowblower? You mean one of those big highway jobs?"

"Yup. We're about to get rescued, Miss Fashion Designer."

Debbie let out a loud war whoop and clapped her hands together. "You think so? I mean you really think so?"

"We're off the main highway," Barry said between gritted teeth. "The only reason they'd be out here on this road would be that they're trying to reach Shadow Creek Ranch. They must be looking for us."

"We're saved. WE'RE SAVED!" The girl flattened herself on the pile of supplies by the cab and shouted into the pipe. "Help! We're down here under the snow. Help! Here we are!"

The giant snow blower moved along the white expanse that was supposed to be a road. Ned Thomas, the driver, carefully guided the big, roaring machine, his eyes searching for familiar landmarks by which to steer.

Beside him sat his work partner, Alex Krueger. Both men studied the space ahead, concentrating on keeping their powerful machine centered on hard, solid ground.

In their wake, they left a cleanly cleared passageway through the drifting snows. A second truck, sporting the markings of the Gallatin County Search and Rescue Squad, followed close behind. It carried two snowmobiles and assorted emergency equipment. Searching for lost travelers was nothing new to the men driving the vehicles. They only hoped they'd find Barry Gordon and Debbie Hanson in time.

The first vehicle sent a steady fountain of snow high into the air. Alex operated the controls of the powerful blower, aiming the spout so as to direct the arching loads of snow away from the road and into areas where they'd be out of the way.

Debbie continued to shout, her mouth pressed against the pipe.

Suddenly, she felt cold snow slam against her face, and the light that had been filtering down the shaft disappeared. The girl fell back into the truck bed, coughing and sputtering, a look of terror in her eyes.

She fumbled for the flashlight and directed its beam at the air shaft. What she saw made her heart stop mid-beat. The pipe had been filled with snow. The very machine sent to save her and Barry had thrown its load high into the air, and, unknown to the drivers, had covered up the only sign of the captives' presence with a fresh blanket of powder. Not only was the light gone, but now the two people buried deep under the drifts were without a fresh supply of air.

Barry closed his eyes, the pain in his chest growing unbearable. He knew Debbie would be unable to get another shaft up through the now hard-packed snows. It was no longer a question of how long before they'd be rescued. It was a question of how long they could stay alive in their icy tomb.

Debbie glanced over at her companion and choked back a sob. The young man didn't hear. He had slipped into unconsciousness.

* * * * *

"They're coming. THEY'RE COMING!" Samantha shouted as she ran down the second floor hallway of

132

the north wing of the Station. She'd been waiting at the window of the room closest to the road that passed above and beside the old hotel.

At first, she'd seen the fountain of snow flowing up and over the trees some distance away. Then suddenly, the lead vehicle had emerged from the man-made blizzard, lights flashing in the early morning gray.

"Joey! John!" Mr. Hanson shouted as he grabbed his pair of snowshoes and stumbled out onto the front porch. "I'll climb up to the road and meet 'em. They'll have another pair of snowshoes for you, John. I talked with the police chief a few minutes ago. He said the rescue squad would be right behind the blower, with snowmobiles and other equipment we might need."

By now the machine was roaring along the road above the Station, its cascade of snow aimed away from the valley and against the side of the mountain. Ned brought the machine to a halt when he saw Mr. Hanson scurrying up the hill toward him.

"I'm sure glad to see you," the lawyer called, extending his hand as the driver hopped down from the work machine.

Ned smiled. "I think we'll be able to continue on up the valley for another two miles or so, toward the Dawson spread." He shouted above the din of the engine. "After that, the snowmobiles will work best on the logging roads." The highway worker pointed at the emergency truck waiting behind the blower.

"We've got two of 'em. Mr. Dawson and a squad member can head into the mountains to dig out Wendy and Merrilee. You and Joey can go back toward the highway with the other. The rescue truck will be tight on your heels."

Mr. Hanson nodded. "Did you see anything at all?"

"Nothing." The man spread his hands in a gesture of helplessness. "The radio dispatcher said no one's found anything along Highway 191—"

"And the police chief just called and said Barry never reached the school," the lawyer interjected. "He and Debbie must've tried for the ranch. That means they've gotta be somewhere between here and the main road." Mr. Hanson started walking in the direction of the emergency vehicle. "We'd better get to work."

"Take this." Ned drew a walkie-talkie from his coat pocket and handed it to Mr. Hanson. "We'll monitor you from the truck. If you find anything, call."

"You'll be the first to know, trust me," the lawyer smiled, then he paused. "They will be OK, won't they?"

Ned nodded. "We'll find them, Tyler. They'll be home in time for lunch."

Mr. Hanson waved weakly and then hurried to lend a hand to the emergency personnel off-loading the snowmobiles. They worked quickly.

Tyler Hanson had a strange feeling in the pit of

his stomach that time might not be on their side. They had to find Barry and Debbie soon. Very soon.

* * * * *

The air in the dark confines of the buried truck grew heavy. Debbie found herself gasping after the slightest exertion. Barry's breathing was steady. He hadn't moved for more than an hour.

"Don't panic!" the girl ordered, trying to convince herself that there was still hope. She lifted the flashlight and shone it around the dark truck bed. "We just need air. That's all. Lots of it up above our heads, so all I've got to do is figure out a way of getting some of it down here. Simple." She closed her eyes. "Not so simple. The passageway is clogged and I can't shove another pipe through the snow. Tried that. Packed too hard."

She rested her head against the cab frame. "The snow has had two days to settle. Then the blower presented us with a fresh load. Who knows how high the new drift is. At least *it* wouldn't be packed hard."

Debbie's chest heaved as her lungs searched for breathable air. She continued to shine the flashlight around the truck bed, not sure of what she was looking for. The beam slipped past the grocery bags, one only half full now. It passed the piles of feed and a collection of leather straps that Barry and Joey were to use to mend some aging harness.

Finally it came to rest on a bundle of smaller PVC pipes, wrapped tightly together with lengths of string. She studied the bundle for a long moment, her mind fighting growing dizziness.

"Pipe. Small pipe." Debbie's head tilted slightly as she continued to gasp for air. "Can't push it through the packed snow. Too hard."

Her eyes closed. "Oh, God, help me. Don't know what to do. Snow's too hard all around. Can't push it through—"

She blinked. "New snow isn't packed. Blower snow's only an hour old." She reached forward, steadying herself with her outstretched hand. "Snow in passageway is new snow. Not packed."

Beads of sweat glistened across the girl's forehead as she crawled along the dark truck bed. "Maybe I can push the smaller pipe up through the big pipe. Maybe I can make a new air passage."

Her hands fumbled with the string that tied the bundles of plastic tubing. "Gotta stay awake. Gotta get some air. Gotta save us."

With her world beginning to spin faster and faster, the girl gathered several of the lengths of pipe. She found the couplings in a nearby box, the same type of couplings Barry had used to join the larger pipes.

Debbie's hands trembled as she twisted the first two lengths together. Her head was pounding now, her brain beginning its one-way journey into oxygen starvation.

"How shall I cap it? Don't have a small piece that

will fit. Snow will get in as I push it through the other pipe." The girl reached up and slipped her woolen ski cap from her head. She held it out in front of her. "There's a cap," she said. Then she began to giggle. "Get it? Cap?"

She started laughing out loud. "That's funny," she chuckled, weaving drunkenly in the darkness. "Need a cap. Got a cap. Right there on my head."

As the oxygen supply continued to dwindle, Debbie wrapped her red cap around the top of the first length of pipe and secured it with a string. She held the plastic tubing out in front of her. "You look like a skinny skier." The girl giggled again, her thoughts fading in and out as she fought the effects of rebreathing her own air. "Up you go, you skinny skier."

The girl pushed the smaller pipe adorned with its woolen cap up into the snow-clogged passageway. The work was not easy. Weaving back and forth, almost losing her balance several times, she managed to attach a third section, then a fourth. By now she was so dizzy that she leaned heavily against the side of the truck bed. She fought waves of nausea.

"Please, Lord," she prayed, her mind dulled with jumbled thoughts and emotions. "Air. Please, air. Gotta get air—"

She fell forward against the pipe and slipped down into a crumpled heap, her face pressed against the open end of the last section of plastic tubing. Her strength was gone, robbed by the carbon dioxide in the buried truck. Before losing consciousness she was able to whisper just two words. "God help."

* * * * *

Wendy looked up from her book and studied the window across the room for a long moment, then returned to her reading.

Seconds later she looked up again. "I heard something," she said.

Merrilee, who was sitting at the dining room table trying to glue a broken saucer back together with some "scientifically improved and space tested" glue, tilted her head slightly. "Just the wind," she yawned.

Wendy shrugged and turned the page. Suddenly they both heard a noise—far away. It sounded like a motor running at high speed. First it would whine, then sputter as if working hard, then run smoothly again.

The two jumped to their feet and hurried up the stairs. They reached the second-floor bedroom window at the same time.

Something was out there all right, and it was coming closer.

Then they saw it—a snowmobile blasting through the drifts on the logging trail beyond the grove of trees that guarded the last bend in the road.

"We're SAVED!" Wendy shouted as she flung open the window. "No more dark nights, with the wind howling like a mad wolf. No more hard floor to sleep on. And—" she closed her eyes savoring the moment, "no more *baked beans!*"

Merrilee grinned broadly as she recognized the passenger on the snowmobile speeding into the yard. "Hurrah for John! My hero!"

Wendy blinked. "And hurrah for whoever's driving. Hey. Didn't any of my family come to save me? Humph. Probably too busy with important things like brushing their teeth or clipping their toenails."

Merrilee laughed as she waved to her husband. "Now, now. Don't be upset. There's only room for two on the snowmobile. Besides, I wouldn't mind if Pueblo the dog came to save us. Just get me back to some place where I can take a shower and sleep on something soft."

Wendy nodded. "You're right. They're probably planning a welcome home party for us as we speak."

The vehicle stopped by the snow-blocked front porch and the driver switched off the engine.

"Hello up there," John called. "You guys all right?"

"A little sunburned, but surviving," Wendy responded cheerfully. "How's everything at the Station?"

A shadow crossed the man's face. "Not too good, I'm afraid. Barry and Debbie never made it back. We don't know where they are. People are out looking for them right now."

"Never made it back?" Merrilee gasped. "You mean—"

"Yeah. Storm got 'em somewhere between Bozeman and the ranch. We believe they got as far as the turnoff, but the road crews haven't found the truck yet. Mr. Hanson and Joey are out searching the stretch between the Station and 191."

Wendy's hands trembled slightly. "Oh, Merrilee. I'm sorry I said what I did about my family not coming to rescue me. Debbie's in real danger and I—"

"It's OK, Wendy," the woman comforted. "You didn't know."

John unstrapped a snowshoe from his back and attached it to his foot. "By the way, this is Doug. He's an emergency medical technician out of Bozeman. Works for the rescue squad. He'll check the two of you out and then drive us, one at a time, back to the Station. Wendy, you'll go first, OK?"

"OK," the girl nodded, then paused. "How's my dad doing, with Debbie missing and all?"

John shook his head. "Let's just say they'd better find her today, and she'd better be safe. It's pretty rough on him." The man smiled gently. "He said to tell you that he loves you very much and for you to pray harder than you've ever prayed before."

Wendy nodded. "Thanks, Mr. Dawson." Turning to Merrilee she said softly, "Will you pray with me? I'm scared."

The two knelt by the window and Wendy closed her eyes tightly. "Our Father in heaven," she whispered, "protect my sister. Keep her safe until someone finds her and Barry. Please, God. I love her. She's my sister and I don't want anything bad to happen to her. Please. Help my dad and Joey find her very, very soon. In Jesus' name, amen."

Merrilee whispered her own "amen" then encircled the youngster in her arms. "God knows where she is. They'll find her. You'll see."

Mr. Dawson studied the two kneeling forms in the upstairs window. After a long moment he called out, "Let's hurry back to the Station so we can welcome Debbie home, OK?"

The girl tried to smile through the fear gripping her young heart. "We'll dig a path from the porch to the snowmobile," she said. "It's pretty deep down there."

Mr. Dawson thrust his loose snowshoe into the drift. It disappeared completely. "Do tell. We've got our work cut out for us. Let's get busy."

Doug and his passenger carefully began to scoop out the snow beside their vehicle as Wendy and Merrilee hurried downstairs. Opening the front door, they started digging away at the drifts that had shut them from the outside world. Wendy worked feverishly as if her actions would somehow assist in the search for her dark-haired missing sister.

* * * * *

Mr. Hanson slowly guided his snowmobile along the snow-blanketed road. The blower had done its work well, blasting a wide path over the old route

141

that connected Shadow Creek Ranch with the main highway three miles to the west.

Joey straddled the machine's back, his feet firmly planted on the runners, fingers gripping his companion's shoulders as he strained to see over the lip of the snow into the drifts that spread out on each side of the road.

Close behind, eyes scanning to the left and right, Don Hixon and Marie Holland strained to catch any sign of the missing vehicle or its young driver and passenger.

"This isn't good," Marie sighed. "They've been out here almost 48 hours. I've seen victims lose their lives in a lot less time."

"I know what you mean," her partner nodded. "Remember last year when we found that couple up in Maudlow? Frozen solid in their car. They'd broken down while out joyriding in a storm. They had moved into the state from Florida and had no idea what cold was. If they'd just taken a few precautions they'd be alive today."

Marie nodded somberly. "These are natives, or at least Barry is. Hope they were better prepared. I wouldn't want to be the one to tell that man up there his daughter won't be coming home for supper— ever."

"You're right. But after two days in a blizzard, I don't hold out much hope. We'd better be prepared for the worst."

The vehicle crept forward as all eyes searched

the roadsides and embankments.

Mr. Hanson twisted the grip on the handle bars and brought the snowmobile to a stop. He reached down and turned the key, allowing the engine to sputter to silence.

He sat heavily on the narrow seat, shoulders sagging. "You see anything, Joey?" he asked.

"Not yet," the lad responded, trying to keep his words hopeful. "We're almost to the main road again, aren't we?"

"Yeah. It's about a quarter mile away. Thought we'd see if we could hear anything."

The lawyer signaled for Don to shut off his truck's motor. The countryside became still as the second engine quieted.

Storm Castle Rock loomed overhead, its proud face of granite bearded with snow. Scattered growths of pine trees thrust green arms out into the morning light, giving the mountain a ragged, disheveled look.

In desperation, Mr. Hanson turned and gazed up at the rocks jutting high into the blue sky overhead. "What did you see?" he pleaded. "Tell me! Did they come this way? Did you notice them? Please tell me."

Joey listened as his friend's voice echoed and re-echoed along the frozen surfaces of the mountainside and across the low, small meadows. "Somebody tell me," the man begged, his voice strained with agony. "Where are they? Where's my little Debbie?"

The boy's eyes filled with tears as his companion's words tore at his heart. He'd never had a father. He'd never known what father love was like. Now, on this narrow, valley road, he was beginning to understand the depth of feeling that a parent has for a child. He'd caught a glimpse of it last spring, when Wendy's horse had come back to the ranch without her. Now the man, his friend, his best friend, was breaking under the weight of another fearful time.

All the words and sermons he'd heard about how God was the Father of everyone on earth were beginning to make sense. Mr. Hanson was demonstrating, on a smaller scale, just how filled with anguish earth's heavenly Father must be as He searches for His children lost in the blizzard of sin.

Joey saw the man fall to his knees, eyes lifted heavenward. "Please," the man pleaded. "We've searched the whole way. They've *got* to be here. They've just got—"

Mr. Hanson paused, studying the tree branches by the side of the road. Joey followed his gaze and noticed several limbs had been snapped in two, as if something heavy had been thrown against them.

The lawyer stumbled to his feet and walked slowly to the edge of the road. Other tree limbs had been broken, all in the same direction. Joey and his companion scrambled up the wall of white snow that bordered the roadway. Don and Marie quickly joined them.

From the top of the bank, the four searchers gazed down into a narrow gully. They recognized that the blower had sprayed snow in this direction as it passed by. But what was most curious was the pattern of destruction through the trees. The broken, twisted limbs and branches pointed like lifeless fingers at an open patch of snow. This was a spot where Joey and Mr. Hanson knew a creek flowed during the summer.

All at once, the man's hand rose trembling and stretched out in front of him. "Look," he whispered.

The others strained to see what their companion was gazing at. There, half hidden in the snow, was a tiny patch of red. Mr. Hanson's voice was hoarse as he spoke. "Debbie . . . Debbie was wearing a red cap when she left. I gave it to her last Christmas."

Don placed his hand on the lawyer's shoulder. "Why don't you let us take care of this, OK?" he said slowly. "You can wait up here on the road."

"NO!" Mr. Hanson said firmly. "She's my daughter. I'll bring her up."

Joey felt sick to his stomach. His hands shook as he helped his friend strap on a pair of snowshoes. Don and Marie ran to the truck and grabbed their own set and hurried back to the side of the road.

Wordlessly, the lawyer eased himself over the lip of the drifts and made his way down into the narrow gully. After what seemed like forever, he reached the spot where the little patch of red jutted from the snow.

"Oh, Debbie," the man whispered. "I'm sorry. I'm so sorry."

He knelt and touched the woolen fibers, totally expecting to feel his beautiful daughter's lifeless head underneath.

Joey saw the man's hand stop, then feel around the cap. The lawyer stood and shouted, "It's attached to some sort of tube. It's Debbie's cap, all right, but how did it get here—"

Mr. Hanson stiffened. "Oh, dear God! It's an air passage. That's what it is." He fell to his knees as Don approached and Marie grabbed the walkie-talkie from her pocket. "It's an air passage from below," the lawyer shouted. "The truck. It's buried. That's what happened. The truck came off the road and broke all those limbs and landed down here. Then the snows covered it up. Hurry! They're buried under here. They may still be alive. HURRY!"

Joey ran to the emergency vehicle and collected an armload of shovels. Moving quickly, he waded through the drifts, his feet sinking deep into the powder as he half fell, half slid down the embankment. Eager hands clutched the tools and began working, following the pipe into the snow.

Mr. Hanson ripped the cap from the tube and shouted down into its dark throat. "DEBBIE! BARRY! WE'RE COMING. WE'RE COMING! HANG ON! JUST HANG ON!"

* * * * *

Wendy saw Grandpa Hanson running for the farm truck as she and the driver of the snowmobile sped down the long driveway toward the Station. Something was up. She knew it.

"Take me to my grandfather, there," she shouted over the din of the conveyance. The driver nodded and altered course to reach the snow-encased farm truck parked by the area the blower had cleared in front of the Station.

Ned was standing nearby, ear pressed against a walkie-talkie. Wendy saw him shake his head, then motion for his companion to follow him.

"What's going on?" the girl called as the snowmobile came to a halt by the porch.

"They think they've found where Barry's truck is," the old man shouted, his hand pulling blocks of snow from his vehicle. " 'Bout a quarter mile from the main road. It's buried."

Wendy gasped. "Buried? Under the snow?"

"Yup." Grandpa Hanson reached out and hugged his youngest granddaughter. "How you doin', Wendy? Glad to see you made it through all right. We kinda figured you would."

"Merrilee and I did fine, once we got some wood for the stove. Have they talked to Debbie?"

"No. There's only an air passage up to the surface, but thank God for that."

Ned and the others added their energies to the task at hand and slowly the old farm truck emerged from the drift. "We've got some more shovels in the

147

blower. We can all help," Ned encouraged. "I've called Bozeman. They're sending a chopper down to Castle Rock. That's where they found the truck. Those two just might need some medical attention when we dig 'em out. Better safe than sorry."

Grandpa Hanson jumped into the farm vehicle and fired up the engine. Wendy and Mr. Krueger scrambled in and together they sped back up the driveway, followed by the ponderous highway blower.

Doug spun his snowmobile round and began his journey back up the mountain toward Merrilee. There were still two people to retrieve from the old homestead.

By the time Wendy and the others arrived at the accident site, Joey, Mr. Hanson, and the emergency crew had just about reached the top of the buried truck. They'd followed the pipe, which could be seen clearly embedded in the wall of snow.

"Daddy!" Wendy called from the road as she shouldered a shovel and started down the embank-ment.

Mr. Hanson looked up and waved. "Hi, honey. One down, two to go," he called. "I'm so glad to see you." He waded through the drifts and engulfed his daughter in a firm hug. "Are you OK?"

"I'm fine, Daddy," Wendy smiled bravely. "Really. Don't worry about me. Let's just get Debbie and Barry out of there."

The two hurried to the site and began digging,

lifting heavy loads of snow as down, down, down they burrowed.

Every so often, Mr. Hanson would stop and hurry to the pipe, removing a section as it was freed and calling down into the darkness of the plastic tubing. "Debbie? Barry? Can you hear me?"

He'd listen, his ear pressed against the opening, then shake his head to the others and everyone would continue digging. Arms and backs ached, but no one complained. The work they were doing was far too important to worry about hurting muscles.

Below, in the darkness of the snow-covered truck bed, a young girl lay unmoving, her face illuminated by the dimming glow of the flashlight she'd dropped as consciousness had faded. Her face was pressed against the round, hard end of the tube, mouth open, eyes closed. Nearby, Barry lay still on his pile of blankets. There was no sound.

"Debbie? Debbie?" High, filtered words rattled in the pipe. They sounded miles away—miles and miles, like the cry of a hawk in some distant valley. The finger on Debbie's left hand twitched slightly.

"Debbie? Can you hear me?"

The girl's eyes fluttered almost imperceptibly as a few flakes of snow struck her face. The feverish work overhead had loosened some of the powder and it had fallen from the larger pipe resting inches from her nose.

"Barry? Can you hear me? Can you answer?"

That voice. It sounded familiar.

"Daddy?" the girl whispered in the darkness. "Daddy?"

"If you can hear me, say something. Anything." The voice was pleading, almost like someone crying and talking at the same time.

"Daddy?" Debbie strained to speak, but her throat was dry, unresponsive. Slowly her hand moved from her side and paused just above her cheek. With all the strength she could muster, she bumped her fingers against the pipe.

Mr. Hanson froze, his eyes opening wide. "Wait!" he ordered. The digging stopped.

"Debbie? Barry? Can you hear me? Did you move the air passage? I felt it move."

The girl's hand rose again and struck the plastic casing by her face. Mr. Hanson felt the jolt. "SOMEONE'S ALIVE DOWN THERE!" he shouted, tears mingling with the cold sweat on his face. "I felt the pipe move. I felt it move twice!" He paused. "There. It bumped again. Someone is hitting the pipe."

"WE'RE COMING!" he shouted into the mouth of the air passage. "HANG ON. WE'RE COMING!"

The workers began digging with renewed determination. There was hope in each heart. Somebody was alive in the buried truck. If one was still breathing, maybe both were.

Debbie's eyes blinked open. She could now hear strange sounds overhead—scraping, bumping, voices, beautiful voices calling her name.

Her lungs burned as she drew in a deep breath.

Cold, fresh air was flowing from the pipe by her face—oxygen, life-giving oxygen.

She tried to move but felt terribly dizzy. Slowly, painfully, she drew in breath after breath, feeling warmth return to her fingers and toes, her arms, legs, and chest.

Pressing her mouth against the pipe she called out in a voice growing in strength. "Daddy. We're here. We're here in the truck."

The man heard the call and cradled the mouth of the pipe in his trembling hands. "Debbie? Did you say something?" He held his breath as the others gathered around.

"Help us," he heard a weak voice call from somewhere far below. "Help us, Daddy."

The lawyer sank to his knees, crying, tears streaming down his face. "Thank You, God. Oh, thank You." He moved to the pipe. "Is Barry OK? Is he alive?"

Debbie nodded sluggishly. "He's hurt. But I think he's still alive. Yes. I can hear him breathing. Hurry, Daddy. Hurry and save us."

"THEY'RE BOTH ALIVE!" the man cried out, grabbing each worker, one after another. "They're both alive, but we must hurry. Barry's hurt and Debbie sounds very weak." He grabbed his shovel and began digging, almost out of control. "Hurry, everybody, hurry. My little girl is alive. SHE'S ALIVE!"

High overhead, a helicopter thundered into view.

It passed over the top of Castle Rock like a dark bird. The pulsating sound of its rotors rushed down the cliffs and settled on the little valley below. The pilot could see activity in a gully by the cleared road. He searched for a place to set down and decided Highway 191, just off to the right, would be best.

With skillful hands he guided his powerful machine and came to rest in a blowing cloud of snow at the turnoff. He'd await further orders there.

CHAPTER 8

WHISPERS

✦ ✦ ✦

Clank. Joey's shovel hit something hard, almost jerking the tool out of his gloved hands.

"Hey," he shouted to the others working all around him. "I think I've got somethin' here."

The workers hurried over to the spot where the boy was kneeling. He pushed aside several handfuls of snow, revealing a shiny expanse of metal. Others dropped to their knees and started digging with their hands, widening the hole and revealing the battered roof of a truck cab.

Mr. Hanson thrust his hand into the snow beside the pipe and felt his fingers break through into open space. Eagerly he pushed aside the last barrier that separated him from his daughter. He dropped onto his stomach to peer into the dark cavity where the driver-side window used to be.

Sunlight filtered into the cab and sent shadowy shafts of light into the dark recesses of the covered bed beyond. He saw a pale, dirt-smudged face and tearful eyes staring back at him.

"Debbie?" he said softly. "I love you."

The girl started to cry as her father pushed his body through the opening and slid into the cab. "Do you know that? I love you." He repeated his gentle greeting as he crawled to where his daughter lay crumpled just inside the dimly lit bed.

Debbie wrapped her arms around the man and held him close for a long, long moment. They wept silently together in the confines of the truck, lost in the unspeakable joy of being reunited after two days of bottomless fear.

Debbie kissed her father's face and smiled into his eyes. "It's not your fault, Daddy," she said, realizing the burden her father carried when anything bad happened to his precious daughters.

The man smiled. "Have I ever told you how much you mean to me?"

Debbie nodded. "That's what kept me going," she whispered. "I knew you'd come and save us. I just knew it."

Mr. Hanson touched his daughter's cheek with the back of his fingers. "If anything had happened to you—anything—"

"I'm OK, Daddy," she said quietly. "But we gotta

help Barry. He's hurt pretty badly."

The lawyer moved to the wrangler's side. "How did it happen?"

"He slammed into the steering wheel," the girl said. "I think something's broken inside—ribs and stuff."

"Can you get around OK?" the man asked.

"I think so."

The two slowly made their way into the cab, then out into the bright, cold sunlight. A cheer arose from those gathered about the small opening as Debbie emerged, shielding her eyes from the brightness.

Gentle hands guided her up to the road, where she was placed on a stretcher. An emergency medical technician began asking her questions and carefully examining her, looking for any signs of hidden injuries.

"I'm OK. Really," she said. "Just help my friend in the truck. He's hurt."

Once it was determined that Debbie was in no immediate danger, all hands joined in the effort to free the unconscious wrangler still buried in the wreck.

Mr. and Mrs. Gordon, summoned from Bozeman, arrived just in time to see their son lifted carefully out of the entombed vehicle and strapped to an air-transport stretcher.

The helicopter rose over the trees and hovered above the accident site. A crewman lowered a long cable, which was quickly grabbed by a member of the rescue squad below. Skillfully they secured the injured man's stretcher to the cable. Everyone held their breath as Barry's warmly wrapped form floated heavenward and was guided in through the open door of the noisy aircraft. With a wave, the pilot of the helicopter adjusted his control yokes and the machine bowed forward and sped away. A medical trauma team at the city hospital had been alerted and were standing by, waiting for their patient to arrive.

As Debbie sat watching the aircraft disappear from view, she felt someone tap her on the shoulder. Turning, she gazed into the eyes of her father. "Better put this on," he said, handing her a red ski cap. "Don't want you to catch cold."

The girl chuckled wearily and held the woolen hat out in front of her. "One of the best Christmas presents I ever received," she said. "Now I just need some gloves to match."

"Oh, brother," Wendy groaned, slipping up beside her father. "Same ol' Debbie. Two days in a deep-freezer and she's still worried about color coordination."

"Hey, Wendy," the older girl smiled, "did you make it through the storm OK?"

"Piece of cake—or should I say, piece of baked beans."

"Huh?"

The younger girl laughed. "I'll tell you about it later, after the doctor finishes transplanting all your organs or whatever he's going to do to you." She paused. "I'm glad you're all right. I was worried."

Debbie blinked. "You? Worried about me? Boy, that storm must've rattled your brains or something."

Wendy frowned. "You're my sister and I . . . I . . . I love you."

Mr. Hanson grinned and ruffled his youngest daughter's hair. "Keep that thought for the next 50 years."

The girl giggled. "Ask Joey how *he* survived the storm. Grandpa said he had to eat horse food."

"It weren't too bad," the boy called from nearby, where he was helping the rescue squad load the snowmobile onto their truck. " 'Cept, now, every time I see a straight stretch of road I have this irresistible urge to gallop."

Debbie laughed. "Sounds like you guys had a tough time, too."

"Nah," Wendy said, waving her hand. "It was nothin'."

As the rescue squad gently helped the dark-haired girl into their vehicle for the drive to the hospital, Wendy leaned forward and asked, "Hey, Debbie. When you were buried down there, where'd you go to the bathroom?"

Mr. Hanson pulled his youngest daughter away from the truck. "Wendy! Leave your poor sister alone. She's trying to recover."

Debbie laughed a tired laugh. "I'll never tell," she teased.

The lawyer reached up and touched his daughter's hand. "We'll be at the hospital just as soon as we can get there. We're going to pick up Grandma and Lizzy. Oh, and Samantha told me on the radio to tell you that if you want, she can bring Pueblo. She says he's very worried about you."

The truck pulled away as Debbie grinned and waved. "I love you guys," she called. "Hurry and come take me home."

The group returned her wave and stood in the empty roadway for a long time, listening to the grind of gears and race of the distant motor.

Slowly the tired rescuers walked back to the old farm truck—all, that is, except Mr. Hanson.

Quietly he slipped from the others and stood looking down into the gully. Packed snow circled a small opening in the drifts where portions of Barry's truck jutted from the white, icy blanket. The man closed his eyes. "Thank You, God," he whispered. "Thank You for keeping Your hand over my precious little girl and Wrangler Barry." He paused. "Lord, make me stronger than I am. Build my faith so that when troubles come, I'll lean more on You and less on fear. Forgive my untrusting heart. Please, Lord. Amen."

The man felt a touch on his shoulder as Grandpa Hanson joined him by the edge of the road. "Faith's a funny thing, Tyler," the old man said softly. "Right when you need it most, it seems to be the weakest. That's when you have to listen, listen for God's whispers."

"Even in a blizzard?"

"Especially then," the older man nodded. "Joey, Wendy, Debbie, you, me—I'm sure we all heard God speak to us in our own ways during the past 48 hours." Grandpa Hanson turned. "I think we should talk about it in the days and weeks to come. Whatta ya say, Tyler?"

The lawyer nodded. "I thought my heart would break, Dad. I didn't think I'd make it through . . . not knowing."

"That's what sin does," Grandpa Hanson continued. "It breaks good people's hearts. But God's an expert at picking up the pieces and bringing confidence back into our lives. We can't live in fear of tomorrow. We have to have faith that no matter what tomorrow brings, God will be by our side, ready and willing to help us get through our times of greatest fear."

"You're right," Mr. Hanson sighed. "I need to learn to listen for the whispers. I guess my fear got in the way—sorta blocked everything else out."

The old man smiled. "Come on, one and only son of mine. Let's get back to the Station and round everybody up. We gotta head into town. Our little Debbie's been separated from us long enough."

The two men hurried to the farm truck and brought the engine to life. As the vehicle roared up the valley toward the distant ranch, silence once again settled over the gully. Storm Castle Rock loomed overhead, its stone face indifferent to what had happened at its feet.

But the inhabitants of Shadow Creek Ranch had learned, once again, that there's a Presence beyond the towering mountains, past the dark line of clouds, above the rumble of thunder.

Up there, where peace reigns, is a God who speaks to all His children, sometimes in words loud and clear. And sometimes in whispers carried by the wind.

HEART
of the Warrior

Charles Mills

Dedication

To my wife, Dorinda,
in whose heart
I find my greatest joy.

Contents

CHAPTER 1

Racing the Wind

Plenty?" The old man's voice carried across the bright, green-carpeted prairie as he strained to catch sight of any movement in the surrounding grassy fields.

"Plenty! This is no time to play games with me. Look to the south. The bus is coming. Don't you see it?"

Only the soft whisper of summer breezes echoed a response to the man's question.

"You'll like it in the mountains," he urged through wrinkled, age-worn hands cupped about his lips. "We might even see a bear. Or maybe a mountain lion. I've heard them often in the night."

He listened. There was no reply except the wind and the occasional thin-whistle call of a circling swainson's hawk.

"Come on, Plenty. You'll meet some very nice people, too. They're kind and they treat me with respect. Not like the others."

A large, sun-faded bus, pulling a tail of dust across

the flatlands, appeared over a small rise a quarter mile away. It began to slow when the driver spotted the old man waiting beside the road, battered suitcases and carefully rolled bundles at his feet.

"PLENTY! You must come now! The bus has arrived. It will not wait for you."

With a grind of gears and squeak of brakes, the vehicle lurched to a stop. The door swung open, revealing a smiling face perched high behind the steering wheel.

"Well, hello, Red Stone," the driver called with a friendly laugh. "You look like you've lost something."

The passenger-to-be nodded and pointed toward the prairie. "It's my great-granddaughter. Disappeared again. Can't find her."

"You mean Plenty?" the driver queried, glancing out across the tall grasses.

"Yes. I'm taking her with me to the mountains this summer. First time." Red Stone lifted a bundle and passed it to waiting hands at the top of the stairs. "At least, I thought I was."

The remainder of the suitcases were quickly stored in the noisy conveyance as the old man called out again and again. Still nothing moved beyond the dusty edges of the arrow-straight road.

"You'd better hop in," the driver urged. "I've got a schedule to keep." He paused. "Tell you what. Maybe this will get her attention." Reaching up, he gave a sharp tug on a chain hanging beside his head.

A sudden blast of air howled through twin horns mounted side by side on the top of the bus. An ear-piercing *blaaaat* screamed across the expanses on every side. The sound reverberated as it rolled through shallow gullies and surged over small rises in the treeless countryside.

By now, all eyes in the bus were searching the distant folds of the earth for any sign of the missing girl.

Suddenly someone called out, "There. To the west. I see something!" Passengers scurried from their seats and pressed sun-tanned faces against the cool glass that lined the side of the bus.

"Yes. I see her!" another shouted. "She's running . . . very fast." Mouths dropped open as one by one the group of travelers caught sight of a lone figure racing across the green carpet of prairie. The form seemed to flow as though it had no contact with the land. Tirelessly it ran northward, parallel to the road.

"Come on!" the driver shouted to the old man still waiting at the base of the steps. "We'll catch her up ahead."

Red Stone grabbed hold of the step rail as the bus lurched forward. He climbed hand over hand, fighting the power of the accelerating vehicle. Passengers cheered, and dust swirled behind rumbling tires.

The old man fought his way to an empty seat and grinned over at the driver. "You won't catch her," he said. "Nothing has ever been invented by a White man or Indian that can keep up with my Plenty."

The man at the wheel laughed as he threw his vibrating bus into high gear.

"She's like the wind," Red Stone continued.

Admiration filled his voice as he studied the distant figure that moved with unrestrained energy over the grasslands. "And you should see her shoot an arrow. State archery champion, you know. Beat out every White man who entered. The whole Crow tribe is proud of her."

"I remember," the driver nodded, holding tightly onto the steering wheel. His body swayed with the movement of the bus. "Our leaders say she'd make a fine warrior, if it were a hundred and fifty years ago, and if she was a boy." The man frowned. "'Course, if it were a hundred and fifty years ago, we wouldn't be stuck on this reservation and warriors could prove themselves in the hunt instead of in some state archery contest."

Red Stone shook his head. "Some things always remain the same," he called above the whine of the gears. "A true Crow Indian knows what he is inside. No government can take that away."

"You're dreaming again, Red Stone," the driver smiled. "But you're an old man. That's your privilege."

Passengers slid open their windows and leaned out into the slipstream of air. "Run, Plenty, run!" they shouted, their eyes watering from the wind in their faces. "Fly like the wind! FLY LIKE THE WIND!"

Plenty smiled to herself. She could see the bus racing along the ribbon of dirt and stone. She could see the arms waving, urging her on, faster and faster.

A narrow ditch flowed in her direction. She lengthened just one stride and slipped over it as easily as a hawk leaps a canyon.

The girl lowered her head a little and sped on, her legs pumping tirelessly, rhythmically, carrying her over the fields with a grace honed by many such runs, in years of racing the winds of southern Montana.

This is home, the girl told herself as a long-eared jackrabbit popped from his hole and glanced in her direction. Out there, beyond the boundaries of the reservation, were people who pointed and whispered, laughed, and turned their faces. But here by the banks of the Bighorn, at the foot of the Rosebud Mountains, along the endless expanses of prairie where fascinating creatures lived and the wind whistled encouragement to 14-year-old girls with hopes no one knew or understood, this was where her heart felt at home. Here she could run and leave the past far behind.

Plenty lifted her arms until they floated wing-like at her side. Oh, if she could only fly like the bird her people were named after. If only she could catch the currents of air racing up the distant mountain sides, she'd hover for hours like the eagle and the osprey. She'd call out her name and no one would laugh. For in the sky any name was beautiful.

But she had no wings, only arms. She couldn't fly, but she could run. She could run faster and faster until the world was a blur, and the only sound she could hear was the pounding of her own heart.

The girl smiled at the thought of the bus racing along beside her. She knew her great-grandfather was sitting inside the bus, watching. He understood why she raced along the prairie. He was wise. He knew secret things, things about the animals and about the earth, and about her.

Yes, she would go to the mountains with him, because he was old, and old was special to her people.

Plenty altered her course and began moving in a direction that would intercept the bus before it crossed the dry stream bed up ahead. She would do it for Great-grandfather. But her heart would stay on the prairie.

* * *

Five-year-old Samantha sat unmoving, staring at her dog, Pueblo. The animal, a mixture of most any canine you'd happen to meet, sat as still as a rock, staring at Samantha. They faced each other on the broad porch of the Station, their ranch home tucked in a beautiful valley amid the folds of the Gallatin National Forest.

The afternoon sun felt warm on their faces. In the bushes that surrounded the old, two-story, broad-beamed hotel, birds sang territorial songs and chased intruders away with chirps and squawks understood only by their own kind.

The hard winter was fast becoming a memory in the minds of those who lived on Shadow Creek Ranch. Not long ago, spring had finally arrived, loosening the icy grip the snow season had held on the land.

Flowers had bloomed with uncommon vigor as if believing their very presence would assure that no more storms would sweep down from the northwest and smother the mountains under deep blankets of white.

14

Now it was summer, and with it would come the guests everyone on the ranch had been eagerly awaiting and discussing.

A tan, muscular boy walked across the footbridge spanning the creek and made his way to the steps that led up to the porch. He paused when he saw his little dark-skinned, adopted sister sitting statue-like before her furry pet.

"Hi, Joey," the girl whispered, not moving her lips.

The young horse wrangler sat down heavily on the top stair and leaned against one of the thick posts that supported the second-floor deck.

"What are you doing?" the just-turned-17-year-old asked.

Samantha didn't move a muscle. "I'm training Pueblo," she whispered.

Joey nodded thoughtfully. "Training him to do what?"

"To stay," the little girl answered.

"Is it working?" Joey asked, a grin playing at the corners of his mouth.

"Oh, yes," Samantha said. "I just tell him to stay and then I sit really still like this. He doesn't move an inch as long as I stare at him."

Joey scratched his head. "But isn't the whole idea of making a dog stay so you can go somewhere and it won't follow?"

The little girl was silent for a long moment. "Maybe," she said quietly.

"Then aren't you training the dog just to stare at

you like some kinda statue?"

Samantha's head tilted slightly to one side. Pueblo's head tilted slightly in the same direction.

Samantha sighed. The dog sighed.

"I'm not doing this right," the little girl moaned.

Joey burst out laughing. "Oh, but you're teaching Pueblo something really neat."

"I am?"

"Sure, you're teaching him to play follow the leader. Not too many dogs know how to do that." Joey smiled at his companion. "Why, I'll bet if you go out to the pasture and run around the cottonwoods, that dog would follow you every step of the way."

"He would?" Samantha gasped. "Hey, that's pretty good, isn't it? I'm teaching my dog to play follow the leader." She jumped to her feet. Pueblo did the same. "Did you see that?" the girl squealed in glee. "I've taught Pueblo pretty good, don't you think?"

"Sure do," Joey said as he rose and walked to the front door. "You're the best dog teacher in Montana."

Samantha fairly burst with excitement. "Watch this," she said. Facing the dog she commanded, "Pueblo, follow me!"

The youngster raced down the steps and headed for the footbridge. Pueblo barked enthusiastically and followed at his young owner's heels.

"Good dog, good dog!" Joey heard Samantha call. "Just wait till I show Wendy and Debbie. They'll be amazed!"

The boy chuckled to himself and glanced up toward the towering mountains that ringed the ranch. Yes, summer had definitely arrived and he wasn't sorry. Not one bit.

"What's all the commotion about?" a voice called from the balcony just over the Station's front door. Joey saw Mr. Hanson step from his office on the second floor, file folder in hand.

"Samantha is teaching Pueblo to follow her everywhere she goes," Joey announced. He stuck his head through the kitchen door and filled his nostrils with the odor of freshly baked bread.

"Doesn't that mutt kinda do that anyway?" the man called from above.

"Yeah, but before, he didn't know he was supposed to," Joey laughed as he headed for the den. "Have you seen Grandpa Hanson?"

The man paused before reentering his office, from where he was constantly connected by fax and phone lines to his company headquarters in New York City. "He went into Bozeman a couple hours ago to pick up Red Stone at the bus station. Should be back around supper. Whatcha need?"

Joey sighed. "I can't find those new saddle blankets—you know, the fancy ones we ordered from Utah."

The man's face appeared above the railing. "What do I know from saddle blankets? I'm a lawyer. I work with computers. They don't leave stuff lying around to step in. I kinda like that."

Joey laughed. "Maybe Wendy's got 'em."

"Now there's a possibility," Mr. Hanson nodded. "Do try to leave her in one piece if she is involved in this latest mystery. She's my daughter and I love her."

Joey waved and headed for the door. "Not to fear, Mr. H. Me and Wendy are best of friends."

"That'll be the day," the lawyer chuckled as he entered his large work room and settled once again before the screen of his powerful computer.

"Wendy?" Joey called, his eyes searching the distant pasture. He saw a horse and rider emerge from behind a stand of trees at the far end of the orchard. "Hey, Wendy. I want to talk to you."

The rider waved and steered her mount down the long driveway that led from the old logging road half a mile away to the Station.

As the pair drew closer, Joey blinked. The blanket tucked neatly between the saddle and the smooth, muscular back of the animal looked strangely familiar. It also looked brand-new.

"I don't believe it," Joey said angrily when Wendy reigned her horse to a stop beside him. "You took one of the new blankets right out of the tack house without even asking me. Those are supposed to be for the mares arriving tomorrow, part of our summer herd."

"So? I just tried it out for you," the girl shrugged. "Big deal."

Joey bit his tongue.

"Besides," Wendy continued, "Early really, really likes this blanket. He says it feels so soft on his back, like velvet."

"Listen, Miss Soft-Like-Velvet," Joey retorted, "you can tell this pitiful excuse for a horse that her old blanket is still plenty good enough. If she has a problem with that, I'll find a nice, big piece of *sandpaper* for you guys to use from now on. Understand!?"

Wendy lifted her chin. "Good grief, Joey. Who died and left you king of the universe?"

"Wrangler Barry, that's who," the boy responded firmly. "Well, he didn't exactly die, but being buried under 12 feet of snow in his wrecked truck with Debbie for three days ain't exactly what I call living."

Wendy swallowed hard. "That scared 10 years off my life, and when you're only 11, that's a lot."

Joey nodded. "Well, Barry's comin' out soon and I want to have everything ready when he gets here. So get my new blanket off that crazy, do-everything-before-everyone-else-does-it horse of yours and don't make a mess in the barn while you're at it."

"OK, OK!" Wendy scowled as she gave Early a gentle kick and started across the footbridge. "Hey, are you sure Barry can work here this summer?" she asked as Joey fell in beside her. "I mean, doesn't he have to use a cane and stuff? Doctors said it'll be a long time before his insides heal."

Joey shrugged. "He's supposed to take it easy and not do any ridin' or liftin' of heavy stuff, like feed sacks and saddles."

"What else does a wrangler do all day?" the young rider asked.

Joey rolled his eyes. "Give me a break, Wendy Hanson," he groaned. "You know how hard we work to keep the ranch livestock healthy and safe. There're lots of jobs he can do. I'll just make sure he doesn't strain himself. After all, he's still the boss, even if he is in bad shape. You'd be using a cane, too, if you had a steering column jammed into your chest at 50 miles an hour."

"Ouch," the girl responded, with a shudder. "Let's not talk about what happened anymore. Makes me feel creepy inside."

"Fine with me," Joey agreed. "Let's just talk about people who steal new saddle blankets." The two continued through the pasture gate and made their way to the horse barn. It would be hard to forget the pain of what happened when the snows came early, especially after Wrangler Barry arrived. His disability would serve as a constant reminder of the fearful days and agonizing nights they'd all experienced.

* * *

Debbie cringed as the physical therapist lifted the patient's right arm slowly, ever so slowly, until it hovered just above his head. "That's one more inch today," the woman wearing the white smock encouraged. "I knew you could do it."

Barry's face was red from the exertion and his breathing came in quick, painful bursts. Debbie watched a tear form at the corner of her friend's eye and slip down his pale cheek.

"That's more than last week," the therapist said, triumphantly. "I'm proud of you, Barry Gordon." She gently lowered the arm to the wrangler's lap. "We're experiencing real improvement here. We'll have you back roping calves and riding bulls in short order." She scribbled some notations on her clipboard.

"Yeah, right," Barry said without emotion, his eyes closed. He waited for the pain to subside.

Debbie smiled and touched the young man's shoulder. "It *was* higher than last time," she said."

"So after eight weeks of agony I'll be able to raise my hand above my head." Barry slipped his arm into the sling that hung loosely from his neck. "Forgive me if I don't throw a party."

"These things take time," the therapist interjected. "Any improvement is a good sign."

The horseman stood and leaned heavily on the stout, wooden cane that had become his constant companion during the four months since he had left the hospital. "I think it's time I face facts," he said coldly. "I've got a useless leg and a useless arm. Period. I can come in here every week and you can put me through your series of Chinese tortures, but it's not going to change anything." He turned toward the door. "For someone who wants to run a ranch someday, being half a man isn't going to cut it." He glanced at Debbie.

"Mr. Gordon," the therapist called out, her voice a little louder than usual. "You had an accident. The steering column of your truck just about broke you into two pieces. You had severe damage to internal organs, your rib cage was crushed, and vital nerve paths were interrupted. I think you should be happy just to be alive."

"Oh, you do?" Barry spun around and moved

menacingly toward the speaker. "Maybe *you* need to learn something. Alive doesn't mean being able to breathe and blink your eyes." Debbie stepped forward but Barry pushed her back against the file cabinet, causing its collection of bottles to clatter against each other and tumble across the metal shelves. "For your information, I'm not alive. I'm dead. When I wake up in the morning and have to have someone help me get out of bed, I'M DEAD! When I try to write my name, and the letters look like they were scribbled by a 3-year-old, I'M DEAD! And when I see my horses running through the north pasture and I can't go along for the ride, I'm as dead as you can get without someone tossing you into the ground and putting a stone over your head.

"You want to help me? Huh?" The wrangler pressed his body against the therapist, pushing her into the wall. "Then get a gun, put it to the side of my head, and pull the trigger so my brain can be as dead as my body. That would be a real improvement. Do you understand?"

"Stop it!" Debbie screamed. "Stop it, Barry. She's just trying to help. We all are."

The young man backed away as sudden sobs shook his thin, bent frame. "I . . . I can't even dream anymore," he moaned. "There's no future for me. No ranch. No horses. Nothing." He turned and faced Debbie. "No one wants half a man."

Debbie glanced at the therapist, who nodded and quickly slipped from the room. As the door closed, the girl moved slowly to her friend's side and placed her arms around his trembling shoulders. She held him for a long moment until his sobs quieted. Then she lifted his chin and gazed into his eyes. "You listen to me, cowboy," she said softly. "You saved my life that night. Even though you were terribly hurt, you took care of me. You pushed that pipe up through the snow so we could have air to breathe. You were so gentle, so caring. Half of Barry Gordon is a whole lot more than *all* of many guys. Do you hear me?"

The wrangler closed his eyes and a painful sigh escaped his lips. "I . . . I wish I could believe that," he whispered. "I really do."

Debbie sat down on the examining table. "Look. You're moving out to Shadow Creek Ranch so I can keep an eye on you. Joey's been counting the days. Even Wendy said she's willing to tolerate you for another summer." A tiny smile lifted the corners of the young man's mouth. "So the only thing you have to *be* this summer is there, with us, with the family who thinks you're the best wrangler in all of Montana."

Debbie waited as her words filtered through the pain that surrounded her friend like a thick, dark curtain.

Barry nodded. "OK," he said. "Maybe I can at least bug Wendy for a few weeks. That'll be fun."

Debbie grinned. "There, you see? Life *is* worth living after all."

The wrangler stood to his feet. "Man, you give a girl a driver's license and she thinks she's Mother Teresa."

"That's right," Debbie nodded as she helped her companion toward the door. "Someone's gotta take care of all the recovering cowboys of the world. This summer, you're at the top of my list."

The two exited, leaving the room silent except for the drip . . . drip . . . drip of spilled liquids escaping the broken bottles in the metal cabinet by the window.

* * *

Lizzy Pierce and Grandma Hanson were sitting on the front porch peeling potatoes when they heard the sound of an approaching automobile.

"Must be your husband with Red Stone," Lizzy said, looking up toward the road that ran above and beside the stately, white Station. "It'll be nice to have the old Indian up there on Freedom Mountain again. Kids love him, and I like his stories about the history of his people."

With a grind of gears, the farm truck turned and rattled up the valley toward the Station, dust swirling about its old, paint-chipped body.

Grandma squinted, then opened her eyes wide in surprise. "I see *three* people in there," she gasped. "Not two."

"You're right," her companion agreed. "Maybe Red Stone was able to talk his great-granddaughter into spending the summer with him on the mountain."

The women rose, brushed off their aprons, and descended the broad steps just as the truck bounced to a halt in its usual parking spot beneath a tall spruce.

"Hello, ranch-type people," a strong, male voice called from the cab. "We come in peace for all mankind."

Grandma Hanson rolled her eyes. "My husband, the astronaut. Get out of that truck, old man, and introduce us to the young lady sitting beside you."

The three clamored from the vehicle and gathered by the front grill. "Red Stone says he wants to do the honors," Grandpa Hanson announced.

The old Indian cleared his throat. English was not an easy language for him. Never had been. It was a far cry from the guttural, almost German-like sounds of his native Crow.

"This my great-granddaughter," he said proudly. "She come with me to Freedom Mountain. Her name is Plenty Crops Growing, but I just say Plenty."

The young girl with the long black hair and dark eyes lifted her chin. "You heard right. My name is Plenty Crops Growing. So you can laugh if you want."

Red Stone spoke a few quick words in Crow then continued. "My great-granddaughter named by tribal council. Usually uncle or aunt gives name to child at birth. But when Plenty was born, there no close relative, so council give name."

Lizzy reached out her hand. "Hello, Plenty," she said. "We're glad you'll be our neighbor this summer."

Plenty stepped back just a little. "My great-grandfather talked me into coming. I didn't want to. This is the White man's world."

Red Stone spoke sharply again, his words understood only by the girl. Plenty nodded. "Thank you for picking us up at the bus station," she said softly. "We'll be going now."

"Won't you stay for supper?" Grandma Hanson urged. "We've got beans baking in the oven. Fresh bread, too. You're certainly welcome to stay. We'll drive you up to the mountain after the dishes are done."

The girl unconsciously licked her lips. She *was* hungry. The trip from the reservation had taken most of the day. She'd only had an apple and small bag of cashew nuts to eat since leaving her prairie home.

Turning to her great-grandfather, she spoke in Crow. The old man nodded enthusiastically. "We'll stay," the girl announced. "But only until after supper."

"Great!" Grandma Hanson responded happily. "Come, you can help us finish peeling the potatoes while Grandpa Hanson and Red Stone load provisions into the truck."

"I'm not your slave," Plenty said flatly, not moving.

"Oh, heaven's no," the old woman called over her shoulder. "But you are going to be our neighbor. And around here, neighbors help each other." She stopped and turned, a smile lighting her face. "It's the White man's way on Shadow Creek Ranch. You'll get use to it."

Plenty blinked and stared at the woman wearing the colorful apron. "Come on, now," Grandma Hanson encouraged. "We need to hurry. The others will be arriving soon, and on this ranch meals are a big thing. If they're not on the table when they're supposed to be . . . well . . . it's not a pretty sight."

With that she continued toward the front porch. Plenty looked at Red Stone, who just shrugged and ambled off beside Grandpa Hanson.

Lizzy stepped forward, a gentle smile on her face. "I'm from New York, Plenty," she said. "It took me a little while to adjust to Shadow Creek Ranch, too. Mrs. Hanson's right. You'll get used to it."

Plenty studied the woman thoughtfully. "You don't mind that I'm an Indian?" she asked.

Lizzy shrugged. "Not if you don't mind that I'm from East Village."

The girl looked out over the pasture and to the mountains beyond. Late afternoon shadows lay long across the forests and meadows. The ringing melody of Shadow Creek filtered through the songs of birds and buzz of unseen insects. "It's not like the prairie," she said softly.

"Tell me about your home," Lizzy invited, slipping her hand around Plenty's arm and urging her toward the Station.

The young Indian brushed long strands of black hair from her eyes. "I, uh . . . I live in Pryor, in a little trailer with my mom and dad. He works for the coal company."

As the two made their way across the green lawn, Red Stone turned and looked over his shoulder. He smiled, then continued in the direction of the shed that stood at the back of the big way station.

* * *

27

As predicted, activity about the ranch increased considerably as suppertime approached. First, Debbie and Wrangler Barry arrived amid much tooting of horns and shouts of welcome. The cowboy found himself the center of attention, with Grandpa and Grandma Hanson, their lawyer son Tyler, and Lizzy making over him like a long-lost relative.

Even Red Stone had heard of the accident and he joined in the welcome with his share of smiles and back-patting.

Plenty remained on the porch, watching the reunion until Lizzy insisted she come down and meet Debbie and her friend.

Joey, who'd been riding his horse, Tar Boy, miles away from Shadow Creek Ranch, suddenly appeared. He thundered full-speed down the long driveway, waving his hat in the air; a joyous grin lit his sun-tanned face.

"Hey, Barry!" he shouted as his large, black stallion skidded to a halt. The boy hopped off as easily as a frog from a lily pad. "Man, am I glad to see you. You're looking great!"

Barry lifted his cane and smiled weakly. "Hey, Joey. How's the herd?"

"Ornery as ever," came the happy reply. "And if one of those new saddle blankets looks a little used, blame Wendy, not me. She stole it when I—" The boy paused when he saw Plenty standing beside Lizzy.

"Who are you?" he asked abruptly.

Plenty jumped as the young rider's attention

28

suddenly landed on her.

Lizzy grinned and whispered. "Don't mind him. He's from New York, too."

"I'm Red Stone's great-granddaughter," the girl said. "Who are you?"

Now it was Joey's time to be nervous. "I . . . I'm Joey Dugan. You're an Indian, aren't you?"

"Yes. Crow. You know, the people you White folks took this land from."

Lizzy quickly stepped forward. "Why don't we all head inside while Joey takes Barry's things to the horse barn? Supper's almost ready."

Joey stared at Plenty, then shook his head. "I didn't take nothin' from anybody," he said flatly. "So don't worry about it."

Debbie lifted her hand. "Say, Plenty, I like that shirt you're wearing. Did you make it yourself?"

"My mother did. She sews."

"I thought so," the older girl gasped. "You just can't find hand-stitching like that in stores nowadays, even at the mall." She slipped her arm around the Indian and led her away from the group. "I sew, too," everyone heard her say. "Well, not a lot of hand-stitching, but I'd like to learn."

Joey looked about, then lifted his hands. "Hey, what's her problem?"

Red Stone stepped forward. "Plenty have anger inside. She no like White man."

"There's a few White men I ain't too fond of, either," Joey countered.

"No," Red Stone continued. "Plenty not like *all*

29

White man. She say they robbed Crow of land many years ago."

The young boy nodded slowly. "I guess that's sorta true."

"She need to learn lesson," the old Indian sighed. "Maybe I teach her this summer. I try."

Joey was silent as he and Wrangler Barry headed over the footbridge toward the barn. When he spoke his words were somber.

"Did you see the way she looked at me? It was like she hated me, and I don't even know her." He paused. "I mean, I've had guys back in New York who didn't like me, but that's 'cause I gave 'em grief—you know, messed with 'em. But Plenty hates me and I ain't done nothin' to her."

Barry leaned heavily on his cane as he walked. "It's not about you. It's about stuff that happened a long time ago, before you or I, or even Grandpa Hanson, were born."

"You mean, how the government took away their lands so the pioneers could build farms and ranches? Lizzy told me about that last winter in home-school history class. She said the White man sorta took over the whole country, even though the Indians were here first."

The older wrangler nodded and sighed. "Yup. That's what it's about. Plenty, like many in her tribe, and most other tribes for that matter, grow up hearing about how the White man spoiled everything. It's a very old hatred that's reborn with each new generation."

Joey reached up and unlatched the big wooden door that led into the horse barn. "But I wasn't there. I didn't do nothin' to the Crow, or Flathead, or Chippewa, or Cree—those Montana Indian tribes I read about."

Barry hobbled inside as Joey unloaded his burden of suitcases and a sleeping bag onto the narrow cot by the worktable under the window. "Think about it," the horseman said, rubbing his ribs gently. "How would you feel if you knew that many, many years ago your great-great-great-grandfather rode into Plenty's great-great-great-grandfather's village and killed women and children, burned down the tents, took the horses, and carried the surviving men off to prison, simply because the tribe insisted that they had a right to live on that particular plot of land?"

Joey kicked at a piece of straw. "I'd feel kinda lousy about that."

"Well, let's just say Plenty is feeling lousy about that too, every morning when she gets up and sees her once-proud people stuck on a reservation. She doesn't know who to blame, so she takes it out on Joey Dugan, and Barry Gordon, and Lizzy Pierce—anyone she sees whose skin is white."

The teenager nodded slowly. "So, what am I supposed to do?"

"Beats me," Barry said, slowly opening the first suitcase and eyeing its contents. "You can't do anything about the past. It's the present you have to worry about." The older wrangler smiled a weak

31

smile and looked out through the open door. "Did I just sound like Debbie?"

"I do that sometimes, too," Joey said thoughtfully. "Scary, ain't it?"

Barry shook his head and chuckled. "Let's get me settled in. I think I smell supper coming from the Station. We'll talk about Indians . . . and other stuff . . . a little later, OK?"

Joey smiled. "Man, I'm glad you're here. Summer on Shadow Creek Ranch just wouldn't be the same without you."

"Yeah," the wrangler nodded, suddenly sad. "It wouldn't be the same."

The horseman walked to the open door and studied the distant patch of cottonwoods at the far end of the pasture. He could see the ranch's herd of horses grazing contentedly on the sweet, summer grasses.

Joey sat down and looked at his friend and mentor for a long moment. "We'll make it work," he said softly. "Don't worry about it, OK?"

"You mean Plenty?"

Joey nodded. "That, too," he said.

CHAPTER 2

Rainbow Trout

What's that?" Mr. Hanson asked, looking up from his book. His father had guided a heavily loaded cart into the den and pushed it to the center of the room.

Evening crickets chirped and buzzed outside as the inhabitants of Shadow Creek Ranch rested in their favorite spots about the large, cozy chamber.

Grandpa Hanson leaned one arm on the oversized box and read the name written across the top. "Says here, 'Please deliver to David Jarboe in care of Shadow Creek Ranch, Montana.'"

"Who?" the children chorused.

The old man smiled. "David Jarboe. He's one of the five guests arriving tomorrow. Return address is Seattle, Washington. Seems my conversation with the police chief of that city last summer paid off."

Wendy arose and ambled over to the mysterious crate. "What's in it?" she asked, eyeing the "Handle With Care" stickers plastered all over the sides and top. "Must be something fragile—or dangerous."

"Down, girl," Mr. Hanson called to his youngest daughter. "Unless your name is David Jarboe, you've got no business snooping around that box. We'll let the boy open it himself when he gets here."

Wendy bent and knocked softly on the wooden slats. "Maybe it's a secret government project that the FBI wants smuggled to Montana so they can test it up in the mountains where no one will see."

Debbie rolled her eyes, then returned to her fashion magazine. "And maybe it's none of your business," she sighed.

Joey stretched tired muscles. "When's the plane arriving?" he asked through a broad yawn.

"Two o'clock sharp," Grandpa Hanson announced. "Ms. Cadena says she'll be there to meet the group and bring them out to the ranch in her van."

All eyes turned to Mr. Hanson. The lawyer looked up sharply. "What?" he asked, spreading his hands.

Debbie smiled. "It'll be nice to have Ms. Cadena out here more often. I've missed her."

Tyler Hanson glanced at his daughter. "Yes, it will," he said matter-of-factly. "As the director of Project Youth Revival, she's a welcome addition to our summer family."

"Oh, brother," Wendy chuckled. "Such formality. She wouldn't happen to be the reason why you bought that new bottle of cologne the other day, would she?"

"Children, children," Mr. Hanson sighed, shaking his head slowly from side to side. "When a man buys a new bottle of cologne it doesn't necessarily mean he's trying to attract the attention of a member of the opposite sex."

"What's it called?" Wendy queried.

Mr. Hanson cleared his throat. "The name of this particular product is . . . 'Mr. Macho.'"

Debbie giggled, then suppressed her outburst. "No, no. You're not trying to attract Ms. Cadena. You just want Tar Boy and Early to think you smell nice."

The lawyer reddened. "I like the aroma of Mr. Macho. Besides, Ruth . . . I mean, Ms. Cadena and I are just friends. She's a warm, intelligent woman with whom I enjoy conversing from time to time."

Grandma Hanson shifted her position and studied her fingernails. "You two sure did a lot of conversing out on the footbridge last spring. One of you must be hard of hearing 'cause you were standing so close together. Shocked me so much I almost dropped my binoculars."

Mr. Hanson lifted his hands. "Such privacy I have on this ranch. Dad? Were you spying on me, too?"

"Couldn't," the old man grinned. "She had my binoculars."

The room erupted with laughter as Mr. Hanson staggered to his feet. "Some parents you are, and in front of the kids!"

"The children were nowhere to be seen," the man's father urged.

"Yeah," Joey agreed. "You don't think we'd sink so low as to spy on you and Ms. Cadena with binoculars, do you? Besides. We didn't need 'em. We could see just fine from the bushes."

The lawyer sank back into his chair. "I live in a fishbowl," he moaned. "Can't even have a quiet conversation with a pleasant woman without the whole Station getting involved."

His mother reached over and patted his hand. "That's the price you pay for being Mr. Macho," she whispered.

Grandpa Hanson settled into his chair by the fireplace and slipped a piece of paper from his shirt pocket. "And, speaking of Ms. Cadena," he said when the giggles had died down, "she gave me this list of names, along with a short description of our guests. If we can stop teasing my son long enough, I'll tell you what she wrote."

Wendy walked over and sat down on her father's lap. She curled up into a ball and pressed her head against the man's chest as Mr. Hanson began stroking her soft, blond hair. "Don't listen to those guys, Daddy," she said softly. "It's OK if you want to talk to Ms. Cadena on the footbridge. She's nice."

"Well, thank you, Wendy," Mr. Hanson responded.

The girl paused. "Are you wearing Mr. Macho right now?"

"Yes, I am."

Wendy closed her eyes. "I like it. Makes you smell like Early."

Debbie's hand shot to her mouth as Mr. Hanson blinked. His youngest daughter snuggled even closer and sighed contentedly. "Thank you . . . again," the young lawyer said, realizing that Wendy's comment, as strange as it sounded, really was meant to be a compliment. He knew there was nothing as important to the little girl resting in his lap as her mare, Early. In this particular case, smelling like a horse was something any father could be proud of.

"As I was saying," Grandpa Hanson continued, trying to keep his own composure, "we're going to have five teens as our guests this summer. Here's what Ms. Cadena says about each one.

"First there's Gina McClintock, from Rochester, New York. She's 14 years old, likes to read books about old trains, has a pet fish called Fin, and was arrested three times for shoplifting and once for setting fire to her high school science lab."

Lizzy shook her head. "Oh, dear. Sounds like someone I used to know." She shot a quick glance in Joey's direction.

The boy grinned. "Ah, the good old days," he said.

"Then there's Alex Slater, 15, enjoys watching baseball games on TV, likes making model airplanes, and is writing a book entitled *How to Get Rich Without Leaving the Comfort of Your Own Cell.* He's been in San Francisco juvenile detention seven times for fencing stolen goods, misuse of the telephone system, destroying public property, and picketing outside City Hall without a permit." The man paused. "There's a note here that says, 'Alex has real potential.'"

"There's that word again," Joey chuckled.

Grandpa Hanson adjusted his reading glasses.

"Then we have David Jarboe. He's coming to us from Seattle. It says here he's 16, likes nature, enjoys reading about wildlife safaris in Africa, and was arrested for stealing an alligator."

"An alligator?" the children chorused.

"That's what it says. He's also been detained for disturbing the peace, invasion of privacy, loitering, and shoplifting."

"Hey, he likes nature," Debbie called out. "I can have him help me with our hikes. Maybe he knows about those weird flowers at the foot of Mount Blackmore. I can't figure out what they are."

"Maybe so," the old man agreed. "Then there're two other kids from Dallas, Texas; Lyle Burns, 16, and Judy Chisko, 14. They're cousins who like to give the police a hard time. Haven't done anything really crazy, but the chief down there thought a few weeks in Montana might do them some good. Sorta head them in a new direction. We'll see."

Lizzy sighed. "Innocent children who've lost their way. It's a shame, really, that there has to be a program like Project Youth Revival. Wouldn't it be nice if all teenagers had happy homes with moms and dads who loved them? Sure would cut out a lot of pain and suffering from the process of growing up."

Grandma Hanson nodded. "I'm glad there're people like Ruth Cadena who've dedicated their lives to helping wayward teens. I'm also glad we can have a little part in what she and her organization are trying to do."

"Me, too," Debbie and Joey agreed.

"How 'bout you, Wendy?" Mr. Hanson queried. "Think we're up to the task?"

Everyone looked in the lawyer's direction and found the normally energetic 11-year-old fast asleep in her father's arms.

"They always look so sweet like this," Mr. Hanson whispered. "Even Wendy."

Joey chuckled. "Don't be fooled. I'll bet she's cooking up some mischief between snores."

Debbie nodded. "Probably planning something diabolical, something that will send her off on another great adventure like finding bones in the attic or discovering an old, abandoned farmhouse in the mountains. There's only one Wendy, that's for sure."

Mr. Hanson smiled as he bent and kissed the sleeping cheek. "Life would be far too boring around here without her."

The crickets continued their late-night sonnets as the man slowly rocked back and forth. His arms encircled the young girl who, despite her strong-willed ways and wild imagination, was deeply loved by all who lived on Shadow Creek Ranch.

* * *

"What time is it?" Joey stood gazing out from the horse barn, a pitchfork in one hand and a bale of straw dangling from the other.

Wrangler Barry laid down the leather strap he was attempting to fashion into a halter and glanced at his watch. "It's about five minutes from the last

39

time you asked," he said.

"Then it's almost 3:30, right?"

"Right."

The boy nodded. "Should be here any minute. Can't wait to meet our new guests. I wonder what they're like."

The older wrangler picked up the strap once again and started carefully cutting along one edge. "Oh, they probably have two feet and two hands and two eyes and—"

"You know what I mean," Joey chuckled. "I wonder if they'll like it out here."

"What's not to like?" Barry asked without looking up. "We've got mountains and creeks and horses and Grandma Hanson's vegetable stew and—"

"You're right," the teenager nodded. "They'll love it." He paused. "I sure wouldn't want to move back to New York City. I'm glad Mr. H let me come west with him. Me and Sam are never going to leave this ranch for as long as we live."

"No, sir," a faint, female voice called from somewhere overhead. "I'm going to stay here until I have as many wrinkles as Lizzy. Maybe even more."

Wrangler Barry and Joey glanced about the dusty, sun-lit room. "Sam?" Joey called. "Where are you?"

"Up on the roof," came the distant reply.

The two horsemen stumbled out of the barn and looked along the slanted surface covering the structure. There, sitting high atop the ridge of the roof was Samantha, her slender arms hugging a metal lightning rod that jutted into the cloudless sky.

"What on earth are you doing up there?" Joey called out, concern in his voice. "You might fall and break every bone in your scrawny little body."

The girl giggled. "Then the doctor can fix me up like he did Wrangler Barry."

"I wouldn't wish that on anyone," the older horseman moaned with a painful grin. "Why don't you come down so we won't have to bother the good doctor today, OK?"

Samantha tightened her grip on the lightning rod. "But I'm watching for Ms. Cadena's van. I wanna be the first to see it."

"Come on, Sam," Joey urged. "We'll watch for it together, down here, where it's safe."

The little girl hesitated, then suddenly stiffened. "Wait," she called. "I see it. I SEE IT!" Samantha let go of the pole and pointed wildly to the west. "It's coming around the cor—"

In her excitement, the speaker forgot where she was. Her body swayed forward, then backward. Then she lost her balance and began sliding down the roof.

Joey shouted, "Samantha, grab something!" but the little form continued to pick up speed as it careened along the smooth, metal surface.

In an instant, Joey was running toward the spot where he calculated his sister would hit the ground. Samantha sailed out into space at the same instant that Joey hurled himself forward, his arms outstretched. They met in mid-air with a resounding *thump*. The impact sent Joey, with the little girl

41

held tightly in his arms, flipping end over end through the open barn door.

The two landed hard against the bale of straw the young wrangler had been holding moments before.

Joey's right leg slammed into the pitchfork that lay beside the bale. The long tool flew straight up, spinning slowly around and around.

Since gravity is as effective in Montana as anywhere else in the world, what goes up must come down. The teenager saw the pointed ends of the pitchfork dropping straight for his head. He had time to shift his position just enough to allow the tool to embed itself with a *twang* deep into the hard-packed earth inches from his face.

Samantha lay very still for a long moment, then opened her eyes. She looked at her brother, then at the pitchfork. After letting out a frustrated sigh she announced, "Man, I'm not going up on the roof again. Getting up's easy. But comin' back down sure is a lot of work."

With that she raced out of the corral and headed for the footbridge, anxious to meet the soon-to-arrive vehicle.

Barry ambled over to where his friend lay sprawled across the barn floor. He studied the pitchfork, which still swayed from its collision with the ground. "You wanted to know when the van was coming," he said. "Well, it's here." Then, with a smile, he added, "You might want to freshen up a bit. I think you're lying in horse poop."

Joey grinned. "Is that what that smell is? I

thought it was Mr. H's new cologne."

Barry laughed as he watched his friend and roommate stumble to his feet. "That was quite a catch," he said.

The younger boy rubbed his elbow. "Remind me to put Sam on a diet. No more peach jam for her." Then, with a chuckle and a shake of his head, he headed for the washbasin.

Ms. Cadena carefully guided her fully-loaded van down the long driveway to the front of the Station. Inside, eager eyes gazed ahead, trying to drink in the incredible beauty of the valley and mountains surrounding it.

"Do they think we're criminals?" a voice called from the back section of the vehicle.

Ms. Cadena smiled. "They know you've all made some bad choices. Who hasn't?"

The driver saw a group of people gathering at the base of the front porch steps. "They also know that people can change if they want to. That's why this place exists—to give you an opportunity to choose a different course for your life, preferably one on the legal side of the law."

The woman stuck her hand out the window and waved. "Give 'em a chance, OK?" she encouraged. "They work hard to show you a good time."

"I've been to rehab joints before," the voice said flatly.

"Not like this one," Ms. Cadena grinned. "There's only one Shadow Creek Ranch."

The van slowed to a stop and was immediately

surrounded by smiling faces. The driver opened the door and hopped out. "Come on, you guys. The fun's out here, not in the van."

The side door slid open and a group of young, self-conscious teenagers tumbled out into the bright sunlight.

Joey and Wrangler Barry joined the group just as Ms. Cadena was beginning introductions. "This is Gina," she announced, pointing to a slender, brown-haired girl with rosy cheeks; blue eyes peered from under a train conductor's cap. She wore striped overalls and a pair of thick-tongued athletic shoes.

"Where'd you get that neat cap?" Debbie asked as she approached the girl."

I went for a ride on a steam train once," Gina said shyly. "They had 'em at the souvenir shop."

"I like it," the older girl said warmly. "Nice overalls, too."

"Thanks," the new guest responded.

"Makes her look like Casey Jones," a voice called from the van. Joey peered inside, his eyes opening wide with surprise.

"What're you looking at, cowboy?" the voice asked. "Ain't you ever seen someone in a wheelchair before?"

"That's Alex," the tall, blond-haired boy standing beside Gina volunteered. "Watch out for him. He'll rip off your last dollar as fast as you can say 'con man.'"

"Now, David," the voice chuckled. "You're turning the whole group against me before they've even had a chance to find out what a wonderful guy I am. If someone will give me a hand, I'll get out of this

44

rolling cattle car and down to business."

Joey and Mr. Hanson reached in and carefully lowered a wheelchair and its occupant to the ground. "There. That's better," the seated teenager said with a smile, his dark eyes scanning the gathering as if looking for something. Curly black hair stood out from his scalp like a forest of crooked pine trees.

"Hello?" he called, catching sight of Debbie. "Babe alert!" He wheeled himself toward the surprised girl. "How 'bout you and me headin' for the pasture to look for wildflowers?"

"How 'bout if you go by yourself and find a poison mushroom?" Debbie responded nonthreateningly.

"Don't play hard to get," the boy pressed. "You know you like me. I can see it in those beautiful eyes of yours. Besides, I've got money. Cold, hard cash. Lots of it."

Wrangler Barry limped to Debbie's side. "Take it easy, hotshot," he said. "I happen to know that this . . . *babe* . . . might be a little more than you bargained for. Why don't you pick on someone your own size, like that vision of beauty standing over there?" He pointed at Wendy. "I happen to know she doesn't have a steady boyfriend at the present."

Wendy looked Alex straight in the eye. "You touch me and I'll rip your arm off and wrap it around your neck three times and stick your fingers up your nose."

Alex blinked and backpedaled his wheelchair. "Whatever you say, little lady. Besides, why should I bother with a guppy when I can have a rainbow trout." He winked in Debbie's direction. "Anytime

45

you're ready to go fishing, let me know."

Ms. Cadena quickly stepped forward. "Why don't we just move on, here?"

Debbie leaned toward Barry and whispered, "Did he call me a fish?"

The horseman nodded. "Yeah. But it was a nice fish."

"That tall, good-lookin' fella over there beside Gina is David Jarboe from Seattle," Ms. Cadena announced.

The boy waved shyly. "I really like your farm . . . I mean, ranch," he said. "Is it OK if I do some shooting up in the mountains?"

Grandpa Hanson cleared his throat. "I'm sorry, David, but we don't allow hunting on my property. We believe that—"

"No, no," the teenager interrupted. "I don't mean with a gun." He reached into the van and pulled out a satchel. "I mean with a camera. I'm into photography. You know, pictures?"

The old man smiled broadly. "Of course, son. You can take all the pictures you want. Can't see how that'll get you into any trouble."

David grinned. "Well, that's not exactly true. I got arrested for taking a picture of Mrs. Thomlinson, my neighbor."

"What's so bad about that?" Joey wanted to know.

"She was . . . sorta . . . taking a bath at the time."

Wendy gasped. "How'd you do it? With a telephoto lens through the window or something?"

Mr. Hanson pressed his palm against his daughter's mouth. "Ah, David, would you mind not telling my youngest how you did what you did? She likes to experiment with new ideas."

Debbie joined in. "Right, unless you want to find yourself as an 8-by-10 hanging on her wall someday."

The boy smiled. "Sure thing. I'll keep my secrets to myself."

"But I want to know about the alligator," Wendy interjected.

David smiled. "That was all a terrible misunderstanding. Although it was kinda neat when my mom found him in our new jacuzzi—"

"And these are the two cousins I told you about," Ms. Cadena interrupted, making a proud sweep with her hand. "Lyle Burns and Judy Chisko. They're from Dallas, Texas, as you'll probably discover."

"Hi, y'all," Lyle called out, waving. "Cousin Judy is kinda shy. But she wants you to know how happy she is to be here."

The girl at his side nodded slightly, her bland expression looking like it was carved in stone.

"Matter of fact, I ain't seen her this worked up since that time her brother drove his car clean through their living room. He was kinda drunk at the time."

All eyes looked at Judy. One brow twitched.

"See what I mean?" Lyle gasped. "Even the mention of that night sets her off."

Samantha walked up to the girl and stared at her. "Is your face broken?" she asked.

"Samantha!" Lizzy called.

The little girl reached up and took Judy's hand

in her own. "You want to see the spider I caught this morning? It's really pretty. Has long legs and yellow spots all over it."

Judy nodded and followed this new friend in the direction of the horse barn. Lyle spread his hands. "Have you ever seen such absolute glee in one person before? I just know Cousin Judy's gonna love this ranch."

The silent teen and the little girl strolled down the path and headed over the footbridge as Ms. Cadena continued her introductions, giving the names of each of the Station inhabitants. Once everyone knew who everyone else was, the job of unloading the van began in earnest. There were rooms to be assigned and suitcases to unpack. Now that the new guests had arrived, summer at Shadow Creek Ranch could officially begin.

All during the process, Wrangler Barry kept a sharp eye on the boy in the wheelchair. He figured if he could keep Debbie safe from a Montana blizzard he could certainly save her from the clutches of this two-wheeled romeo. Or die trying.

CHAPTER 3

Master of the Morning

🦅 🦅 🦅

Somewhere, far away, water was dripping. It wasn't a quick or steady sound, the kind a leaky faucet makes. Rather, a soft *splat . . . splat*. The sound reverberated along dark corridors and reached the ears of the waking girl only occasionally, randomly, as if time had stolen the urgency from the noise and left it to disturb the silence at its own pace.

Dark eyes fluttered open and stared into the half-light of dawn. What was this place? What were those sounds?

Plenty sat up quickly, her breathing stopped, her mouth open.

Then she remembered. Red Stone. The mountains. The cave.

Even though it had been a few days since she and her great-grandfather left the comfortable, secure surroundings of their prairie reservation, the girl hadn't quite adjusted to waking up somewhere other than in her cozy bed. Sleeping on a pile of pine needles was going to take some getting used to.

She looked about the shadowed chamber. Embers from last night's fire still glowed beneath the large, cast-iron pot that hung from a metal frame by the far wall. Rough, wooden chairs rested beside the small stack of suitcases she and her white-haired companion had brought with them. Other than a few containers stuffed with food, and several plastic milk jugs filled with water fetched from a nearby stream, the cave was empty.

Plenty lay back down on her blanket and closed her eyes. She thought of her father, tall and handsome, walking out to his battered pickup truck in the early morning light as he did day after day, year after year. Mother would leave soon thereafter, heading for her parttime job as clerk in Pryor's only business establishment—a small grocery store a few doors from their mobile home. The woman would always pause and gaze at the mountains rising to the west, then continue on her way.

It was a morning ritual the young Indian girl had witnessed for as long as she could remember— her father heading for the coal fields, and her mother walking to the grocery store down the dusty street.

But Plenty had thoughts of neither coal fields nor mountains. Her mind continually wandered across the table-flat lands to the east, where the winds rustled the grasses and whispered words only she could hear.

"Come, Plenty." A familiar voice shattered her reverie. "It's time. Hurry, or you'll miss it."

The girl sighed and tried to ignore the invitation.

"Come quickly," the voice called again. "It's going to be more beautiful than yesterday."

Plenty rose on one elbow and looked toward the mouth of the cave where Red Stone sat, wrapped in a blanket, gazing intently out across the mountaintops.

"I've seen it before," the girl said.

"Oh, but it's always different, always new," Red Stone encouraged. "A Crow warrior must greet the sun or the day will turn against him."

Plenty shook her head. "I'm not a warrior, Great-grandfather. And neither are you."

Even as she spoke those last words she knew they'd hurt the old man at the cave entrance. Quickly she added, "Because we're not on the reservation. Indians are warriors only when they watch the sun rise over their own land."

"But this *is* my land," the old man retorted. "The people at Shadow Creek Ranch gave it to me."

"It was not theirs to give!" Plenty shot back, her words angry. "How can a man offer something to someone else if it's not his to begin with?"

"Just come," Red Stone insisted. "It'll happen any moment now. You must see it. You must greet the sun when it rises. It's the duty of every warrior."

Plenty sighed and tossed back her thin blanket. "OK, Great-grandfather," she moaned. "I will watch the sunrise with you, if it'll make you happy."

"Good," Red Stone smiled. "It's good that you do it."

The young girl shuffled to the entrance of the cave and sat down heavily beside the old man. She glanced to the east, where the mountains rolled like an angry sea in the soft, gray light of dawn.

Mt. Blackmore stood somber and silent, its summit still wearing the white, winter cap left by the storms that had raged across the region not many months before.

"There," Red Stone whispered. "Do you see it?"

Plenty nodded slowly. "Yes, Great-grandfather. I see it."

At first it was a tiny flicker, like a candle glowing far, far away. Then it spread, becoming a ball of flame, casting long, straight shafts of light high into the sky, piercing the shadows, brushing the mountaintops with yellow and gold hues.

The trees seemed to burst into smokeless flame as the brilliant circle of the sun continued to rise above the eastern lip of the land. Higher and higher the glowing sphere ascended until all reminders of night had vanished, leaving the mountain ranges, forest, and meadows bathed in the pure, radiant glare of a new day.

Red Stone stood to his feet and lifted his hands, his arms spread apart like an eagle in flight. "Master of the Morning!" he called out in words gathered from the ancient, timeless vocabulary of the Crow nation. "I greet you. I welcome you. Guide my steps during your journey across the sky. Bless my day with understanding. And may my heart be filled with compassion for all who walk in your light."

Golden rays pierced the cave entrance and touched every rock, every stone, with a glow no man-made invention could duplicate. The old Indian remained standing, letting the warmth of the light caress his face as it had for decades past.

Ever since he was a little boy running to keep up with his father through these very mountains, and spending the summer months in this very cave, he'd felt the warmth of the rising sun on his face. It was here he'd first heard the mournful cry of a hawk, the bark of a coyote, the snarl of a mountain lion. Right here, at the entrance to this cave, he'd watched his father stand and greet the morning, using the solemn, sacred words he'd just repeated.

But now there were no warriors left to welcome the rising sun—only men with jobs to drive to, mortgages to pay, duties to perform. When daylight broke across the land, no one took notice, and the Master of the Morning had to arrive unwelcomed, unheralded, unannounced.

Red Stone let his gaze fall to the forests below. The tradition would end with him. There was no one to take his place. No one, except Plenty.

* * *

"What's this stuff supposed to be?" Alex wrinkled his nose and pushed his spoon through the steaming mound in his breakfast bowl.

Grandma Hanson chuckled as she passed a jar of honey to the teenager sitting beside her. "It's bear mush," she announced.

53

"Bear what?" Alex exclaimed, dropping his utensil and backing away from the table.

"Bear mush. Haven't you ever heard of it in San Francisco?"

The boy shook his head. "We don't eat bears in California."

Wendy ladled a thick layer of honey over her liberal helping of the morning fare. "It's made from ground-up grizzly," she announced. "Claws and all. Here, honey helps cover the taste."

The boy's eyes opened wider. "I'm not eating a bear, no matter how much honey you dump on it."

Joey burst out laughing. "It's not made out of bear meat. We're all vegetarians on Shadow Creek Ranch."

Grandma Hanson grinned. "I'm sorry. I didn't mean to startle you with that rather unusual name. It's just made out of wheat. Why it's called bear mush I haven't a clue."

Alex relaxed a little. "Are there any more strange names I should know about before I get started?"

Debbie shook her head. "Nope. That's milk, that's peach jam, those are blueberry muffins, Gina's got the butter, and those sausages over there are made from soy beans."

The boy smiled and lifted a muffin and inspected it carefully. "I was thinkin', Debbie. How 'bout you and me goin' on a picnic today? Just the two of us. We could get—shall we say—better acquainted?"

Debbie picked up her spoon and blew softly on its steaming contents. "I've got an even better idea, Alex," she said.

54

The boy looked first one way, then another. Leaning forward, he spoke invitingly. "And what would that be?"

"Why don't we all take our first riding lesson? There's a horse out in the pasture who'd love to show you the sights."

The boy frowned. "And just how am I supposed to ride a horse? I'm in a wheelchair, if you haven't noticed."

"You'll see," Debbie smiled sweetly.

"*I* want to learn how to ride," David interjected from the far end of the food-laden table. "The only time I was ever on a horse was at a county fair. I was just 9 years old and this guy led us around for about 10 minutes. Wasn't very exciting."

Joey swallowed a glass of milk and wiped the white mustache it left above his lip with the back of his sleeve. "No one's gonna lead you around here," he said firmly. "These ain't kiddie horses. They're the real thing."

"Great!" David grinned excitedly. "May I bring my camera?"

"Sure," the young wrangler nodded. "You can stick it in your saddle bag and take it with you wherever you go."

Mr. Hanson cleared his throat. "Ah . . . David. That big box we received before you came. Is everything in it OK?"

"Yup."

The man nodded. "Nothing was . . . ah . . . broken . . . or wrinkled . . . or cracked?"

"Nope. Everything was just fine, thank you."

Wendy lifted her finger. "Wouldn't want anything bad to happen to . . . whatever's inside."

David smiled. "I appreciate that."

The girl paused. "Do you need any help unloading . . . or assembling . . . or painting . . . or arranging what's inside?"

David chuckled, enjoying the mystery his box seemed to have created in the minds of his new friends. "What I really need is a room, a room with no windows in it. But it has to have electricity. Is that possible?"

Grandpa Hanson scratched his head. "You want a room with no windows?"

"Yeah. And close to a bathroom."

Lizzy blinked. "A bathroom?"

"If it's not too much trouble."

Grandpa Hanson shrugged. "Well, we do have a storeroom at the end of the hall. Bathroom's just next door. Will that be OK?"

"Perfect!" David grinned. "Joey, could you help me put my box in that storeroom right after breakfast?"

The young horseman nodded slowly. "Sure thing, . . . David."

With that piece of business taken care of, the excited group hungrily devoured the delicious meal Grandma Hanson and Lizzy had prepared. Occasionally, Wendy would glance in David's direction and stop chewing. Then she'd shake her head and continue with her breakfast. Whatever was in the box would have to remain a mystery for a little while longer, as painful as the wait might be.

When all had cleaned their plates, Mr. Hanson stood to his feet. "Attention, everyone," he said with a smile. "I'd like to talk to you for a few moments." Voices stilled into attentive silence.

"This is the very first full day of your visit. I just want you to know how happy we are that you've agreed to spend a few weeks with us out here on the ranch.

"You're probably wondering why we do this sorta thing—working with Project Youth Revival, and all. The answer is simple. My father and I, along with my mother and Lizzy Pierce, firmly believe that this world has far too much sadness, violence, and hate in it. Crowded cities and drug-filled streets tend to support those unpleasant facts.

"But here on Shadow Creek Ranch we've dedicated our summers to showing teens like you that the world can be a pleasant place, a safe place. We're Christians. We believe in a God who says we should love our neighbors, and do unto others as we want them to do to us.

"The most important lesson we want you to learn during the next six weeks is that it *is* possible to live without hatred, without violence and fear, and that any sadness you may carry in your heart can be shared, and we won't laugh or make fun. Do you understand?"

Heads around the table nodded slowly.

"We're not perfect. We make mistakes. But we're

trying to help you as best we can. So, Gina, Alex, David, Lyle, and Judy, welcome to Montana, and welcome to Shadow Creek Ranch."

A cheer rose from those gathered about the table as chairs slid back and happy voices ushered in the new day. With excitement building, the group rushed out of the Station and headed for the pasture, where the ranch's small herd of horses waited by the corral.

Joey and David carefully carried Alex and his wheelchair down the porch steps and the three hurried in the direction of the footbridge.

"How am I going to ride a horse?" the handicapped boy kept saying over and over again. "I'll probably fall off the dumb animal and paralyze the rest of me."

Lizzy shook her head and smiled as she watched the happy procession from her kitchen window. Then, as she was turning around to attack the piles of breakfast dishes waiting by the sink, she jumped. Gina was standing in the doorway.

"Oh, you startled me! I thought everyone was heading for the corral."

The girl smiled shyly. "I'm not all that interested in horses," she said. "Is that OK?"

"Sure. We learned that lesson last summer." Lizzy lowered a wobbly tower of bowls into the suds. "Had a boy who spent most of his time glued in front of Mr. Hanson's computers."

"I'm not into computers much, either," the youngster admitted. "But I do like trains, you know, steam locomotives, coal cars, stuff like that."

Lizzy nodded. "I've ridden on a few choo-choos. And that was before they were considered a novelty in this country."

"You did?" Gina stepped to the sink and thrust her hands into the soap bubbles, searching for a dishrag. "I've only ridden on one steam train, down in Pennsylvania. It didn't go very far. But the sound and the power was really somethin'. I loved the smoke and embers blowing past the window and the rattle of those big iron wheels. It was really neat."

Lizzy took in a deep breath and gazed out the window as if searching for some long-forgotten memory. "I'd go to upstate New York with my aunt every summer. I was just a kid—5, 6 years old. But I remember the hissing, belching steam engine that pulled the cars. To tell you the truth, it scared me to death. I'd close my eyes until we were safe in our seats and the doors had been locked."

Gina sighed. "I wish I was born a long time ago like you." Her words softened. "Then maybe I could be someone else."

"Is there anything in particular wrong with being Gina McClintock?"

"Well, to begin with, that's not my real name."

"It isn't?"

The girl shook her head. "I'm adopted. Mr. and Mrs. McClintock raised me since I was a baby."

Lizzy tilted her head slightly. "Don't you mean 'Mom and Dad' raised you?"

"I used to call them that," the girl sighed. "Not anymore. They've changed."

"How?"

"Well, for starters, they treat me differently. They're always making up rules that I'm supposed to follow, you know. Like, when I'm supposed to come in at night, who I can and can't see, the clothes I can wear, the kind of music I should listen to. I don't have any freedom. They treat me like a little baby." The teenager wiped strands of brown hair from her forehead with the back of her hand. "I don't like it."

Lizzy nodded slowly as she carefully dried a serving bowl and lifted it into the cupboard. "Growing up's not easy. Take it from me, a young person needs all the help he or she can get. Maybe your adoptive parents are just trying to keep you safe, trying to keep you from making painful mistakes."

The girl's upper lip tightened. "Well, I don't see it that way. They just bug me. I hate them."

"Gina. You can't mean that. It seems to me like they want what's best for you."

The girl turned sharply. "You sound just like they do. They're always saying, 'We're only doing what's best for you. We're only doing what's best for you.' They're ruining my life! That's what they're doing. My birth mother wouldn't be like that. She'd be kind and loving. She'd be my friend. She'd understand what it's like to be me, because I'm part of her."

Sudden tears spilled down the girl's flushed cheeks. "And you don't understand, either. You're the same as they are!"

Gina threw the wet dishrag into the pile of suds, sending soapy water cascading against the window and open cupboards. "I came out here only to get away from my parents." She stormed to the doorway and stopped, her back to Lizzy. "I know what I have to do. And no one can stop me."

Lizzy watched the girl rush from the room and listened as her footsteps echoed through the lobby and out onto the porch. The front door slammed shut, leaving the old woman standing, dish in hand, alone in the kitchen.

Mr. Hanson appeared on the upper balcony. "Mrs. Pierce? Is everything all right?"

Lizzy walked out of the kitchen and stood at the base of the stairs. "I'm afraid not," the woman said softly. "We've got a problem with Gina. I've seen that kind of rage before." She turned and looked up at her friend. "In Joey."

Mr. Hanson lifted his eyebrows. "What're we going to do?"

"I'm not sure, Tyler. I need to talk with Ms. Cadena about this. Is she coming out today?"

"At 3:00."

Lizzy nodded. "Good."

With that she turned and headed for the kitchen. There were dishes to wash, and plans to make.

* * *

Alex looked down from his lofty perch and frowned. It seemed to him that he was at least 20 feet in the air when, in reality, the horse's back wasn't

61

more than five and a half feet above the ground.

Joey rubbed his chin and nodded slowly. "I think it'll work."

"You *think*?" Alex gasped. "No, no. That's not good. You gotta *know* this contraption that you and Montana Slim over there threw together is going to keep me from killing myself. It's my rear end on the line here."

Joey chuckled. "My partner's name is Barry Gordon. He's the head wrangler. I'm his assistant."

"Forget the politics. Just guarantee me that this . . . this . . . gizmo whatchacallit is gonna save my hide when Rover here decides to gallop into the sunset with me strapped to his backbone."

The young wrangler laughed again. "Your horse's name isn't Rover. It's Lightning."

Alex's face paled. "You've got me bolted onto a horse named Lightning? Listen, I changed my mind. Get me down from here and I'll never do another bad thing as long as I live. I'll become a monk, a missionary, a preacher! Just don't let me die in Montana on a horse named after a destructive discharge of static electricity."

Wrangler Barry limped over and stood beside the animal. "What's the problem here?" he asked, throwing a quick wink in Joey's direction.

"So you're the head honcho around here," Alex said, his hands tightly gripping the oversized saddle horn. "How come you weren't at breakfast? I thought everyone ate together in this outfit."

"Didn't have time," Barry announced. "Was too

busy building the gizmo whatchacallit you're sitting on."

Alex glanced at Joey. "Whatta guy. Gave up his bear mush so I could die on a dumb animal called Lightning."

Joey shook his head. "You're not gonna die. Barry and I just made some adjustments so you won't slip, that's all. Most riders use their legs for balance and to keep themselves from falling off the back of their horses."

"But since my legs are useless," Alex interrupted, "you had to make this stupid glorified infant seat for me." The boy sighed. "I suppose you think I should be thankful."

"Don't strain yourself," Barry said coldly. "Wouldn't want to see you left behind when everyone heads for the sunset." The wrangler turned, then paused. "Lightning's a good horse. He'll watch out for you." Barry stabbed the ground with his cane. "And stop complaining. At least you can ride."

"Hey," Alex called. "Like you can't? I don't see you stuck in a wheelchair."

The wrangler lifted his chin as if to respond, then hobbled toward the corral.

"Take it easy, Alex," Joey whispered. "Barry *can't* ride. The bouncing hurts his guts too much. He had an accident last winter and he ain't healed yet. So don't go messin' with him, OK?"

Alex watched the young man with the cane move carefully through the entrance to the horse barn.

63

"He can work some," Joey continued. "He can do stuff at the bench with his hands, but he can't ride, pitch hay, or even saddle the horses." The speaker's eyes narrowed. "He's my best friend, anyway. So just don't mess with him, you understand me?"

Alex nodded. "Whatever you say, cowboy. You're in charge. But don't try to make me feel sorry for Roy Rogers over there. I've got problems of my own."

Joey shook his head and was about to offer a response using a few choice words he'd learned on the streets of New York when he remembered a phrase Lizzy Pierce often repeated. "Silence is the best defense." Even Grandpa Hanson had read a verse in the Bible that said something about a soft answer turning away wrath. So Joey held his tongue and smiled up at the boy through gritted teeth. "Looks like the others are about ready to go. We'd better join them." He spoke with as much enthusiasm as he could muster.

"Why not?" Alex muttered. "At least I'll have a chance to bug ol' Debbie some more. I think she likes me but is just too shy to admit it."

Joey hid a grin as he led Lightning toward the cottonwoods, where the others waited. Debbie? Shy? Yeah, right.

* * *

The morning went well, considering that Lyle and Judy kept getting their horses tangled up with each other, David rode under a tree and emerged with a mouthful of leaves, Gina could never keep her feet in the stirrups, and Alex kept telling Debbie how wonderful she looked with her long, dark hair tied up in a pony tail.

Joey suggested to Alex that maybe he should concentrate a little more on learning to ride his horse.

Debbie said she was flattered but, no, she didn't want to run off to Las Vegas with him just yet.

Wendy told him to shut up.

But by lunch time, each of the new arrivals had grown accustomed to the somewhat unpredictable movements horses make as they trot through meadows and along forest trails. The group traveled in a big circle around the valley, always within a short distance of the Station. The route had been carefully designed to challenge the new riders, yet allow them ample space to learn the most effective ways of informing their horses what direction to go and how fast to get there.

At noon, sack lunches were delivered to a pre-selected meadow by Grandpa Hanson, and the group gathered in the shade of a tall hardwood to enjoy the delicious meal Grandma Hanson and Lizzy had prepared.

"Do you know what I think?" David called out, moving his words around a mouthful of wheat bread piled with lettuce and tomatoes.

Lyle, savoring the flavor of an enormous red apple, sighed a contented sigh. "I think we're all about to find out," he teased good-naturedly.

David grinned. "Someday, I'm going to move to

Montana and open a photo shop in a little town and take pictures for *National Geographic.*"

Joey raised his eyebrows. "Sounds like a great idea. You could specialize in photographing horses for ranchers. I'd even hire you to take a picture of Tar Boy, after I cleaned him up a bit." He admired the large, black animal grazing with the other horses nearby.

Alex shook his head. "You wanna show me how you can tell a clean horse from a dirty horse? They all look the same to me."

Wendy chuckled as she carefully folded a sandwich wrapper and returned it to her sack. "Tar Boy's always dirty. Early's always clean. That's how you can tell."

"Well, I think that's a wonderful idea," Debbie said with a smile. "David could open his shop up in Deer Lodge, or somewhere near Flathead Lake. Lots of tourists head that direction in the summer." She turned. "How 'bout you, Gina? What're you going to do after you finish high school?"

The girl shrugged. "I'm gonna be rich. I won't have to work."

"You are?" Debbie asked. "Do your folks have lots of money?"

Gina tossed her half-eaten sandwich back into her bag. "The McClintocks?" She laughed. "I'm not going to be like them. They're always working and saving and making big plans about how they're going to send me to some stupid college and buy me a stupid computer and all. Well, they won't have to bother. They can keep their nickels and dimes. I'm going to be so rich I can do whatever I please."

Debbie grinned. "You got an uncle who owns a gold mine or something?"

The girl with the rosy cheeks and blue eyes brushed bread crumbs from her lap. "Yeah, somethin' like that."

"Cousin Judy's grandfather had a gold mine once," Lyle announced with a big, Texas grin, his words heavily edged with a southern drawl. "Made more money than he knew what to do with. Then he died. Went to bed one night and didn't wake up. Butler found him the next morning stiff as a board."

"Really?" Wendy gasped, leaning forward. "An honest-to-goodness gold mine? Where is it?"

"That's the problem," Lyle continued. "He never told anyone where it was. The families have been searching for years, and all anybody comes up with are rattlesnakes and sagebrush. Ain't that right, Cousin Judy?"

The girl sitting beside him moved her head in what looked like a gesture of agreement. "See how distraught my cousin is?" Lyle shook his head sadly. "It's something we don't talk about too often. Shakes her up pretty bad, as you can see."

Wendy and the others stared at the silent, unmoving girl.

"Don't worry," Lyle encouraged with a smile. "She'll get it out of her system soon enough. We'll just have to be patient, that's all."

67

After a few moments, the girl lifted her hand to her mouth and took a bite of her sandwich. "There," Lyle announced, "the worst is over."

Wendy blinked. "Your cousin is a very interesting person."

"Isn't she, though?" the boy agreed. "She's always been a real inspiration to me and my whole family."

Joey glanced at Wendy, then at Debbie. "Well, enough chatter. Let's get back on our horses and continue our riding lessons. David and Lyle, you wanna help me get ol' Alex back up on Lightning?"

Lunch sacks were quickly collected and stowed in worn saddle bags. Before long, the meadow stood empty except for a small pile of bread crumbs left for the furry creatures that Joey, Wendy, and Debbie knew were waiting at the edge of the forest.

Unseen by the departing riders, several bushes trembled at the far end of the meadow and a shadowy form moved silently behind the tree line. The picnickers, every movement had been watched, their words overheard, their laughter noticed by a young, unseen visitor. A crow called overhead, then flapped away, its wings dark against the blue, cloudless sky.

CHAPTER 4

First Prisoner

Evening shadows lengthened across the folds of the mountain range as Plenty sat gazing at the valley far below. From her vantage point, she could see all of Shadow Creek Ranch—the Station, horse barn, tack house, pasture, and the silvery creek that wound through it like a weaver's thread.

The air was chill, as it always was this high in the Gallatins. To her back, beyond the meadow where the grasses swayed in the evening breezes, stood Mount Blackmore, eternal snows softening its jagged summit. Up range and much closer waited Freedom Mountain, its crest too low to wear winter's coat during summer months.

Plenty sighed and let her gaze settle on the distant way station. Everyone had gone inside about an hour ago. She'd seen them, moving slowly along the driveway. Her eyes, accustomed to the vast spaces of the prairie, had become very adept at seeing details from far away. Red Stone had often commented on the sharpness of her eyesight. "A warrior needs clear vision," the old man would say proudly.

Warrior. The word seemed to taste bad in Plenty's mouth whenever she spoke it. It didn't describe her, that was for sure. She was just a young girl who spent her days on the Crow Indian reservation in south-central Montana.

A warrior would never live as she did. He'd be free, free to pitch his tent where he chose. Free to run across the flatlands, to move silently in the night, to hunt where no barbed-wire fences divided the pastures, where no White-man buildings stood, where no logging roads felt the rumble of trucks, where no chain saws shaved away the forests, leaving the land naked, scarred.

No, she wasn't a warrior. Never could be. The past had stripped her people of such noble beings, leaving behind mere shadows of the men and women who used to roam this land, who used to splash in mountain streams and fall in love under unpolluted skies.

Her once-proud Crow nation, survivors of blizzards, droughts, and prairie fires, had fallen victim to the worst kind of disaster—the encroachment of White people from the east, across tribal lands, across sacred mountains, across dreams.

The sun slipped below the horizon, leaving behind a golden glow that slowly faded until night stars blinked to life across the vast canopy of sky. Plenty turned and faced Freedom Mountain. She lingered for just a moment, studying the dark outline beyond the meadow. "All the warriors are gone, Great-grandfather," she whispered, knowing no one heard. "They're all gone."

With a sigh, the girl began to walk along the path she knew would lead her directly to the cave. It was a path Red Stone had worn through the years as he'd come to sit alone, gazing down at the valley where his memories lived, where he'd spent summer days with his father.

A deep sadness crept into the teenager's heart, a feeling as cold as the air she breathed. Why did she have to be born an Indian? Why did she have to live with a past filled with such pain, such heartache?

She melted into the shadows as, far below, lights glowed from the Station windows.

*　*　*

Five tired, dirt-stained but happy teenagers slumped into the high-ceilinged den and collapsed at selected spots around the cozy room. China and silver clanked down the hall as Grandma Hanson and Lizzy waged war with the piles of dirty dishes.

The women smiled at each other, knowing this would be the last night they'd have to attack the job alone. Starting tomorrow morning, two of the five visitors would be assigned as their helpers for the summer. The adults had decided that, for the first full day of their visit, the new arrivals could just play.

"I think my legs are going to fall off," David moaned, rubbing his thighs. "Do you have any narrower horses I can ride?"

Joey laughed. "You'll get use to it."

Lyle shook his head. "Judy and I are beat." Everyone glanced at the girl who sat bolt upright in her chair by the window. "Just look at her," Lyle continued. "She's really done in. Don't be too surprised if she's not her usual, bubbly self this evening."

Wendy blinked. "Oh, we won't."

"Comin' through!" Alex burst into the room, his wheelchair sending Samantha and Mr. Hanson scattering for safety. "Man, I ate like a pig," the boy announced. He stopped in the middle of the room and spun his chair around and around on its large main wheels. "Those two women sure know how to whip up a tasty pile of chow."

Mr. Hanson chuckled. "I'll be sure that the women hear of your kind compliment."

Alex nodded. "Hey, your honor. How's the lawyering business? Hung any bad guys today?"

The man paused for just a moment. "Not yet," he said.

Gina pressed her face against the window glass and gazed out across the front lawn. "Sure gets dark around here."

Samantha tilted her head to one side. "Don't you have night where you come from?"

Joey laughed and grabbed his sister, smothering her with hugs. "Of course, she has night," he said. "But in the city, there're so many lights, it's hard to tell. Don't you remember what it was like in New York?"

The little girl shrugged. "I don't remember New

York anymore. I only remember Shadow Creek Ranch."

"Good," the boy responded. "I wish I could do that."

Grandpa Hanson strode into the room and took his place by the hearth. "I see everyone survived their first day with us. Hope you all had a good time."

Heads nodded enthusiastically around the room.

"Terrific. Tomorrow, we get down to the business of running a ranch. Each of you will be given a main task to perform while you're guests here. I've studied you carefully during our short time together and have assigned you work based on what I think you'll get the most benefit from.

"We'll begin with Gina. I noticed at supper that you were quite taken by the vegetarian dishes we served. You said you were amazed that meatless foods could taste so good. That's why I'm assigning you as assistant cook. You'll be working with Mrs. Pierce in the kitchen for one meal a day."

Gina lifted her hand to protest, then lowered it. Of all the jobs she imagined a ranch to contain, this one might be the least offensive. At least she wouldn't be shoveling horse manure out in the corral.

"I talked to David earlier and he showed me some of the pictures he'd taken in the Seattle area—the ones where people were fully clothed," the old man continued with a grin. "They're very good. So, Mr. Jarboe, I'm making you the official photographer of the group. Your job is to create a scrapbook for each of us to enjoy in the coming years—sort of a report, if you know what I mean. Ms. Cadena says she could always use pictures of Project Youth Revival in action. I understand that your box will come in handy for this purpose."

Wendy looked up sharply. "Box? Did you say box?" She glanced over at David. "I can help. I'll be your assistant. We can begin by unpacking that box, OK?"

David chuckled. "Thanks, Grandpa Hanson. I'd like that. 'Cept I don't have much film. It's kinda expensive."

Tyler Hanson cleared his throat. "I've opened an account for you at the photo store in Bozeman. You can get what you need there."

"Wow!" David enthused. "You mean anything?"

"Within reason," the young lawyer grinned. "Let's keep in mind that we have to eat around here."

David sat back in his chair, an excited smile creasing his slightly sunburned face. "I'm going to try all the films I've read about in my magazines. Man! This is going to be my best summer ever!"

Grandpa Hanson nodded. "Good. Now, Alex." The boy spun his wheelchair around until he was facing the speaker. "I don't know nothin' about food or photography," he said. "But I'm great on dates. How 'bout assigning me as personal bodyguard and escort for Miss Debbie. I'll take good care of her. Really."

The old man chuckled. "That's not exactly what I had in mind. Joey tells me you handled yourself fairly well on Lightning today. He said you may be a natural horseman."

Alex looked at Grandpa Hanson sideways. "I don't

74

think I like where this conversation is leading."

"So," the man continued, "I'm assigning you as assistant wrangler for the summer."

"WHAT! You want me to take care of horses? I can't do that. I'm . . . I'm . . . handicapped, unless you haven't noticed."

"Oh, I've noticed," Grandpa Hanson said matter-of-factly. "I've also noticed that you're kinda pale around the cheeks. You need to be outdoors, in the fresh air, working those arm muscles instead of sittin' around watching baseball games on TV or"—he paused and looked the young man squarely in the eyes—"or using the phone to raise funds for nonexistent charities."

Alex grinned. "You know about that, huh?"

"Yeah. So that's why we're going to teach you a new trade, out in the horse barn, where there are no phones. And you don't have to worry about TV either. Only get one station around here. PBS."

The teenager rolled his eyes. "Documentaries. I hate documentaries."

"Great, so it's settled. Report to Barry Gordon first thing tomorrow morning after breakfast."

Alex nodded with a frown. "Whatever you say."

"How 'bout Judy and me?" Lyle called. "Whatcha got planned for us?"

"Glad you asked," Grandpa Hanson smiled. "You two are going to help with the housework—you know, clothes washing, floor sweeping, trash collecting. Even with Joey and Wrangler Barry sleeping in the horse barn, that leaves 12 people living in the

75

Station. We need all the domestic help we can get."

"Say no more," Lyle beamed. "Cousin Judy and I will gladly lend a hand to the daily chores of this fine establishment. We'd be honored to keep everything in tip-top condition, right, Cousin Judy?" The girl lowered her head slightly. "She's as honored as I am," Lyle announced.

"Fantastic," Grandpa Hanson responded enthusiastically. "Now everyone has a job to do. Your duties won't take but an hour and a half a day, at the most. We'll also have two of you help with the dishes every meal. I'll post a schedule so you'll know when it's your turn. After your chores are done, you're free to enjoy whatever the ranch has to offer."

Alex yawned. "Right now the only thing I'd like to enjoy is my bed. Any objections?"

"Sounds good to me," Joey replied, rising. "Wrangler Barry's probably snoring already. Guess I'll join him. We make a great duet."

David glanced over at Wendy. "Hey, partner," he said. "We'll open the box first thing tomorrow, OK?"

"OK!" Wendy smiled. "Right after breakfast. And there'd better not be an alligator in there."

"You'll have to wait and see," David teased.

One by one, sleepy people stumbled from the room, calling goodnights to each other. Soon the Station settled into silence as a full moon looked down from above, washing the valley with soft, silver light.

* * *

Rumble . . . rumble . . . CRASH! Thunder shook

the Station as dawn arrived cold and gray. Rain fell heavily from dark, rolling clouds, obscuring the mountains and filling the creek bed with muddy torrents of water.

Wrangler Barry stirred, awakened from a dream about a time long past when he was a little boy. He was searching for his pony, Trotter. He couldn't find him anywhere. He kept calling his name over and over until the thunder snatched sleep from his mind.

The young man pushed himself up on one elbow and stared into the dimly lit workshop. Saddles hung neatly on low beams of wood. Colorful blankets moved in the occasional gust that whistled through the long, narrow boards forming the back wall of the corral.

He was startled to see Joey sitting on his cot by the workbench, staring at him.

"Hey, Joey." The wrangler greeted his friend with a not-quite-awake grin. "What're you doin' up so early?"

"Who's Trotter?" his young companion asked from across the room.

Barry chuckled. "Sometimes I dream too loudly."

Another bolt of lightning lit the cracks in the wall. This was followed quickly by a window-rattling thump of thunder.

"He was my first pony," the older wrangler yawned. "Brown. Speckled. Loved to eat my mom's roses."

"Bet she appreciated that," Joey grinned.

"Oh, yeah. They were best of pals."

Wrangler Barry stretched his good arm and

began massaging his other. This was something he had to do each day to get the injured limb to operate with any degree of success.

"Did they tell him?"

Joey nodded. "Yup."

"How'd he take it?"

The younger boy shrugged. "How do you think?"

Barry grimaced as he rose slowly to his feet. "There's something about Alex that bothers me. Not just his big mouth or his high regard for himself. It's . . . how he says what he says. His attitude."

Joey stretched and yawned. "I used to know guys like him in New York."

"What'd you do about it?"

"Beat the tar out of 'em. 'Course, that was the old Joey Dugan."

Barry collected his cane and shuffled across the room and sat down on a bundle of straw. "I know what it's like to . . . to not be able to do things."

Joey nodded.

"I figured if anybody here could help him, I could. 'Cept I don't have a clue how to go about it. I haven't exactly worked things out myself."

The younger wrangler lay back on his bunk. "Dizzy used to tell me it took a whole lot less energy to be kind than to be nasty. I used to work very hard at being nasty. She's right. Wears you out."

Barry smiled. "Strange. I can't picture you as a street punk." The horseman paused. "What made the change?"

Joey thought for a long moment. "Someone

believed in me when I didn't believe in myself."

"You mean Mr. Hanson?"

"Yeah. And Grandpa Hanson. Dizzy." Joey glanced at his companion. "And you."

Barry nodded slowly. It seemed so simple. Show someone you have faith in them, and they'll change. Right? But what if you don't have enough faith in yourself? What if the very person you're trying to help carries the same hurt in his heart as you do? It would be like the blind leading the blind. Or in this case, the cripple leading the cripple.

THUMP. An object slammed against the corral door, making Joey and Barry jump. "What was that?" the boy on the cot called.

The wrangler hobbled to the wide doorway. "It sounded like something hit the corral."

Joey hurried over and lifted the metal latch. Rain stung his face as he eased open the door and peered into the dim light of dawn. He could see nothing.

Lightning flashed, freezing the raindrops in mid-air like a camera captures an image. In the sudden light he thought he saw a figure running along the line of cottonwoods, but he wasn't sure.

Turning to close the door, he gasped. "Barry! Look at this!"

The wrangler stumbled out into the downpour and stood gazing at the boards that formed the entrance to the horse barn. There, embedded in the stout, rough-hewn wood, was a handmade arrow. Joey reached up and worked the shaft free, then rushed back into the barn, Barry limping at his heels.

The two stood staring at the carefully crafted object, neither speaking. When Joey found words, they were spoken with a quiet fear. "I think we have a problem here," he said. "A big, big problem."

* * *

Mr. Hanson rubbed his unshaved chin and slowly turned the arrow over and over in his hands. It was a work of art; finely chiseled stone point on one end and precisely positioned feathers fastened securely at the other end. Someone had taken great care in creating the deadly piece.

"You didn't see anyone at all?" the man repeated, his bathrobe hanging loosely over his shoulders.

Joey shook his head. "Just a movement at the tree line. Could've been a shadow. It wasn't light enough yet, and the storm was pretty intense."

The lawyer sighed. "We can't let the others know about this. It'll scare our guests half to death."

"Ain't exactly making me feel warm and fuzzy inside," Joey admitted. "I don't like having people shooting arrows at me. What if I'd opened the barn door at that very moment? Next Halloween I wouldn't have to buy one of those fake arrow-through-the-head gags. I'd have one for real."

Wrangler Barry tapped his cane on the floor. "Do you think it was one of the new arrivals playing a joke or something?"

"No way," Mr. Hanson said. "They wouldn't know how to construct such a beautiful piece as this, much less fire it with any degree of accuracy from the tree line. No, as far as I'm concerned, only someone who is a student of true Indian folklore would have the knowledge necessary to construct this arrow."

Joey looked at Barry, then at Mr. Hanson. "You're not thinking Red Stone, are you? He's our friend. You and your dad gave him a whole mountain last year. He wouldn't—" The speaker stopped mid-sentence as an unsettling thought gripped his mind.

Wrangler Barry, sensing the same conclusion, walked to the office window and gazed out across the rain-swept lawn and pasture. "Why would *she* do it?"

Mr. Hanson shrugged. "She's not exactly a fan of the White man. Sometimes the past pain of a tribe can surface among the young—violently. There've been many of what the newspapers call 'uprisings' on reservations during the past 100 years. People have died, Indian and White. This is no matter to be taken lightly."

Joey sat down heavily on the nearby office chair. "It's just like the streets. You do somethin' bad to me so I'm going to do somethin' bad to you."

"Revenge is nasty medicine," the lawyer responded. "I deal with it in almost every case I try. No one wins. Everyone loses."

"What're we going to do?" Barry asked, still watching the rain falling beyond the windowpane.

Joey stood. "Let me talk to Red Stone. I'm sure he doesn't even know what happened."

Mr. Hanson frowned. "Maybe we should just contact the leaders of her tribe at Crow Agency. They wouldn't want one of their own trying to take on the

White man single-handedly."

"Just let me try," Joey insisted. "I'll go up the mountain first thing after breakfast. It's too wet for riding lessons. Besides, maybe it was all just a practical joke."

Mr. Hanson studied the arrow lying across his hands. "You don't fire a deadly weapon as a joke, especially if you're an Indian."

Joey nodded. "Just let me talk to Red Stone, OK?"

The lawyer sighed a long sigh. "OK," he said quietly. "But Joey, be careful."

"Hey," the teenager responded with a determined grin. "I'm from East Village, remember?"

Mr. Hanson smiled. "I remember. Just watch your backside. I kinda like having you around. Don't ask me why."

Joey chuckled as he turned to leave. "As I've told you before, it's my shy, innocent nature. You can't help yourself."

"Your humility, too," the lawyer called after the disappearing horseman. "Just be careful."

"You got it," Joey's voice answered from the hallway.

Wrangler Barry shook his head. "I don't like this," he said.

Mr. Hanson tossed the arrow onto his desk and sighed. "What a way to start a summer."

* * *

Gina stood in the doorway of the kitchen, unsure of the welcome she'd receive. Her last visit had not gone well at all.

She looked about the spotlessly clean room and its brightly tiled floor. Carefully arranged pots and pans hung from a rectangular wooden frame suspended above a solidly built work island. A big four-burner range stood at one end of a long counter, sporting a copper heat vent like an oversized hat.

A huge refrigerator hummed quietly off to one side, keeping its store of food cold, ready for future meals.

Under the window rested the double sink, its white enamel worn down to metal in several places, testimony to the years of use it had sustained.

To her left, two microwave ovens sat side by side atop an old ice chest pushed up against the wall. Their modern, high-tech faces looked strangely out of place beside an even older dry sink that formed a serving platform for dishes headed for the dining room. An arched entryway separated the kitchen from the large eating area.

The kitchen had a look of efficiency and homeyness—a look the girl had admired the first time she'd seen it.

Several aprons hung from hooks on the pantry door. Gina ambled over to the closet-like alcove and studied the contents that burdened the thick shelves. Columns of canned goods wrapped in colorful pictures enticed the viewer to try what was inside. Cereal boxes stood tightly packed together on the next row while, just above, round, plastic containers offered abundant supplies of dried goods such as noodles and brown wheat flour.

The other wall sported well-braced shelves brimming with skillets, serving dishes, and canning jars.

The pantry was clean and orderly, just like the kitchen, just like the entire Station. These people were serious about their ranch, and their lives. Of this, Gina was sure. Seemed everything had a place, a purpose, a job to do.

"Hot cereal or omelettes?" a voice called from across the room. Gina turned to find Lizzy opening a cupboard and staring up at its contents.

"What?" Gina responded nervously.

"Should we make hot cereal or omelettes this morning?" the woman repeated.

Gina shrugged. "I like cheese omelettes. With hot sauce on them."

Lizzy nodded. "So do I. Sorta like Mexico meets France. Good choice."

Gina walked over to the sink and glanced out the window, not wanting to make eye contact with the woman. "Raining today," she said. "Can't go riding."

"Nope," Lizzy agreed, reaching for an apron and tossing it in the girl's direction. "There's only one word to describe a teenager who'd go horseback riding on a day like this."

"What's that?" Gina asked.

"Wet."

The girl blinked. "What?"

"Wet. You know. Un-dry?"

A grin played at the corners of Gina's mouth. "Yeah. Good word."

84

Lizzy fastened her own apron around her waist and brushed out its wrinkles. "So you want to learn how to cook vegetarian dishes, huh?"

"I guess so."

"The animals of the world thank you."

Gina's grin widened. "You think so?"

"Trust me," Lizzy called, heading into the pantry. "There are celebrations going on at slaughter houses around the world even as we speak." She emerged with a box of powdered milk in one hand, a mixing bowl in the other.

"Eggs are in the fridge. I'll fire up the burner. We don't fix eggs too much 'round here. Cholesterol, you know. But it's OK once in a while. Cheese, you say?"

"Yes. Lots of cheese."

"How 'bout just enough cheese to give the omelette flavor without clogging everyone's arteries? Deal?"

Gina nodded. "Deal."

Lizzy placed the ingredients on the work island. "Vegetarian, or health-conscious cooking, isn't just about not eating flesh foods. It's about being careful with whatever we put in our bodies. I guess it's possible to overdose on green beans or tossed salads. So, I'm going to teach you how to plan a balanced menu, how to bring out the natural taste of vegetables, and how to control the amount of sugar we dump down people's throats. Still interested?"

"Yes," Gina said enthusiastically. "I want to be healthy so I can—" She paused. "So I can have a good future."

"Noble cause," Lizzy agreed. "I've given Grandma Hanson the morning off so it'll be just you and me preparing breakfast, and lunch if you want." She motioned toward the refrigerator. "You get the eggs, I'll mix the milk. We'll have this breakfast on the table in no time flat."

Gina studied the energetic woman thoughtfully. Her real mother was probably just like that—funny, intense, caring. Maybe Shadow Creek Ranch wasn't going to be so bad, after all.

The girl pulled open the refrigerator door and began searching for the egg cartons. Maybe they'd even help her in her plan. But she'd better wait a little longer. Sometimes people aren't what they appear to be.

* * *

Thunder shook the ground as Joey guided Tar Boy along the narrow mountain trail. A steady rain beat the forest unmercifully, causing the leaves to quiver as if they too felt the uneasy fear the young horseman carried in his heart.

He'd faced troubles before. He couldn't count the number of times he'd walked down dark alleys and deserted city streets late at night, hurrying to meet a challenge thrown down by a rival gang member in East Village.

But this was different. He was going to have to face a young girl, an Indian no less, one who seemed to be very good with a bow and arrow.

He carried no weapon, except a small hunting

knife he always kept strapped to his belt. The knife was not for defense but for safety in the wilds. One never knew when it would be necessary to cut up a few small twigs for an emergency fire, or dig in the ground for life-sustaining roots, or try to deter a bobcat or other predator from attempting to turn you into a snack. He'd never had to use the knife in such an emergency, and as far as he was concerned, he wasn't about to begin using it now.

Tar Boy's big hooves slipped slightly in the mud as the two continued their journey along one of the few abandoned logging roads that led up Freedom Mountain. The rain increased, sending miniature waterfalls cascading over the lip of Joey's broad-rimmed hat and down the slick surface of his flapping raincoat.

"There it is," the boy whispered over the sound of the falling rain. "Do you see it, Tar Boy?"

The horse shook his head as if in response and lifted his young rider over the top of a small rise. At the crest of the mountain, beyond the dark-trunked forest, waited Red Stone's cave, its mouth yawning broadly through the deluge.

Joey stopped and studied the scene for a long moment. Nothing moved, except for the trees bending at the passage of each cold gust of wind.

Slowly, the boy dismounted and tied his horse's reigns loosely around a nearby bush.

He moved nervously toward the mouth of the grotto, glancing about for any signs of human life as he went.

Reaching the lip of the cave, he peered inside. He could see the blankets and cooking pot, the small collection of suitcases. Smoke rose from the hot ashes and half-burned wood of a still-flickering fire.

Joey stepped inside, listening, straining to hear any sound other than the wind-whipped rain falling behind him.

"Red Stone . . . Stone . . . Stone . . . Stone?" His call echoed and reechoed along unseen corridors in the darkness of the cave. "Hello . . . lo . . . lo . . . lo? Anybody here . . . ody here . . . ody here . . . ody here?"

There was no answer. Nothing moved in the shadows.

Joey turned and looked out into the rain. Tar Boy stood grazing on a collection of leaves, the long hairs of his mane wrinkled and clumped, his shoulders shining black and silver.

"No one's here, Tar Boy," Joey called from the cave entrance. "Must be out hunting or something."

He stepped forward. "Guess we may as well—"

Thump! An arrow sliced the air and struck deep into a tree trunk inches from the boy's head. Joey froze, watching the shaft vibrate, sending little sprays of water arching into the damp air.

"That's not funny," he called, motionless. "Someone could get hurt."

Thump! Another arrow pierced the bark just below the first.

"Stop it!" Joey demanded. "I mean it. This is stupid."

"Don't tell me the White man is scared?" a

young, female voice called from somewhere beyond the sheets of rain.

"I don't like being shot at," Joey countered. He waited for a response. There was none.

Slowly, he turned and faced the woods as rain drummed against his hat and coat. There was no movement among the bushes and low-lying branches.

"I don't want to fight you," he called. "Fighting only gets people hurt. It doesn't prove nothin'."

"I think it does," the unseen speaker responded, this time far to the right. Joey spun around. Squinting through the deluge, he could just make out the form of a girl standing atop a large rock about 50 feet away. In her grip, an arrow poised at full tension behind a straining, wooden bow.

Joey remained motionless. "Where's Red Stone?" he asked, trying not to let the form on the rock see his hands trembling.

"At the river," came the reply. "We saw you ride by. I knew you'd be coming. My great-grandfather is old and not very fast on his feet."

Joey shook his head. "Why don't you stop with the cowboy and Indian routine, Plenty? I just want to talk to you and Red Stone. That's all."

"What about?"

The boy laughed nervously. "What about? Well, let's see. The weather? Sports? The economy? Come on, Plenty. You're standing there with an arrow aimed at my head and you wonder what I want to talk to you about?"

Joey saw the girl lower the bow just a little, then raise it again. "You shouldn't be here. This is my great-grandfather's mountain."

"Well, you shouldn't shoot arrows into our barn, either. Why'd you do it? You got Mr. H all worked up. He's really worried. We've got guests down there, city kids. How'd it look if Project Youth Revival had to tell some juvenile delinquent's mother that her pride and joy is in the hospital because he was attacked by an Indian?"

Plenty shrugged. "The same things Indian moms were told after the White man raided villages and killed all their children."

"That was a long time ago!" Joey shouted, frustration forming his words. "We weren't even born yet. Our parents weren't even born, for goodness sake."

"Doesn't matter," the girl called through the rain. "I'm still Indian and you're still White. Nothing's changed. Nothing."

"Plenty?" An old man's voice called from down the path. "Plenty, is someone there with you?"

The girl turned. At that moment Joey let out a shrill whistle and started running in Tar Boy's direction. The big horse's head shot up, pulling the bush he was tied to clean out of the ground. With a bolt, the animal surged forward, running parallel with his master.

Before Plenty could reaim her arrow, she saw the young wrangler leap from a rock and arch through the air, landing hard on Tar Boy's broad back.

Joey's feet slammed into the stirrups as he bent low over the surging animal and, in an instant, both disappeared into the forest.

Red Stone entered the clearing and stopped to catch his breath. "Did I hear a horse?" he asked. "Did Joey come for a visit?"

Plenty lowered her bow and shook her head. "I was just target shooting," she said. "Maybe you heard my arrows hitting the tree. The horse and rider must've gone somewhere else after we saw them."

Red Stone shielded his eyes from the rain. At the mouth of the cave he could see two arrows jutting from the wet bark of a spruce.

"That must have been it," he said. "Sounded like horses' hooves. But in this rain, who can tell?" He continued walking up the path. "I was hoping young Dugan would pay us a visit. He's nice. Likes to hear my stories."

Plenty nodded and followed her great-grandfather to the mouth of the cave. Pausing by the tree, she carefully removed the arrows and returned them to the leather quiver strapped to her back.

She glanced in the direction Joey had headed and studied the quaking leaves through the blowing rain. He'd be back. The girl knew Joey Dugan was not the type to run away from a fight. They'd meet again. She just knew it.

* * *

Wendy stood beside the mysterious box as David eased a long table against the wall. Grandpa

Hanson had brought the table down from the attic for him. Stepping back, the boy gave a satisfied sigh.

"This is great," he said. "Should do fine."

His companion glanced about the windowless room with a degree of apprehension. "Why's it have to be so dark?" she asked. Then her eyes brightened and she leaned forward. "Do you work for the government?"

David laughed. "Hardly. They're always trying to lock me up."

"Oh, yeah," the girl nodded. "I forgot."

David rubbed his hands together. "Now, how 'bout we see what's in the box?"

Wendy stepped back just a little. "Don't let it bite me or I'll rip out its teeth."

"Don't worry," the boy chuckled. "What's inside doesn't have that many teeth."

With a yank David flipped open the top of the crate, revealing a sea of shredded newspapers. Confidently he thrust his hand through the pile and grabbed something underneath. Slowly, carefully, he lifted a long object into the light that spilled in from the open door.

Wendy saw two shiny parallel poles about three feet long and 12 inches apart. They were held together by a flat metal plate. A stubby handle jutted from the object; at the base of the poles she noticed a large, rectangular piece of wood.

"It's a launching pad for a rocket, right?" Wendy asked excitedly.

"Nope."

The boy buried his hands in the shredded newspaper again. This time they emerged with a round item that looked like it had accordion bellows built into it.

"It's a heart pump or a lung machine to help wounded soldiers on the battlefield!"

"Nope."

David fastened the bizarre object to the flat plate that straddled the parallel bars, leaving it suspended above the wooden base. Next he withdrew a small box from the shredded paper and opened it slowly. "This is the secret," he whispered. "This is what makes everything work." In his hand he held a small, metal cylinder filled with gently curving layers of glass.

"A lens," Wendy breathed. "Is it for your camera?"

Wordlessly, the boy screwed the device into a hole at the bottom of the accordion-like bellows, then stood back to admire his work.

"That, my dear Wendy Hanson, is the finest photographic enlarger money, or in this case my mom's credit card, can buy."

The girl's mouth dropped open. "It's, it's beautiful," she said. "It looks so . . . elegant." Wendy blinked. She didn't think she'd *ever* hear herself describe something as "elegant."

"Sure is," David agreed, running his hand along the cold, metal contours of the enlarger. "With this baby, I can capture time. I can steal faces right off of people and plaster them up on my walls. I can make a 10-foot daisy or a three-inch skyscraper. Why, I can make you and your sister and everyone on Shadow Creek Ranch smile, or frown, or laugh, or even cry

93

forever with this machine and a simple little negative taken from my camera. Whatta ya think of that?"

Wendy, for the first time in her young life, was absolutely speechless. This was better than any ol' alligator. She'd never, ever, ever been introduced to such a marvelous machine—not in New York, not in Montana.

Oh, she'd seen photographs before. Who hadn't? But here, resting on the table right before her eyes, stood the magic behind the images, the power that controlled what everyone remembered of the family vacation or the visit to a faraway land. The girl fairly trembled with the possibilities. Stepping forward she reached out and touched the cylinder, feeling its cold face. "Teach me how to do it," she breathed. "Teach me how to make magic with your machine."

David moved close to his companion, his eyes locked on the enlarger. "Together," he whispered solemnly, "you and I are going to capture moments, snatch events, grab pieces of time like leaves falling from a tree. Then we'll hurry into this very room and print those prisoners trapped by my camera, and we won't stop until the images are perfect, flawless, beautiful."

"Yes, beautiful," the girl repeated, her head nodding slowly. She looked up at her companion. "I'll remember this summer forever."

David lifted his hand and Wendy reached up and smacked her palm against his. "Let's begin with Early," she said.

"Early it is," David nodded, drawing in a deep breath. "He'll be our very first prisoner."

The Power of Another

Over the course of the next few weeks, life at the Station settled into its summer schedule with enthusiasm. The five new members of the working ranch began to realize that this wasn't going to be a simple vacation away from the city, away from the past. Every activity, no matter how spontaneous, seemed to have a purpose built into it.

This was the result of Ms. Cadena's tireless planning sessions with Grandpa Hanson and the other adults during the spring. They had met, sometimes late into the night, to review, discuss, clarify objectives, and encourage each other. They would be dealing with teenagers' futures. Nothing was more important than that.

Joey, Wrangler Barry, and Mr. Hanson kept the secret of the uninvited arrow to themselves, believing that the more people who knew about the incident, the greater chance there'd be to respond in a wrong way. Problem is, they couldn't come up with a right way.

Joey insisted he could handle the situation alone. After hearing of his encounter on the mountain, Mr. Hanson wasn't quite so sure.

"She could've nailed me to a tree," the boy insisted. "But she didn't. I don't think she really wants to hurt nobody. She's just mad and doesn't know what to do about it."

Mr. Hanson finally agreed to give him one more chance. "Then we're calling Crow Agency," he warned.

The summer guests quickly fell into a routine. Lyle and Judy cheerfully went about their household chores, with Samantha as their unofficial helper.

Occasionally, the little girl would stop and stare at the expressionless Judy for a long moment. Then she'd shake her head and busy herself with the task at hand.

Gina's interest in cooking grew, as did her respect for Lizzy Pierce. She'd even presented dishes of her own creation on several occasions. Debbie's description of the girl's first attempt at rice pudding was "unusual, but interesting." Joey smiled gamely at his bean and onion casserole and suggested that it needed a pinch of salt. Wendy said her potato salad tasted like cardboard.

But Gina wasn't deterred. Lizzy assured her that people have different tastes and to not worry about Wendy's reaction one bit. "She's the only person I know who puts catsup on chocolate ice cream," the old woman encouraged.

David's darkroom at the end of the hall was now fully operational. He and his young assistant spent hours stalking the valleys and mountainsides, camera in hand, looking for images to capture and rush to the marvelous machine that waited in the orangish gloom back in the Station.

Together they developed roll after roll of black-and-white film, pouring first one liquid chemical then another into the round, plastic developing tank the boy had brought with him from Seattle. After washing the strips thoroughly in the bathroom sink, David and Wendy examined the negatives over a light table and made contact sheets so they could see their pictures as positive duplicates.

Then with much whispering and earnest discussion, they slipped a selected piece of film into the enlarger and shone the hard-earned likeness onto a large sheet of photographic paper held tightly across the flat base of the device.

Next came the magic, the moment they'd been waiting for. Carefully, oh, so carefully, the paper was submerged in the slightly yellowish liquid in the first of three wide developing trays. Their heads bent low, watching, waiting, searching for a first glimpse of the emerging photograph as the powerful chemicals did their work.

Mysteriously, portions of the picture began to appear. If it was a person or animal that had been photographed, eyes usually materialized before anything else. This might be followed by an ear, or patch of hair.

Then, suddenly, the entire image sprang into view, prompting muffled gasps of joy and shouts of victory to echo down the Station hallway.

"Look at that!" Wendy called. "It's beautiful. It's marvelous. It's—"

"Too dark," David groaned. "We'd better do it again and use eight seconds instead of 10."

But they didn't mind reexposing the image. It gave them a chance to witness the magic all over again.

Alex, on the other hand, wasn't having as much fun.

One bright, warm day frustrated words sounded from the confines of the barn.

"This horse doesn't like me," the teenager announced.

Wrangler Barry looked up from the worktable. "Whadda ya mean, he doesn't like you?"

The boy in the wheelchair reached out and ran a big brush down the side of the chestnut mare. "See? She keeps moving away. I have to unlock my wheels, scoot forward, lock the wheels again, then brush. She moves further. I move further. We end up going around and around like slow-motion ball-room dancers."

Barry chuckled. "Now, what'd I tell you about that?"

"I know, I know. I'm supposed to talk to the dumb animal and brush her with my hand first so she'll get used to me being here."

"So what's the problem?"

Alex shook his head. "I never know what to say to a horse."

"What would you say if she was a beautiful girl?"

The boy paused. "You want me to ask this four-footed hay cruncher for a date?"

Barry rolled his eyes. "Just say nice things like 'Good girl, pretty girl.'"

Alex stared at the horse that stood patiently in front of him. Raising his brush he cooed, "Good girl pretty girl stay put don't move you gorgeous thing you're marvelous you're wonderful I hate your guts."

The animal's tail swung around and knocked the boy's hat off.

"Hey," he cried. "Did you see that? She punched me with her tail. Ain't fair."

Wrangler Barry shook his head. "Alex, what *is* your problem?"

The younger boy's lips tightened. "I'm supposed to be a wrangler and I'm sitting in a wheelchair, *that's* my problem."

Barry shrugged. "Hasn't stopped me."

"Oh, really?" Alex twisted his chair around and moved toward the open door. "I see you looking at us when we go riding in the afternoon. I know what you're feeling. Don't try to play doctor with me."

Barry paused in his work. "You don't hear me complaining, do you?"

"I don't have to hear it, buddy, ol' pal. We're both freaks of nature and always will be."

"THAT'S NOT TRUE!" Wrangler Barry shouted angrily, then regained his composure. "That's not true. We both have to make allowances for our handicaps, but that shouldn't stop us from doing

99

what we want to do."

Alex's eyes narrowed. "It stops us from *being* what we want to *be*. Give it up, cowboy. You can't teach me anything I don't already know. You may be a few years older than I am, but I've had a lot more practice at being a cripple. Just like me, you'll learn what it takes to get by."

"By breaking the law?" the wrangler challenged. "You call that getting by?"

"Hey, I do what I gotta do."

Barry threw down the screwdriver he was holding. It bounced across the top of the workbench, scattering wood shavings and pieces of leather. "You're wrong, Alex! You're wrong to think that way. There are people who want to help you. People who care."

Alex turned sharply. "Maybe for you. Maybe out here on this fancy dude ranch there are people who'll take the time to listen to you rant and rave about how sorry you are for yourself.

"But I ain't got nobody to listen to me. My mom works hard. She's never home. And I ain't exactly mobile sitting in this rotten contraption. So when I feel afraid, when I feel like I'm the only crippled teenager on my block, which I am, I get mad. I do dumb stuff. But it keeps me from losin' it. And I have a little fun in the process.

"So don't think for one minute that showing me how to talk to a horse is going to make my day. Show me how to stop being angry inside every time I see someone run across a baseball field and snag a fly. Show me how to live without being terrified everyday that I'll be left in the middle of nowhere with no one around to push me home.

"You wanna heal me, cowboy? Heal yourself first. Then we'll talk."

Alex angrily maneuvered his chair to the door and slipped outside, his hands and arms straining against the resistance of mud and manure. He floundered 10 feet from the door, unable to move any further.

Wrangler Barry closed his eyes, feeling wet tears creep down his cheeks. The boy's words had cut like a knife, not because they were angry but because they were true.

The horseman lifted his cane from the table and hobbled to the doorway. "Alex," he called, his voice uncertain, "I'm sorry. I really don't know what to do for you . . . or for me. All I know is that I care. The people on this ranch have taught me to care. I can't help myself. They're always talking about God and His love and how we're supposed to share it with others. It makes sense, even though it's not easy sometimes.

"So I guess you're stuck with me. Are you listening? I'm not going to give up on you, Alex. I'm not going to let you go back to San Francisco and continue breaking the law and getting into trouble. The things you do are wrong. I don't want you to do them anymore."

Alex leaned his head against the back of his wheelchair, eyes tightly closed. He felt helpless, a feeling he'd experienced often. Even now, he was stuck, his wheels buried six inches in mud, in front of a horse barn in Montana. There was nothing he could do to help himself.

Angry tears stung his eyes. Why? Why would he have to spend his life depending on other people? Why would he have to be afraid of the simplest trip to town or to school? Why would he always be forced to sit and watch life pass him by, a life filled with people who could laugh, who could hope—who could walk?

The boy felt something hard hit his back and shoulder. Looking down he saw one end of a thick rope resting in his lap. "Tie it low on your chair," a determined voice called.

Glancing back he noticed Wrangler Barry slowly swinging the chestnut mare around inside the barn workshop.

Alex bent and fastened the stout cord to the seat frame of his wheelchair. Barry painfully wrapped his end of the rope around the horse's neck. Then with a soft command, the wrangler, leaning heavily on his cane, guided the large animal back toward the stalls.

Alex felt the rope tighten, then he found himself moving slowly across the damp, muddy ground. In moments he was slipping along the solid boards that formed the horse barn's floor.

Unfastening the rope, he saw Wrangler Barry hobbling in his direction. The two paused and looked at each other for a long moment, understanding that they'd just accomplished something quite unusual. A person who couldn't strain on a rope had just pulled another person who couldn't walk, out of the mud. All they had done was borrow the power of another.

Barry smiled shyly. "Not bad for a couple freaks of nature, huh?"

"What did you say to the horse to make her do that?" Alex questioned.

The older boy shrugged. "Just two words. 'Help us.'"

Alex grinned a tired grin. "You sure know how to talk to horses." Then he looked down at the floor. "Would you teach me?"

Barry studied his companion as the soft sound of shuffling hooves on fresh straw drifted from the far end of the stalls. He lifted his hands and spoke quietly. "I may not know how to do it right."

The boy in the wheelchair nodded. "I need your help, Barry. Where else can I go to find someone who speaks horse?"

* * *

Lizzy looked up from her bread dough in surprise when she saw who'd just walked into her kitchen. "Hey, Gina, aren't you going with the group to visit Red Stone? They're about to leave."

The girl ambled to the sink window and glanced out toward the pasture where Joey and Wrangler Barry were making sure the ranch's young riders were properly mounted on their eager steeds. Alex could be heard calling out instructions from atop Lightning.

"Nah. I'm not in the mood to ride today," Gina sighed.

"Well, that's OK," Lizzy smiled. "You can keep me

103

company. Grandma Hanson went to Bozeman with Tyler, and Grandpa Hanson's up in the mountains, visiting our neighbors, John and Merrilee Dawson. I'm stuck here at home, baking some bread for tomorrow. Wanna help?"

Gina grinned and twisted one of the knobs on the faucet. "I was hoping you'd say that," she replied, lathering her hands with soap. "It's not that I don't like horses. I just didn't feel like bouncing around all day."

"I understand," Lizzy nodded. "I'm not much of a cowgirl myself. Guess I'm gettin' too old for such goin's on."

Gina powdered her fingers with flour and thrust them into a large lump of wheat dough. "You're not old. You're . . . you're experienced in years."

Lizzy paused. "What a lovely way of putting it. Thanks."

The teenager bent to her work. "Do you have any children, Lizzy?"

"Nope. Never did. My young, dashing husband was killed in the Second World War. Airplane pilot. Shot down over France."

Gina shook her head. "That's sad. I'm sorry."

"So was I. So sorry, I guess, that I never married again. Kinda foolish of me—trying to stay faithful to a dead man."

The teenager squeezed another lump of dough and slapped it on the table. "You would've been a great mother," she said. "You make kids laugh. And you're patient."

"Had to get that way pretty fast when I began

104

teaching school in New York City. Without a sense of humor and the patience of Job, you'd be climbing the walls before the second bell.

"Then I met Joey when his parents moved into the same apartment as mine." The speaker paused. "Joey. Now there's a good kid. Heart as big as all of Montana and Wyoming combined. 'Cept he didn't know it at the time. He figured he had to be a tough guy, so he was. After little Samantha showed up in his life, he had a real problem. How do you play the tough street hood and take care of a tiny child at the same time? It was a battle for him."

Gina smiled. "My mother is like you."

The old woman lifted her lump of dough and dropped it into a deep baking pan. "Which one?" she asked, not looking up.

"My *real* one, of course. She's rich. And very smart."

"Really? Have you talked to her?"

Gina shook her head. "Nah. A couple years ago I convinced my adopted parents to help me locate her. I wrote her a letter, but she didn't reply. Too busy making money for us."

"Us?"

"Yeah. The way I see it, she's going to save up until she has enough in the bank for us to travel around the world together. Egypt, India, Africa. We'll have a great time. She's not far—" Gina hesitated. "I mean, she's president of a big corporation. Tells everyone what to do. But she loves me. I just know it. And she's got plans for us." The girl chuckled playfully. "After all, I *am* her daughter."

Lizzy slipped several bread pans into the oven and adjusted the temperature control. "I'm sure she thinks of you often."

The two were silent for a moment. Outside the window, the last of the riders disappeared from view as the happy group headed for Freedom Mountain. Samantha could be heard playing with Pueblo by the footbridge, encouraging the dog to climb a tree to see if there were any eggs in the nest clinging to "the third limb from the right, the one with the bump on it."

"We're going to be very happy together," Gina added softly. "She'll understand me. She'll treat me like an adult, not a child."

Lizzy sprayed a thin layer of cooking oil on a pan and set it down gently. "Have you told the McClintocks about your dream?"

"It's not a dream," the girl tensed. "It's real."

"Don't you think they should know what you're planning? I mean, they've invested a lot in you—not only time, but money, too. They have the right to know when you'll be leaving."

Gina nodded slowly. "They know I'm not happy living with them anymore."

"But why, Gina?" Lizzy pressed. "Please explain to me what it is you don't like about the McClintocks." Seeing her companion's face begin to cloud, she added quickly, "Because, they might want to know so they won't make the same mistakes with their next daughter."

The teenager's expression softened. "Perhaps you're right. I guess they deserve at least that much."

Lizzy closed her eyes momentarily, knowing how close she'd come to making her young friend angry again.

"OK. I'll tell you." The girl sighed as she walked to the window and gazed out into the late-morning sunshine. "When I was little, everything was fine. They treated me great. We'd go on camping trips to the Adirondacks, drive through New England in the fall to see the colorful leaves, spend a week at the beach every summer."

"And they stopped doing that?"

"No. But for the last couple years they've gotten bossy, you know, telling me everything I'm supposed to do. 'Clean up your room . . . lengthen your skirt . . . don't hang around with so-and-so . . . be home by 9:00 . . . don't watch that video.'" The girl straightened. "That's not love. That's dictatorship. I'm not free to do what I want anymore."

Lizzy nodded. "So you do things like shoplifting and getting in trouble with the law to show them who's boss, right?"

"You bet. No one's going to rule my life."

The old woman dropped another lump of dough into a pan and carried it to the oven. "We had a girl here last summer whose father abused her, physically and otherwise. Project Youth Revival arranged for her and her sister to have a new home with a caring couple. She writes to Debbie, boasting about how her new parents do the very same things you're talking about, except this girl is amazed that two people could love her so much they'd bother noticing the length of her skirts and who her friends were. Why do you think you and she see things so differently?"

Gina was silent for a long moment. When she spoke, her words were cold. "I'm not concerned about what other girls may or may not think. I just know there are going to be some changes in my life. Very soon, too."

With that she turned and walked quickly from the room, leaving Lizzy standing, her hands covered with flour, by the open oven.

* * *

Red Stone's smile broadened when he saw Joey and the others emerge from the forest and ride to the entrance of the cave.

"Welcome," the old Indian called as Debbie waved. "Welcome to my mountain."

Joey dismounted and hurried over to his friend. "I've brought you some more listeners for your stories," he grinned. "Think you might have some ready for us?"

Red Stone nodded. "Always have story for boy and girl."

Judy and Lyle slipped from their saddles and tied their horses to a tree limb as they'd been taught. "Nice to meet you," Lyle said, extending his hand. "I ain't never met a real-live Indian before."

Red Stone looked over at Joey. "This boy talk funny. Like you, only different."

108

The young wrangler laughed. "He's from Texas and I'm from New York. I guess we both have pretty weird accents—at least that's what Montana people say."

Judy stood and looked at the Indian thoughtfully as Lyle grinned. "My cousin here ain't never seen an Indian before, either," Lyle offered. "We've met lots of Mexicans, being from Texas and all, but no Indians."

Judy blinked and continued staring. Red Stone returned her gaze. "Does girl know how to talk?" he asked.

"Sure she does," Lyle laughed. "But she likes to save up her words for special occasions. Then she rattles off like a train at a crossing. Yak, yak, yak. Can't shut her up for love nor money."

Click. The old Indian turned to see Wendy and a boy peering from behind a camera. "Did you get 'em?" Wendy asked.

"Yup," David nodded. "The sun's just in the right place too, sorta back-lighting him and Joey."

"You opened up enough for the shadowed areas, didn't you?"

"Yeah. Gave it a full stop. Should be a keeper."

Red Stone nudged Joey. "What Wendy and boy talk about?"

The teenager grinned. "That's David, one of our guests. He's teaching Wendy how to take pictures, and they're making a photo album, all about Shadow Creek Ranch. I'll bring you a copy when it's done."

Wendy waved. "Hi, Red Stone. Where's the best place to get a good view of Mount Blackmore?"

The old Indian pointed to his left. "Up there," he said. Wendy and David hurried away, camera and exposure meter in hand.

"What am I, a permanent fixture up here?" Alex lifted his arms and dropped them with a sigh.

Joey and Lyle hurried to Lightning's side. "Sorry 'bout that, Alex," Joey chuckled. "We forgot all about you."

"Well, I guess so," Alex teased. "But Wrangler Barry's teachin' me how to put up with just such incompetence. He says I should politely express my needs. I'm pretty good at expressin', but the polite part still could use some work."

The two boys gently carried their friend into the cave and deposited him on a pile of blankets. "You're doin' just fine," Lyle encouraged. "You haven't even hit on ol' Debbie for goin' on 20 minutes now."

"And I appreciate that," another voice called from the group of horses. The girl in question walked up and gave Red Stone a friendly hug. She paused, a shadow crossing her face. "You losin' some weight, Red Stone? And you look just a little pale."

The old man grinned. "No, no! Don't you know that *White* man is paleface? Not Indian. We're redskin."

Debbie giggled. "So what color do you get when you're not feeling good?"

Red Stone thought for a moment. "Pink," he said. "Yes. That's right. Pink."

"Well, then," Debbie pressed, looking into the kind eyes of the old Indian. "You're looking a little pink. Maybe these cold nights up here are gettin' to ya. Why don't you let my grandpa take you to see the doctor? Perhaps he can make you . . . red again."

Red Stone laughed. "I'm strong as grizzly. Don't worry. Plenty look after me."

Just then Wendy and David returned from their short journey to the overlook. "Sun's not right," the boy sighed. "We'll try again later."

Everyone settled themselves at the mouth of the cave as Red Stone poked a stick into a small fire. Although it had been warm in the valley, Freedom Mountain rose to where the air was always cooler, especially to the old Indian whose body was worn by years.

"Tell us about Shadow Creek when it wasn't Shadow Creek," Wendy encouraged.

Red Stone nodded. "You mean Valley of Laughing Waters?" He opened his mouth to continue but paused as another person entered the cave. Joey looked up to see Plenty standing silhouetted against the bright forest sky.

"Come, Great-granddaughter!" the old Indian called happily. He wanted all to understand his invitation. "Sit by me and listen. I tell about my father's valley to my new friends." His hand swept the air. "They have journeyed up Freedom Mountain to listen."

Joey watched the girl slip her quiver from her shoulder and lean her bow against the cave wall. "Whatever you say, Great-grandfather." She moved among the gathering and knelt beside him. Never once did her eyes glance in Joey's direction.

The young horseman studied the girl thoughtfully. What would she do next? What plan was circulating in her mind even as she sat beside the old storyteller there in the cave, listening to adventures from long ago?

The afternoon passed quickly, too quickly for the visitors on Red Stone's mountain. They were carried, again and again, to another time, when this part of the Gallatins rang with the joyous voices of children. These children were members of the Mountain Crow tribe, a people honored to be overseers of this corner of nature's pure and unspoiled wilderness.

The old Indian drew his listeners from the present and gave them front-row seats to a way of life that had vanished forever under the uncaring tread of modern civilization. Lyle, Judy, Alex, David, and the others sat spellbound as the age-worn voice of their guide painted graphic work-pictures of the way life used to be. In beautiful detail, he told how his own laughter used to mingle with that of other tribal children as they splashed through mountain streams and lay dreaming under summer stars.

Evening shadows were beginning to creep across the land as Joey and the others bade farewell to their old friend and turned their horses homeward. Plenty stood with her great-grandfather at the entrance to the cave, silent, her expression emotionless. Joey could feel her hatred, even though she had tried to act civil for her great-grandfather's sake.

As they rode away, the young wrangler glanced one last time over his shoulder. Plenty was looking directly at him. He waved. She did not respond.

* * *

A few days later, the phone rang in Mr. Hanson's office, as it often did during the day. He picked up the receiver and pressed it to his ear, his other hand still tapping on his computer keys.

"Hanson here," he said.

The voice on the other end of the line sounded friendly. "Mr. Hanson of Shadow Creek Ranch?" it questioned.

"One and the same," the lawyer sang out.

"I just wanted you to know that your girl got off safe and sound."

"I beg your pardon?"

"Your girl. She left right on time. Put her on board myself."

The lawyer's hand froze above the keyboard. "What are you talking about?"

The voice paused. "You are Tyler Hanson of Shadow Cr—"

"Yes, yes. That's me. What girl?"

"She said you'd made the arrangements, Mr. Hanson. Even brought a letter signed by you. Has your business address and phone number on it."

"Wait a minute, friend," Mr. Hanson chuckled, running his fingers through his hair. "You've lost me. Where are you calling from?"

"Bozeman. The train station. I put your girl on the 4:00 limited to Denver, just as you requested. My company has a policy of calling to confirm when

113

a minor is placed on board."

The lawyer's mouth dropped open. "What was her name?" he gasped.

The voice on the line hesitated.

"HER NAME!" Mr. Hanson commanded.

"Gina. Gina Hanson, your daughter."

The man slammed the phone down on its cradle and bolted for the door. Reaching the top of the stairs, he shouted, "Mrs. Pierce! MRS. PIERCE! Is Gina with you?"

"No, Tyler," came the reply from downstairs. "I think she went to town with Debbie earlier this afternoon." Lizzy appeared at the bottom step. "Whatever is the matter?"

"I just got a call from the train station telling me that my daughter, Gina Hanson, was put aboard the 4:00 limited to Denver."

"Oh, my; oh, my!" the woman gasped. "What are we going to do?"

Mr. Hanson lifted his hands. "First Joey disappeared last fall, now Gina. Doesn't anyone want to *stay* on this ranch?!" Racing back into his office he shouted over his shoulder, "I'm calling Ruth Cadena. Find my dad. Looks like we've got another teenager to track down."

CHAPTER 6

The Mistake

Traffic jammed the streets, and harried pedestrians jostled for position along downtown sidewalks and crossing zones. Car horns blared their drivers' impatience at busy intersections and parking lots.

Motors raced, trucks and taxis inched forward, and the smell of burnt diesel fuel mixed with the odor of strong coffee. Gina moved with the flow of people, past small restaurants that cowered at the bases of towering glass-and-steel structures.

It was morning. Her long rail journey had come to an end. The girl had watched the sunrise through a dusty window at Union Station and was now making her way along 8th Avenue toward an address she'd memorized months before.

Gina hadn't bothered to eat breakfast. She was far too excited. Today was going to be the beginning of a whole new life for her, a life of freedom with the woman who had brought her into this world, a woman whose face she'd imagined a million times.

A street number glowed in golden letters across

the glass entrance to a tall office building on the corner of 8th and Broadway. This was it! This was the correct address. To make sure her excitement wasn't clouding her mind, she dug into her change purse and found the paper with those magic words scrawled across them. L & R Media Productions, 49789 8th Avenue, Denver, Colorado. Gina smiled. She knew the "L" stood for Lynda, her birth mother's first name.

The young girl exited the elevator at the eighteenth floor and stood looking around the tastefully decorated lobby. "May I help you?" The receptionist smiled up at her.

"Yes," Gina said, returning the smile. "I'm looking for Lynda Ellis. She's the president of L & R Media Productions."

The receptionist nodded. "Does she know you're coming? I mean, do you have an appointment?"

"No. It's a . . . surprise visit."

"Ms. Ellis doesn't get too many young visitors," the woman reported. Leaning forward she pointed as she spoke. "Head down that hallway to the end, turn right, and Ms. Ellis's secretary will be sitting behind the desk by the window. She'll find out if she can see you."

"Oh, she'll see me," Gina grinned confidently. Turning to leave, she paused. "Do you work for her?"

The receptionist laughed. "Young lady, everyone on this floor works for Lynda Ellis."

Gina smiled. "She must be a wonderful boss."

There was a short pause. "She gets the job done,"

the receptionist said flatly.

The hallway was lined with office doors, each with a different name and title printed neatly on the frosted glass—Adam Tarrance: West Coast Sales; Elaine LeClair: Accounting; George Digman: Photography; Samuel Aikens: Copy Editing; Sharon Daily: Desktop Publishing. On and on they went; musicians, sound recordists, videographers, editors, writers. Every few seconds a door would burst open and someone would rush by as if on an urgent mission.

The secretary's desk waited right where the receptionist said it would be. A woman was furiously typing at a computer as Gina approached.

"Yes?" she asked, not looking up.

"I'd like to see Ms. Ellis, please."

The secretary chuckled. "Take a number."

"What?"

"Everyone wants to see Ms. Ellis."

Gina frowned. "No. I'm not here on business."

The secretary pressed some keys on her computer keyboard and a laser printer whirred to life by her elbow. "Today's not a good day. Try next Wednesday."

Gina stepped forward. "You don't understand. I've got to see her right away."

The secretary stopped working and studied the young visitor who stood before her desk. "Look, she's busy. She's always busy. Leave your number and I'll have her call you later. Besides, auditions have closed."

"But I'm not auditioning for anything. I just want to see her. I've come a long—"

117

"Listen, I don't mean to be rude, but Ms. Ellis is an extremely busy woman." The secretary pointed in the direction of a thick, wooden door across the small lobby. "She's in a committee right now, trying to figure out how one of her pet projects went 'way over budget.' She doesn't have time for social calls from nice young women. So if you'll just come back in a few days, she might be able to see you. OK?"

Gina fought back a strong urge to scream out her demands. "But I have to—"

"Thanks for stopping by. Now, you must leave."

The girl nodded slowly and turned. After walking a few paces she glanced back just as the phone rang. The secretary picked up the receiver and began a heated conversation with someone on the other end of the line. So engrossed was she in her call that she didn't see the young visitor crack open the big, wooden door and slip inside.

Gina found herself in a small hallway lined with award plaques and autographed photos of celebrities. The girl recognized the pictures of many Hollywood and television actors along the brightly-lit gallery.

"What do you mean, you had to shoot another day?" A woman's voice drifted from the archway at the end of the hall. "Cost us $15,000 and we were already over budget."

"We had no choice," a man's voice pleaded. "It rained."

"It's not supposed to rain in Los Angeles in June. I think it's the law." Gina heard people laugh.

"The studios were booked solid," the unseen man

continued. "We had to stay on location for an additional day and that's that. Period. What's done is done. It was either shoot or postpone the product launch date two weeks. Marketing would've had my liver for lunch."

Gina heard the woman sigh. "Just plan a little better from now on, OK? We're in this business to *make* money, not spend it. Now, everyone get outta here and do some magic with the WebCore account. We'll try to recover our losses by milking them for another $50,000, but don't put me in this position again or *I'll* take a few bites of your liver."

The girl heard chairs bump and the muffled voices of people approaching. She ducked behind a large plastic plant beside a statue of a lion; she waited as eight or nine sets of highly polished shoes shuffled by. Then all was quiet.

Peeking around the plant, Gina could just make out the slender form of the woman seated at a wide, expensive-looking desk. She had tied her dark brown hair up behind her head, leaving long, curving strands that cascaded over her ears and forehead. She wore a red dress, tightly fitted. The sun's rays, piercing the long, lacy curtains with warm, morning light struck the side of her face, illuminating it with a soft glow.

She was beautiful, with smooth skin and practiced grace, just like Gina had imagined.

A couch stood nearby, and an overstuffed chair. A rolled-up newspaper balanced on the broad back of the chair, probably left by one of the employees who'd just departed.

Gina stepped from behind the plant and stood in full view, staring in wonder at the president of L & R Media Productions.

"Who are you?" the woman asked when she saw the teenager in the archway.

"I'm Gina."

"Auditions were yesterday. We'll let you know when—"

"I'm Gina," the girl repeated. "Your daughter."

The woman paused, then smiled. "I don't have a daughter."

"Yes, you do. Me."

The woman reached for the phone, then hesitated. "What makes you think that?"

Gina stepped forward. "I checked. This is the address, and you're Lynda Ellis. That means you're my mother."

The woman rose slowly and walked around her desk until she stood before it. "How old are you?"

"Fourteen. Almost 15. I'll be 15 in September."

Gina could see her companion make some quick, mental calculations. Suddenly, she saw her expression harden. "Why have you come here?"

"Because," Gina replied, smiling, "I want to live with you."

The woman laughed out loud. "You want to live with me? Listen, . . . whoever you are. I want you to understand something. You're not a part of my life. You never were."

"You carried me inside you."

The woman glanced out the window. "Fourteen years ago I made a mistake. Then I fixed that mistake by turning it over to the proper authorities. What's done is done. Now, go back to wherever you came from and leave me alone."

The words hit Gina like flying pieces of glass. She almost staggered under their impact.

"You're my mother! You carried me for nine months and then gave birth to me. I'm not a mistake. I'm a person, a person who loves you and wants to—"

"I don't have time for this," the woman interrupted, glancing at her watch and turning back to her desk. "You mustn't come here anymore. Please leave."

"But Mother—"

"DON'T CALL ME THAT! Never . . . call me that." The woman turned around, her eyes narrow, cold. "You have no right to barge into my office and demand anything of me. I did what's best for you 14 years ago. It's still best. Nothing has changed."

Gina braced herself under the full weight of the woman's words. "But you love me," she encouraged. "I know you do. We can be happy together. We can travel, see things. I can tell you what's in my heart. You can listen and hold me when—"

Gina stopped talking as she realized her words were not being accepted by the lovely lady standing behind the desk.

"I'm not your mother," the woman said firmly. "I may have given birth to you, but I'm not your mother. I never will be. Do you understand?"

Tears moistened the corners of Gina's eyes. There was nothing between them. No warmth. No understanding. It was as if they were separated by a bottomless canyon, uncrossable, unchangeable, unseen.

"Don't you care for me just a little?" she whispered. "Don't you ever think about me, how I'm doin', what I look like?"

"That's not my responsibility," the woman replied. "I gave up that privilege when I let you go. I refused to hold you in my arms then. And I refuse to hold you in my thoughts now. So, you see, as far as I'm concerned, you don't exist. Believe me, it's best for both of us."

The woman moved across the room and brushed by the teenager without looking at her. She continued out into the hallway and paused at the big, wooden door. "You must go now," Gina heard her say. "Don't be here when I return."

The room fell silent except for the soft whistle of air passing through the air-conditioner ducts somewhere overhead. Gina walked to the window and stared out across the city to the Rocky Mountains beyond. Some summits still carried their winter coats, the snow looking as cold and distant as the woman had been.

The girl trembled slightly, too sad to cry. Her dreams had been crushed, her carefully planned future destroyed. She'd lived each day in preparation for a new life with the woman who worked at the corner of 8th Avenue and Broadway. Now she felt terribly alone, cast aside like so much rubbish—unwanted by the very woman who had given her life.

"Gina?" A soft voice called from the doorway. The girl didn't turn.

"We're here, Gina. Both of us. We came as soon as we heard."

Mr. and Mrs. McClintock stood together at the far end of the office, their expressions shaped by the deep concern that filled their hearts. "Are you all right?"

Gina closed her eyes as a sob rocked her body. "Do you hate me now?" she asked, her words barely audible.

"No!" came the quick reply. "No. We could never hate you. We love you, more than you'll ever understand."

Gina turned slowly, looking down at the thick carpet at her feet. "She said I was a mistake. She said she didn't ever think about me."

Mrs. McClintock began to cry. "You're not a mistake, Gina. You're a treasure, to us, to our home."

The man stepped forward. "We're not perfect parents," he said, fighting back his own tears. "But we're there when you need us. We never had such a wonderful little girl before. We just don't want anything bad to happen to you. That's why we try so hard to keep you safe from the pain we know waits all around."

The girl allowed her gaze to rise until she was looking into the kind, loving eyes of the couple by the door. "Will you forgive me?" she whispered. "Will you forgive me for causing so much trouble?"

Gina rushed forward and fell into waiting arms. They cried together for a long time, lost in the unspeakable joy that a parent feels when a child accepts the love they offer, and when a child learns just how far a parent's heart will reach to forgive.

* * *

The cozy den was silent as Mr. Hanson finished his report. It was evening. Crickets sang and buzzed outside in the darkness. The quarter moon hung just above the trees, its silver light touching the ripples playing along the banks of Shadow Creek.

He'd just gotten off the phone with the McClintocks, who were back in Rochester with their daughter. Lizzy reached up and wiped her eyes with a handkerchief. "This whole episode reminds me of something Grandpa Hanson said earlier this year during one of our planning sessions with Ms. Cadena."

"I remember," Debbie nodded, smiling over at the old man sitting by the hearth. "You said we were all like children-lost in a world of sin with no one to love us. Then God offers to adopt us, so we can be part of a loving family again."

Joey sighed. "I know what it's like to feel alone and rejected, like Gina. But I also remember how great it felt when Dizzy offered to be my friend and when Mr. H chased me down in that old warehouse and said he'd never leave me again. Believe you me,

124

there's nothin' like it in the whole world."

Grandpa Hanson glanced about the room, letting his gaze pause at each of the ranch's remaining summer guests. "Listen, guys. I don't care what kind of mess you're in. Doesn't matter what you've done, or where you've gone, or who you've hurt. God says, 'Come back home to Me. You're always welcome at My supper table. And if you'll listen, I'll teach you how to avoid trouble, how to right the wrongs you've done, how to bring peace back into your heart.'" The old man sighed. "So few people take Him up on His offer. They just keep on hurting themselves, and others, until the law, or their own guilt, sentences them to a lifetime of sorrow."

David fingered the controls of his ever-present camera. "The other day Wendy and I were up in the mountains, past Merrilee. We were looking for a small patch of nodding onions—you know, the little pink jobs? Debbie had said wildlife really likes 'em and we were hoping to see a bear or elk or something.

"Anyway, while we were huntin' around, we heard this chirp . . . chirp . . . chirping coming from a bush. We figured we might get a shot of some baby birds for our book, so we headed in that direction. On the way we saw this pile of feathers on the ground, like there'd been a fight—and the bird lost. We looked up the feather patterns in our bird field guide and decided it was a horned lark, or at least it used to be.

"When we got to the nest, guess what? Baby horned larks. It made us sad to think that the

125

mother bird wouldn't be bringing breakfast to the nest anymore. The babies were way too small to save, so we had to leave 'em. I can still hear them chirping and chirping, calling for their mom as we left the area. Gina's story sorta reminds me of that."

"At least Gina has a new mother and father who love her," Lyle added. "Some kids don't."

Alex nodded. "Seems to me that bein' a mother is more than giving birth to a baby. It means stickin' by that kid, day in and day out. It's lovin' him even when he does something stupid like go off on his own like Gina did. Guess she didn't know just how good things were for her back in Rochester. Somethin' tells me she's kinda figuring that out now.

"You know, I learned something awhile back." He glanced at Wrangler Barry. "I learned that you shouldn't try to do everything alone. You need parents, or at least someone to help you with your problems. Know what I mean? Some people are smarter than you are, although in my case, that may be hard to believe." Barry grinned as the boy continued. "And the smartest thing that you can do, is shut your mouth and listen. It's amazing what can happen."

Lyle lifted his hand. "You know what I'm going to do when I get back to Texas? I'm going to give my mom and dad a great big kiss right on their noses." Everyone giggled. "No, really. I am. This whole thing with Gina made me appreciate what they do for me. It's true they get on my nerves from time to time, probably always will. But instead of going off and doing something dumb, I'm going to stop and think. At least they're there. They may not be perfect, but neither am I. Why should I get all bent out of shape when they screw up and then expect them to be loving and forgiving when I do something really dumb? I gotta be fair. Yeah, that's it. I gotta be fair with my parents. That means letting the other guy make mistakes without calling in the National Guard. Know what I mean?"

"Yes," Judy said firmly. Everyone gasped as the girl who'd not said one audible word since arriving on the ranch smiled over at her cousin. She nodded and looked around the room. "Must be fair."

Lyle threw up his hands. "See what I mean? Once she gets started, you can't get a word in edgewise."

The den exploded with laughter as Grandpa Hanson shook his head and smiled broadly. He knew something was stirring in the hearts of the teenagers who had, as expected, become part of the Shadow Creek Ranch family. The seeds had been planted. Now it was up to the Holy Spirit to help them grow.

CHAPTER 7

Light of the New Day

🦅 🦅 🦅

Dawn was just beginning to tinge the eastern sky when Plenty stirred. She'd been dreaming. At least, she thought she had. There was such a feeling of joy filling her body that she closed her eyes again, trying to recapture the fading images, but it was too late. Sleep had slipped away, like the night beyond the entrance to her great-grandfather's cave.

Her companion coughed a quiet cough, the sound rattling in his throat like pebbles in a jar. It was a comforting sound, like the creak of an old floor or squeak of a back door in a home lived in for many years.

The weeks had flown by, days tumbling over each other in rapid succession. She'd found her frequent walks with Red Stone had become more relaxed, more enjoyable. His gentle words, patient training, and constant encouragement were beginning to chip away at her stony heart.

His often repeated stories began to take on fresh meaning as she experienced the mountains firsthand.

When he spoke of the things of nature, she didn't have to imagine them anymore. She'd seen the graceful gait of a white-tailed deer. She'd heard the throaty trumpet of the bull elk, listened to the clatter of pronghorn sheep's hooves on slabs of granite, watched red squirrels playing tag high in the forest canopy, and witnessed the silent flight of the great horned owl.

From her perch above Shadow Creek Ranch, she'd seen the summer guests take their leave amid happy calls and tearful waves. They'd driven away in a little red minivan, trailing a cloud of dust in their wake.

The valley seemed empty to her now. She went less often to sit and gaze down at the Station.

Red Stone rose on one elbow as he did each morning, then stumbled to his feet, taking a little longer than usual.

"Are you OK, Great-grandfather?" Plenty asked, yawning.

"Oh, yes. I'm fine. Just a little stiff, that's all." The girl reluctantly slipped from beneath her warm blanket and helped her great-grandfather to the mouth of the cave. Then she took her usual place at his feet. The morning ritual, something she was now very familiar with, was about to begin. She understood it was part of Red Stone's life, and although she didn't exactly feel the need to greet the morning sun when it decided to rise, she'd play along if only to keep him happy.

As the first rays of the sun pierced the dark sky, setting the horizon on fire, Red Stone lifted his arms. "Master of the Morning," he sang out, his voice a little more labored than usual. "I greet you. I welcome you." The man swayed and caught himself. Plenty tensed as he continued. "Guide my steps during your . . . during your journey across . . . the sky."

"Great-grandfather. What's wrong?"

"Bless my day . . . my day . . ."

The old man's right arm slammed into his chest as his knees buckled, almost toppling him.

"GREAT-GRANDFATHER! WHAT'S WRONG?"

"And my. . . my heart . . . be filled . . . be filled—"

The words choked in Red Stone's throat as he stumbled backward into the cave, weaving drunkenly, bumping against stone walls. Plenty screamed as the frail, aged body tumbled into a twisted heap by the fire. The man's face was ash-white, his eyes wide with terror.

"WHAT IS IT?" Plenty shrieked, rushing to Red Stone's side. "WHAT IS IT, GREAT-GRANDFATHER?"

The old man jerked in agony, his hand gripping the young girl's arm. "Plenty! PLENTY!"

"I'm here. I'M HERE! What's the matter? What's happening?"

Red Stone closed his eyes tightly as stabbing pains racked his chest and limbs. His face trembled, teeth grinding together, sounding like sandpaper digging into wood. The torturing agony eased just long enough for him to whisper, "Get help."

In one quick movement, Plenty gathered her bow and arrows and was out of the cave, her feet a blur over the frosty ground. She ran faster than she'd ever

130

run before, arms pumping, legs pounding the earth. The path turned into a flowing river of movement, colors blending together, details lost in the rush.

The girl's heart hammered against her ribs, not only from the extreme exertion but also from the fear of what was happening back at the cave. Red Stone had been growing weaker during the last couple days. Plenty had thought it was just a touch of the flu. Now she knew it was something much more serious, much more deadly.

Her breath was coming in great heaves when she arrived at the overlook. All was quiet in the valley. Nothing moved, except the gentle sparkle of the creek as it threaded its way beside the pasture and past the large, white way station resting far beyond the cottonwoods.

With trembling hands, Plenty slipped an arrow from her quiver and placed it between her teeth. Reaching up she gathered several strands of hair and yanked hard, closing her eyes at the sharp pain.

Twisting the long fibers around the middle of the shaft, she tied a quick knot. Then she slipped the arrow into the bow.

Back, back, back she pulled, the wooden weapon straining under the powerful tension the girl placed on it. Her mind calculated the distances, the winds, the drift, the vast sea of space that separated her from the ranch in the valley. Then, with one last tug on the string, she let the arrow fly.

Up, up, up it sailed, silent, free, piercing the cool mountain air like a rocket fired into space. But the girl didn't watch it for long. Another arrow was quickly jammed between her teeth, another length of hair was yanked from her head. Even before the first missile slammed into the thick, wooden door of the barn a second was already arching through the sky, its smooth, polished skin glistening in the early morning light.

THUMP!

Joey jumped as the sound rattled the horse barn, causing him to drop the bucket of oats he was carrying.

"Not again," he moaned, glancing in Wrangler Barry's direction. "That Plenty just doesn't give up. She's beginning to get on my nerves. She won't talk to me, won't—"

THUMP!

"Give me a break!" the boy called angrily as he rushed to the door and flung it open. "So you can shoot a barn," he shouted out across the pasture. "Big deal."

"Wait a minute." Barry hurried over to his companion's side, eying the two arrows jutting from the wooden planks. "Look at them. They're at an incredible angle, like they dropped out of the sky."

Joey reached up and retrieved one of the shafts and held it out in front of him. "And what's this? Looks like hair or something tied to the middle."

Barry gasped. "Get your grandfather. Quickly!"

"Why?" Joey questioned, moving obediently in the direction of the pasture gate.

"The hair tied around the arrow. I read about that in a book on Indian lore. It means something . . . something bad has happened."

132

Joey broke into a run. Strange, he thought. The arrow had arrived at such an extreme angle. It must have been shot from somewhere far away, somewhere high— He skidded to a stop and spun around. Somewhere like the overlook!

The morning sun glared down with brilliant rays. Squinting, he searched the ring of mountains to the east, looking for the pattern of rocks and trees that marked the spot where he knew Red Stone's path ended at the lip of a towering granite formation.

Then he saw her. A lone figure standing against the distant sky, arms waving frantically, desperately, back and forth. He couldn't see Plenty's expression. He didn't have to. Her movements said it all. Something was terribly wrong on Freedom Mountain.

"GRANDPA HANSON!" Joey screamed, racing up the steps. "Come quickly. Plenty needs help!"

The old man stumbled from the kitchen where he'd been helping his wife prepare breakfast.

"What's the matter, Joey?" he shouted.

"Red Stone! Maybe something's happened to Red Stone! He must be hurt or sick."

Grandpa Hanson turned. "I'll call the doctor in Gallatin Gateway. If he takes the logging road behind Blackmore, he can be at the cave in 45 minutes."

"Right!" Joey called, heading back toward the front door. "I'm taking Tar Boy. You come in the truck."

The boy exploded from the Station and flew down the steps. He pressed his fingers between his lips and created a piercing whistle. Tar Boy's head jerked up and the stallion immediately galloped

133

away from the ranch herd at the far end of the pasture. In seconds, the powerful horse and his rider were thundering up the long driveway, filling the quiet valley with the pounding of hooves.

Wrangler Barry waved his good arm in the air and shouted, "Hurry, Joey! HURRY!"

Plenty was waiting at the cave when the black horse finally burst from the woods and slid to a stop. Joey was off his mount and running even before the animal had come to a complete halt.

"What is it?" he shouted. "What's the matter?"

"My great-grandfather. Something's wrong. He stopped breathing right before you got here."

Joey hurried into the cave. One look told the story. Wordlessly he dropped to the ground beside the man.

"Red Stone!" he shouted, shaking the old Indian's shoulders. "Red Stone! Can you hear me?" There was no response. Joey repeated the question. Nothing.

Joey tilted Red Stone's head back slightly and pressed his mouth against his friend's lips. He blew firmly, filling the prone victim's lungs with air. Red Stone's chest rose and fell with each breath.

Then the boy carefully measured a short space from the man's top chest bone to a spot over his left breast. Placing one hand over the other, Joey pushed down—once, twice, three times, four times, five times. Then he bent and breathed into Red Stone's mouth once again.

This he did several times before shouting, "Breathe or pump?"

"What?" Plenty questioned, her hands trembling.

"Breathe or pump?" Joey shouted again, his voice raspy from the exertion. "Which one do you want to do? Come on, Plenty. I need your help."

"Breathe. I'll breathe."

Joey positioned himself where he could get the best leverage and continued pressing down onto the prone man's chest. Plenty sealed Red Stone's nostrils with her fingers as she'd seen Joey do and began forcing breaths of air into her great-grandfather's lungs.

"They taught us how to do this back in East Village, at my high school," the boy gasped, his arms pumping rhythmically. "Glad I showed up that week."

Plenty fought back tears as she worked to keep oxygen flowing into the old man's lungs. "Is he going to die?"

"I don't know," Joey answered, his voice uneven as he continued pressing down on Red Stone's chest. "He was always telling us that the heart of the warrior is strong. I sure hope he's right. Grandpa Hanson and the others should be here soon. Doctor's on his way, too. We just gotta keep him alive until they get here. Keep breathing for him, Plenty, and I'll keep his heart pumping. It's all we can do right now."

Plenty nodded and bent again, placing her mouth over the weathered, wrinkled lips of the old Indian. "Please," Joey heard her whisper. "Please be strong. Don't die. I love you, Great- grandfather. I love you."

* * *

The hospital corridor was quiet as late afternoon

shadows caressed the flowered wallpaper and framed pictures on the walls. Somewhere, in the distance, the staccato beep . . . beep . . . beep of a machine announced that a patient's heart was still operating normally.

Occasionally a phone rang. Quiet voices spoke and footsteps echoed down the long passageway as doctors, nurses, and visitors passed one another, each lost in separate concerns.

Plenty sat with her chin resting on the smooth, metal railing that encircled the bed like a fence, keeping the sleeping form safely centered under the covers.

A series of red and yellow lights moved silently across the shiny face of an instrument beside the bed, recording the heartbeat, breathing rate, blood pressure, and temperature of the patient. A plastic bottle hung overhead, sending drips of clear liquid down a tube and into the man's arm.

The girl remained motionless. She'd been sitting there for hours, ever since the nurses had brought her great-grandfather up from the emergency room three floors below.

Everyone else had left to get a bite to eat in the cafeteria. Plenty didn't even know where it was. She didn't care.

The doctor had explained everything. Red Stone had suffered a heart attack, a "massive" one. A clot had cut off the flow of blood to one of the chambers in his heart, causing that part of the muscle to die. Lack of oxygen had done damage elsewhere, too.

Muscles scattered about the old man's body had been starved of the life-giving gas. Her great-grandfather would never be the same again. Someone would have to care for him night and day.

Plenty had spoken with her mother and father on the phone earlier. They'd offered to come as soon as they could get off work, but the girl had assured them that everything that could be done was being done. Red Stone was out of danger.

She and he would return to the reservation when his condition was stable enough for him to travel. Plenty understood that jobs were hard to come by for her people and that it was best, under the circumstances, for her parents not to take on his care. They must keep their bosses happy and not jeopardize their small but steady incomes.

Joey appeared at the door and leaned against the frame. "How's he doin'?"

Plenty nodded. "OK, still."

The boy let his gaze fall on the sleeping form. "I'm sorry he got sick. Really I am."

"I know," Plenty said. Then she added, "You saved his life. That's what the doctor said. He said you kept him from dying."

"*We* did," the boy urged. "We both did."

Plenty laid her chin back against the railing. After a long moment she spoke. "Why do things have to happen? You know. Bad things?"

The boy understood the question included a lot more than Red Stone's heart attack. Plenty's words came from deep in her heart, where hurt and hate lived.

137

"Just life, I guess," Joey sighed. "Bad things happen to everyone." He sat down in an empty chair. "But he's going to be OK. We'll take care of him. We can bring him to Freedom Mountain each summer and he can tell us stories—"

"No," Plenty interrupted. "He can't. He'll be too . . . too tired."

Joey nodded. "Then we'll come visit him. Summers just wouldn't be the same without your great-grandfather. He's my friend. We all love him very much."

The girl closed her eyes. "He talks about you often. Even back at the reservation, he's always telling me how well Joey rides the big black horse and how funny Wendy is and how much he likes Debbie's smile. I'd be jealous, 'cept I understand."

The girl reached over and stroked the man's cheek. "'A true warrior loves all people,' he'd tell me. That's what he wanted me to be, a warrior, a brave, strong—"

Tears slipped down Plenty's dark cheeks. "But I refused. I just wouldn't let myself be that kind of person."

Joey gazed at the old man sleeping on the pillow, his wrinkled face surrounded by thin strands of white hair. "Red Stone loves the mountains," he said quietly. "He can tell you the song of every bird and the call of every animal. There's something in the mountains and valleys that can change a person. Grandpa Hanson says the Creator God put it there, and I believe him. It changed me, forever.

Maybe it can change you, too."

The boy sighed. "We'd better go, Plenty. We'll come back tomorrow, first thing. OK? Doctor said Red Stone should rest now."

Plenty nodded and stood. Moving to the head of the bed, she bent and kissed the withered cheek of the man. "Good night, Great-grandfather," she whispered. "I'll be back tomorrow."

Joey smiled as the two teenagers slipped from the room, leaving the old Indian alone as the last rays of the sun faded, and the lights of the city blinked on.

* * *

"Are you all right?" Wrangler Barry walked over to the girl who stood in the moonlight, looking down at the sparkling waters below.

Debbie nodded. "I'm OK. Just thinking about Red Stone and Plenty. It's so sad."

Barry leaned against the railing. "Yeah, I know. Tough break. I like the old man."

The two were silent for a long moment, then the horseman spoke. "Debbie, there's something I've been meaning to talk to you about. Do you have a minute?"

"You're not going to yell at me for interfering in your life again, are you?" the girl said, a hint of coolness in her voice. "I've been trying to stay out of your way all summer."

Barry tapped his cane on the wooden supports holding them above the creek. "That's what I want

139

to talk to you about. I mean, I want you to know that . . . oh, I'm not very good at saying things from inside."

Debbie worked a splinter free from the railing and tossed it into the creek. "You mean you *have* an inside?"

"OK, I deserve that. I haven't been very good company since the accident."

The girl nodded. "I miss the old Barry Gordon," she said, "the one who laughed at me all the time and made me feel like I was 9 years old."

"You liked that?"

"It was better than nothing."

Barry sighed. "I just didn't want to think of you as older because . . ."

"Because?"

"Because you're beautiful and wise and caring. You made my heart do stupid things."

Debbie turned. Barry noticed how the moonlight touched her cheek and shone through the carefully combed strands of her dark hair.

"I'm just a cowboy. I don't know fashion and high society and all that New York stuff. That was bad enough. Now I can't even ride a horse. As Joey would say, 'I ain't got nothin' goin' for me 'cept my incredible good looks and endless charm.' I'm not too sure about those, either."

Debbie grinned. "The charm could use a little work, but you aren't too shabby in the looks department. In fact, I think you're kinda cute, in a horse-about-to-have-a-foal sorta way."

"Yeah?"

"Yeah."

Barry shook his head. "Wait. Now I'm gettin' off the track. I just want you to know that . . . well . . . I'm sorry for being so cold to you this summer. I mean, here I was tellin' Alex how to accept himself and I was going around with a giant chip on my shoulder—"

"Beam."

"What?"

Debbie pointed at the young man's face. "*Beam* in your *eye*. That's what Grandpa Hanson would call it. It's in the Bible."

"Yeah . . . well . . . so here I have this beam in my eye and I can't see how lucky I am to have someone like you who wants to be around me even though I can't do stuff anymore like I used to and I guess what I'm trying to say is that I need you to—"

The horseman felt lips press against his, shutting off his rambling words. Arms gently encircled him as the creek sang its sweet song below his feet.

After what seemed like a very long time, he felt the pressure ease and stood looking into the soft eyes of the girl. "What were you saying, cowboy?"

Barry blinked. "I . . . um . . ." He smiled and touched her cheek. "I think I was about to say that . . . I love you."

Debbie grinned. "See? You're not as dumb as you think."

The two stood facing each other as the moon continued its journey across the night sky. Debbie's heart sang with the music of the waters. Now she knew her cowboy would be OK, as long as she was there to hold his hand and fill his life with hope.

* * *

Dawn was still an hour away when Joey drifted from sleep and opened his eyes. His first thoughts were about Plenty and the pain she was feeling. All her anger and hate had been masked by the terrible events of the day before. Would they return, this time only stronger? Would she ever stop blaming him and all other White people for robbing her great-grandfather of his mountain heritage?

Joey got up and slipped into his work clothes. He walked slowly from the barn just as the sky began to blush beyond the distant mountains.

Entering the Station, he ambled into the den, his mind searching for answers. What could he do to change the way Plenty looked at the world, her world? What could he say?

Sure, he'd been there to help save her great-grandfather. But they'd be returning to the reservation soon. Plenty would live among daily reminders of what other White people had done in the past. Every time she gazed at the mountains she'd be reminded that her people were once free to roam the hills and valleys, to hunt amid the peaks.

He saw Wendy sitting curled up with her ever-present photo album, the one she and David had produced during the summer. Joey smiled. That girl was always up before anyone else stirred.

"Hey, Wendy," he called quietly.

The girl blinked. "Well, Mr. Dugan. Is it noon already?"

Joey chuckled. "Couldn't sleep. Kept thinking about Plenty."

Wendy nodded. "Yeah. I know what you mean." She sighed. "Maybe you can talk to her some more when she gets back."

"Gets back? Whatta ya mean?"

"She left. About 20 minutes ago. Took one of the horses. Didn't think you'd mind."

Joey's brow furrowed. "Where'd she go?"

"I don't know. Rode down the drive and headed that way." The girl pointed. "Maybe she just needed to think for a while."

Joey scratched his head. "But she's sad. She shouldn't be all alone. What if she gets lost or confused?"

Wendy shrugged. "Maybe you should try to find her. She did look kinda tired and all. I would be, too, if my great-grandfather was bad sick."

The young horseman nodded. "Think I will. Tell your dad I'll be back as soon as I find her."

Wendy watched as Joey trotted down the steps and hurried across the lawn. He gave a short whistle and Tar Boy galloped over to meet him at the gate. Soon they were moving through the half light of dawn away from the Station in the direction of Freedom Mountain.

The trail became clearer and clearer as the eastern sky continued to brighten, transforming the

143

horizon from a dark, amber hue to a lighter yellow. Tar Boy's hooves clattered over the stones and soil as the big animal carried his rider higher, higher, higher into the mountains.

What would he find once they reached the cave? He was sure that's where Plenty had gone. Would she greet him with arrow feathers poised at her cheek? What would he say to her? It couldn't go on anymore. The deep hatred in her heart had to stop. It just had to. She'd need her full energies to care for the old man who lay in the hospital bed in Bozeman.

Just before emerging from the tree line that surrounded Red Stone's cave, Joey reigned in his horse and slipped to the ground. Slowly he pushed back the branches that guarded the clearing.

As the first rays of the sun arched across the sky, Joey saw a movement at the cave entrance. A form stood, arms raised. Through the cold, mountain air a voice called in a language he couldn't understand.

As the morning chased the shadows away, Plenty's tear-stained face turned toward the rising sun, her determined smile greeting the brilliant light.

Joey paused, not sure of what was happening. As he watched, the girl's voice rose in strength until her strange words echoed through the forests and meadows, filling the mountaintop with sound.

Suddenly, he understood. Red Stone would never again come to his mountain. But his heart, the heart of the warrior, would continue to beat strong and true within the young girl who stood at the mouth of the cave, welcoming the new day.

144